CODE TO ZERO

KEN FOLLETT

CODE TO ZERO

PAN BOOKS

First published 2000 by Macmillan

First published in paperback 2001 by Pan Books

This edition published 2010 by Pan Books
an imprint of Pan Macmillan, a division of Macmillan Publishers Limited
Pan Macmillan, 20 New Wharf Road, London N1 9RR
Basingstoke and Oxford
Associated companies throughout the world
www.panmacmillan.com

ISBN 978-0-330-52679-1

5 7 9 8 6 4

A CIP catalogue record for this book is available from
the British Library.

Typeset by SetSystems Ltd, Saffron Walden, Essex
Printed and bound by CPI Group (UK) Ltd, Croydon, CR0 4YY

Historical note: The launch of the first American space satellite, Explorer I, was originally scheduled for Wednesday 29 January, 1958. Late that evening, it was postponed to the following day. The reason given was the weather. Observers at Cape Canaveral were puzzled: it was a perfect, sunny Florida day. But the army said that a high-altitude wind called the jet stream was unfavourable.

Next night, there was another postponement, and the same reason was given.

The launch was finally attempted on Friday 31 January.

'... from its beginning in 1947, the Central Intelligence Agency ... has spent millions of dollars on a major program of research to find drugs and other esoteric methods to bring ordinary people, willing and unwilling alike, under complete control – to act, to talk, to reveal the most precious secrets, even to forget on command.'

Thomas Powers, from the Introduction to
The Search for the 'Manchurian Candidate':
The CIA and Mind Control by John Marks

PART 1

5 A.M.

The Jupiter C missile stands on the launch pad at Complex 26, Cape Canaveral. For secrecy, it is draped in vast canvas shrouds that hide everything but its tail, which is that of the Army's familiar Redstone rocket. But the rest of it, under the concealing cloak, is quite unique . . .

He woke up scared.

Worse than that: he was terrified. His heart was pounding, his breath came in gasps, and his body was taut. It was like a nightmare, except that waking brought no sense of relief. He felt that something dreadful had happened, but he did not know what it was.

He opened his eyes. A faint light from another room dimly illuminated his surroundings, and he made out vague shapes, familiar but sinister. Somewhere nearby, water ran in a cistern.

He tried to make himself calm. He swallowed, took regular breaths, and attempted to think straight. He was lying on a hard floor. He was cold, he hurt everywhere, and he had some kind of hangover, with a headache and a dry mouth and a feeling of nausea.

He sat upright, shaking with fear. There was an

3

unpleasant smell of damp floors washed with strong disinfectant. He recognized the outline of a row of washbasins.

He was in a public toilet.

He felt disgusted. He had been sleeping on the floor of a men's room. What the hell had happened to him? He concentrated. He was fully dressed, wearing some kind of topcoat and heavy boots, though he had a feeling that these were not his clothes. His panic was subsiding, but in its place came a deeper fear, less hysterical but more rational. What had happened to him was very bad.

He needed light.

He got to his feet. He looked around, peering into the gloom, and guessed where the door might be. Holding his arms out in front of him in case of invisible obstacles, he made his way to a wall. Then he walked crabwise, his hands exploring. He found a cold glassy surface he guessed was a mirror, then there was a towel roller, then a metal box that might be a slot machine. At last his fingertips touched a switch, and he turned it on.

Bright light flooded white-tiled walls, a concrete floor, and a line of toilets with open doors. In a corner was what looked like a bundle of old clothes. He asked himself how he got here. He concentrated hard. What had happened last night? He could not remember.

The hysterical fear began to return as he realized *he could not remember anything at all.*

He clenched his teeth to stop himself crying out.

Yesterday . . . the day before . . . nothing. What was his name? He did not know.

He turned toward the row of basins. Above them was a long mirror. In the glass he saw a filthy hobo, dressed in rags, with matted hair, a dirty face, and a crazy, pop-eyed stare. He looked at the hobo for a second, then he was hit by a terrible revelation. He started back, with a cry of shock, and the man in the mirror did the same. The hobo was himself.

He could no longer hold back the tide of panic. He opened his mouth and, in a voice that shook with terror, he shouted: 'Who am I?'

* * *

The bundle of old clothes moved. It rolled over, a face appeared, and a voice mumbled: 'You're a bum, Luke, pipe down.'

His name was Luke.

He was pathetically grateful for the knowledge. A name was not much, but it gave him a focus. He stared at his companion. The man wore a ripped tweed coat with a length of string around the waist for a belt. The grimy young face had a crafty look. The man rubbed his eyes and muttered: 'My head hurts.'

Luke said: 'Who are you?'

'I'm Pete, you retard, can't you see?'

'I can't—' Luke swallowed, holding down the panic. 'I've lost my memory!'

'I ain't surprised. You drank most of a bottle of liquor yesterday. It's a miracle you didn't lose your entire mind.' Pete licked his lips. 'I didn't get hardly any of that goddamn bourbon.'

Bourbon would explain the hangover, Luke thought. 'But why would I drink a whole bottle?'

Pete laughed mockingly. 'That's about the dumbest question I ever heard. To get drunk, of course!'

Luke was appalled. He was a drunken bum who slept in public toilets.

He had a raging thirst. He bent over a washbasin, ran the cold water, and drank from the tap. It made him feel better. He wiped his mouth, then forced himself to look in the mirror again.

The face was calmer now. The mad stare had gone, replaced by a look of bewilderment and dismay. The reflection showed a man in his late thirties, with dark hair and blue eyes. He had no beard or moustache, just a heavy growth of dark stubble.

He turned back to his companion. 'Luke what?' he said. 'What's my last name?'

'Luke . . . something, how the hell am I supposed to know?'

'How did I get this way? How long has it been going on? Why did it happen?'

Pete got to his feet. 'I need some breakfast,' he said.

Luke realized he was hungry. He wondered if he had any money. He searched the pockets of his clothes: the raincoat, the jacket, the pants. All were empty. He had no money, no wallet, not even a handkerchief. No assets, no clues. 'I think I'm broke,' he said.

'No kidding,' Pete said sarcastically. 'Come on.' He stumbled through a doorway.

Luke followed.

When he emerged into the light, he suffered another shock. He was in a huge temple, empty and eerily silent. Mahogany benches stood in rows on the marble floor, like church pews waiting for a ghostly congregation. Around the vast room, on a high stone lintel atop rows of pillars, surreal stone warriors with helmets and shields stood guard over the holy place. Far above their heads was a vaulted ceiling richly decorated with gilded octagons. The insane thought crossed Luke's mind that he had been the sacrificial victim in a weird rite that had left him with no memory.

Awestruck, he said: 'What is this place?'

'Union Station, Washington, DC,' said Pete.

A relay closed in Luke's mind, and the whole thing made sense. With relief he saw the grime on the walls, the chewing gum trodden into the marble floor, and the candy wrappers and cigarette packs in the corners, and he felt foolish. He was in a grandiose train station, early in the morning before it filled up with passengers. He had scared himself, like a child imagining monsters in a darkened bedroom.

Pete headed for a triumphal arch marked 'Exit', and Luke hurried after him.

An aggressive voice called: 'Hey! Hey, you!'

Pete said: 'Oh-oh.' He quickened his step.

A stout man in a tight-fitting railroad uniform bore down on them, full of righteous indignation. 'Where did you bums spring from?'

Pete whined: 'We're leaving, we're leaving.'

Luke was humiliated to be chased out of a train station by a fat official.

The man was not content just to get rid of them. 'You been sleeping here, ain't you?' he protested, following hard on their heels. 'You know that ain't allowed.'

It angered Luke to be lectured like a schoolboy, even though he guessed he deserved it. He *had* slept in the damn toilet. He suppressed a retort and walked faster.

'This ain't a flophouse,' the man went on. 'Damn bums, now scram!' He shoved Luke's shoulder.

Luke turned suddenly and confronted the man. 'Don't touch me,' he said. He was surprised by the quiet menace in his own voice. The official stopped short. 'We're leaving, so you don't need to do or say anything more, is that clear?'

The man took a big step backward, looking scared.

Pete took Luke's arm. 'Let's go.'

Luke felt ashamed. The guy was an officious twerp, but Luke and Pete were vagrants, and a railroad employee had the right to throw them out. Luke had no business intimidating him.

They passed through the majestic archway. It was dark outside. A few cars were parked around the traffic circle in front of the station, but the streets were quiet. The air was bitterly cold, and Luke drew his ragged clothes closer about him. It was winter, a frosty morning in Washington, maybe January or February.

He wondered what year it was.

Pete turned left, apparently sure where he was

going. Luke followed. 'Where are we headed?' he asked.

'I know a gospel shop on H Street where we can get free breakfast, so long as you don't mind singing a hymn or two.'

'I'm starving, I'll sing a whole oratorio.'

Pete confidently followed a zigzag route through a low-rent neighbourhood. The city was not yet awake. The houses were dark and the stores shuttered, the greasy spoons and the news-stands not yet open. Glancing at a bedroom window hung with cheap curtains, Luke imagined a man inside, fast asleep under a pile of blankets, his wife warm beside him; and he felt a pang of envy. It seemed that he belonged out here, in the pre-dawn community of men and women who ventured into the cold streets while ordinary people slept on: the man in work clothes shuffling to an early-morning job; the young bicycle rider muffled in scarf and gloves; the solitary woman smoking in the brightly lit interior of a bus.

His mind seethed with anxious questions. How long had he been a drunk? Had he ever tried to dry out? Did he have any family who might help him? Where had he met Pete? Where did they get the booze? Where did they drink it? But Pete's manner was taciturn, and Luke controlled his impatience, hoping Pete might be more forthcoming when he had some food inside him.

They came to a small church standing defiantly between a cinema and a smoke shop. They entered by a side door and went down a flight of stairs to the basement. Luke found himself in a long room with a low ceiling – the crypt, he guessed. At one end he saw an upright piano and a small pulpit; at the other, a kitchen range. In between were three rows of trestle tables with benches. Three bums sat there, one at each table, staring patiently into space. At the kitchen end, a dumpy woman stirred a big pot. Beside her, a grey-bearded man wearing a clerical collar looked up from a coffee urn and smiled. 'Come in, come in!' he said cheerfully. 'Come into the warm.' Luke regarded him warily, wondering if he was for real.

It *was* warm, stiflingly so after the wintry air outside. Luke unbuttoned his grubby trench coat. Pete said: 'Morning, Pastor Lonegan.'

The pastor said: 'Have you been here before? I've forgotten your name.'

'I'm Pete, he's Luke.'

'Two disciples!' His bonhomie seemed genuine. 'You're a little early for breakfast, but there's fresh coffee.'

Luke wondered how Lonegan maintained his cheery disposition when he had to get up this early to serve breakfast to a roomful of catatonic deadbeats.

The pastor poured coffee into thick mugs. 'Milk and sugar?'

Luke did not know whether he liked milk and sugar in his coffee. 'Yes, thank you,' he said, guessing. He accepted the mug and sipped the coffee. It tasted sickeningly creamy and sweet. He guessed he normally took it black. But it assuaged his hunger, and he drank it all quickly.

'We'll have a word of prayer in a few minutes,' said the pastor. 'By the time we're done, Mrs Lonegan's famous oatmeal should be cooked to perfection.'

Luke decided his suspicion had been unworthy. Pastor Lonegan was what he seemed, a cheerful guy who liked to help people.

Luke and Pete sat at the rough plank table, and Luke studied his companion. Until now, he had noticed only the dirty face and ragged clothes. Now he saw that Pete had none of the marks of a long-term drunk: no broken veins, no dry skin flaking off the face, no cuts or bruises. Perhaps he was too young – only about twenty-five, Luke guessed. But Pete was slightly disfigured. He had a dark red birthmark that ran from his right ear to his jawline. His teeth were uneven and discoloured. The dark moustache had probably been grown to distract attention from his bad teeth, back in the days when he cared about his appearance. Luke sensed suppressed anger in him. He guessed that Pete resented the world, maybe for making him ugly, maybe for some other reason. He probably had a theory that the country was being ruined by some group he hated: Chinese immigrants, or uppity Negroes, or a shadowy club of ten rich men who secretly controlled the stock market.

'What are you staring at?' Pete said.

Luke shrugged and did not reply. On the table was a newspaper folded open at the crossword, and a stub of pencil. Luke glanced idly at the grid, picked up the pencil, and started to fill in the answers.

More bums drifted in. Mrs Lonegan put out a stack

of heavy bowls and a pile of spoons. Luke got all the crossword clues but one: 'Small place in Denmark,' six letters. Pastor Lonegan looked over his shoulder at the filled-out grid, raised his eyebrows in surprise, and said quietly to his wife: 'Oh, what a noble mind is here o'erthrown!'

Luke immediately got the last clue – Hamlet – and wrote it in. Then he thought: 'How did I know that?'

He unfolded the paper and looked at the front page for the date. It was Wednesday, 29 January 1958. His eye was caught by the headline U.S. MOON STAYS EARTHBOUND. He read on:

Cape Canaveral, Tuesday: The U.S. Navy today abandoned a second attempt to launch its space rocket, Vanguard, after multiple technical problems.

The decision comes two months after the first Vanguard launch ended in humiliating disaster when the rocket exploded two seconds after ignition.

American hopes of launching a space satellite to rival the Soviet Sputnik now rest with the Army's rival Jupiter missile.

The piano sounded a strident chord, and Luke looked up. Mrs Lonegan was playing the introductory notes of a familiar hymn. She and her husband began to sing 'What a Friend We Have in Jesus', and Luke joined in, pleased he could remember it.

Bourbon had a strange effect, he thought. He could do the crossword and sing a hymn from memory, but he did not know his mother's name. Perhaps he had been drinking for years, and had damaged his brain. He wondered how he could have let such a thing happen.

After the hymn, Pastor Lonegan read some Bible verses, then told them all that they could be saved. Here was a group that really needed saving, Luke thought. All the same, he was not tempted to put his faith in Jesus. First he needed to find out who he was.

The pastor extemporized a prayer, they sang grace, then the men lined up and Mrs Lonegan served them hot oatmeal with syrup. Luke ate three bowls. Afterwards, he felt much better. His hangover was receding fast.

Impatient to resume his questions, he approached the pastor. 'Sir, have you seen me here before? I've lost my memory.'

Lonegan looked hard at him. 'You know, I don't believe I have. But I meet hundreds of people every week, and I could be mistaken. How old are you?'

'I don't know,' Luke said, feeling foolish.

'Late thirties, I'd say. You haven't been living rough very long. It takes its toll on a man. But you walk with a spring in your step, your skin is clear under the dirt, and you're still alert enough to do a crossword puzzle. Quit drinking now, and you could lead a normal life again.'

Luke wondered how many times the pastor had said that. 'I'm going to try,' he promised.

'If you need help, just ask.' A young man who

appeared to be mentally handicapped was persistently patting Lonegan's arm, and he turned to him with a patient smile.

Luke spoke to Pete. 'How long have you known me?'

'I don't know, you been around a while.'

'Where did we spend the night before last?'

'Relax, will you? Your memory will come back sooner or later.'

'I have to find out where I'm from.'

Pete hesitated. 'What we need is a beer,' he said. 'Help us think straight.' He turned for the door.

Luke grabbed his arm. 'I don't want a beer,' he said decisively. Pete did not want him to dig into his past, it seemed. Perhaps he was afraid of losing a companion. Well, that was too bad. Luke had more important things to do than keep Pete company. 'In fact,' he said, 'I think I'd like to be alone for a while.'

'What are you, Greta Garbo?'

'I'm serious.'

'You need me to look out for you. You can't make it on your own. Hell, you can't even remember how old you are.'

Pete had a desperate look in his eyes, but Luke was unmoved. 'I appreciate your concern, but you're not helping me find out who I am.'

After a moment Pete shrugged. 'You got a right.' He turned to the door again. 'See you around, maybe.'

'Maybe.'

Pete went out. Luke shook Pastor Lonegan's hand. 'Thank you for everything,' he said.

'I hope you find what you're looking for,' said the pastor.

Luke went up the stairs and out into the street. Pete was on the next block, speaking to a man in a green gaberdine raincoat with a matching cap – begging the price of a beer, Luke guessed. He walked in the opposite direction and turned around the first corner.

It was still dark. Luke's feet were cold, and he realized he was not wearing socks under his boots. As he hurried on, a light flurry of snow fell. After a few minutes, he eased his pace. He had no reason to rush. It made no difference whether he walked fast or slow. He stopped, and took shelter in a doorway.

He had nowhere to go.

6 A.M.

The rocket is surrounded on three sides by a service gantry that holds it in a steel embrace. The gantry, actually a converted oilfield derrick, is mounted on two sets of wheels that run on wide-gauge rails. The entire service structure, bigger than a town house, will be rolled back three hundred feet before the launch.

Elspeth woke up worrying about Luke.

She lay in bed for a few moments, her heart heavy with concern for the man she loved. Then she switched on the bedside lamp and sat upright.

Her motel room was decorated with a space-programme theme. The floor lamp was shaped like a rocket, and the pictures on the walls showed planets, crescent moons and orbital paths in a wildly unrealistic night sky. The Starlite was one of a cluster of new motels that had sprouted among the sand dunes in the area of Cocoa Beach, Florida, eight miles south of Cape Canaveral, to accommodate the influx of visitors. The decorator had obviously thought the outer-space theme appropriate, but it made Elspeth feel as if she were borrowing the bedroom of a ten-year-old boy.

She picked up the bedside phone and dialled

Anthony Carroll's office in Washington, D.C. At the other end, the phone rang unanswered. She tried his home number with the same result. Had something gone wrong? She felt sick with fear. She told herself that Anthony must be on his way to the office. She would call again in half an hour. It could not take him longer than thirty minutes to drive to work.

As she showered, she thought about Luke and Anthony when she had first known them. They were at Harvard when she was at Radcliffe, before the war. The boys were in the Harvard Glee Club: Luke had a nice baritone voice and Anthony a wonderful tenor. Elspeth had been the conductor of the Radcliffe Choral Society and had organized a joint concert with the Glee Club.

Best friends, Luke and Anthony had made an odd couple. Both were tall and athletic, but there the resemblance ended. The Radcliffe girls had called them Beauty and the Beast. Luke was Beauty, with his wavy black hair and elegant clothes. Anthony was not handsome, with his big nose and long chin, and he always looked as if he were wearing someone else's suit, but girls were attracted to his energy and enthusiasm.

Elspeth showered quickly. In her bathrobe, she sat at the dressing table to do her make-up. She put her wristwatch beside the eyeliner so that she would know when thirty minutes was up.

She had been sitting at a dressing table wearing a bathrobe the first time she ever spoke to Luke. It was during a panty raid. A group of Harvard boys, some drunk, had climbed into the dormitory building

17

through a ground-floor window late one evening. Now, almost twenty years later, it seemed incredible to her that she and the other girls had feared nothing worse than having their underwear stolen. Had the world been more innocent then?

By chance, Luke had come to her room. He was a math major, like her. Although he was wearing a mask, she recognized his clothes, a pale grey Irish tweed jacket with a red spotted cotton handkerchief in the breast pocket. Once alone with her, Luke had seemed embarrassed, as if it had just occurred to him that what he was doing was foolish. She had smiled, pointed to the closet, and said: 'Top drawer.' He had taken a pair of pretty white panties with a lace edging, and Elspeth felt a pang of regret – they had been expensive. But the next day he asked her for a date.

She tried to concentrate on her make-up. The job was more difficult than usual this morning, because she had slept badly. Foundation smoothed her cheeks and salmon-pink lipstick brightened her mouth. She had a math degree from Radcliffe, but still she was expected to look like a mannequin at work.

She brushed her hair. It was reddish brown, and cut in the fashionable style: chin-length and turned under at the back. She dressed quickly in a sleeveless shirtwaist dress of green-and-tan striped cotton with a wide dark brown patent-leather belt.

Twenty-nine minutes had elapsed since she had tried to call Anthony.

To pass the last minute, she thought about the number 29. It was a prime number – it could not be divided by any number except itself and 1 – but otherwise it was not very interesting. The only unusual thing about it was that 29 plus $2x^2$ was a prime number for every value of x up to 28. She calculated the series in her head: 29, 31, 37, 47, 61, 79, 101, 127 . . .

She picked up the phone and dialled Anthony's office again.

There was no reply.

1941

Elspeth Twomey fell in love with Luke the first time he kissed her.

Most Harvard boys had no idea how to kiss. They either bruised your lips with a brutal smackeroo, or opened their mouths so wide you felt like a dentist. When Luke kissed her, at five minutes to midnight in the shadows of the Radcliffe Dormitory Quad, he was passionate yet tender. His lips moved all the time, not just on her mouth but on her cheeks and her eyelids and her throat. The tip of his tongue probed gently between her lips, politely asking permission to come in, and she did not even pretend to hesitate. Afterwards, sitting in her room, she had looked into the mirror and whispered to her reflection: 'I think I love him.'

That had been six months ago, and the feeling had grown stronger since. Now she was seeing Luke almost every day. They were both in their senior year. Every day they either met for lunch or studied together for a couple of hours. Weekends they spent almost all their time together.

It was not uncommon for Radcliffe girls to get engaged in their final year, to a Harvard boy or a young professor. They would marry in the summer, go on a long honeymoon, then move into an apartment when they returned. They would start work, and a year or so later have their first baby.

But Luke had never spoken about marriage.

She looked at him now, sitting in a booth at the back of Flanagan's bar, arguing with Bern Rothsten, a tall graduate student with a bushy black moustache and a hardbitten look. Luke's dark hair kept falling forward over his eyes, and he pushed it back with his left hand, a familiar gesture. When he was older, and had a responsible job, he would put goop on his hair to make it stay in place, and then he would not be quite so sexy, she thought.

Bern was a communist, like many Harvard students and professors. 'Your father's a banker,' he said to Luke with disdain. 'You'll be a banker, too. Of course you think capitalism is great.'

Elspeth saw a flush rise at Luke's throat. His father had recently been featured in a *Time* magazine article as one of ten men who had become millionaires since the Depression. However, she guessed he was blushing not because he was a rich kid, but because he was fond of his family, and resented the implied criticism of his father. She felt angry for him, and said indignantly: 'We don't judge people by their parents, Bern!'

Luke said: 'Anyway, banking is an honourable job. Bankers help people to start businesses and provide employment.'

'Like they did in 1929.'

'They make mistakes. Sometimes they help the

21

wrong people. Soldiers make mistakes – they shoot the wrong people – but I don't accuse you of being a murderer.'

It was Bern's turn to look wounded. He had fought in the Spanish Civil War – he was older than the rest of them by three or four years – and Elspeth now guessed he was remembering some tragic error.

Luke added: 'Anyway, I don't aim to be a banker.'

Bern's dowdy girlfriend, Peg, leaned forward, interested. Like Bern, she was intense in her convictions, but she did not have his sarcastic tongue. 'What, then?'

'A scientist.'

'What kind?'

Luke pointed upward. 'I want to explore beyond our planet.'

Bern laughed scornfully. 'Space rockets! A schoolboy fantasy.'

Elspeth leaped to Luke's defence again. 'Knock it off, Bern, you don't know what you're talking about.' Bern's subject was French literature.

However, Luke did not appear to have been stung by the sneer. Perhaps he was accustomed to having his dream laughed at. 'I think it's going to happen,' he said. 'And I'll tell you something else. I believe science will do more than communism for ordinary people in our lifetime.'

Elspeth winced. She loved Luke, but she felt he was naive about politics. 'Too simple,' she said to him. 'The benefits of science are restricted to the privileged elite.'

'That's just not true,' Luke said. 'Steamships make life better for seamen as well as for transatlantic passengers.'

Bern said: 'Have you ever been in the engine room of an ocean liner?'

'Yes, and no one was dying of scurvy.'

A tall figure cast a shadow over the table. 'Are you kids old enough to drink alcoholic liquor in public?' It was Anthony Carroll, wearing a blue serge suit that looked as if he had slept in it. With him was someone so striking that Elspeth uttered an involuntary murmur of surprise. She was a small girl with a petite figure, fashionably dressed in a short red jacket and a loose black skirt, with curls of dark hair escaping from under a little red hat with a peak. 'Meet Billie Josephson,' said Anthony.

Bern Rothsten said to her: 'Are you Jewish?'

She was startled to be asked so directly. 'Yes.'

'So you can marry Anthony, but you can't join his country club.'

Anthony protested: 'I don't belong to a country club.'

'You will, Anthony, you will,' said Bern.

Luke stood up to shake hands, nudged the table with his thighs, and knocked over a glass. It was unusual for him to be clumsy, and Elspeth realized with a twinge of annoyance that he was instantly taken with Miss Josephson. 'I'm surprised,' he said, giving her his most charming smile. 'When Anthony said his date was called Billie, I imagined someone six feet tall and built like a wrestler.'

Billie laughed merrily and slid into the booth beside Luke. 'My name is Bilhah,' she said. 'It's biblical, she was the handmaiden of Rachel and the mother of Dan. But I was brought up in Dallas, where they called me Billie-Jo.'

Anthony sat next to Elspeth and said quietly: 'Isn't she pretty?'

Billie was not exactly pretty, Elspeth thought. She had a narrow face, with a sharp nose and large, intense, dark brown eyes. It was the whole package that was so stunning: the red lipstick, the angle of the hat, the Texas accent, and most of all her animation. While she talked to Luke, telling him some story about Texans now, she smiled, frowned, and pantomimed all kinds of emotion. 'She's cute,' Elspeth said to Anthony. 'I don't know why I never noticed her before.'

'She works all the time, doesn't go to many parties.'

'So how did you meet her?'

'I noticed her in the Fogg Museum. She was wearing a green coat with brass buttons and a beret. I thought she looked like a toy soldier fresh out of the box.'

Billie was not any kind of toy, Elspeth thought. She was more dangerous than that. Billie laughed at something Luke had said and swiped his arm in mock admonishment. The gesture was flirtatious, Elspeth thought. Irritated, she interrupted them and said to Billie: 'Are you planning to beat the curfew tonight?'

Radcliffe girls were supposed to be in their dormitories by ten o'clock. They could get permission to stay out later, but they had to put their name in a book, with details of where they planned to go and what time they would be back; and their return time was checked. However, they were clever women, and the complex rules only inspired them to ingenious deceptions. Billie said: 'I'm supposed to be spending the night with a visiting aunt who has taken a suite at the Ritz. What's your story?'

'No story, just a ground-floor window that will be open all night.'

Billie lowered her voice. 'In fact, I'm staying with friends of Anthony's in Fenway.'

Anthony looked sheepish. 'Some people my mother knows, who have a large apartment,' he said to Elspeth. 'Don't give me that old-fashioned look, they're terribly respectable.'

'I should hope so,' Elspeth said primly, and she had the satisfaction of seeing Billie blush. Turning to Luke, she said: 'Honey, what time is the movie?'

He looked at his wristwatch. 'We've got to go,' he said.

Luke had borrowed a car for the weekend. It was a two-seater Ford Model A roadster, ten years old, its sit-up-and-beg shape looking antiquated beside the streamlined cars of the early forties.

Luke handled the old car skilfully, obviously enjoying himself. They drove into Boston. Elspeth asked herself if she had been bitchy to Billie. Maybe, a little, she decided, but she was not going to shed any tears.

They went to see Alfred Hitchcock's latest film, *Suspicion*, at Loew's State Theatre. In the darkness,

Luke put his arm around Elspeth, and she laid her head on his shoulder. She felt it was a pity they had chosen a film about a disastrous marriage.

Around midnight they returned to Cambridge and pulled off Memorial Drive to park facing the Charles River, next to the boathouse. The car had no heater, and Elspeth turned up the fur collar of her coat and leaned against Luke for warmth.

They talked about the movie. Elspeth thought that in real life the Joan Fontaine character, a repressed girl brought up by stuffy parents, would never be attracted to the kind of ne'er-do-well Cary Grant had played. Luke said: 'But that's why she fell for him – because he was dangerous.'

'Are dangerous people attractive?'

'Absolutely.'

Elspeth turned away from him and looked at the reflection of the moon on the restless surface of the water. Billie Josephson was dangerous, she thought.

Luke sensed her annoyance and changed the subject. 'This afternoon, Professor Davies told me I could do my master's degree right here at Harvard if I want.'

'What made him say that?'

'I mentioned that I was hoping to go to Columbia. He said: "What for? Stay here!" I explained that my family's in New York, and he said: "Family. Huh!" Like that. Like I couldn't possibly be a serious mathematician if I cared about seeing my little sister.'

Luke was the eldest of four children. His mother

was French. His father had met her in Paris at the end of the First World War. Elspeth knew that Luke was fond of his two teenage brothers and doted on his eleven-year-old sister. 'Professor Davies is a bachelor,' she said. 'He lives for his work.'

'Have you thought about doing a master's?'

Elspeth's heart missed a beat. 'Should I?' Was he asking her to go to Columbia with him?

'You're a better mathematician than most of the Harvard men.'

'I've always wanted to work at the State Department.'

'That would mean living in Washington.'

Elspeth was sure Luke had not planned this conversation. He was just thinking aloud. It was typical of a man, to talk without a moment's forethought about matters that affected their whole lives. But he seemed dismayed that they might move to different cities. The solution to the dilemma must be as obvious to him as it was to her, she thought happily.

'Have you ever been in love?' he said suddenly. Realizing he had been abrupt, he added: 'It's a very personal question, I don't have any right to ask.'

'That's okay,' she said. Any time he wanted to talk about love, it was fine with her. 'As a matter of fact, I have been in love.' She watched his face in the moonlight, and was gratified to see the shadow of displeasure flicker across his expression. 'When I was seventeen, there was a steelworks dispute in Chicago. I was very political, in those days. I went to help, as a volunteer, carrying messages and making coffee. I worked for a young organizer called Jack Largo, and I fell in love with him.'

'And he with you?'

'Goodness, no. He was twenty-five, he thought of me as a kid. He was kind to me, and charming, but he was like that with everyone.' She hesitated. 'He kissed me once, though.' She wondered whether she should be telling Luke this, but she felt the need to unburden herself. 'We were alone in the back room, packing leaflets in boxes, and I said something that made him laugh, I don't even remember what it was. "You're a gem, Ellie," he said – he was one of those men who shorten everyone's name, he would have called you Lou for sure. Then he kissed me, right on the lips. I nearly died of joy. But he just went on packing leaflets as though nothing had changed.'

'I think he did fall in love with you.'

'Maybe.'

'Are you still in touch with him?'

She shook her head. 'He died.'

'So young!'

'He was killed.' She fought back sudden tears. The last thing she wanted was for Luke to think she was still in love with the memory of Jack. 'Two off-duty policemen, hired by the steelworks, got him in an alley and beat him to death with iron bars.'

'Jesus Christ!' Luke stared at her.

'Everyone in town knew who had done it, but nobody was arrested.'

He took her hand. 'I've read about that kind of stuff in the papers, but it never seemed real.'

'It's real. The mills must keep rolling. Anyone who gets in the way has to be rubbed out.'

'You make it sound as if industry were no better than organized crime.'

'I don't see a big difference. But I don't get involved any more. That was enough.' Luke had started talking about love, but she had stupidly moved the conversation on to politics. She switched back. 'What about you?' she said. 'Have you ever been in love?'

'I'm not sure,' he said hesitantly. 'I don't think I know what love is.' It was a typical boy's answer. Then he kissed her, and she relaxed.

She liked to touch him with her fingertips while they kissed, stroking his ears and the line of his jaw, his hair and the back of his neck. Every now and again he stopped to look at her, studying her with the hint of a smile, making her think of *Hamlet*'s Ophelia saying: 'He fell to such perusal of my face, as a would draw it.' Then he would kiss her again. What made her feel so good was the thought that he liked her this much.

After a while he drew away from her and sighed heavily. 'I wonder how married people ever get bored,' he said. 'They never have to stop.'

She liked this talk of marriage. 'Their children stop them, I guess,' she said with a laugh.

'Do you want to have children, some day?'

She felt her breath come faster. What was he asking her? 'Of course I do.'

'I'd like four.'

The same as his parents. 'Boys or girls?'

'A mixture.'

There was a pause. Elspeth was afraid to say anything. The silence stretched out. Eventually he turned to her with a serious look. 'How would you feel about that? Having four children?'

It was the cue she had been waiting for. She smiled happily. 'If they were yours, I'd love it,' she said.

He kissed her again.

Soon it became too cold to stay where they were, and reluctantly they drove back towards the Radcliffe dorms.

As they were passing through Harvard Square, a figure waved to them from the side of the road. 'Is that Anthony?' Luke said incredulously.

It was, Elspeth saw. Billie was with him.

Luke pulled over, and Anthony came to the window. 'I'm glad I spotted you,' he said. 'I need a favour.'

Billie stood behind Anthony, shivering in the cold night air, looking furious. 'What are you doing here?' Elspeth asked Anthony.

'There's been a muddle. My friends in Fenway have gone away for the weekend – they must have got the dates mixed up. Billie has nowhere to go.'

Billie had lied about where she was spending the night, Elspeth recalled. Now she could not return to her dorm without revealing her deception.

'I took her to the House.' He meant Cambridge House, where he and Luke lived. Harvard men's dormitories were called 'Houses'. 'I thought she could sleep in our room, and Luke and I could spend the night in the library.'

Elspeth said: 'You're crazy.'

Luke put in: 'It's been done before. So what went wrong?'

'We were seen.'

'Oh, no!' Elspeth said. For a girl to be found in a man's room was a serious offence, especially at night. Both the man and the woman could be expelled from the university.

Luke said: 'Who saw you?'

'Geoff Pidgeon and a whole bunch of men.'

'Well, Geoff's all right, but who was with him?'

'I'm not sure. It was half dark and they were all drunk. I'll talk to them in the morning.'

Luke nodded. 'What are you going to do now?'

'Billie has a cousin who lives in Newport, Rhode Island,' Anthony said. 'Would you drive her there?'

'What?' said Elspeth. 'But it's fifty miles away!'

'So it will take an hour or two,' Anthony said dismissively. 'What do you say, Luke?'

'Of course,' Luke said.

Elspeth had known he would comply. It was a matter of honour for him to help out a friend, regardless of inconvenience. But she was angry all the same.

'Hey, thanks,' Anthony said lightly.

'No problem,' Luke said. 'Well, there is a problem. This car is a two-seater.'

Elspeth opened the door and got out. 'Be my guest,' she said sulkily. She felt ashamed of herself for being so bad-tempered. Luke was right to rescue a friend in trouble. But she hated the thought of him spending two hours in this little car with sexy Billie Josephson.

Luke sensed her displeasure and said: 'Elspeth, get back in, I'll drive you home first.'

She tried to be gracious. 'No need,' she said. 'Anthony can walk me to the dorm. And Billie looks as if she might freeze to death.'

'Okay, if you're sure,' Luke said.

Elspeth wished he had not agreed quite so fast.

Billie kissed Elspeth's cheek. 'I don't know how to thank you,' she said. She got into the car and closed the door without saying goodbye to Anthony.

Luke waved and drove off.

Anthony and Elspeth stood and watched the car recede into the darkness.

'Hell,' said Elspeth.

6.30 A.M.

Stencilled on the side of the white rocket is the designation 'UE' in huge black letters. This is a simple code –

H	U	N	T	S	V	I	L	E	X
1	2	3	4	5	6	7	8	9	0

– so UE is missile number 29. The purpose of the code is to avoid giving clues as to how many missiles have been produced.

Daylight crept stealthily over the cold city. Men and women came out of the houses, narrowing their eyes and pursing their lips against the biting wind, and hurried through the grey streets, heading for the warmth and bright lights of the offices and stores, hotels and restaurants where they worked.

Luke had no destination: one street was as good as another when none of them meant anything. Maybe, he thought, he would turn the next corner and know, in a flash of revelation, that he was some place familiar – the street where he was brought up, or a building where he had worked. But every corner disappointed him.

As the light improved, he began to study the people he passed. One of these could be his father, his sister, even his son. He kept hoping that one of them would catch his eye, and stop, and embrace him, and say: 'Luke, what happened to you? Come home with me, let me help you!' But perhaps a relative would turn a cold face to him and pass by. He might have done something to offend his family. Or they might live in another town.

He began to feel he was not going to be lucky. No passer-by would embrace him with glad cries, and he was not suddenly going to recognize the street where he lived. Simply walking around fantasizing about a lucky break was no kind of strategy. He needed a plan. There must be some way to discover his identity.

Luke wondered if he might be a Missing Person. There was a list, he felt sure, of such people, with a description of each. Who kept the list? It had to be the police.

He seemed to remember passing a precinct house a few minutes earlier. He turned abruptly to go back. As he did so, he bumped into a young man in an olive-coloured gaberdine raincoat and matching cap. He had a feeling he might have seen the man before. Their eyes met, and, for a hopeful moment, Luke thought he might have been recognized; but the man looked away, embarrassed, and walked on.

Swallowing his disappointment, Luke tried to retrace his steps. It was difficult, because he had turned corners and crossed streets more or less at random.

However, he had to come across a police station sooner or later.

As he walked, he tried to deduce information about himself. He watched a tall man in a grey Homburg hat light a cigarette and take a long, satisfying drag, but he had no desire for tobacco. He guessed he did not smoke. Looking at cars, he knew that the racy, low-slung designs he found attractive were new. He decided he liked fast cars, and he was sure he could drive. He also knew the make and model names of most of the cars he saw. That was the kind of information he had retained, along with how to speak English.

When he glimpsed his reflection in a shop window, what he saw was a bum of indeterminate years. But when he looked at passers-by, he could tell if they were in their twenties, thirties, or forties, or older. He also found he automatically classified people as older or younger than himself. Thinking about it, he realized that people in their twenties seemed younger than he, and people in their forties older; so he had to be somewhere in between.

These trifling victories over his amnesia gave him an inordinate sense of triumph.

But he had completely lost his way. He was on a tawdry street of cheap shops, he saw with distaste: clothing stores with windows full of bargains, used-furniture stores, pawnbrokers, and grocery stores that took food stamps. He stopped suddenly and looked back, wondering what to do. Thirty yards behind him, he saw the man in a green gaberdine raincoat and cap, watching the TV in a store window.

Luke frowned, thinking: 'Is he shadowing me?'

A shadow was always alone, rarely carried a briefcase or shopping bag, and inevitably appeared to be loitering rather than walking with a set purpose. The man in the olive cap matched the specification.

It was easy enough to check.

Luke walked to the end of the block, crossed the street, and walked back along the side. When he reached the far end he stood at the kerb and looked both ways. The olive raincoat was thirty yards behind him. Luke crossed again. To allay suspicion, he studied doors, as if looking for a street number. He went all the way back to where he had started.

The raincoat followed.

Luke was mystified, but his heart leaped with hope. A man who was following him must know something about him – maybe even his identity.

To be sure he was being followed, he needed to travel in a vehicle, forcing his shadow to do the same.

Despite his excitement, a cool observer in the back of his mind was asking: 'How come you know exactly how to check whether you're being followed?' The method had popped into his head immediately. Had he done some kind of clandestine work before he became a bum?

He would think about that later. Now he needed bus fare. There was nothing in the pockets of his ragged clothes; he must have spent every last cent on booze. But that was no problem. There was cash everywhere: in people's pockets, in the stores, in taxicabs and houses.

He began to look at his surroundings with different eyes. He saw news-stands to be robbed, handbags that could be snatched, pockets ready to be picked. He glanced into a coffee shop where a man stood behind the counter and a waitress served the booths. The place would do as well as anything. He stepped inside.

His eyes raked the tables, looking for change left as tips, but it was not going to be that easy. He approached the counter. A radio was playing the news. 'Rocket experts claim America has one last chance of catching up with the Russians in the race to control outer space.' The counterman was making espresso coffee, steam billowing from a gleaming machine, and a delicious fragrance made Luke's nostrils flare.

What would a bum say? 'Any stale doughnuts?' he asked.

'Get out of here,' the man said roughly. 'And don't come back.'

Luke contemplated leaping the counter and opening the cash register, but it seemed extreme when all he wanted was bus fare. Then he saw what he needed. Beside the till, within easy reach, was a can with a slit in the top. Its label showed a picture of a child and the legend: 'Remember Those Who Cannot See.' Luke moved so that his body shielded the box from the customers and the waitress. Now he just had to distract the counterman.

'Gimme a dime?' he said.

The man said: 'Okay, that's it, you get the bum's

rush.' He put down a jug with a clatter and wiped his hands on his apron. He had to duck under the counter to get out, and for a second he could not see Luke.

In that moment, Luke took the collection box and slipped it inside his coat. It was disappointingly light, but it gave a rattle, so it was not empty.

The counterman grabbed Luke by the collar and propelled him rapidly across the café. Luke did not resist until, at the door, the man gave him a painful kick in the ass. Forgetting his act, Luke spun round, ready to fight. The man suddenly looked scared and backed inside.

Luke asked himself what he had to be angry about. He had gone into the place begging, and had not left when asked to. Okay, the kick was unnecessary, but he deserved it – he had stolen the blind children's money!

All the same, it took an effort for him to swallow his pride, turn around, and slink away like a dog with its tail between its legs.

He ducked into an alleyway, found a sharp stone, and attacked the can, venting his anger. He soon busted it open. The money inside, mostly pennies, amounted to two or three dollars, he guessed. He put it in his coat pocket and returned to the street. He thanked heaven for charity and made a silent promise to give three bucks to the blind if he ever got straight.

All right, he thought, thirty bucks.

The man in the olive raincoat was standing by a news-stand, reading a paper.

A bus pulled up a few yards away. Luke had no idea where it went, but that did not matter. He boarded.

The driver gave him a hard look, but did not throw him off. 'I want to go three stops,' Luke said.

'Don't matter where you want to go, the fare is seventeen cents, unless you got a token.'

Luke paid with some of the change he had stolen.

Maybe he was not being shadowed. As he walked towards the back of the bus, he looked anxiously out the window. The man in the raincoat was walking away with his newspaper tucked under his arm. Luke frowned. The man should have been trying to hail a taxicab. Maybe he was not a shadow, after all. Luke felt disappointed.

The bus pulled away, and Luke took a seat.

He wondered again how come he knew about all this stuff. He must have been trained in clandestine work. But what for? Was he a cop? Perhaps it was to do with the war. He knew there had been a war. America had fought against the Germans in Europe and the Japanese in the Pacific. But he could not remember whether he had been in it.

At the third stop, he got off the bus with a handful of other passengers. He looked up and down the street. There were no taxicabs in sight, and no sign of the man in the olive raincoat. As he hesitated, he noticed that one of the passengers who had got off the bus with him had paused in a shop doorway and was fumbling in his pockets. As Luke watched, he lit a cigarette and took a long, satisfying drag.

He was a tall man, wearing a grey Homburg hat.

Luke realized he had seen him before.

7 A.M.

The launch pad is a simple steel table with four legs and a hole in the middle through which the rocket jet passes. A conical deflector beneath spreads the jet horizontally.

Anthony Carroll drove along Constitution Avenue in a five-year-old Cadillac Eldorado that belonged to his mother. He had borrowed it a year ago, to drive to Washington from his parents' place in Virginia, and had never gotten around to returning it. His mother had probably bought another car by now.

He pulled into the parking lot of Q Building in Alphabet Row, a strip of barracks-like structures hastily erected, during the war, on parkland near the Lincoln Memorial. It was an eyesore, no question, but he liked the place, for he had spent much of the war here, working for the Office of Strategic Services, precursor of the CIA. Those were the good old days, when a clandestine agency could do more or less anything, and did not have to check with anyone but the President.

The CIA was the fastest-growing bureaucracy in Washington, and a vast multimillion dollar headquarters was under construction across the Potomac

River in Langley, Virginia. When it was completed, Alphabet Row would be demolished.

Anthony had fought hard against the Langley development, and not merely because Q Building held fond memories. Right now the CIA had offices in thirty-one buildings in the government-dominated downtown neighbourhood known as Foggy Bottom. That was the way it should be, Anthony had argued vociferously. It was very difficult for foreign agents to figure out the size and power of the Agency when its premises were scattered and mixed up with other government offices. But when Langley opened, anyone would be able to estimate its resources, manpower, and even budget simply by driving past.

He had lost that argument. The people in charge were determined to manage the CIA more tightly. Anthony believed that secret work was for daredevils and buccaneers. That was how it had been in the war. But nowadays it was dominated by pen-pushers and accountants.

There was a parking slot reserved for him and marked: 'Head of Technical Services', but he ignored it and pulled up in front of the main door. Looking up at the ugly building, he wondered if its imminent demolition signified the end of an era. He was losing more of these bureaucratic battles nowadays. He was still a hugely powerful figure within the Agency. 'Technical Services' was the euphemistic name of the division responsible for burglary, phone tapping, drug testing and other illegal activities. Its nickname was Dirty Tricks. Anthony's position was founded on his record as a war hero and a series of Cold War coups. But some people wanted to turn the CIA into what the public imagined it to be, a simple information-gathering agency.

Over my dead body, he thought.

However, he had enemies: superiors he had offended with his brash manners, weak and incompetent agents whose promotion he had opposed, pen-pushers who disliked the whole notion of the government doing secret operations. They were ready to destroy him as soon as he made a slip.

And today his neck was stuck out farther than ever before.

As he strode into the building, he deliberately put aside his general worries and focused on the problem of the day: Dr Claude Lucas, known as Luke, the most dangerous man in America, the one who threatened everything Anthony had lived for.

He had been at the office most of the night, and had gone home only to shave and change his shirt. Now the guard in the lobby looked surprised and said: 'Good morning, Mr Carroll – you back already?'

'An angel appeared unto me in a dream and said: "Get back to work, you lazy son of a bitch." Good morning.'

The guard laughed. 'Mr Maxell's in your office, sir.'

Anthony frowned. Pete Maxell was supposed to be with Luke. Had something gone wrong?

He ran up the stairs.

Pete was sitting in the chair opposite Anthony's

desk, still dressed in ragged clothes, a smear of dirt partly covering the red birthmark on his face. As Anthony walked in he jumped up, looking scared.

'What happened?' Anthony said.

'Luke decided he wanted to be alone.'

Anthony had planned for this. 'Who took over?'

'Simons has him under surveillance, and Betts is there for back-up.'

Anthony nodded thoughtfully. Luke had got rid of one agent, he could get rid of another. 'What about Luke's memory?'

'Completely gone.'

Anthony took off his coat and sat behind his desk. Luke was causing problems, but Anthony had expected as much, and he was ready.

He looked at the man opposite. Pete was a good agent, competent and careful, but inexperienced. However, he was fanatically loyal to Anthony. All the young agents knew that Anthony had personally organized an assassination: the killing of the Vichy French leader Admiral Darlan, in Algiers on Christmas Eve in 1942. CIA agents did kill people, but not often, and they regarded Anthony with awe. But Pete owed him a special debt. On his job application form, Pete had lied, saying he had never been in trouble with the law, and Anthony had later found out that, as a student in San Francisco, he had been fined for soliciting a prostitute. Pete should have been fired for that, but Anthony had kept the secret and Pete was eternally grateful.

Now Pete was miserable and ashamed, feeling he had let Anthony down. 'Relax,' Anthony said, adopting a fatherly tone. 'Just tell me exactly what happened.'

Pete looked grateful, and sat down again. 'He woke up crazy,' he began. 'Yelling "Who am I?" and stuff like that. I got him calmed down ... but I made a mistake. I called him Luke.'

Anthony had told Pete to observe Luke but not to give him any information. 'No matter – it's not his real name.'

'Then he asked who I was, and I said: "I'm Pete." It just came out, I was so concerned to stop him yelling.' Pete was mortified to confess these blunders, but in fact they were not grave and Anthony waved aside his apologies. 'What happened next?'

'I took him to the gospel shop, just the way we planned it. But he asked shrewd questions. He wanted to know if the pastor had seen him before.'

Anthony nodded. 'We shouldn't be surprised. In the war, he was the best agent we ever had. He's lost his memory, but not his instincts.' He rubbed his face with his right hand, tiredness catching up with him.

'I kept trying to steer him away from inquiring into his past. But I think he figured out what I was doing. Then he told me he wanted to be alone.'

'Did he get any clues? Did anything happen that might lead him to the truth?'

'No. He read an article in the paper about the space programme, but it didn't seem to mean anything special to him.'

'Did anyone notice anything strange about him?'

'The pastor was surprised Luke could do the crossword. Most of those bums can't even read.'

This was going to be difficult, but manageable, as Anthony had expected. 'Where is Luke now?'

'I don't know, sir. Steve will call in as soon as he gets a chance.'

'When he does, get back there and join up with him. Whatever happens, Luke mustn't get away from us.'

'Okay.'

The white phone on Anthony's desk rang, his direct line. He stared at it for a moment. Not many people had the number.

He picked it up.

'It's me,' said Elspeth's voice. 'What's happened?'

'Relax,' he said. 'Everything is under control.'

7.30 A.M.

The missile is 68 feet 7 inches high, and it weighs 64,000 pounds on the launch pad – but most of that is fuel. The satellite itself is only 2 feet 10 inches long, and weighs just 18 pounds.

The shadow followed Luke for a quarter of a mile as he walked south on 8th Street.

It was now full light and, although the street was busy, Luke easily kept track of the grey Homburg hat bobbing among the heads crowded together at street corners and bus stops. But after he crossed Pennsylvania Avenue, it disappeared from view. Once again, he wondered if he might be imagining things. He had woken up in a bewildering world where anything might be true. Perhaps the notion that he was being tailed was only a fantasy. But he did not really believe that, and a minute later he spotted the green raincoat coming out of a bakery.

'*Toi, encore,*' he said under his breath. 'You again.' He wondered briefly why he had spoken in French, then he put the thought out of his mind. He had more pressing concerns. There was no further room for doubt: two people were following him in a smoothly executed relay operation. They had to be professionals.

He tried to figure out what that meant. Homburg and Raincoat might be cops – he could have committed a crime, murdered someone while drunk. They could be spies, KGB or CIA, although it seemed unlikely that a deadbeat such as he could be involved in espionage. Most probably he had a wife he had left many years ago, who now wanted to divorce him and had hired private detectives to get proof of how he was living. (Maybe she was French.)

None of the options was attractive. Yet Luke felt exhilarated. They probably knew who he was. Whatever the reason for their tailing him, they must know something about him. At the very least, they knew more than he did.

He decided he would split the team, then confront the younger man.

He stepped into a smoke shop and bought a pack of Pall Malls, paying with some of the change he had stolen. When he went outside, Raincoat had disappeared and Homburg had taken over again. He walked to the end of the block and turned the corner.

A Coca-Cola truck was parked at the kerb, and the driver was unloading crates and carrying them into a diner. Luke stepped into the road and walked to the far side of the truck, positioning himself where he could watch the street without being seen by anyone coming around the corner.

After a minute, Homburg appeared, walking

quickly, checking in the doorways and windows, looking for Luke.

Luke dropped to the ground and rolled under the truck. Looking along the sidewalk at ground level, he picked out the blue suit pants and tan Oxfords of his shadow.

The man quickened his pace, presumably concerned that Luke had disappeared off the street. Then he turned and came back. He went into the diner and came out a minute later. He walked around the truck, then returned to the sidewalk and continued on. After a moment, he broke into a run.

Luke was pleased. He did not know how he had learned this game, but he seemed to be good at it. He crawled to the front of the truck and scrambled to his feet. He looked around the nearside fender. Homburg was still hurrying away.

Luke crossed the sidewalk and turned the corner. He stood in the doorway of an electrical store. Looking at a record player with an eighty bucks price tag, he opened the pack of cigarettes, took one out, and waited, keeping an eye on the street.

Raincoat appeared.

He was tall – about Luke's height – and his build was athletic, but he was about ten years younger, and his face wore an anxious look. Luke's instinct told him the man was not very experienced.

He spotted Luke, and gave a nervous start. Luke looked straight at him. The man looked away and continued walking, edging to the outside of the sidewalk to pass Luke, as anyone might to avoid contact with a bum.

Luke stepped into his path. He put the cigarette into his mouth and said: 'Got a light, buddy?'

Raincoat did not know what to do. He hesitated, looking worried. For a moment, Luke thought he would walk by without speaking; but then he made a quick decision, and stopped. 'Sure,' he said, trying to act casual. He reached into the pocket of his raincoat, took out a book of matches and struck one.

Luke took the cigarette out of his mouth and said: 'You know who I am, don't you?'

The young man looked scared. His training course had not prepared him for a surveillance subject who started to question the shadow. He stared at Luke, dumbstruck, until the match burned down. Then he dropped it and said: 'I don't know what you're talking about, pal.'

'You're following me,' Luke said. 'You must know who I am.'

Raincoat continued to act innocent. 'Are you selling something?'

'Am I dressed like a salesman? Come on, level with me.'

'I'm not following anyone.'

'You've been behind me for an hour, and I'm lost!'

The man made a decision. 'You're out of your mind,' he said. He tried to walk past Luke.

Luke moved sideways, blocking his path.

'Excuse me, please,' Raincoat said.

Luke was not willing to let the man go. He grabbed him by the lapels of the raincoat and slammed him against the shop window, rattling the glass. Frustration and rage boiled over. '*Putain de merde!*' he yelled.

Raincoat was younger and fitter than Luke, but he offered no resistance. 'Get your damn hands off me,' he said in a level voice. 'I'm not following you.'

'Who am I?' Luke screamed at him. 'Tell me, who am I?'

'How should I know?' He grasped Luke by the wrists, trying to shake his hold on the lapels of the raincoat.

Luke shifted his grip and took the man by the throat. 'I'm not taking your bullshit,' he rasped. 'You're going to tell me what's going on.'

Raincoat lost his cool, eyes widening in fear. He struggled to loosen Luke's grip on his throat. When that failed, he began to punch Luke's ribs. The first blow hurt, and Luke winced, but he retained his hold and moved in close, so that subsequent punches had little force. He pressed his thumbs into his opponent's throat, choking him. Terror showed in the man's eyes as his breath was cut off.

Behind Luke, the frightened voice of a passer-by said: 'Hey, what's going on here?'

Suddenly Luke was shocked at himself. He was killing the guy! He relaxed his grip. What was the matter with him? Was he a murderer?

Raincoat broke Luke's hold. Luke was dismayed at his own violence. He let his hands fall to his side.

The guy backed away. 'You crazy bastard,' he said. The fear had not left his eyes. 'You tried to kill me!'

'I just want the truth, and I know you can tell me it.'

Raincoat rubbed his throat. 'Asshole,' he said. 'You're out of your goddamn mind.'

Luke's anger rose once more. 'You're lying!' he yelled. He reached out to grab the man again.

Raincoat turned and ran away.

Luke could have chased him, but he hesitated. What was the point? What would he do if he caught the guy – torture him?

Then it was too late. Three passers-by had stopped to watch the fracas and were now standing at a safe distance, staring at Luke. After a moment, he walked away, heading in the direction opposite to that taken by his two shadows.

He felt worse than ever, shaky after his violent outburst and sick with disappointment at the result. He had met two people who probably knew who he was, and he had got no information.

'Great job, Luke,' he said to himself. 'You achieved precisely nothing.'

And he was alone again.

8 A.M.

The Jupiter C missile has four stages. The largest part is a high-performance version of the Redstone ballistic missile. This is the booster, or first stage, an enormously powerful engine that has the gargantuan task of freeing the missile from the mighty pull of Earth's gravity.

Dr Billie Josephson was running late.

She had got her mother up, helped her into a quilted bathrobe, made her put on her hearing aid, and sat her in the kitchen with coffee. She had woken her seven-year-old, Larry, praised him for not wetting the bed, and told him he had to shower just the same. Then she returned to the kitchen.

Her mother, a small, plump woman of seventy known as Becky-Ma, had the radio on loud. Perry Como was singing 'Catch a Falling Star'. Billie put sliced bread in the toaster, then laid the table with butter and grape jelly for Becky-Ma. For Larry she poured cornflakes into a bowl, sliced a banana over the cereal, and filled a jug with milk.

She made a peanut-butter-and-jelly sandwich and put it in Larry's lunch box with an apple, a Hershey bar and a small bottle of orange juice. She put the lunch box in his school bag and added his home-reading book and his baseball glove, a present from his father.

On the radio, a reporter was interviewing sightseers on the beach near Cape Canaveral who were hoping to see a rocket launch.

Larry came into the kitchen with his shoelaces untied and his shirt buttons done up awry. She straightened him out, got him started on his cornflakes, and began to scramble eggs.

It was eight-fifteen, and she was almost caught up. She loved her son and her mother, but a secret part of her resented the drudgery of taking care of them.

The radio reporter was now interviewing an army spokesman. 'Aren't these rubbernecks in danger? What if the rocket goes off course and crash-lands right here on the beach?'

'There's no danger of that, sir,' came the reply. 'Every rocket has a self-destruct mechanism. If it veers off course it will be blown up in mid-air.'

'But how can you blow it up after it's already taken off?'

'The explosive device is triggered by a radio signal sent by the range safety officer.'

'That sounds dangerous in itself. Some radio ham fooling around might accidentally set it off.'

'The mechanism responds only to a complex signal, like a code. These rockets are expensive, we don't take any risks.'

Larry said: 'I have to make a space rocket today. Can I take the yoghurt pot to school?'

'No, you can't, it's half full,' she told him.

'But I have to take some containers! Miss Page will be mad if I don't.' He was near to tears with the suddenness of a seven-year-old.

'What do you need containers for?'

'To make a space rocket! She told us last week.'

Billie sighed. 'Larry, if you had told *me* last week, I would have saved a whole bunch of stuff for you. How many times must I ask you not to leave things until the last minute?'

'Well, what am I gonna do?'

'I'll find you something. We'll put the yoghurt in a bowl, and . . . what kind of containers do you want?'

'Rocket shape.'

Billie wondered if schoolteachers ever thought about the amount of work they created for busy mothers when they blithely instructed children to bring things from home. She put buttered toast on three plates and served the scrambled eggs, but she did not eat her own. She went around the house and got a tube-shaped cardboard detergent container, a plastic liquid-soap bottle, an ice-cream carton, and a heart-shaped chocolate box.

Most of the packaging showed the products being used by families – generally a pretty housewife and two happy kids, with a pipe-smoking father in the background. She wondered if other women resented the stereotype as much as she did. She had never lived in a family like that. Her father, a poor tailor in Dallas, had died when she was a baby, and her mother had brought up five children in grinding poverty. Billie herself had been divorced since Larry was two. There were plenty of families without a man, where the mother was a widow, a divorcee, or what used to be called a fallen woman. But they did not show such families on the cornflakes boxes.

She put all the containers in a shopping bag for Larry to carry to school.

'Oh, boy, I bet I have more than anyone!' he said. 'Thanks, Mom.'

Her breakfast was cold, but Larry was happy.

A car horn tooted outside, and Billie quickly checked her appearance in the glass of a cupboard door. Her curly black hair had been hastily combed, she had no make-up on except the eyeliner she had failed to remove last night, and she was wearing an oversize pink sweater ... but the effect was kind of sexy.

The back door opened and Roy Brodsky came in. Roy was Larry's best friend, and the boys greeted one another joyously, as if they had been apart for a month instead of just a few hours. Billie had noticed that all Larry's friends were boys now. In kindergarten it had been different, boys and girls playing together indiscriminately. She wondered what psychological change took place, around the age of five, that made children prefer their own gender.

Roy was followed by his father, Harold, a good-looking man with soft brown eyes. Harold Brodsky was a widower: Roy's mother had died in a car wreck. Harold taught chemistry at the George Washington University. Billie and Harold were dating. He looked at her adoringly and said: 'My God, you look gorgeous.' She grinned and kissed his cheek.

Like Larry, Roy had a shopping bag full of cartons. Billie said to Harold: 'Did you have to empty half the containers in your kitchen?'

'Yes. I have little cereal bowls of soap flakes, chocolates, and processed cheese. And six toilet rolls without the cardboard cylinder in the middle.'

'Darn, I never thought of toilet rolls!'

He laughed. 'I wonder, would you like to have dinner at my place tonight?'

She was surprised. 'You're going to cook?'

'Not exactly. I thought I'd ask Mrs Riley to make a casserole that I could warm up.'

'Sure,' she said. She had not had dinner at his house before. They normally went to the movies, to concerts of classical music, or to cocktail parties at the homes of other university professors. She wondered what had prompted him to invite her.

'Roy's going to a cousin's birthday party tonight, and he'll sleep over. We'll have a chance to talk without interruption.'

'Okay,' Billie said thoughtfully. They could talk without interruption at a restaurant, of course. Harold had another reason for inviting her to his house when his child would be away for the night. She glanced at him. His expression was open and candid – he knew what she was thinking. 'That'll be great,' she said.

'I'll pick you up around eight. Come on, boys!' He shepherded the children out through the back door. Larry left without saying goodbye, which Billie had learned to take as a sign that all was well. When he was anxious about something, or coming down with an infection, he would hang back and cling to her.

'Harold is a good man,' her mother said. 'You should marry him soon, before he changes his mind.'

'He won't change his mind.'

'Just don't deal him in before he puts his stake on the table.'

Billie smiled at her mother. 'You don't miss much, do you, Ma?'

'I'm old, but I'm not stupid.'

Billie cleared the table and threw her own breakfast in the trash. Rushing now, she stripped her bed, Larry's, and her mother's, and bundled the sheets into a laundry bag. She showed Becky-Ma the bag and said: 'Remember, all you have to do is hand this to the laundry man when he calls, okay, Ma?'

Her mother said: 'I don't have any of my heart pills left.'

'Jesus Christ!' She rarely swore in front of her mother, but she was at the end of her rope. 'Ma, I have a busy day at work today, and I don't have time to go to the goddamn pharmacist!'

'I can't help it, I ran out.'

The most infuriating thing about Becky-Ma was the way she could switch from being a perceptive parent to a helpless child. 'You could have told me *yesterday* that you were running out – I shopped yesterday! I can't shop every day, I have a job.'

Becky-Ma burst into tears.

Billie relented immediately. 'I'm sorry, Ma,' she

said. Becky-Ma cried easily, like Larry. Five years ago, when the three of them had set up house together, Ma had helped take care of Larry. But nowadays she was barely able to look after him for a couple of hours when he came home from school. Everything would be easier if Billie and Harold were married.

The phone rang. She patted Ma on the shoulder and picked it up. It was Bern Rothsten, her ex-husband. Billie got on well with him, despite the divorce. He came by two or three times a week to see Larry; and he cheerfully paid his share of the cost of bringing up the boy. Billie had been angry with him, once, but it was a long time ago. Now she said: 'Hey, Bern – you're up early.'

'Yeah. Have you heard from Luke?'

She was taken aback. 'Luke Lucas? Lately? No – is something wrong?'

'I don't know, maybe.'

Bern and Luke shared the intimacy of rivals. When they were young they had argued endlessly. Their discussions often seemed acrimonious, yet they had remained close at college and all through the war. 'What's happened?' Billie said.

'He called me on Monday. I was kind of surprised. I don't hear from him often.'

'Nor do I.' Billie struggled to remember. 'Last time I saw him was a couple of years ago, I think.' Realizing how long it was, she wondered why she had let their friendship lapse. She was just busy all the time, she guessed. She regretted that.

'I got a note from him last summer,' Bern said. 'He'd been reading my books to his sister's kid.' Bern was the author of *The Terrible Twins*, a successful series of children's books. 'He said they made him laugh. It was a nice letter.'

'So why did he call you on Monday?'

'Said he was coming to Washington and wanted to see me. Something had happened.'

'Did he tell you what?'

'Not really. He just said: "It's like the stuff we used to do in the war".'

Billie frowned anxiously. Luke and Bern had been in OSS during the war, working behind enemy lines, helping the French resistance. But they had been out of that world since 1946 – hadn't they? 'What do you think he meant?'

'I don't know. He said he would call me when he reached Washington. He checked into the Carlton Hotel on Monday night. Now it's Wednesday, and he hasn't called. And his bed wasn't slept in last night.'

'How did you find that out?'

Bern made an impatient noise. 'Billie, you were in OSS too, what would you have done?'

'I guess I would have given a chambermaid a couple of bucks.'

'Right. So he was out all night and he hasn't come back.'

'Maybe he was cattin' around.'

'And maybe Billy Graham smokes reefer, but I don't think so, do you?'

Bern was right. Luke had a powerful sex drive, but he craved intensity, not variety, Billie knew. 'No, I don't think so,' she said.

'Call me if you hear from him, okay?'

'Sure, of course.'

'Be seeing you.'

'Bye.' Billie hung up.

Then she sat at the kitchen table, her chores forgotten, thinking about Luke.

1941

Route 138 meandered south through Massachusetts towards Rhode Island. There was no cloud, and the moon shone on the country roads. The old Ford had no heater. Billie was wrapped up in coat, scarf and gloves, but her feet were numb. However, she did not really mind. It was no great hardship to spend a couple of hours in a car alone with Luke Lucas, even if he was someone else's boyfriend. In her experience beautiful men were tediously vain, but this one seemed to be an exception.

It was taking for ever to drive to Newport, but Luke seemed to be enjoying the long journey. Some Harvard men were nervous with attractive women, and chain-smoked, or drank from hip flasks, smoothed their hair all the time and kept straightening their ties. Luke was relaxed, driving without apparent effort and chatting. There was little traffic, and he looked at her as much as at the road.

They talked about the war in Europe. That morning in Radcliffe Yard, rival student groups had set up stalls and handed out leaflets, the Interventionists passionately advocating that America should enter the war, the America Firsters arguing the opposite with equal fervour. A crowd had gathered, men and women, students and professors. The knowledge that Harvard boys would be among the first to die made the discussions highly emotional.

'I have cousins in Paris,' Luke said. 'I'd like us to go over there and rescue them. But that's kind of a personal reason.'

'I have a personal reason too, I'm Jewish,' Billie said. 'But rather than send Americans to die in Europe, I'd open our doors to refugees. Save lives instead of killing people.'

'That's what Anthony believes.'

Billie was still fuming about the night's fiasco. 'I can't tell you how mad I am at Anthony,' she said. 'He should have made sure we could stay at his friends' apartment.'

She was hoping for sympathy from Luke, but he disappointed her. 'I guess you both were a little too casual about the whole thing.' He said it with a friendly smile, but there was no mistaking the note of censure.

Billie was stung. However, she was indebted to him for this ride, so she swallowed the retort that sprang to her lips. 'You're defending your friend, which is fine,' she said gently. 'But I think he had a duty to protect my reputation.'

'Yes, but so did you.'

She was surprised he was so critical. Until now he had been all charm. 'You seem to think it was my fault!'

'It was bad luck, mainly,' he said. 'But Anthony put

you in a position where a little bad luck could do you a lot of damage.'

'That's the truth.'

'And you let him.'

She found herself dismayed by his disapproval. She wanted him to think well of her – though she did not know why she cared. 'Anyway, I'll never do that again, with any man,' she said vehemently.

'Anthony's a great guy, very smart, kind of eccentric.'

'He makes girls want to take care of him, brush his hair and press his suit and make him chicken soup.'

Luke laughed. 'Could I ask you a personal question?'

'You can try.'

He met her eyes for a moment. 'Are you in love with him?'

That was sudden – but she liked men who could surprise her, so she answered candidly. 'No. I'm fond of him, I enjoy his company, but I don't love him.' She thought about Luke's girlfriend. Elspeth was the most striking beauty on campus, a tall woman with long coppery hair and the pale, resolute face of a Nordic queen. 'What about you? Are you in love with Elspeth?'

He returned his gaze to the road. 'I don't think I know what love is.'

'Evasive answer.'

'You're right.' He threw a speculative look at her, then seemed to decide that she could be trusted. 'Well, to be honest, this is as close to love as I've ever come, but I still don't know if it's the real thing.'

She felt a pang of guilt. 'I wonder what Anthony and Elspeth would think of us having this conversation,' she said.

He coughed, embarrassed, and changed the subject. 'Damn shame you ran into those men at the House.'

'I hope Anthony won't be found out. He could be expelled.'

'He's not the only one. You might be in trouble, too.'

She had been trying not to think about that. 'I don't believe anyone knew who I was. I heard one of them say "tart".'

He shot a surprised glance at her.

She guessed that Elspeth would not have used the word 'tart', and she wished she had not repeated it. 'I suppose I deserved it,' she added. 'I was in a men's House at midnight.'

He said: 'I don't think there's ever any real excuse for bad manners.'

It was a reproach to her as much as to the man who had insulted her, she thought with annoyance. Luke had a sharp edge. He was angering her – but that made him interesting. She decided to take the gloves off. 'What about you?' she said. 'You're very preachy about Anthony and me, aren't you? But didn't you put Elspeth in a vulnerable situation tonight, keeping her out in your car until the early hours?'

To her surprise, he laughed appreciatively. 'You're right, and I'm a pompous idiot,' he said. 'We all took risks.'

'That's the truth.' She shuddered. 'I don't know what I'd do if I got thrown out.'

'Study somewhere else, I guess.'

She shook her head. 'I'm on a scholarship. My father's dead, my mother's a penniless widow. And if I were expelled for moral transgression, I'd have little chance of getting another scholarship. Why do you look surprised?'

'To be honest, I'd have to say you don't dress like a scholarship girl.'

She was pleased he had noticed her clothes. 'It's the Leavenworth Award,' she explained.

'Wow.' The Leavenworth was a famously generous grant, and thousands of outstanding students applied for it. 'You must be a genius.'

'I don't know about that,' she said, gratified by the respect in his voice. 'I'm not smart enough to make sure I have a place to stay the night.'

'On the other hand, being thrown out of college is not the worst thing in the world. Some of the cleverest people drop out – then go on to become millionaires.'

'It would be the end of the world for me. I don't want to be a millionaire, I want to help sick people get well.'

'You're going to be a doctor?'

'Psychologist. I want to understand how the mind works.'

'Why?'

'It's so mysterious and complicated. Things like logic, the way we think. Imagining something that isn't there in front of us – animals can't do that. The ability to remember – fish have no memory, did you know that?'

He nodded. 'And why is it that just about everyone can recognize a musical octave?' he said. 'Two notes, the frequency of one being double that of the other – how come your brain knows that?'

'You find it interesting, too!' She was pleased that he shared her curiosity.

'What did your father die of?'

Billie swallowed hard. Sudden grief overwhelmed her. She struggled against tears. It was always like this: a chance word, and from nowhere came a sorrow so acute she could barely speak.

'I'm really sorry,' Luke said. 'I didn't mean to upset you.'

'Not your fault,' she managed. She took a deep breath. 'He lost his mind. One Sunday morning he went bathing in the Trinity River. The thing is, he hated the water, and he couldn't swim. I think he wanted to die. The coroner thought so too, but the jury took pity on us and called it an accident, so that we'd get the life insurance. It was a hundred dollars. We lived on that for a year.' She took a deep breath. 'Let's talk about something else. Tell me about math.'

'Well.' He thought for a moment. 'Math is as weird as psychology,' he said. 'Take the number *pi*. Why should the ratio of circumference to diameter be three point one four two? Why not six, or two and a half? Who made that decision, and why?'

'You want to explore outer space.'

'I think it's the most exciting adventure mankind has ever had.'

'And I want to map the mind.' She smiled. The grief of bereavement was leaving her. 'You know, we have something in common – we both have big ideas.'

He laughed, then braked the car. 'Hey, we're coming to a crossroads.'

She switched on the flashlight and looked at the map on her knee. 'Turn right,' she said.

They were approaching Newport. The time had passed quickly. She felt sorry the trip was coming to an end. 'I have no idea what I'm going to tell my cousin,' she said.

'What's he like?'

'He's queer.'

'Queer? In what way?'

'In the homosexual way.'

He shot her a startled look. 'I see.'

She had no patience with men who expected women to tiptoe around the subject of sex. 'I've shocked you again, haven't I?'

He grinned at her. 'As you would say – that's the truth.'

She laughed. It was a Texan colloquialism. She was glad he noticed little things about her.

'There's a fork in the road,' he said.

She consulted the map again. 'You'll have to pull up, I can't find it.'

He stopped the car and leaned across to look at the

map in the light of the flash. He reached out to turn the map a little, and his touch was warm on her cold hand. 'Maybe we're here,' he said, pointing.

Instead of looking at the map, she found herself staring at his face. It was deeply shadowed, lit only by the moon and the indirect torchlight. His hair fell forward over his left eye. After a moment he felt her gaze, and glanced up at her. Without thinking, Billie lifted her hand and stroked his cheek with the outside edge of her little finger. He stared back at her, and she saw bewilderment and desire in his eyes.

'Which way do we go?' she murmured.

He moved away suddenly and put the car in gear. 'We take . . .' He cleared his throat. 'We take the left fork.'

Billie wondered what the hell she was doing. Luke had spent the evening smooching with the most beautiful girl on campus. Billie had been out with Luke's room-mate. What was she thinking about?

Her feelings for Anthony had not been strong, even before tonight's calamity. All the same, she *was* dating him, so she certainly should not be toying with his best friend.

'Why did you do that?' Luke said angrily.

'I don't know,' she said. 'I didn't intend to, it just happened. Slow down.'

He took a bend too fast. 'I don't want to feel like this about you!' he said.

She was suddenly breathless. 'Like what?'

'Never mind.'

The smell of the sea came into the car, and Billie realized they were close to her cousin's home. She recognized the road. 'Next left,' she said. 'If you don't slow down you'll miss it.'

Luke braked and turned on to a dirt road.

Half of Billie wanted to arrive at the destination and get out of the car and leave behind this unbearable tension. The other half wanted to drive with Luke for ever.

'We're here,' she said.

They stopped outside a neat one-storey frame house with gingerbread eaves and a lamp by the door. The Ford's headlights picked out a cat sitting motionless on a windowsill, looking at them with a calm gaze, disdainful of the turmoil of human emotion.

'Come in,' Billie said. 'Denny will make some coffee to keep you awake on the return trip.'

'No, thanks,' he said. 'I'll just wait here until you're safely inside.'

'You've been very kind to me. I don't think I deserve it.' She held out her hand to shake.

'Are we friends?' he said, taking her hand.

She lifted his hand to her face, kissed it, and pressed it against her cheek, closing her eyes. After a moment she heard him groan softly. She opened her eyes and found him staring at her. His hand moved behind her head, he pulled her to him, and they kissed. It was a gentle kiss, soft lips and warm breath and his fingertips light on the back of her neck. She held the lapel of his rough tweed coat and pulled him closer. If he grabbed her now, she would not resist, she knew. The thought made her burn with desire. Feeling wild, she took his lip between her teeth and bit.

She heard Denny's voice. 'Who's out there?'

She pulled away from Luke and looked out. There were lights on in the house, and Denny stood in the doorway, wearing a purple silk dressing gown.

She turned back to Luke. 'I could fall in love with you in about twenty minutes,' she said. 'But I don't think we can be friends.'

She stared at him a moment longer, seeing in his eyes the same churning conflict she felt in her heart. Then she looked away, took a deep breath, and got out of the car.

'Billie?' said Denny. 'For heaven's sake, what are you doing here?'

She crossed the yard, stepped on to the porch and fell into his arms. 'Oh, Denny,' she murmured. 'I love that man, and he belongs to some woman!'

Denny patted her back with a delicate touch. 'Honey, I know *just* how you feel.'

She heard the car move, and turned to wave. As it swung by, she saw Luke's face – and the glint of something shiny on his cheeks.

Then he disappeared into the darkness.

8.30 A.M.

Perched on top of the pointed nose of the Redstone rocket is what looks like a large birdhouse with a steeply pitched roof and a flagpole stuck through its centre. This section, about thirteen feet long, contains the second, third and fourth stages of the missile – and the satellite itself.

Secret agents in America had never been as powerful as they were in January 1958.

The Director of the CIA, Allen Dulles, was the brother of John Foster Dulles, Eisenhower's Secretary of State – so the Agency had a direct line into the administration. But that was only half the reason.

Under Dulles were four Deputy Directors, only one of whom was important – the Deputy Director for Plans. The Plans Directorate was also known as CS, for Clandestine Services, and this was the department that had carried out coups against left-leaning governments in Iran and Guatemala.

The Eisenhower White House had been amazed and delighted by how cheap and bloodless these coups were, especially by comparison with the cost of a real war such as that in Korea. Consequently, the guys in Plans enjoyed enormous prestige in government circles

– though not among the American public, who had been told by their newspapers that both coups were the work of local anti-communist forces.

Within the Plans Directorate was Technical Services, the division that Anthony Carroll headed. He had been hired when the CIA was set up in 1947. He had always planned to work in Washington – his major at Harvard had been government – and he had been a star of OSS in the war. Posted to Berlin earlier in the fifties, he had organized the digging of a tunnel from the American sector to a telephone conduit in the Soviet zone, and had tapped into KGB communications. The tunnel remained undiscovered for six months, during which the CIA amassed a mountain of priceless information. It had been the greatest intelligence coup of the Cold War, and Anthony's reward had been the top job.

Technical Services was theoretically a training division. There was a big old farmhouse down in Virginia where recruits learned how to break into houses and plant concealed microphones, to use codes and invisible ink, to blackmail diplomats and browbeat informers. But 'training' also served as an all-purpose cover for covert actions inside the USA. The fact that the CIA was prohibited, by law, from operating within the United States was no more than a minor inconvenience. Just about anything Anthony wanted to do, from bugging the phones of union bosses to testing truth drugs on prison inmates, could be labelled a training exercise.

The surveillance of Luke was no exception.

Six experienced agents were gathered in Anthony's office. It was a large, bare room with cheap wartime furniture: a small desk, a steel filing cabinet, a trestle table and a set of folding chairs. No doubt the new headquarters at Langley would be full of upholstered couches and mahogany panelling, but Anthony liked the Spartan look.

Pete Maxell passed around a mug shot of Luke and a typed description of his clothes while Anthony briefed the agents. 'Our target today is a middle-ranking State Department employee with a high security clearance,' he said. 'He's having some kind of nervous breakdown. He flew in from Paris on Monday, spent Monday night in the Carlton Hotel, and went on a drinking binge on Tuesday. He stayed out all last night, and went to a shelter for homeless people this morning. The security risk is obvious.'

One of the agents, 'Red' Rifenberg, put up a hand. 'Question.'

'Go ahead.'

'Why don't we just pull him in, ask him what the hell goes on?'

'We will, eventually.'

Anthony's office door opened, and Carl Hobart came in. A plump, bald man with spectacles, he was head of Specialized Services, which included Records and Decrypting as well as Technical Services. In theory, he was Anthony's immediate boss. Anthony groaned inwardly and prayed that Hobart would not interfere with what he was doing, today of all days.

Anthony continued with his briefing. 'But before we

tip our hand, we want to see what the subject does, where he goes – who he contacts, if anyone. A case like this, he may just be having trouble with his wife. But it could be that he's giving information to the other side, either for ideological reasons or because they're blackmailing him, and now the strain has gotten to be too much for him. If he's involved in some kind of treason, we need all the information we can get *before* we pick him up.'

Hobart interrupted. 'What's this?'

Anthony turned to him slowly. 'A little training exercise. We're conducting surveillance on a suspect diplomat.'

'Give it to the FBI,' Hobart said abruptly.

Hobart had spent the war in Naval Intelligence. For him, espionage was a plain matter of finding out where the enemy was and what he was doing there. He disliked OSS veterans and their dirty tricks. The split went right down the middle of the Agency. The OSS men were buccaneers. They had learned their trade in wartime, and had scant respect for budgets and protocol. The bureaucrats were infuriated by their nonchalance. And Anthony was the archetypal buccaneer: an arrogant daredevil who got away with murder because he was so good at it.

Anthony gave Hobart a cool look. 'Why?'

'It's the FBI's job, not ours, to catch communist spies in America – as you know perfectly well.'

'We need to follow the thread to its source. A case like this can unlock a horde of information if we handle it right. But the Feds are only interested in getting publicity for putting Reds in the electric chair.'

'It's the law!'

'But you and I know it's horseshit.'

'Makes no difference.'

One thing shared by the rival groups within the CIA was a hatred of the FBI and its megalomaniac director, J. Edgar Hoover. So Anthony said: 'Anyway, when was the last time the FBI gave us anything?'

'The last time was never,' Hobart said. 'But I've got another assignment for you today.'

Anthony began to feel angry. Where did this asshole get off? It was not his job to hand out assignments. 'What are you talking about?'

'The White House has called for a report on ways to deal with a rebel group in Cuba. There's a top-level meeting later this morning. I need you and all your experienced people to brief me.'

'You're asking me for a briefing on Fidel Castro?'

'Of course not. I know all about Castro. What I need from you are practical ideas for dealing with insurgency.'

Anthony despised this kind of mealy-mouthed talk. 'Why don't you say what you mean? You want to know how to take them out.'

'Maybe.'

Anthony laughed scornfully. 'Well, what else would we do – start a Sunday School for them?'

'That's for the White House to decide. Our job is to present options. You can give me some suggestions.'

Anthony maintained a show of indifference, but inside he was worried. He had no time for distractions today, and he needed all his best people to keep an eye on Luke. 'I'll see what I can do,' Anthony said, hoping Hobart might be satisfied with a vague assurance.

He was not. 'My conference room, with all your most experienced agents, at ten o'clock – and no excuses.' He turned away.

Anthony made a decision. 'No,' he said.

Hobart turned at the door. 'This is not a suggestion,' he said. 'Just be there.'

'Watch my lips,' said Anthony.

Reluctantly, Hobart stared at Anthony's face.

Enunciating carefully, Anthony said: 'Fuck off.'

One of the agents sniggered.

Hobart's bald head reddened. 'You'll hear more about this,' he said. 'A lot more.' He went out and slammed the door.

Everyone burst out laughing.

'Back to work,' Anthony said. 'Simons and Betts are with the subject at this moment, but they're due to be relieved in a few minutes. As soon as they call in, I want Red Rifenberg and Ackie Horwitz to take over the surveillance. We'll run four shifts of six hours each, with a back-up team always on call. That's all for now.'

The agents trooped out, but Pete Maxell stayed back. He had shaved and put on his regular business suit with a narrow Madison Avenue tie. Now his bad teeth and the red birthmark on his cheek were more noticeable, like broken windows in a new house. He was shy and unsociable, perhaps because of his appearance, and he was devoted to his few friends. Now he looked concerned as he said to Anthony: 'Aren't you taking a risk with Hobart?'

'He's an asshole.'

'He's your boss.'

'I can't let him close down an important surveillance operation.'

'But you lied to him. He could easily find out that Luke isn't a diplomat from Paris.'

Anthony shrugged. 'Then I'll tell him another story.'

Pete looked doubtful, but he nodded assent and moved to the door.

Anthony said: 'But you're right. I'm sticking my neck all the way out. If something goes wrong, Hobart won't miss a chance to chop my head off.'

'That's what I thought.'

'Then we'd better make sure nothing goes wrong.'

Pete went out. Anthony watched the phone, making himself calm and patient. Office politics infuriated him, but men such as Hobart were always around. After five minutes the phone rang and he picked it up. 'Carroll here.'

'You've been upsetting Carl Hobart again.' It was the wheezy voice of a man who has been smoking and drinking enthusiastically for most of a lifetime.

'Good morning, George,' said Anthony. George Cooperman was Deputy Chief of Operations and a wartime comrade of Anthony's. He was Hobart's immediate superior. 'Hobart should stay out of my way.'

'Get over here, you arrogant young prick,' George said amiably.

'Coming.' Anthony hung up. He opened his desk drawer and took out an envelope containing a thick sheaf of Xerox copies. Then he put on his topcoat and walked to Cooperman's office, which was in P Building, next door.

Cooperman was a tall, gaunt man of fifty with a prematurely lined face. He had his feet on his desk. There was a giant coffee mug at his elbow and a cigarette in his mouth. He was reading the Moscow newspaper *Pravda*: he had majored in Russian literature at Princeton.

He threw down the paper. 'Why can't you be nice to that fat fuck?' he growled. He spoke without removing the cigarette from the corner of his mouth. 'I know it's hard, but you could do it for my sake.'

Anthony sat down. 'It's his own fault. He should have realized by now that I only insult him if he speaks to me first.'

'What's your excuse this time?'

Anthony tossed the envelope on to the desk. Cooperman picked it up and looked at the Xerox copies. 'Blueprints,' he said. 'Of a rocket, I guess. So what?'

'They're top secret. I took them from the surveillance subject. He's a spy, George.'

'And you chose not to tell Hobart that.'

'I want to follow this guy around until he reveals his whole network – then use his operation for disinformation. Hobart would hand the case over to the FBI, who would pick the guy up and throw him in jail, and his network would fade to black.'

'Hell, you're right about that. Still, I need you at this meeting. I'm chairing it. But you can let your team carry on the surveillance. If anything happens they can get you out of the conference room.'

'Thanks, George.'

'And listen. This morning you fucked Hobart up the ass in front of a room full of agents, didn't you?'

'I guess so.'

'Next time, try and do it gently, okay?' Cooperman picked up *Pravda* again. Anthony got up to leave, taking the blueprints. Cooperman said: 'And make damn sure you run this surveillance right. If you screw up on top of insulting your boss, I may not be able to protect you.'

Anthony went out.

He did not return to his office right away. The row of condemned buildings that housed this part of the CIA filled a strip of land between Constitution Avenue and the mall with the reflecting pool. The motor entrances were on the street side, but Anthony went out through a back gate into the park.

He strolled along the avenue of English elms, breathing the cold fresh air, soothed by the ancient trees and the still water. There had been some bad moments this morning, but he had held it together, with a different set of lies for each party in the game.

He came to the end of the avenue and stood at the halfway point between the Lincoln Memorial and the Washington Monument. This is all your fault, he thought, addressing the two great presidents. You made men believe they could be free. I'm fighting for your ideals. I'm not even sure I believe in ideals any more – but I guess I'm too ornery to quit. Did you guys feel that way?

The presidents did not answer, and after a while Anthony returned to Q Building.

In his office he found Pete with the team that had been shadowing Luke: Simons, in a navy topcoat, and Betts, wearing a green raincoat. Also there were the team that should have relieved them, Rifenberg and Horwitz. 'What the hell is this?' Anthony said with sudden fear. 'Who's with Luke?'

Simons was carrying a grey Homburg hat, and it shook as his hand trembled. 'Nobody,' he said.

'What happened?' Anthony roared. 'What the fuck happened, you assholes?'

After a moment, Pete answered. 'We, uh . . .' He swallowed. 'We've lost him.'

PART 2

PART 2

9 A.M.

The Jupiter C has been built for the Army by the Chrysler Corporation. The large rocket engine that propels the first stage is manufactured by North American Aviation, Inc. The second, third and fourth stages have been designed and tested by the Jet Propulsion Laboratory in Pasadena.

Luke was angry with himself. He had handled things badly. He had found two people who probably knew who he was – and he had lost them again.

He was back in the low-rent neighbourhood near the gospel shop on H Street. The winter daylight was brightening, making the streets look more grimy, the buildings older, the people shabbier. He saw two bums in the doorway of a vacant store, passing a bottle of beer. He shuddered and walked quickly by.

Then he realized that was strange. An alcoholic wanted booze any time. But to Luke, the thought of beer this early in the day was nauseating. Therefore, he concluded with enormous relief, he could not be an alcoholic.

But, if he was not a drunk, what was he?

He summed up what he knew about himself. He was in his thirties. He did not smoke. Despite

83

appearances, he was not an alcoholic. At some point in his life he had been involved in clandestine work. And he knew the words of 'What a Friend We Have in Jesus.' It was pathetically little.

He had been walking around looking for a police station, but he had not come across one. He decided to ask for directions. A minute later, as he passed a vacant lot fenced with broken corrugated-iron sheeting, he saw a uniformed cop step through a gap in the sheeting on to the sidewalk. Seizing the chance, Luke said to him: 'How do I get to the nearest precinct house?'

The cop was a beefy man with a sandy moustache. He gave Luke a look of contempt and said: 'In the trunk of my cruiser, if you don't get the fuck out of my sight.'

Luke was startled by the violence of his language. What was the man's problem? But he was tired of tramping the streets, and he needed directions, so he persisted. 'I just need to know where the station house is.'

'I won't tell you again, shitbrain.'

Luke was annoyed. Who did he think he was? 'I asked you a polite question, Mister,' he snapped.

The cop moved surprisingly fast for a heavy man. He grabbed Luke by the lapels of his ragged coat and shoved him through the gap in the sheeting. Luke staggered and fell on a patch of rough concrete, hurting his arm.

To his surprise he was not alone. Just inside the lot was a young woman. She had dyed blonde hair and heavy make-up, and she wore a long coat open over a loose dress. She had high-heeled evening shoes and torn stockings. She was pulling up her panties. Luke realized she was a prostitute who had just serviced the patrolman.

The cop came through the gap and kicked Luke in the stomach.

He heard the whore say: 'For Christ's sake, Sid, what did he do, spit on the sidewalk? Leave the poor bum alone!'

'Fucker has to learn some respect,' the cop said thickly.

Out of the corner of his eye, Luke saw him draw his nightstick and raise it. As the blow came down, Luke rolled to one side. He was not quite fast enough, and the end of the stick glanced off his left shoulder, numbing his arm momentarily. The cop raised the nightstick again.

A circuit closed in Luke's brain.

Instead of rolling away, he threw himself towards the cop. The man's forward momentum brought him crashing to the ground, and he dropped the nightstick. Luke sprang up nimbly. As the cop got up, Luke stepped close to him, waltzing inside his reach so that the man could not punch him. He grabbed the lapels of the uniform coat, pulled the man forward with a sharp jerk, and butted him in the face. There was a snapping sound as the cop's nose broke. The man roared with pain.

Luke released his grip on the lapels, pirouetted on one foot, and kicked the man in the side of the knee.

His battered shoes were not rigid enough to break bones, but the knee has little resistance to a blow from the side, and the cop fell.

A part of Luke's mind wondered where the hell he had learned to fight like this.

The cop was bleeding from the nose and mouth, but he raised himself on his left elbow and drew his gun with his right hand.

Before it was out of the holster, Luke was on him. Grabbing the man's right forearm, he banged the hand on the concrete once, very hard. The gun immediately fell from the cop's grasp. Then Luke pulled the cop upright and twisted his arm so that he rolled onto his front. Bending the arm up behind the man's back, Luke dropped, driving both knees into the small of the cop's back, knocking the breath out of his lungs. Finally, he took the cop's forefinger and bent it all the way back.

The cop screamed. Luke bent the finger farther. He heard it snap, and the cop fainted.

'You won't beat up any more bums for a while,' Luke said. 'Shitbrain.'

He stood up. He picked up the gun, ejected all the shells, and threw them across the lot.

The whore was staring at him. 'Who the fuck are you, Elliott Ness?' she said.

Luke looked back at her. She was thin, and under the make-up her complexion was bad. 'I don't know who I am,' he told her.

'Well, you ain't no bum, that's for sure,' she said. 'I

never saw an alky that could punch out a big fat prick like Sidney here.'

'That's what I've been thinking.'

'We better get out of here,' she said. 'He's going to be mad when he comes round.'

Luke nodded. He was not afraid of Sidney, mad or otherwise, but before long there would be more cops on the scene, and he needed to be elsewhere. He stepped through the gap in the fence on to the street and walked away quickly.

The woman followed him, stiletto heels clicking on the sidewalk. He slowed his pace to let her catch up, feeling a kind of camaraderie with her. They had both been abused by Sidney the patrolman.

'It was kind of nice to see Sidney come up against someone he couldn't push around,' she said. 'I guess I owe you.'

'Not at all.'

'Well, next time you're feeling horny, it's on the house.'

Luke tried not to show his revulsion. 'What's your name?'

'Dee-Dee.'

He raised an eyebrow at her.

'Well, Doris Dobbs, really,' she admitted. 'But what kind of name is that for a good-time girl?'

'I'm Luke. I don't know my surname. I've lost my memory.'

'Wow. That must make you feel, like . . . strange.'

'Disoriented.'

'Yeah,' she said. 'That's the word was on the tip of my tongue.'

He glanced at her. There was a wry grin on her face. He realized she was making fun of him, and he liked her for it. 'It's not just that I don't know my name and address,' he explained. 'I don't even know what kind of person I am.'

'What do you mean?'

'I wonder if I'm honest?' Maybe it was foolish, he thought, to pour out his heart to a whore on the street, but he had no one else. 'Am I a loyal husband and a loving father and a reliable workmate? Or am I some kind of gangster? I hate not knowing.'

'Honey, if that's what's bothering you, I know what kind of guy you are already. A gangster would be thinking am I rich, do I slay the broads, are people scared of me?'

That was a point. Luke nodded. But he was not satisfied. 'It's one thing to want to be a good person – but maybe I don't live up to what I believe in.'

'Welcome to the human race, sweetheart,' she said. 'We all feel that way.' She stopped at a doorway. 'It's been a long night. This is where I get off the train.'

'So long.'

She hesitated. 'Want some advice?'

'Sure.'

'If you want people to stop treating you like a piece of shit, you better smarten yourself up. Have a shave, comb your hair, find yourself a coat that doesn't look like you stole it off a carthorse.'

Luke realized she was right. No one would take any

notice of him, let alone help him discover his identity, while he looked like a crazy person. 'I guess you're right,' he said. 'Thanks.' He turned away.

She called after him: 'And get a hat!'

He touched his head, then looked around. He was the only person on the street, male or female, without a hat. But how could a bum get a new suit of clothes? The handful of change in his pocket would not buy much.

The solution came fully formed into his head. Either it was an easy question, or he had been in this situation before. He would go to a train station. A station was generally full of people carrying complete changes of clothing, together with shaving tackle and other toiletries, all neatly packed in suitcases.

He went to the next corner and checked his location. He was on A Street and Seventh. On leaving Union Station early this morning, he had noticed that it was near the corner of F and Second.

He headed that way.

10 A.M.

The first stage of the missile is attached to the second by explosive bolts wrapped around with coil springs. When the booster is burned out, the bolts will detonate and the springs push the redundant first stage away.

The Georgetown Mind Hospital was a red-brick Victorian mansion with a flat-roofed modern extension at the back. Billie Josephson parked her red Ford Thunderbird in the parking lot and hurried into the building.

She hated to arrive this late. It seemed disrespectful of her work and her colleagues. What they were doing was vitally important. Slowly, painstakingly, they were learning to understand the mechanisms of the human mind. It was like mapping a distant planet, the surface of which could be seen only through breaks in the cloud layer that were tantalizingly brief.

She was late because of her mother. After Larry left for school, Billie had gone to get the heart pills and returned home to find Becky-Ma lying on her bed, fully dressed, gasping for breath. The doctor had come right away, but he had nothing new to say. Becky-Ma had a weak heart. If she felt breathless, she should lie

90

down. She must remember to take her pills. Any stress was bad for her.

Billie wanted to say: 'What about me? Isn't stress bad for me, too?' But instead she resolved anew to walk on eggshells around her mother.

She stopped by the admissions office and glanced at the overnight register. A new patient had been brought in late yesterday, after she had left: Joseph Bellow, a schizophrenic. The name rang a bell, but she could not recall why. Surprisingly, the patient had been discharged during the night. That was odd.

She passed through the day room on the way to her office. The TV was on, and a reporter standing on a dusty beach was saying: 'Here at Cape Canaveral, the question on everyone's lips is: "When will the army attempt to launch its own rocket?" It must be within the next few days.'

The subjects of Billie's research sat around, some watching TV, some playing games or reading, a few gazing vacantly into space. She waved to Tom, a young man who did not know the meaning of words. 'How are you, Tommy?' she called. He grinned and waved back. He could read body language well, and often responded as if he knew what people were saying, so it had taken Billie months to figure out that he did not understand a single word.

In a corner Marlene, an alcoholic, was flirting with a young male nurse. She was fifty years old, but she could not remember anything that had happened since she was nineteen. She thought she was still a young girl, and refused to believe that the 'old man' who loved and cared for her was her husband.

Through the glass wall of an interview room she saw Ronald, a brilliant architect who had suffered head injuries in a car crash. He was doing tests on paper. His problem was that he had lost the ability to deal with numbers. He would count with excruciating slowness on his fingers in the attempt to add three and four.

Many patients had forms of schizophrenia, an inability to relate to the real world.

Some of the patients could be helped, by drugs or electric-shock treatment or both; but Billie's job was to trace the exact contours of their disabilities. By studying minor mental handicaps, she was outlining the functions of the normal mind. Ronald, the architect, could look at a group of objects on a tray and say whether there were three or four of them, but if there were twelve and he had to count them, he would take a long time and might make a mistake. This suggested to Billie that the ability to see at a glance how many items are in a small group is a separate skill from the ability to count.

In this way, she was slowly charting the depths of the mind, locating memory here, language there, mathematics somewhere else. And if the disability was related to minor brain damage, Billie could speculate that the normal ability was located in the part of the brain that had been destroyed. Eventually, her conceptual picture of the mind's functions would be mapped on to a physical diagram of the human brain.

At her present rate of progress, it would take about two hundred years. However, she was working alone. With a team of psychologists she could progress much faster. She might see the map completed in her lifetime. That was her ambition.

It was a long way from her father's suicidal depression. There were no quick cures in mental illness. But the mind was still largely a mystery to scientists. It would be much better understood if Billie could speed up her work. And then, perhaps, people like her father could be helped.

She went up the stairs to the next floor, thinking about the mystery patient. Joseph Bellow sounded like Joe Blow, the kind of name someone might make up. And why had he been discharged in the middle of the night?

She reached her office and looked out of the window on to a building site. A new wing was being added to the hospital – and a new post was to be created to go with it: Director of Research. Billie had applied for the job. But so had one of her colleagues, Dr Leonard Ross. Len was older than Billie, but she had wider experience and had published more: several articles and a textbook, *An Introduction to the Psychology of Memory*. She felt sure she could beat out Len, but she did not know who else might be in the running. And she wanted the job badly. As Director, she would have other scientists working under her.

On the building site she noticed, among the workmen, a small group of men in business clothes – wool topcoats and Homburgs instead of overalls and hard hats. They looked as if they might be getting a tour. Looking more closely, she saw that Len Ross was with them.

She spoke to her secretary. 'Who are those guys being shown around the site by Len Ross?'

'They're from the Sowerby Foundation.'

Billie frowned. The Foundation was financing the new post. They would have a big say in who got the job. And there was Len making nice to them. 'Did we know they were coming today?'

'Len said he had sent you a note. He came by this morning to pick you up, but you weren't here.'

There had never been a note, Billie felt sure. Len had deliberately failed to warn her. And she had been late.

'Damn,' Billie said with feeling. She rushed out to join the party on the building site.

She did not think about Joseph Bellow again for several hours.

11 A.M.

Because the missile was put together in a rush, the upper stages use a rocket motor that has been in production for some years, rather than a new design. The scientists have chosen a small version of the tried-and-tested Sergeant rocket. The upper stages of the missile are powered by clustered assemblies of these small rockets, known as Baby Sergeants.

As Luke negotiated the grid of streets leading to Union Station, he found himself checking, every minute or two, to see whether he was being followed.

He had lost his shadows more than an hour ago, but they might now be searching for him. The thought made him fearful and bewildered. Who were they and what were they doing? His instincts told him they were malevolent. Otherwise, why watch him secretly?

He shook his head to clear it. This baseless speculation was frustrating. There was no point in guessing. He had to find out.

First he had to clean himself up. His plan was to steal a suitcase from a train passenger. He felt sure he had done this before, at some time in his life. When he tried to remember, French words came into his head: 'La valise d'un type qui descend du train.'

It would not be easy. His dirty, ragged clothing would stand out in a crowd of respectable travellers. He would have to move fast to get away. But he had no alternative. Dee-Dee the whore had been right. No one would listen to a bum.

If he were arrested, the police would never believe he was anything but a deadbeat. He would end up in jail. The thought made him shiver with fear. It was not prison itself that scared him so much as the prospect of weeks or months of ignorance and confusion, not knowing who he was and helpless to make any progress finding out.

Ahead of him on Massachusetts Avenue he saw the white granite arcade of Union Station, like a Romanesque cathedral transplanted from Normandy. Thinking ahead, he figured that after the theft he would have to disappear fast. He needed a car. The knowledge of how to steal one came into his mind immediately.

Close to the station, the street was lined with parked cars. Most would belong to people who had taken trains. He slowed his pace as a car pulled into a slot ahead of him. It was a two-tone Ford Fairlane, blue and white, new but not ostentatious. It would do fine. The starter would be operated with a key, not a handle, but it would be easy to pull out a couple of wires behind the dash and bypass the ignition.

He wondered how he knew that.

A man in a dark topcoat got out of the Ford, took a briefcase from the trunk, locked the car, and headed for the station.

How long would he be gone? It was possible he had some business at the station and would be back in a few minutes. Then he would report his car stolen. Driving around in it, Luke would be in danger of arrest at any minute. That was no good. He had to find out where the man was going.

He followed him into the station.

The grand interior, which this morning had seemed like a disused temple, was now bustling. He felt conspicuous. Everyone else seemed so clean and well dressed. Most people averted their eyes, but some looked at him with expressions of disgust or contempt. It occurred to him that he might run into the officious man who had thrown him out earlier. Then there would be a fuss. The guy was sure to remember.

The owner of the Ford joined a line at a ticket window. Luke got in line too. He looked at the ground, not meeting anyone's eye, hoping no one would notice him.

The line shuffled forward and his mark reached the window. 'Philadelphia, one-day return,' he said.

That was enough for Luke. Philadelphia was hours away. The man would be out of town all day. His car would not be reported stolen before he returned. Luke would be safe in it until tonight.

He left the line and hurried away.

It was a relief to be outside. Even bums had the right to walk the streets. He returned to Massachusetts Avenue and found the parked Ford. To save time later, he would unlock it now. He looked up and down the street. Cars and pedestrians were passing constantly.

The trouble was that he looked like a criminal. But if he waited until there was no one about, he could be here all day. He would just have to be quick.

He stepped into the road, walked around the car, and stood at the driver's door. Pressing his hands flat against the glass of the window, he pushed down. Nothing happened. His mouth felt dry. He looked quickly to either side: no one was paying him any attention yet. He stood on tiptoe, to add the weight of his body to the pressure on the window mechanism. At last the pane of glass slid slowly down.

When the window was fully open, he reached in and unlocked the door. He opened it, wound up the window, and closed the door again. Now he was ready for a fast getaway.

He considered starting the car now and leaving the engine running, but that might draw the attention of a passing patrolman or even just an inquisitive passer-by.

He returned to Union Station. He worried constantly that a railroad employee would notice him. It did not have to be the man he had clashed with earlier – any conscientious official might take it in to his head to throw him out, the way such a man might pick up a candy wrapper. He did everything he could to make himself inconspicuous. He walked neither slow nor fast, tried to keep close to walls when he could, took care not to cross anyone's path, and never looked anyone in the eye.

The best time to steal a suitcase would be immediately after the arrival of a large, crowded train, when the concourse was thronged with hurrying people. He studied the information board. An express from New York was due in twelve minutes. That would be perfect.

As he looked at the board, checking which track the train would come in on, the hairs on the back of his neck stood up.

He looked around. He must have seen something out of the corner of his eye, something that had triggered an instinctive warning. What? His heart beat faster. What was he afraid of?

Trying to be inconspicuous, he strolled away from the board and stood at the news-stand, examining a rack of daily papers. He took in the headlines:

ARMY ROCKET BLAST SOON
SLAYER OF 10 IS NABBED
DULLES ASSURES BAGHDAD GROUP
LAST CHANCE AT CAPE CANAVERAL

After a moment he looked back over his shoulder. A couple of dozen people criss-crossed the concourse, hurrying to or from suburban trains. A larger number sat on the mahogany benches or stood around patiently, relatives and chauffeurs waiting to meet passengers off the New York train. A maître d' stood outside the door of the restaurant, hoping for early lunch customers. There were five porters in a group, smoking . . .

And two agents.

He was quite certain what they were. Both were

young men, neatly dressed in topcoats and hats, their wingtip shoes well shined. But it was not their appearance so much as their attitude that gave them away. They were alert, raking the station concourse with their eyes, studying the faces of the people they passed, looking everywhere ... except at the information board. The one thing they were not interested in was travel.

He was tempted to speak to them. Thinking about it, he was overwhelmed by a need for simple human contact with people who knew him. He longed for someone to say: 'Hi, Luke, how are you? Good to see you again!'

These two would probably say: 'We are FBI agents and you are under arrest.' Luke felt that would almost be a relief. But his instincts warned him off. Every time he thought of trusting them, he asked himself why they would follow him around surreptitiously if they meant him no harm.

He turned his back to them and walked away, trying to keep the news-stand between him and them. In the shadow of a grand archway he risked a backwards look. The two men were crossing the open concourse, walking from east to west across his field of vision.

Who the hell were they?

He left the station, walked a few yards along the grand arcade of its front, and re-entered the main hall. He was in time to see the backs of the two agents as they headed for the west exit.

He checked the clock. Ten minutes had passed. The New York express was due in two minutes. He hurried to the gate and waited, trying to fade into the background.

As the first passengers emerged, a frigid calm descended on him. He watched the arrivals intently. It was a Wednesday, the middle of the week, so there were many businessmen and military types in uniform, but few tourists, and only a sprinkling of women and children. He looked for a man his own size and build.

As passengers poured through the gate, the people waiting surged forward and a traffic jam formed. The crowd around the gate thickened, then spread, with people pushing through irritably. Luke saw a young man of his size, but he was wearing a duffel coat and a wool watch cap: he might not have a spare suit in his haversack. Likewise, Luke dismissed an elderly traveller who was the right height but too thin. He saw a man who looked just right but carried only a briefcase.

By this time at least a hundred passengers had emerged, but there seemed to be many more to come. The concourse filled up with impatient people. Then he saw the right man. He was Luke's height, build and age. His grey topcoat was unbuttoned to show a tweed sport coat and flannel pants – which meant he probably had a business suit in the tan leather case he carried in his right hand. His face wore an anxious look, and he walked quickly, as if he were late for an appointment.

Luke slipped into the crowd and shoved his way through until he was directly behind the man.

The throng was dense and slow-moving, and Luke's target moved in fretful stops and starts. Then the crowd thinned a little, and the man stepped quickly into a gap.

That was when Luke tripped him. He hooked his foot firmly around the ankle in front of him. As the man moved forward, Luke kicked upward, bending the target's leg at the knee.

The man cried out and fell forward. He let go of both briefcase and suitcase, and threw his hands out in front of him. He crashed into the back of a woman in a fur coat and she, too, stumbled, giving a little scream, and fell. The man hit the marble floor with an audible thump, his hat rolling away. A split second later the woman went down on both knees, dropping a handbag and a chic white leather suitcase.

Other passengers quickly gathered around, trying to help, saying: 'Are you all right?'

Luke calmly picked up the tan leather suitcase and walked quickly away. He headed for the nearest exit arch. He did not look back, but he listened intently for shouted accusations or sounds of pursuit. If he heard anything, he was ready to run: he was not going to give up his clean clothes easily, and he felt he could probably outrun most people, even carrying a suitcase. But his back felt like a bull's-eye target as he walked briskly toward the doors.

At the exit, he glanced back over his shoulder. The crowd was milling around the same spot. He could not see the man he had tripped, nor the woman in the fur coat. But a tall man with an authoritative air was scanning the concourse keenly, as if looking for something. His head swivelled suddenly toward Luke.

Luke stepped quickly through the door.

Outside, he headed down Massachusetts Avenue. A minute later he reached the Ford Fairlane. He went automatically for the trunk, so that he could hide the stolen suitcase – but the trunk was locked. He recalled seeing the owner lock it. He looked back toward the station. The tall man was running across the traffic circle in front of the station, dodging cars, heading Luke's way. Who was he – off-duty cop? Detective? Nosy Parker?

Luke went quickly around to the driver's door, opened it, and slung the bag onto the back seat. Then he got in and slammed the door.

He reached under the dash and found the wires on either side of the ignition lock. He pulled them out and touched them together. Nothing happened. He felt sweat on his forehead, despite the cold. Why was this not working? The answer came into his head: Wrong wire. He felt under the dash again. There was another wire to the right of the ignition. He pulled it out and touched it to the wire on the left.

The engine started.

He pressed the gas pedal, and the engine raced.

He put the transmission into drive, released the parking brake, flicked the indicator, and pulled out. The car was pointing towards the station, so he did a U-turn. Then he drove off.

A smile crossed his face. Unless he was very unlucky, he had a complete set of fresh clothes in the bag. He felt he had begun to take charge of his life.

Now he needed somewhere to shower and change.

12 NOON

The second stage consists of eleven Baby Sergeant rockets in an annular ring around a central tube. The third stage has three Baby Sergeant motors held together by three transverse bulkheads. On top of the third stage is the fourth, a single rocket, with the satellite in its nose.

The countdown stood at X minus 630 minutes, and Cape Canaveral was buzzing.

Rocket men were all the same: they would design weapons, if the government wanted, but what they dreamed about was outer space. The Explorer team had built and launched many missiles, but this would be the first of them to break free of the Earth's pull and fly beyond the atmosphere. For most of the team, tonight's launch would be the fulfilment of a lifetime's hopes. Elspeth felt the same way.

They were based in Hangar D and Hangar R, which were side by side. The standard aircraft hangar design had been found to be well suited to missiles: there was a large central space where the rockets could be checked out, with two-storey wings either side for offices and smaller laboratories.

Elspeth was in Hangar R. She had a typewriter and

a desk in the office of her boss, Willy Fredrickson, the launch conductor, who spent almost all his time elsewhere. Her job was to prepare and distribute the launch timetable.

Trouble was, the timetable changed constantly. Nobody in America had sent a rocket into space before. New problems arose all the time, and the engineers were forever improvising ways to jury-rig a component or bypass a system. Here, duct tape was called missile tape.

So Elspeth produced regular updates of the timetable. She had to stay in touch with every group on the team, record changes of plan in her shorthand notebook, then transfer her notes to typed and Xeroxed sheets and distribute them. The job required her to go everywhere and know almost everything. When there was a hitch, she learned of it right away; and she was among the first to know about the solution, too. Her title was secretary, and she was paid a secretary's wages, but no one could have done the job without a science degree. However, she did not resent the low pay. She was grateful for a job that challenged her. Some of her Radcliffe classmates were still taking dictation from men in grey flannel suits.

Her noon update was ready, and she picked up the stack of papers and set out to distribute them. She was rushed off her feet, but that suited her today: it stopped her worrying constantly about Luke. If she followed her inclination, she would be on the phone to Anthony every few minutes, asking if there was any news. But that would be stupid. He would contact her if anything went wrong, she told herself. Meanwhile she should concentrate on her work.

Elspeth went first to the press department, where public relations officers were working the phones, telling trusted reporters that there would be a launch tonight. The army wanted journalists on the scene to witness their triumph. However, the information was not to be released until after the event. Scheduled launches were often delayed, or even cancelled, as unforeseen snags arose. The missile men had learned, from bitter experience, that a routine postponement to solve technical problems could be made to look like an abject failure when the newspapers reported it. So they had a deal with all the major news organizations. They gave advance notification of launches only on condition that nothing would be published until there was 'fire in the tail', which meant that the rocket engine had been ignited.

It was an all-male office, and several men stared at Elspeth as she walked across the room and handed a timetable to the chief press officer. She knew she was attractive, with her pale Viking looks and tall, statuesque figure; but there was something formidable about her – the determined set of her mouth, maybe, or the dangerous light in her green eyes – that made men who were inclined to whistle, or call her 'Honeybunch', think again.

In the Missile Firing Laboratory she found five shirt-sleeved scientists standing at a bench, staring worriedly at a flat piece of metal that looked as if it had been in a fire. The group leader, Dr Keller, said: 'Good afternoon, Elspeth.' He spoke in heavily accented English. Like most of the scientists, he was a German who had been captured at the end of the war and brought to America to work on the missile programme.

She handed him a copy of her update, and he took it without looking at it. Elspeth nodded at the object on the table and said: 'What's that?'

'A jet vane.'

Elspeth knew that the first stage was steered by vanes inside the tail. 'What happened to it?'

'The burning fuel erodes the metal,' he explained. His German accent became stronger as he warmed to his subject. 'This always happens, to some extent. However, with normal alcohol fuel, the vanes last long enough to do their job. Today, by contrast we are using a new fuel, Hydyne, that has a longer burning time and higher exhaust velocity – but it may erode the vanes so much that they become ineffective for steering.' He spread his hands in a gesture of exasperation. 'We have not had time to run sufficiently many tests.'

'I guess all I need to know is whether this is going to delay the launch.' She felt she could not stand a postponement. The suspense was already killing her.

'That's what we're trying to decide.' Keller looked around at his colleagues. 'And I think our answer is going to be: Let's take the chance.' The others nodded gloomily.

Elspeth felt relieved. 'I'll keep my fingers crossed,' she said, turning to leave.

'That's about as useful as anything we can do,' Keller said, and the others laughed ruefully.

She went outside into the scorching Florida sun. The hangars stood in a sandy clearing hacked out of the low scrub that covered the Cape – palmetto palms and scrub oaks and sharp sandspur grass that would cut your skin if you walked barefoot. She crossed a dusty apron and entered Hangar D, its welcome shade falling across her face like the touch of a cool breeze.

In the telemetry room Elspeth saw Hans Mueller, known as Hank. He pointed a finger at her and said: 'One hundred thirty-five.'

It was a game they played. She had to say what was unusual about the number. 'Too easy,' she said. 'Take the first digit, add the square of the second digit, plus the cube of the third, and you get the number you first thought of.' She gave him the equation:

$$1^1+3^2+5^3=135$$

'All right,' he said. 'So what is the next-highest number that follows the pattern?'

She thought hard, then said: 'One hundred and seventy-five.'

$$1^1+7^2+5^3=175$$

'Correct! You win the big prize.' He fished in his pocket and brought out a dime.

She took it. 'I'll give you a chance to win it back,' she said. 'One hundred thirty-six.'

'Ah.' He frowned. 'Wait. Sum the cubes of its digits.'

$$1^3+3^3+6^3=244$$

'Now repeat the process, and you get the number you first thought of!'

$$2^3+4^3+4^3=136$$

She gave him back his dime, and a copy of her update.

As she went out, her eye was caught by a telegram pinned to the wall: I'VE HAD MY LITTLE SATELLITE, NOW YOU HAVE YOURS. Mueller noticed her reading it and explained: 'It's from Stuhlinger's wife.' Stuhlinger was chief of research. 'She had a baby boy.' Elspeth smiled.

She found Willy Fredrickson in the communications room with two army technicians, testing the teletype link to the Pentagon. Her boss was a tall, thin man, bald with a fringe of curly hair, like a medieval monk. The teletype machine was not working, and Willy was frustrated, but as he took the update he gave her a grateful look and said: 'Elspeth, you are twenty-two-carat gold.'

A moment later, two people approached Willy: a young army officer carrying a chart, and Stimmens, one of the scientists. The officer said: 'We got a problem.' He handed Willy the chart, and went on: 'The jet stream has moved south, and it's blowing at 146 knots.'

Elspeth's heart sank. She knew what this meant. The jet stream was a high-altitude wind in the stratosphere between 30,000 and 40,000 feet. It did not normally extend over Cape Canaveral, but it could move. And if it was too fierce, it might throw the missile off course.

Willy said: 'How far south is it?'

'All over Florida,' the officer replied.

Willy turned to Stimmens. 'We've allowed for this, haven't we?'

'Not really,' Stimmens said. 'It's all guesswork, of course, but we figure the missile can withstand winds up to 120 knots, no higher.'

Willy turned back to the officer. 'What's the forecast for tonight?'

'Up to 177 knots, and no sign of the jet stream moving back north.'

'Hell.' Willy ran a hand over his smooth pate. Elspeth knew what he was thinking. The launch might have to be postponed until tomorrow. 'Send up a weather balloon, please,' he ordered. 'We'll review the forecast again at five o'clock.'

Elspeth made a note to add the weather-review meeting to her timetable, then she left, feeling despondent. They could solve engineering problems, but there was nothing they could do about the weather.

Outside, she got into a jeep and drove to Launch Complex 26. The road was a dusty, unpaved track through the brush, and the jeep bounced on the ruts. She startled a white-tailed deer that was drinking from a ditch, and it bounded off into the bushes. There was a lot of wildlife on the Cape, hiding in the low scrub. People said there were alligators and Florida panthers, but Elspeth had never seen either.

She pulled up outside the blockhouse and looked across to Launch Pad 26B, three hundred yards away. The gantry was a derrick from an oil rig, adapted for this purpose and coated with orange rust-resistant paint to protect it from corrosion by the humid, salty Florida air. At one side was an elevator for access to the platforms. The whole edifice was brutally practical, quite without grace, Elspeth thought; a functional structure bolted together with no regard for how it looked.

The long white pencil of the Jupiter C rocket seemed caught in the tangle of orange girders like a dragonfly in a spiderweb. The men called it 'she', despite its phallic shape, and Elspeth too thought of the rocket as female. A bridal veil of canvas covers had concealed the upper stages from prying eyes since it arrived here; but that had now been removed, and the missile stood fully revealed, sunshine gleaming off its spotless paintwork.

The scientists were not very political, but even they knew that the eyes of the world were on them. Four months ago, the Soviet Union had stunned the world by sending up the first space satellite, the Sputnik. In all the countries where the tug-of-war between capitalism and communism was still going on, from Italy to India, throughout Latin America and Africa and Indochina, the message was heard: Communist science is best. A month later the Soviets had sent up a second satellite, Sputnik 2, with a dog on board. Americans were devastated. A dog today, a man tomorrow.

President Eisenhower promised an American satellite before the end of the year. On the first Friday in December, at fifteen minutes to noon, the US Navy launched its Vanguard rocket in front of the world's press. It rose a few feet into the air, burst into flames, toppled sideways and smashed to pieces on the concrete. IT'S A FLOPNIK! said one headline.

The Jupiter C was America's last hope. There was no third option. If this failed today, the United States was out of the space race. The propaganda defeat was the least of the consequences. The American space programme would be in total disarray, and the USSR would control outer space for the foreseeable future.

All that, Elspeth thought, resting on this one rocket.

Vehicles were banned from the launch-pad area, except for essential ones such as fuel trucks, so she left her car and walked across the open space between blockhouse and gantry, following the line of a metal conduit that housed the cables linking the two locations. Attached to the back of the derrick at ground level was a long steel cabin, the same orange colour, containing offices and machinery. Elspeth entered by a metal door at the rear.

The gantry supervisor, Harry Lane, sat on a folding chair, wearing a hard hat and engineer boots, studying a blueprint. 'Hi, Harry,' she said brightly.

He grunted. He did not like to see women around the launch pad, and no sense of courtesy constrained him from letting her know it.

She dropped an update on a metal table and left. She returned to the blockhouse, a low white building with slit windows of thick green glass. The blast doors stood open, and she walked inside. There were three compartments: an instrumentation room, which ran the width of the building, and two firing rooms, A on the left and B on the right, angled towards the two launch pads served by this blockhouse. Elspeth stepped into Firing Room B.

The strong sunlight coming through the green glass cast a weird light over the whole place, so that it looked like the inside of an aquarium. In front of the windows, a row of scientists sat at a bank of control panels. They all wore short-sleeved shirts, she noticed, as if it were a uniform. They had headsets through which they could talk to the men on the launch pad. They could look over their panels and see the rocket through the windows, or check the colour television screens that showed the same picture. Along the back wall of the firing room, a row of pen recorders stood shoulder to shoulder, tracking temperatures, pressures in the fuel system, and electrical activity. In the far corner was a scale showing the weight of the missile on the launch pad. There was an air of quiet urgency as the men murmured into their headsets and worked their panels, turning a knob here, throwing a switch there, constantly checking the dials and counters. Over their heads, a countdown clock showed the minutes left to ignition. As Elspeth looked, the hand clicked down from 600 to 599.

She handed out her update and left the building. Driving back to the hangar, her mind turned to Luke and she realized she had a perfect excuse for calling

Anthony. She would tell him about the jet stream, then ask about Luke.

That perked her up, and she hurried into the hangar and up the stairs to her office. She dialled Anthony's direct line and got him right away. 'The launch is likely to be postponed until tomorrow,' she told him. 'There are strong winds in the stratosphere.'

'I didn't know there were winds up there.'

'There's one, it's called the jet stream. The postponement isn't definite, there's a weather-review meeting at five. How's Luke?'

'Let me know the upshot of that meeting, okay?'

'Of course. How's Luke?'

'Well, we have a problem there.'

Her heart missed a beat. 'What kind of a problem?'

'We've lost him.'

Elspeth felt cold. 'What?'

'He slipped away from my men.'

'Jesus help us,' she said. 'Now we're in trouble.'

1941

Luke arrived back in Boston at dawn. He parked the old Ford, slipped in through the back door of Cambridge House, and climbed the service stairs to his room. Anthony was fast asleep. Luke washed his face and fell into bed in his underwear.

Next thing he knew, Anthony was shaking him, saying: 'Luke! Get up!'

He opened his eyes. He knew that something bad had happened, but he could not recall what it was. 'What's the time?' he mumbled.

'It's one o'clock, and Elspeth is waiting for you downstairs.'

The mention of Elspeth's name jogged his memory, and he recalled what the calamity was. He did not love her any more. 'Oh, God,' he said.

'You'd better go down and see her.'

He had fallen in love with Billie Josephson. That was the disaster. It would make a train wreck of all their lives: his own, Elspeth's, Billie's and Anthony's.

'Hell,' he said, and he got up.

He stripped off his underwear and took a cold shower. When he closed his eyes he saw Billie, her dark eyes flashing, her red mouth laughing, her white throat. He pulled on a pair of flannels, a sweater, and tennis shoes, then staggered downstairs.

Elspeth was waiting in the lobby, the only part of the building where girls were allowed, except on specially designated Ladies' Afternoons. It was a spacious hall with a fireplace and comfortable chairs. She was as eye-catching as ever, in a wool dress the colour of bluebells and a big hat. Yesterday, the sight of her would have gladdened his heart; today, the knowledge that she had dressed up for him just made him feel even more wretched.

She laughed when she saw him. 'You look like a small boy who can't wake up!'

He kissed her cheek and slumped into a chair. 'It took hours to get to Newport,' he said.

'You've obviously forgotten you're supposed to take me to lunch!' Elspeth said brightly.

He looked at her. She was beautiful, but he did not love her. He did not know whether he had loved her before, but he was sure he did not now. He was the worst kind of heel. She was so gay this morning, and he was going to ruin her happiness. He did not know how to tell her. He felt so ashamed it was like a pain in his heart.

He had to say something. 'Can we skip lunch? I haven't even shaved.'

A troubled shadow crossed her pale, proud face, and he realized that she knew perfectly well something was wrong; but her reply was carefree. 'Of course,' she said. 'Knights in shining armour need their beauty sleep.'

He told himself he would have a serious talk with her, and be completely honest, later in the day. 'I'm sorry you got dressed up for nothing,' he said miserably.

'It wasn't for nothing – I saw you. And your fellow housemen seemed to like my outfit.' She stood up. 'Anyway, Professor and Mrs Durkham are having a jolly-up.' That was Radcliffe slang for a party.

Luke stood and helped her into her coat. 'We could meet later.' He had to tell her today – it would be deceitful to let any more time pass without revealing the truth.

'That'll be fine,' she said gaily. 'Pick me up at six.' She blew him a kiss and walked out like a movie star. He knew she was faking, but it was a good act.

He returned woefully to his room. Anthony was reading the Sunday paper. 'I made coffee,' he said.

'Thanks.' Luke poured a cup.

'I owe you big time,' Anthony went on. 'You saved Billie's hide last night.'

'You'd do the same for me.' Luke sipped his coffee and began to feel better. 'Seems we got away with it. Has anyone said anything to you this morning?'

'Not a thing.'

'Billie's quite a gal,' Luke said. He knew it was dangerous to talk about her, but he could not help it.

'Isn't she great?' Anthony said. Luke observed with dismay the look of pride on his room-mate's face. Anthony went on: 'I kept asking myself: "Why shouldn't she go out with me?" But I didn't think she would. I don't know why, maybe because she's so neat and pretty. And when she said yes, I couldn't believe my ears. I wanted to ask for it in writing.'

Extravagant overstatement was Anthony's way of being amusing, and Luke forced a smile, but secretly he was appalled. To steal someone else's girlfriend was despicable in any circumstances, but the fact that Anthony was obviously crazy about Billie made everything even worse.

Luke groaned, and Anthony said: 'What's the matter?'

Luke decided to tell him half the truth. 'I'm not in love with Elspeth any more. I think I have to end it.'

Anthony looked shocked. 'That's too bad. You two are quite an item.'

'I feel like a jerk.'

'Don't crucify yourself. It happens. You're not married – not even engaged.'

'Not officially.'

Anthony raised his eyebrows. 'Have you proposed?'

'No.'

'Then you're not engaged, officially or unofficially.'

'We've talked about how many children we'll have.'

'You're still not engaged.'

'I guess you're right, but all the same I feel like a rotter.'

There was a tap at the door, and a man Luke had never seen before came in. 'Mr Lucas and Mr Carroll, I presume?' He wore a shabby suit, but had a haughty manner, and Luke guessed he was a college proctor.

Anthony leaped to his feet. 'We are,' he said. 'And

you must be Doctor Uterus, the famous gynaecologist. Thank God you've come!'

Luke did not laugh. The man was carrying two white envelopes, and Luke had a pessimistic feeling he knew what they were.

'I'm the clerk to the Dean of Students. He's asked me to hand you these notes in person.' The clerk gave them an envelope each and left.

'Hell,' Anthony said as the door closed. He ripped open his envelope. 'God damn it.'

Luke opened his and read the short note inside.

Dear Mr Lucas,
 Please be good enough to come and see me in my study at three o'clock this afternoon.
 Yours sincerely,
 Peter Ryder
 Dean of Students

Such letters always meant disciplinary trouble. Someone had reported to the Dean that there had been a girl in the House last night. Anthony would probably be expelled.

Luke had never seen his room-mate afraid – his insouciance always seemed unshakeable – but now he was pale with shock. 'I can't go home,' he whispered. He had never said much about his parents, but Luke had a vague picture of a bullying father and a long-suffering mother. Now he guessed the reality might be worse than he had imagined. For a moment, Anthony's expression was a window into a private hell.

Then there was a knock at the door, and in came Geoff Pidgeon, the amiable, chubby occupant of the room opposite. 'Did I just see the Dean's clerk?'

Luke waved his letter. 'Too damn right.'

'You know, I haven't said a word to anyone about seeing you with that girl.'

'But who did?' Anthony said. 'The only sneak in the House is Jenkins.' Paul Jenkins was a religious zealot whose mission in life was to reform the morals of Harvard men. 'But he's away for the weekend.'

'No, he's not,' Pidgeon said. 'He changed his plans.'

'Then it's him, damn his eyes,' Anthony said. 'I'm going to strangle the son of a bitch with my own hands.'

If Anthony were expelled, Luke realized suddenly, Billie would be free. He felt ashamed of such a selfish thought when his friend's life was about to be ruined. Then it struck him that Billie might be in trouble too. He said: 'I wonder if Elspeth and Billie have had letters.'

Anthony said: 'Why would they?'

'Jenkins probably knows the names of our girl-friends – he takes a prurient interest in such things.'

Pidgeon said: 'If he knows the names, we can be sure he reported them. That's what he's like.'

Luke said: 'Elspeth is safe. She wasn't here, and no one can prove she was. But Billie could be expelled. Then she'll lose her scholarship. She explained it to me last night. She won't be able to study anywhere else.'

'I can't worry about Billie now,' Anthony said. 'I have to figure out what I'm going to do.'

Luke was shocked. Anthony had got Billie into trouble, and by Luke's code he should be more worried about her than about himself. But Luke saw a pretext to talk to Billie, and he could not resist it. Suppressing a guilty feeling, he said: 'Why don't I go to the girls' dorm and see whether Billie's back from Newport yet?'

'Would you?' Anthony said. 'Thanks.'

Pidgeon went out. Anthony sat on the bed, smoking gloomily, while Luke quickly shaved and changed his clothes. Although he was in a hurry, he dressed with care, in a soft blue shirt, new flannel pants, and his favourite grey tweed jacket.

It was two o'clock when he reached the Radcliffe dormitory quadrangle. The red-brick buildings were arranged around a small park where students strolled in pairs. This was where he had kissed Elspeth, he recalled unhappily, at midnight on a Saturday at the end of their first date. He detested men who switched loyalties as readily as they changed their shirts, yet here he was doing the thing he disdained – and he could not stop.

A uniformed maid let him into the lobby of the dorm. He asked for Billie. The maid sat at a desk, picked up a speaking-tube of the kind used on ships, blew into the mouthpiece, and said: 'Visitor for Miss Josephson.'

Billie came down wearing a dove-grey cashmere

sweater and a plaid skirt. She looked lovely but
distraught, and Luke longed to take her in his arms
and comfort her. She, too, had been summoned to the
office of Peter Ryder, and she told him that the man
who had delivered her letter had also left one for
Elspeth.

She showed him into the smoking room, where girls
were allowed to receive male visitors. 'What am I going
to do?' she said. Her face was drawn with distress. She
looked like a grieving widow.

Luke found her even more ravishing than yesterday.
He longed to tell her that he would make everything
all right. But he could not think of a way out. 'Anthony
could say it was someone else in the room, but he'd
have to produce the girl.'

'I don't know what I'm going to tell my mother.'

'I wonder if Anthony would pay a woman, you know,
a street woman, to say it was she.'

Billie shook her head. 'They wouldn't believe it.'

'And Jenkins would tell them it was the wrong girl.
He's the sneak that reported you.'

'My career is over.' With a bitter smile, she said: 'I'll
have to go back to Dallas and be a secretary to an oil
man in cowboy boots.'

Twenty-four hours ago Luke had been a happy man.
It was hard to believe.

Two girls in coats and hats burst into the lounge.
Their faces were flushed. 'Have you heard the news?'
said one.

Luke was not interested in news. He shook his head.
Billie said desultorily: 'What's happened?'

'We're at war!'

Luke frowned. 'What?'

'It's true,' said the second girl. 'The Japanese have bombed Hawaii!'

Luke could hardly take it in. 'Hawaii? What the heck for? What's in Hawaii?'

Billie said: 'Is this true?'

'Everyone's talking about it on the street. People are stopping their cars.'

Billie looked at Luke. 'I'm frightened,' she said.

He took her hand. He wanted to say he would take care of her, no matter what.

Two more girls rushed in, talking excitedly. Someone brought a radio downstairs and plugged it in. There was an expectant silence while they waited for it to warm up. Then they heard an announcer's voice. 'The battleship *Arizona* is reported destroyed and the *Oklahoma* sunk in Pearl Harbor. First reports say that more than one hundred US aircraft were crippled on the ground at the Naval Air Station on Ford Island and at Wheeler Field and Hickam Field. American casualties are estimated to be at least two thousand dead and a thousand more injured.'

Luke felt a surge of rage. 'Two thousand people killed!' he said.

More girls came into the lounge, talking excitedly, and were rudely told to shut up. The announcer was saying: 'No warning was given for the Japanese attack, which began at seven fifty-five a.m. local time, just before one p.m. Eastern Standard Time.'

Billie said: 'It means war, doesn't it.'

'You bet it does,' Luke said angrily. He knew it was stupid and irrational to hate a whole nation, but he felt that way all the same. 'I'd like to bomb Japan flat.'

She squeezed his hand. 'I don't want you to be in a war,' she said. There were tears in her eyes. 'I don't want you hurt.'

His heart felt ready to burst. 'I'm so happy you feel that way.' He smiled ruefully. 'The world is falling apart, and I'm happy.' He looked at his watch. 'I suppose we all have to see the Dean, even though we're at war.' Then he was struck by a thought, and he fell silent.

'What?' Billie said. 'What is it?'

'Maybe there *is* a way for you and Anthony to stay at Harvard.'

'How?'

'Let me think.'

* * *

Elspeth was nervous, but she told herself that she did not need to be afraid. She had broken the curfew last night, but she had not been caught. She was almost certain this was nothing to do with her and Luke. Anthony and Billie were the ones who were in trouble. Elspeth hardly knew Billie, but she cared for Anthony, and she had a dreadful feeling he was going to be thrown out.

The four of them met outside the Dean's study. Luke said: 'I've got a plan,' but before he could explain, the Dean opened the door and summoned them inside. Luke had time only to say: 'Leave the talking to me.'

The Dean of Students, Peter Ryder, was a fussy, old-fashioned man in a neat suit of black coat and waistcoat with grey striped pants. His bow tie was a perfect butterfly, his boots gleamed with polish, and his oiled hair looked like black paint on a boiled egg. With him was a grey-haired spinster called Iris Rayford who was responsible for the moral welfare of Radcliffe girls.

They sat in a circle of chairs, as if for a tutorial. The Dean lit a cigarette. 'Now, you boys had better tell the truth, like gentlemen,' he said. 'What happened in your room last night?'

Anthony ignored Ryder's question and acted as if he were in charge of the proceedings. 'Where's Jenkins?' he said curtly. 'He's the sneak, isn't he?'

'No one else has been asked to join us,' the Dean said.

'But a man has a right to be confronted by his accuser.'

'This isn't a court, Mr Carroll,' the Dean said testily. 'Miss Rayford and I have been asked to establish the facts. Disciplinary proceedings, if such prove necessary, will follow in due course.'

'I'm not sure that's acceptable,' Anthony said haughtily. 'Jenkins should be here.'

Elspeth saw what Anthony was doing. He hoped Jenkins would be scared to repeat his accusation to Anthony's face. If that happened, the college might have to drop the matter. She did not think it would work, but perhaps it was worth a try.

However, Luke cut the discussion short. 'Enough of

this,' he said with an impatient gesture. He addressed the Dean. 'I brought a woman into the House last night, sir.'

Elspeth gasped. What was he talking about?

The Dean frowned. 'My information is that it was Mr Carroll who invited the woman in.'

'I'm afraid you've been misinformed.'

Elspeth burst out: 'That's not true!'

Luke gave her a look that chilled her. 'Miss Twomey was in her dorm by midnight, as the dormitory mistress's overnight book will show.'

Elspeth stared at him. The book *would* show that, because a girlfriend had forged her signature. She realized she had better shut up before she talked herself into trouble. But what was Luke up to?

Anthony was asking himself the same question. Staring at Luke, mystified, he said: 'Luke, I don't know what you're doing, but—'

'Let me tell the story,' Luke said. Anthony looked doubtful, and Luke added: 'Please.'

Anthony shrugged.

The Dean said sarcastically: 'Please carry on, Mr Lucas. I can't wait.'

'I met the girl at the Dew Drop Inn,' Luke began.

Miss Rayford spoke for the first time. 'The Dew Drop Inn?' she said incredulously. 'Is that a pun?'

'Yes.'

'Carry on.'

'She's a waitress there. Her name is Angela Carlotti.'

The Dean plainly did not believe a word. He said: 'I

was told that the person seen in Cambridge House was Miss Bilhah Josephson here.'

'No, sir,' Luke said in the same tone of immovable certitude. 'Miss Josephson is a friend of ours, but she was out of town. She spent last night at the home of a relative in Newport, Rhode Island.'

Miss Rayford spoke to Billie. 'Will the relative confirm that?'

Billie shot a bewildered look at Luke, then said: 'Yes, Miss Rayford.'

Elspeth stared at Luke. Did he really intend to sacrifice his career to save Anthony? It was crazy! Luke was a loyal friend, but this was taking friendship too far.

Ryder said to Luke: 'Can you produce this . . . waitress?' He pronounced 'waitress' with distaste, as if he were saying 'prostitute'.

'Yes, sir, I can.'

The Dean was surprised. 'Very well.'

Elspeth was astonished. Had Luke bribed a town girl to pretend to be the culprit? If he had, it would never work. Jenkins would swear it was the wrong girl.

Then Luke said: 'But I don't intend to bring her into this.'

'Ah,' said the Dean. 'In that case, you make it difficult for me to accept your story.'

Now Elspeth was baffled. Luke had told an implausible tale and had no way to back it up. What was the point?

Luke said: 'I don't think Miss Carlotti's evidence will be necessary.'

'I beg to differ, Mr Lucas.'

Then Luke dropped his bombshell. 'I'm leaving the college tonight, sir.'

Anthony said: 'Luke!'

The Dean said: 'It will do you no good to leave before you can be sacked. There will still be an investigation.'

'Our country is at war.'

'I know that, young man.'

'I'm going to join the army tomorrow morning, sir.'

Elspeth cried: 'No!'

For the first time, the Dean did not have an answer. He stared at Luke with his mouth open.

Elspeth realized that Luke had been clever. The college could hardly pursue a disciplinary action against a boy who was risking his life for his country. And if there were no investigation, then Billie was safe.

A mist of grief obscured her vision. Luke had sacrificed everything – to save Billie.

Miss Rayford might still demand testimony from Billie's cousin, but he would probably lie for her. The key point was that Radcliffe could hardly expect Billie to produce the waitress Angela Carlotti.

But none of that mattered to Elspeth now. All she could think of was that she had lost Luke.

Ryder was muttering about making his report and leaving others to decide. Miss Rayford made a big fuss about writing down the address of Billie's cousin. But it was all camouflage. They had been outwitted, and they knew it.

At last the students were dismissed.

As soon as the door closed, Billie burst into tears. 'Don't go to war, Luke!' she said.

Anthony said: 'You saved my life.' He put his arms around Luke and embraced him. 'I'll never forget this,' Anthony said. 'Never.' He detached himself from Luke and took Billie's hand. 'Don't worry,' he said to her. 'Luke's too smart to get killed.'

Luke turned to Elspeth. When he met her eye he flinched, and she realized that her rage must be plainly visible. But she did not care. She stared at him for a long moment, then she raised her hand and slapped his face, once, very hard. He let out an involuntary gasp of pain and surprise.

'You fucking bastard,' she said.

Then she turned and walked away.

1 P.M.

Each Baby Sergeant motor is four feet long and six inches in diameter, and weighs fifty-nine pounds. Its motor burns for just six and a half seconds.

Luke was looking for a quiet residential street. Washington was totally unfamiliar to him, as if he had never been here before. Driving away from Union Station he had chosen a direction at random, and headed west. The road had taken him further into the centre of the city, a place of striking vistas and grandiose government buildings. Perhaps it was beautiful, but he found it intimidating. However, he knew that if he kept going in a straight line he must eventually come to a place where normal families lived in regular houses.

He crossed a river and found himself in a charming suburb of narrow streets lined with trees. He passed a building with a sign that read 'Georgetown Mind Hospital', and he guessed the neighbourhood was called Georgetown. He turned into a tree-lined street of modest houses. This was promising. People here would not have full-time household help, so there was a good chance of finding a place empty.

The street turned a corner and immediately dead-ended in a cemetery. Luke parked the stolen Ford facing the way he had come, in case he had to make a fast getaway.

He needed some simple tools, a chisel or screwdriver and a hammer. There was probably a small tool kit in the trunk – but the trunk was locked. He could pick the lock if he could find a piece of wire. Otherwise he would have to drive to a hardware store and buy or steal what he required.

He reached into the back and picked up the stolen bag. Rummaging through the clothes, he found a folder containing papers. He took out a paper clip and closed the case.

It took him about thirty seconds to open the trunk. As he had hoped, there were a few tools in a tin box next to the jack. He chose the largest screwdriver. There was no hammer, but there was a heavy adjustable wrench that would serve. He put them in the pocket of his ragged raincoat and slammed the lid of the trunk.

He took the stolen bag from inside the car, closed the door, and walked around the corner. He knew he was conspicuous, a ragged bum walking in a nice neighbourhood with an expensive suitcase. If the local busybody called the cops, and the cops had nothing much to do this morning, he could be in trouble in minutes. On the other hand, if all went well he might be washed and shaved and dressed like a respectable citizen in half an hour's time.

He drew level with the first house in the street. He crossed a small front yard and knocked at the door.

* * *

Rosemary Sims saw a nice blue-and-white car drive slowly past her house, and she wondered whose it was. The Brownings might have bought a new car, they had plenty of money. Or Mr Cyrus, who was a bachelor and did not have to stint himself. Otherwise, she reasoned, it must belong to a stranger.

She had good eyesight still, and she could watch most of the street from her comfy chair by the second-floor window, especially in winter when the trees were bare of leaves. So she saw the tall stranger when he came walking around the corner. And 'strange' was the word. He wore no hat, his raincoat was torn, and his shoes were tied up with string to stop them falling apart. Yet he carried a new-looking suitcase.

He went to Mrs Britsky's door and knocked. She was a widow, living alone, but she was no fool – she would make short work of the stranger, Mrs Sims knew. Sure enough, Mrs Britsky looked out the window and waved him away with a peremptory gesture.

He went next door and knocked at Mrs Loew's. She opened up. She was a tall, black-haired woman, who was too proud, in Mrs Sims's opinion. She spoke a few words with the caller, then slammed the door.

He went to the next house, apparently intending to work his way along the street. Young Jeannie Evans came to the door with baby Rita in her arms. She fished in the pocket of her apron and gave him something, probably a few coins. So he was a beggar.

Old Mr Clark came to the door in his bathrobe and carpet slippers. The stranger got nothing out of him.

The owner of the next house, Mr Bonetti, was at

work, and his wife Angelina, seven months pregnant, had left five minutes ago, carrying a string bag, obviously heading for the store. The stranger would get no answer there.

* * *

By now, Luke had had time to study the doors, which were all the same. They had Yale locks, the kind with a tongue on the door side and a metal socket in the jamb. The lock was operated by a key from outside and by a knob inside.

Each door had a small window of frosted glass at head height. The easiest way in would be to break the glass and reach inside to turn the knob. But a broken window would be visible from the street. So he decided to use the screwdriver.

He glanced up and down the street. He had been unlucky, having to knock on five doors to find an empty house. By now he might have attracted attention, but he could see no one. Anyway, he had no choice. He had to take the risk.

* * *

Mrs Sims turned away from the window and lifted the handset of the phone beside her seat. Slowly and carefully, she dialled the number of the local police station, which she knew by heart.

* * *

Luke had to do this fast.

He inserted the screwdriver's blade between the

door and the jamb at the level of the lock. Then he struck the handle of the screwdriver with the heavy end of the adjustable wrench, trying to force the blade into the socket of the lock.

The first blow failed to move the screwdriver, which was jammed up against the steel of the lock. He wiggled the screwdriver, trying to find a way in. He used the wrench again, harder this time. Still the screwdriver would not slip into the socket. He felt perspiration break out on his forehead, despite the cold weather.

He told himself to stay calm. He had done this before. When? He had no idea. It did not matter. The technique worked, he was sure of that.

He wiggled the screwdriver again. This time, it felt as if a corner of the blade had caught in a notch. He hammered again, as hard as he could. The screwdriver sank in an inch.

He pulled sideways on the handle, levering the tongue of the lock back out of the socket. To his profound relief, the door opened inward.

The damage to the frame was too slight to be seen from the street.

He stepped quickly inside and closed the door behind him.

* * *

When Rosemary Sims finished dialling the number, she looked out the window again, but the stranger had vanished.

That was quick.

The police answered. Feeling confused, she hung up the phone without speaking.

Why had he suddenly stopped knocking on doors? Where had he gone? Who was he?

She smiled. She had something to occupy her thoughts all day.

* * *

It was the home of a young couple. The place was furnished with a mixture of wedding presents and junk-shop purchases. They had a new couch and a big TV set in the living room, but they were still using orange crates for storage in the kitchen. An unopened letter on the hall radiator was addressed to Mr G. Bonetti.

There was no evidence of children. Most probably, Mr and Mrs Bonetti both had jobs and would be out all day. But he could not count on it.

He went quickly upstairs. There were three bedrooms, only one of which was furnished. He threw the suitcase on the neatly made bed. Inside it he found a carefully folded blue chalk-stripe suit, a white shirt and a conservative striped tie. There were dark socks, clean underwear, and a pair of polished black wingtips that looked only about half a size too big.

He stripped off his filthy clothes and kicked them into a corner. It gave him a spooky feeling, to be naked in the home of strangers. He thought of skipping the shower, but he smelled bad, even to himself.

He crossed the tiny landing to the bathroom. It felt great to stand under the hot water and soap himself all over. When he got out, he stood still and listened carefully. The house was silent.

He dried himself with one of Mrs Bonetti's pink bath towels – another wedding present, he guessed – and put on undershorts, pants, socks and shoes from the stolen bag. Being at least half dressed would speed his getaway if something went wrong while he was shaving.

Mr Bonetti used an electric shaver, but Luke preferred a blade. In the suitcase he found a safety razor and a shaving brush. He lathered his face and shaved quickly.

Mr Bonetti did not have any cologne, but maybe there was some in the suitcase. After stinking like a pig all morning, Luke liked the idea of smelling sweet. He found a neat leather toiletry case and unzipped it. There was no cologne inside – but there was a hundred dollars in twenties, neatly folded: emergency money. He pocketed the cash, resolving to pay the man back one day.

After all, the guy was not a collaborator.

And what the heck did that mean?

Another mystery. He put on the shirt, tie and jacket. They fitted well: he had been careful to choose a victim his own size and build. The clothes were of good quality. The luggage tag gave an address on Central Park South, New York. Luke guessed the owner was a corporate big shot who had come to Washington for a couple of days of meetings.

There was a full-length mirror on the back of the bedroom door. He had not looked at his reflection

since early this morning, in the men's room at Union Station, when he had been so shocked to see a filthy hobo staring back at him.

He stepped to the mirror, bracing himself.

He saw a tall, fit-looking man in his middle thirties, with black hair and blue eyes; a normal person, looking harassed. A weary sense of relief swept over him.

Take a guy like that, he thought. What would you say he does for a living?

His hands were soft, and now that they were clean they did not look like those of a manual worker. He had a smooth indoor face, one that had not spent much time out in bad weather. His hair was well cut. The guy in the mirror looked comfortable in the clothes of a corporate executive.

He was not a cop, definitely.

There was no hat or coat in the bag. Luke knew he would be conspicuous without either, on a cold January day. He wondered if he might find them in the house. It was worth taking a few extra seconds to look.

He opened the closet. There was not much inside. Mrs Bonetti had three dresses. Her husband had a sport coat for weekends and a black suit he probably wore to church. There was no topcoat – Mr Bonetti must be wearing one, and he could not afford two – but there was a light raincoat. Luke took it off the hanger. It would be better than nothing. He put it on. It was a size small, but wearable.

There was no hat in the closet, but there was a

tweed cap that Bonetti probably wore with the sport coat on Saturday. Luke tried it on. It was too small. He would have to buy a hat with some of the money from the sponge bag. But the cap would serve for an hour or so—

He heard a noise downstairs. He froze, listening.

A young woman's voice said: 'What happened to my front door?'

Another voice, similar, replied: 'Looks like someone tried to break in!'

Luke cursed under his breath. He had stayed too long.

'Jeepers – I think you're right!'

'Maybe you should call the cops.'

Mrs Bonetti had not gone to work, after all. Probably she had gone shopping. She had met a friend at the store and invited her home for coffee.

'I don't know . . . looks like the thieves didn't get in.'

'How do you know? Better check if anything's been stolen.'

Luke realized he had to get out of there fast.

'What's to steal? The family jewels?'

'What about the TV?'

Luke opened the bedroom window and looked out on to the front yard. There was no convenient tree or drainpipe down which he could climb.

'Nothing's been moved,' he heard Mrs Bonetti say. 'I don't believe they got in.'

'What about upstairs?'

Moving silently, Luke crossed the landing to the

bathroom. At the back of the house there was nothing but a leg-breaking drop to a paved patio.

'I'm going to look.'

'Aren't you scared?'

There was a nervous giggle. 'Yes. But what else can we do? We'll look pretty silly if we call the cops and there's no one here.'

Luke heard footsteps on the stairs. He stood behind the bathroom door.

The footsteps mounted the staircase, crossed the landing and entered the bedroom. Mrs Bonetti gave a little scream.

Her friend's voice said: 'Whose bag is that?'

'I've never seen it before!'

Luke slipped silently out of the bathroom. He could see the open bedroom door, but not the women. He tiptoed down the stairs, grateful for the carpet.

'What kind of burglar brings luggage?'

'I'm calling the cops right now. This is spooky.'

Luke opened the front door and stepped outside.

He smiled. He had done it.

He closed the door quietly and walked quickly away.

* * *

Mrs Sims frowned, mystified. The man leaving the Bonetti house had on Mr Bonetti's black raincoat and the grey tweed cap he wore to watch the Redskins, but he was larger than Mr Bonetti, and the clothes did not quite fit.

She watched him walk down the street and turn the corner. He would have to come back: it was a dead end. A minute later the blue-and-white car she had noticed earlier came around the corner, going too fast. She realized then that the man who had left the house was the beggar she had been watching. He must have broken in and stolen Mr Bonetti's clothes!

As the car passed her window, she read the licence plate and memorized the number.

1.30 P.M.

The Sergeant motors have undergone 300 static tests, 50 flight tests and 290 ignition-system firings without a failure.

Anthony sat in the conference room, fuming with impatience and frustration.

Luke was still running around Washington. No one knew what he might be up to. But Anthony was stuck here, listening to a State Department time-server drone on about the need to combat rebels massing in the mountains of Cuba. Anthony knew all about Fidel Castro and Che Guevara. They had fewer than a thousand men under their command. Of course they could be wiped out – but there was no point. If Castro were killed, someone else would take his place.

What Anthony wanted to do was get out on the street and look for Luke.

He and his staff had put in calls to most of the police stations in the District of Columbia. They had asked the precincts to call in details of any incidents involving drunks or bums, any mention of a perpetrator who talked like a college professor, and anything at all out of the ordinary. The cops were happy to cooperate with the CIA: they liked the thought that they might be involved with international espionage.

The State Department man finished his talk, and a round-table discussion began. Anthony knew that the only way to prevent someone like Castro taking over was for the US to support a moderate reformist government. Fortunately for the communists, there was no danger of that.

The door opened and Pete Maxell slipped in. He gave a nod of apology to the chairman at the head of the table, George Cooperman, then sat next to Anthony and passed him a folder containing a batch of police reports.

There was something unusual at just about every station house. A beautiful woman arrested for picking pockets at the Jefferson Memorial turned out to be a man; some beatniks had tried to open a cage and free an eagle at the zoo; a Wesley Heights man had attempted to suffocate his wife with a pizza with extra cheese; a delivery truck belonging to a religious publisher had shed its load in Petworth, and traffic on Georgia Avenue was being held up by an avalanche of Bibles.

It was possible that Luke had left Washington, but Anthony thought it unlikely. Luke had no money for train or bus fares. He could steal it, of course, but why would he bother? He had nowhere to go. His mother lived in New York and he had a sister in Baltimore, but he did not know that. He had no reason to travel.

While Anthony speed-read the reports, he listened

with half an ear to his boss, Carl Hobart, talking about the US ambassador to Cuba, Earl Smith, who had worked tirelessly to undermine church leaders and others who wanted to reform Cuba by peaceful means. Anthony sometimes wondered if Smith were in fact a Kremlin agent, but more likely he was just stupid.

One of the police reports caught his eye, and he showed it to Pete. 'Is this right?' he whispered incredulously.

Pete nodded. 'A bum attacked and beat up a patrolman on A Street and Seventh.'

'A *bum* beat up a *cop*?'

'And it's not far from the neighbourhood where we lost Luke.'

'This might be him!' Anthony said excitedly. Carl Hobart, who was speaking, shot him a look of annoyance. Anthony lowered his voice to a whisper again. 'But why would he attack a patrolman? Did he steal anything – the cop's weapon, for example?'

'No, but he beat him up pretty good. The officer was treated in hospital for a broken forefinger on his right hand.'

A tremor ran through Anthony like an electric shock. 'That's him!' he said loudly.

Carl Hobart said: 'For Christ's sake!'

George Cooperman said good-humouredly 'Anthony – either shut the fuck up, or go outside and talk, why don't you?'

Anthony stood up. 'Sorry, George. Back in a flash.' He stepped out of the room, and Pete followed. 'That's him,' Anthony repeated as the door shut. 'It was his trademark, in the war. He used to do it to the Gestapo – break their trigger fingers.'

Pete looked puzzled. 'How do you know that?'

Anthony realized he had made a blunder. Pete believed that Luke was a diplomat having a nervous breakdown. Anthony had not told Pete that he knew Luke personally. Now he cursed himself for carelessness. 'I didn't tell you everything,' he said, forcing a casual tone. 'I worked with him in OSS.'

Pete frowned. 'And he became a diplomat after the war.' He gave Anthony a shrewd look. 'He's not just having trouble with his wife, is he.'

'No. I'm pretty sure it's more serious.'

Pete accepted that. 'Sounds like a cold-blooded bastard, to break a guy's finger, just like that.'

'Cold-blooded?' Anthony had never thought of Luke that way, though he did have a ruthless streak. 'I guess he was, when the chips were down.' He had covered up his mistake, he thought with relief. But he still had to find Luke. 'What time did this fight occur?'

'Nine-thirty.'

'Hell. More than four hours ago. He could be anywhere in the city by now.'

'What'll we do?'

'Send a couple of men down to A Street to show the photo of Luke around, see if you can get any clues where he might have been headed. Talk to the cop, too.'

'Okay.'

'And if you get anything, don't hesitate to bust in on this stupid fucking meeting.'

'Gotcha.'

Anthony went back inside. George Cooperman, Anthony's wartime buddy, was speaking impatiently. 'We should send in a bunch of Special Forces tough guys, clean up Castro's ragtag army in about a day and a half.'

The State Department man asked nervously: 'Could we keep the operation secret?'

'No,' George said. 'But we could disguise it as a local conflict, like we did in Iran and Guatemala.'

Carl Hobart butted in. 'Pardon me if this is a dumb question, but why is it a secret what we did in Iran and Guatemala?'

The State Department man said: 'We don't want to advertise our methods, obviously.'

'Excuse me, but that's stupid,' Hobart said. 'The Russians know it was us. The Iranians and the Guatemalans know it was us. Hell, in Europe the newspapers openly said it was us! No one was fooled except the American people. Now, why do we want to lie to *them*?'

George answered with mounting irritation. 'If it all came out, there would be a Congressional inquiry. Fucking politicians would be asking if we had the right, was it legal, and what about the poor Iranian shitkicking farmers and Spic banana-pickers.'

'Maybe those aren't such bad questions,' Hobart persisted stubbornly. 'Did we really do any good in

Guatemala? It's hard to tell the difference between the Armas regime and a bunch of gangsters.'

George lost his temper. 'The hell with this!' he shouted. 'We are not here to feed starving Iranians and give civil liberties to South American peasants, for Christ's sake. Our job is to promote American interests – and *fuck* democracy!'

There was a moment's pause, then Carl Hobart said: 'Thank you, George. I'm glad we got that straightened out.'

2 P.M.

Each Sergeant motor has an igniter that consists of two electrical matches, wired in parallel, and a jellyroll of metal oxidant encased in a plastic sheath. The igniters are so sensitive that they have to be disconnected if an electrical storm comes within twelve miles of Cape Canaveral, to avoid accidental firing.

In a Georgetown menswear store, Luke bought a soft grey felt hat and a navy wool topcoat. He wore them out of the store and felt, at last, that he could look the world in the eye.

Now he was ready to attack his problems. First he had to learn something about memory. He wanted to know what caused amnesia, whether there were different kinds, and how long it might last. Most importantly, he needed information on treatment and cures.

Where did one go for information? A library. How did one find a library? Look at a map. He got a street map of Washington at the news-stand next to the menswear store. Prominently displayed was the Central Public Library, at the intersection of New York and Massachusetts Avenues, back across town. Luke drove there.

It was a grand classical building raised above ground level like a Greek temple. On the pediment above the pillared entrance were carved the words:

SCIENCE–POETRY–HISTORY

Luke hesitated at the top of the steps, then remembered that he was now a normal citizen again, and walked in.

The effect of his new appearance was immediately apparent. A grey-haired librarian behind the counter stood up and said: 'Can I help you, sir?'

Luke was pathetically grateful to be treated so courteously. 'I want to look at books on memory,' he said.

'That'll be the psychology section,' she said. 'If you'd like to follow me, I'll show you where it is.' She led him up a grand staircase to the next floor and pointed to a corner.

Luke looked along the shelf. There were plenty of books on psychoanalysis, child development, and perception, none of which were any use. He picked out a fat tome called *The Human Brain* and browsed through it, but there was not much about memory, and what there was seemed highly technical. There were some equations, and a certain amount of statistical material, which he found easy enough to understand; but much of the rest assumed a knowledge of human biology he did not have.

His eye was caught by *An Introduction to the Psychology of Memory* by Bilhah Josephson. That sounded more promising. He pulled it out and found a chapter on disorders of the memory. He read:

The common condition in which the patient 'loses his memory' is known as 'global amnesia'.

Luke was elated. He was not the only person to whom this had happened.

Such a patient does not know his identity and will not recognize his own parents or children. However, he remembers a great deal else. He may be able to drive a car, speak foreign languages, strip down an engine, and name the Prime Minister of Canada. The condition would be more appropriately called 'autobiographical amnesia'.

This was exactly what had happened to him. He could still check whether he was being tailed and start a stolen car without the key.

Dr Josephson went on to outline her theory that the brain contained several different memory banks, like separate filing cabinets, for different kinds of information.

The autobiographical memory records events we have experienced personally. These are labelled with time and place: we generally know not only what happened, but when and where.

The long-term semantic memory holds general knowledge such as the capital of Romania and how to solve quadratic equations.

The short-term memory is where we keep a phone number for the few seconds in between looking it up in the phone book and dialling it.

She gave examples of patients who had lost one filing cabinet but retained others, as Luke had. He felt profound relief, and gratitude to the author of the book, as he realized that what had happened to him was a well-studied psychological phenomenon.

Then he was struck by an inspiration. He was in his thirties, so he must have followed some occupation for a decade. His professional knowledge should still be in his head, lodged in his long-term semantic memory. He ought to be able to use it to figure out what line of work he did. And that would be the beginning of discovering his identity!

Looking up from the book, he tried to think what special knowledge he had. He did not count the skills of a secret agent, for he had already decided, judging by his soft indoor skin, that he was not a cop of any kind. What other special knowledge did he have?

It was maddeningly difficult to tell. Accessing the memory was not like opening the refrigerator, where you could see the contents at a glance. It was more like using a library catalogue – you had to know what you were looking for. He felt frustrated, and told himself to be patient and think this through.

If he were a lawyer, would he be able to remember thousands of laws? If a doctor, should he be able to look at someone and say: 'She has appendicitis'?

This was not going to work. Thinking back over the last few minutes, the only clue he noticed was that he had easily understood the equations and statistics in *The Human Brain*, even though he had been puzzled by other aspects of psychology. Maybe he was in a profession that involved numbers: accountancy or insurance, perhaps. Or he might be a math teacher.

He found the math section and looked along the shelves. A book called *Number Theory* caught his attention. He browsed through it for a while. It was clearly presented, but some years out of date . . .

Suddenly he looked up. He had discovered something. He understood number theory.

That was a major clue. Most pages of the book in his hand contained more equations than plain text. This was not written for the curious layman. It was an academic work. And he understood it. He had to be some kind of scientist.

With mounting optimism, he located the chemistry shelf and picked out *Polymer Engineering*. He found it comprehensible, but not easy. Next he moved to physics and tried *A Symposium on the Behaviour of Cold and Very Cold Gases*. It was fascinating, like reading a good novel.

He was narrowing it down. His job involved math and physics. What branch of physics? Cold gases were interesting, but he did not feel that he knew as much as the author of the book. He scanned the shelves and stopped at geophysics, remembering the newspaper story headlined U.S. MOON STAYS EARTHBOUND. He picked out *Principles of Rocket Design*.

It was an elementary text, but nevertheless there was an error on the first page he looked at. Reading on, he found two more—

'Yes!' he said aloud, startling a nearby schoolboy who was studying a biology text. If he could recognize mistakes in a textbook, he had to be an expert. He was a rocket scientist.

He wondered how many rocket scientists there were in the United States. He guessed a few hundred. He hurried to the information desk and spoke to the grey-haired librarian. 'Is there any kind of list of scientists?'

'Sure,' she said. 'You need the *Dictionary of American Scientists*, right at the beginning of the science section.'

He found it easily. It was a heavy book, but nevertheless it could not include every single American scientist. It must just be the prominent ones, he thought. Still, it was worth looking at. He sat at a table and went through the index, searching for anyone named Luke. He had to control his impatience and force himself to scan carefully.

He found a biologist called Luke Parfitt, an archaeologist called Lucas Dimittry, and a pharmacologist called Luc Fontainebleu, but no physicist.

Double-checking, he went through geophysicists and astronomers, but found no one with any version of Luke as a first name. Of course, he thought despondently, he was not even certain that Luke was his name. It was only what he had been called by Pete. For all he knew, his real name might be Percival.

He felt disappointed, but he was not ready to give up.

He thought of another approach. Somewhere, there were people who knew him. The name Luke might not be his own, but his face was. The *Dictionary of American Scientists* carried photos of only the most prominent men, such as Dr Wernher von Braun. But

Luke figured he must have friends and colleagues who would recognize him, if only he could find them. And now he knew where to start looking – for some of his acquaintances must be rocket scientists.

Where did one find scientists? At a university.

He looked up Washington, DC in the encyclopedia. The entry included a list of universities in the city. He picked Georgetown University because he had been in Georgetown earlier and knew how to get back there. He looked for the university on his street map, and saw that it had a large campus covering at least fifty city blocks. It would probably have a big physics department with dozens of professors. Surely one of them would know him?

Full of hope, he left the library and got back into his car.

2.30 P.M.

The igniters were not originally designed to be fired in a vacuum. For the Jupiter rocket, they have been redesigned so that: (i) the entire motor is sealed in an airtight container; (ii) in case that container should be breached, the igniter itself is also in a sealed container; and (iii) the igniter should fire in a vacuum anyway. This multiple fail-safe is an application of a design principle known as 'redundancy'.

The Cuba meeting took a coffee break, and Anthony ran back to Q Building for an update, praying his team would have come up with something, any clue to Luke's whereabouts.

Pete met him on the stairs. 'Here's something weird,' he said.

Anthony's heart jumped with hope. 'Give!'

'A report from the police in Georgetown. A housewife comes back from the store to find that her home has been broken into and her shower has been used. The intruder has disappeared, leaving behind a suitcase and a pile of filthy old clothes.'

Anthony was electrified. 'At last – a break!' he said. 'Give me the address.'

'You think this is our guy?'

'I'm sure of it! He's fed up with looking like a bum, so he's broken into an empty house, showered, shaved, and put on some decent clothes. That's characteristic, he would hate to be badly dressed.'

Pete looked thoughtful. 'You know him pretty well, I guess.'

Anthony realized he had slipped again. 'No, I don't,' he snapped. 'I read his file.'

'Sorry,' Pete said. After a moment he went on: 'I wonder why he left stuff behind?'

'My guess is, the housewife came home before he was quite finished.'

'What about the Cuba meeting?'

Anthony stopped a passing secretary. 'Please call the conference room in P Building and tell Mr Hobart that I was taken ill with stomach pains and Mr Maxell had to drive me home.'

'Stomach pains,' she said, deadpan.

'Right,' he said, walking away. Over his shoulder he called: 'Unless you can think of something better.'

He left the building with Pete following, and they jumped into his old yellow Cadillac. 'This may need delicate handling,' he said to Pete as he headed for Georgetown. 'The good news is that Luke has left us some clues. Our problem is that we don't have a hundred men to chase up leads. So, my plan is to get the Washington Police Department working for us.'

'Good luck,' Pete said sceptically. 'What should I do?'

'Be nice to the cops, and leave the talking to me.'

'I believe I can handle that.'

Anthony drove fast and quickly found the address in the police report. It was a small one-family home on a quiet street. A police cruiser was parked outside.

Before going into the house, Anthony studied the opposite side of the street, scrutinizing the houses. After a moment he spotted what he was looking for: a face in an upstairs window, watching him. It was an elderly woman, with white hair. She did not step back from the window when she caught his eye, but returned his stare with unabashed curiosity. She was just what he needed, a neighbourhood busybody. He smiled and gave her a salute, and she inclined her head in acknowledgement.

He turned away and approached the house that had been broken into. He could see scratches and a little splintering on the door jamb where the lock had been forced; a neat, professional job with no unnecessary damage, he thought. That fitted Luke.

The door was opened by an attractive young woman who was expecting a baby – pretty soon, he guessed. She took Anthony and Pete into her living room where two men were sitting on the couch, drinking coffee and smoking. One was a uniformed patrolman. The other, a young man in a cheap sharkskin suit, was probably a detective. In front of them was a splayed-leg coffee table with a red Formica top. An open suitcase was on the table.

Anthony introduced himself. He showed his identification to the cops. He did not want Mrs Bonetti – and all her friends and neighbours – to know that the CIA was interested in the case, so he said: 'We're colleagues of these police officers.'

The detective was Lewis Hite. 'You know something about this?' he said guardedly.

'I think we may have some information that will help you. But first, I need to know what you've got.'

Hite spread his hands in a gesture of bafflement. 'We got a suitcase belongs to a guy named Rowley Anstruther, Junior, from New York. He breaks into Mrs Bonetti's house, takes a shower, and goes away, leaving his suitcase behind. Go figure!'

Anthony studied the case. It was a good-quality tan leather bag, less than half full. He looked through the contents. There were clean shirts and underwear, but no shoes, pants or jackets.

'Looks like Mr Anstruther arrived in Washington from New York today,' he said.

Hite nodded, but Mrs Bonetti said admiringly: 'How do you know that?'

Anthony smiled. 'Detective Hite will tell you.' He did not want to offend Hite by stealing his limelight.

'The bag contains clean underwear but no laundry,' Hite explained. 'The guy hasn't changed his clothes, so he probably hasn't yet spent a night away. That means he left home this morning.'

Anthony said: 'I believe some old clothes were also left behind.'

The patrolman, whose name was Lonnie, said: 'I got 'em.' He lifted a cardboard box from beside the couch. 'Raincoat,' he said, sorting through the contents. 'Shirt, pants, shoes.'

Anthony recognized them. They were the rags Luke had been wearing. 'I don't believe Mr Anstruther came to this house,' Anthony said. 'I think the bag was stolen from him this morning, probably at Union Station.' He looked at the patrolman. 'Lonnie, would you call the precinct nearest the railroad station and ask if such a theft has been reported? That's if Mrs Bonetti will permit us to use the phone.'

'Of course,' she said. 'It's in the hall.'

Anthony added: 'The theft report should list the contents of the bag. I believe you'll find they include a suit and a pair of shoes that are not here now.' They were all staring at him in astonishment. 'Please make a careful note of the description of the suit.'

'Okay.' The patrolman went into the hallway.

Anthony felt good. He had managed to take command of the investigation without offending the police. Detective Hite now looked at him as if waiting for instructions. 'Mr Anstruther must be a man of six foot one or two, about 180 pounds, athletic build,' he said. 'Lewis, if you check the size of those shirts, you'll probably find they're sixteen neck, thirty-five sleeve.'

'They are – I already checked,' Hite said.

'I should have known you'd be ahead of me.' Anthony flattered him with a wry smile. 'We have a picture of the man we believe stole the suitcase and broke into this house.' Anthony nodded to Pete, who handed Hite a sheaf of photographs. 'We don't have a name for him,' Anthony lied. 'He's six foot one, 180 pounds, athletic build, and he may pretend to have lost his memory.'

'So what's the story?' Hite was intrigued. 'This guy wanted Anstruther's clothes, and he came here to change?'

'Something like that.'

'But why?'

Anthony looked apologetic. 'I'm sorry, I can't tell you.'

Hite was pleased. 'Classified, huh? No problem.'

Lonnie came back. 'Dead right about the theft. Union Station, eleven-thirty this morning.'

Anthony nodded. He had impressed the hell out of the two cops. 'And the suit?'

'Navy blue, with a chalk stripe.'

He turned to the detective. 'So, you can put out a photo and description including the clothes he's wearing.'

'You think he's still in town.'

'Yes.' Anthony was not as sure as he pretended, but he could not think of any reason for Luke to leave Washington.

'I presume he's in a car.'

'Let's find out.' Anthony turned to Mrs Bonetti. 'What's the name of the white-haired lady who lives across the street, a couple of doors down?'

'Rosemary Sims.'

'She spends a lot of time looking out her window?'

'We call her Nosy Rosie.'

'Excellent.' He turned to the detective. 'Shall we have a word with her?'

'Yep.'

They crossed the street and knocked on Mrs Sims's

door. She opened it instantly – she had been waiting in the hall. 'I saw him!' she said immediately. 'He went in there looking like a bum, and came out dressed to the nines!'

Anthony made a gesture indicating that Hite should ask the questions. Hite said: 'Did he have a car, Mrs Sims?'

'Yes, a nice little blue-and-white model. I thought it didn't belong to anyone in this street.' She looked at them slyly. 'I know what you're going to ask me next.'

'Did you happen to notice the licence plate?' Hite asked.

'Yes,' she said triumphantly. 'I wrote it down.'

Anthony smiled.

3 P.M.

The upper stages of the missile are contained in an aluminium tub with a cast magnesium base. The upper-stage tub rests on bearings, allowing it to spin during flight. It will rotate at about 550 revolutions per minute to improve accuracy.

On 37th Street at the end of O Street, the iron gates of Georgetown University stood open. Around three sides of a muddy lawn were Gothic buildings of rusticated grey stone, and students and faculty hurried from one building to another in their cold-weather coats. As Luke drove slowly in, he imagined that someone might catch his eye, recognize him, and say: 'Hey, Luke! Over here!' And the nightmare would be over.

Many of the professors wore clerical collars, and Luke realized this must be a Catholic university. It also appeared to be all-male.

He wondered whether he was Catholic.

He parked in front of the main entrance, a triple-arched portico marked 'Healy Hall'. Inside he found a reception desk and the first woman he had seen here. She said that the physics department was directly below where he stood, and told him to go outside and turn down a flight of steps that led beneath the portico. He felt he was coming nearer to the heart of the mystery, like a treasure hunter penetrating the chambers in an Egyptian pyramid.

Following her directions, he found a large laboratory with benches down the centre and doors on either side that led to smaller offices. At one of the benches, a group of men were working with the components of a microwave spectrograph. They all wore eyeglasses. Judging by their ages, Luke thought they were professors and graduate students. Some of them might easily be people he knew. He approached them with an expectant look.

One of the older men caught his eye, but there was no flash of recognition. 'Can I help you?'

'I hope so,' Luke said. 'Is there a department of geophysics here?'

'Goodness, no,' he said. 'At this university, even physics is considered a minor subject.' The others laughed.

Luke gave them all a chance to look at him, but none seemed to know him. He had chosen badly, he thought despondently; he probably should have gone to George Washington University. 'What about astronomy?'

'Why, yes, of course. The heavens, we study. Our observatory is famous.'

His spirits lifted. 'Where is it?'

The man pointed to a door at the back of the lab. 'Go to the other end of this building and you'll see it on the far side of the baseball diamond.' He returned his attention to the bench.

Luke followed a long, dark, dirty corridor that ran the length of the building. Seeing a stooped man in professorial tweeds coming the other way, Luke looked him in the eye, a smile ready to break out if the professor recognized him. But a nervous expression came over the man's face and he hurried by.

Undaunted, Luke walked on, giving the same look to everyone he passed who might possibly be a scientist; but no one showed any sign of recognition. Leaving the building, he saw tennis courts and a view of the Potomac river and, to the west across the sports field, a white dome.

He approached it with mounting anticipation. On the flat roof of a small two-storey house was a large revolving observatory, its dome having a sliding roof section. It was an expensive facility that indicated a serious astronomy department. Luke stepped inside the building.

The rooms were arranged around a massive central pillar that supported the enormous weight of the dome. Luke opened a door and saw an empty library. He tried another, and found an attractive woman about his own age sitting behind a typewriter. 'Good morning,' he said. 'Is the professor in?'

'You mean Father Heyden?'

'Uh, yes.'

'And you are?'

'Um . . .' Luke had stupidly not foreseen that he would have to give a name. Now his hesitation caused the secretary to raise her eyebrows distrustfully. 'He won't know me,' Luke said. 'That is . . . he will know me, I hope, but not by name.'

Her suspicion grew. 'Still, you do have a name.'

'Luke. Professor Luke.'

'To which university are you attached, Professor Luke?'

'Um . . . New York.'

'Any particular one of New York's many institutions of higher learning?'

Luke's heart sank. In his enthusiasm he had failed to plan for this encounter, and now he saw that he was making a mess of it. When you were in a hole, it was best to stop digging, he thought. He turned off his friendly smile and spoke coldly. 'I didn't come here to be cross-examined,' he said. 'Just tell Father Heyden that Professor Luke, the rocketry physicist, has dropped by and would like a word with him, would you?'

'I'm afraid that won't be possible,' she said firmly.

Luke left the room, slamming the door. He was angry with himself more than with the secretary, who was only protecting her boss from being pestered by an apparent nutcase. He decided to look around, opening doors until either someone recognized him or he was thrown out. He went up the stairs to the second floor. The building seemed to be deserted. He climbed a wooden stair with no handrail and entered the observatory. It, too, was empty. He stood admiring the large revolving telescope with its complex system of cogs and gears, a real masterpiece of engineering, and wondered what the hell he was going to do next.

The secretary came up the stairs. He prepared himself for a row, but instead she spoke sympathetically. 'You're in some kind of trouble, aren't you,' she said.

Her kindness brought a lump to his throat. 'It's very embarrassing,' he said. 'I've lost my memory. I know I'm in the rocketry field, and I was hoping to run into someone who might recognize me.'

'There's nobody here right now,' she said. 'Professor Larkley is giving a lecture on rocket fuels at the Smithsonian Institution, as part of International Geophysical Year, and all the faculty are there.'

Luke felt a surge of hope. Instead of one geophysicist he could meet a whole roomful. 'Where's the Smithsonian Institute?'

'It's downtown, right in the Mall, around 10th Street.'

He had driven around Washington enough today to know that that was not far away. 'What time is the lecture?'

'It started at three.'

Luke checked his watch. It was three-thirty. If he hurried, he could get there by four. 'The Smithsonian,' he repeated.

'Actually, it's in the Aircraft Building, around the back.'

'How many people will be at the lecture, do you know?'

'About a hundred and twenty.'

Surely one of them would know him!

'Thank you!' he said, and he ran down the stairs and out of the building.

3.30 P.M.

Rotating the second-stage tub stabilizes the flight path by averaging the variations between the eleven individual small rocket motors in the cluster.

Billie was furious with Len Ross for trying to ingratiate himself with the people from the Sowerby Foundation. The post of Director of Research ought to go to the best scientist – not the most oleaginous. She was still annoyed that afternoon when the chief executive's secretary called and asked her to come to his office.

Charles Silverton was an accountant, but he understood the needs of scientists. The hospital was owned by a trust whose twin aims were to understand and alleviate mental illness. He saw his job as making sure that administrative and financial problems did not distract the medical people from their work. Billie liked him.

His office had been the dining room of the original Victorian mansion, and it still had the fireplace and the ceiling mouldings. He waved Billie to a chair and said: 'Did you speak to the people from the Sowerby Foundation this morning?'

'Yes. Len was showing them around, and I joined the party. Why?'

He did not answer her question. 'Do you think you could have said anything to offend them?'

She frowned, mystified. 'I don't think so. We just talked about the new wing.'

'You know, I really wanted you to get the job of Director of Research.'

She was alarmed. 'I don't like your use of the past tense!'

He went on: 'Len Ross is a competent scientist, but you're exceptional. You've achieved more than him and you're ten years younger.'

'The Foundation is backing Len for the job?'

He hesitated, looking awkward. 'I'm afraid they're insisting on it, as a condition of their grant.'

'The hell they are!' Billie was stunned.

'Do you know anyone connected with the Foundation?'

'Yes. One of my oldest friends is a trustee. His name is Anthony Carroll, he's godfather to my son.'

'Why is he on the board? What does he do for a living?'

'He works for the State Department, but his mother is very wealthy, and he's involved with several charities.'

'Does he have a grudge against you?'

For a moment, Billie slipped back in time. She had been angry with Anthony, after the catastrophe that led to Luke's leaving Harvard, and they never dated again. But she forgave him because of how he behaved toward Elspeth. Elspeth had gone into a decline, letting her academic work slide, and was in danger of failing to graduate. She walked around in a daze, a pale ghost with long red hair, getting thinner and missing classes. It was Anthony who rescued her. They became close, though the relationship was a friendship rather than a romance. They studied together, and she caught up enough to pass. Anthony won back Billie's respect, and they had been friends ever since.

Now she told Charles: 'I got kind of mad at him, back in 1941, but we made it up long ago.'

'Maybe someone on the board admires Len's work.'

Billie considered. 'Len's approach is different from mine. He's a Freudian, he looks for psychoanalytical explanations. If a patient suddenly loses the ability to read, he assumes they have some unconscious fear of literature, a fear that is being suppressed. I would always look for damage to the brain as the likeliest cause.'

'So there might be a keen Freudian on the board who is against you.'

'I guess.' Billie sighed. 'Can they do this? It seems so unfair.'

'It's certainly unusual,' Charles said. 'Foundations normally make a point of not interfering with decisions requiring professional expertise. But there's no law against it.'

'Well, I'm not going to take this lying down. What reason did they give?'

'I got an informal call from the chairman. He told me the board feels Len is better qualified.'

Billie shook her head. 'There has to be another explanation.'

'Why don't you ask your friend?'

'That's exactly what I'm going to do,' she said.

3.45 P.M.

A stroboscope was used to determine exactly where weights should be placed so that the spinning tub would be perfectly balanced – otherwise the inner cage would vibrate within the outer frame, causing the whole assembly to disintegrate.

Luke had looked at his street map of Washington before leaving the Georgetown University campus. The Institute was in a park called the Mall. He checked his watch as he drove along K Street. He would be at the Smithsonian in about ten minutes. Assuming it took him another five to find the lecture theatre, he should arrive as the talk was ending. Then he would find out who he was.

It was almost eleven hours since he had awakened to this horror. Yet, because he could remember nothing from before five o'clock this morning, it seemed to have been going on all his life.

He turned right on 9th Street, heading south towards the Mall with high hopes. A few moments later, he heard a police siren blip once, and his heart skipped a beat.

He looked in his rear-view mirror. A police cruiser was on his tail, lights flashing. There were two cops on the front seat. One pointed toward the right-hand kerb and mouthed: 'Pull over.'

Luke was devastated. He had almost made it.

Could it be that he had committed some minor traffic violation, and they wanted to ticket him? Even if that were all, they would still ask for his driving licence, and he had no kind of identification. Anyway, this was not about a minor traffic violation. He was driving a stolen car. He had calculated that the theft would go unreported until the owner got back from Philadelphia later tonight, but something had gone wrong. They intended to arrest him.

But they would have to catch him first.

He clicked into escape mode. Ahead of him on the one-way street was a long truck. Without further thought, he stamped on the gas pedal and pulled around the truck.

The cops switched on their siren and followed.

Luke pulled in front of the truck, going fast. Acting on instinct now, he yanked the parking brake and spun the wheel hard to the right.

The Ford went into a long skid, turning as it did so. The truck swerved left to avoid it, forcing the patrol car all the way over to the left side of the street.

Luke shifted into neutral to prevent the car stalling. It came to rest facing the wrong way. He put it into drive again and stepped on the gas, heading against the traffic on the one-way street.

Cars veered wildly left and right to avoid a head-on collision. Luke swung right to miss a city bus, then clipped a station wagon, but ploughed on amid a chorus of indignant horns. An old pre-war Lincoln swung onto the sidewalk and hit a lamp post. A motorcyclist lost control and fell off his machine. Luke hoped he was not badly hurt.

He made it to the next crossing and swung right onto a broad avenue. He raced two blocks, running red lights, then looked in his mirror. There was no sign of the police car.

He turned again, heading south now. He was lost, but he knew the Mall was to his south. Now that the patrol car was out of sight, he would have been safer to drive normally. However, it was four o'clock, and he was farther away from the Smithsonian than he had been five minutes ago. If he was late, the audience would have gone. He stepped on the gas again.

The southbound street he was on dead-ended, and he was forced to turn right. He tried to watch for street names as he sped along, swerving around slower vehicles. He was on D Street. After a minute he came to 7th and turned south.

His luck changed. All the lights were green. He hit seventy crossing Constitution Avenue, and he was in the park.

Across the lawn to his right, he saw a big dark-red building like a castle in a fairy tale. It was exactly where the map said the museum would be. He stopped the car and checked his watch. It was five past four. The audience would be leaving. He cursed and jumped out.

He ran across the grass. The secretary had told him the lecture was in the Aircraft Building around the back. Was this the front or the back? It looked like the front. To the side of the building was a path through a little garden. He followed it and came out on a wide two-way avenue. Still running, he found an elaborate iron gateway leading to the back entrance of the museum. To his right, beside a lawn, was what looked like an old aircraft hangar. He went inside.

He looked around. All kinds of aircraft were suspended from the ceiling: old biplanes, a wartime jet, and even the sphere of a hot-air balloon. At floor level were glass cases of aircraft insignia, flight clothing, aerial cameras, and photographs. Luke spoke to a uniformed guard. 'I'm here for the lecture on rocket fuels.'

'You're too late,' the man said, looking at his watch. 'It's ten past four, the lecture's over.'

'Where was it held? I might still catch the speaker.'

'I think he's gone.'

Luke stared hard at him and spoke slowly. 'Just answer the fucking question. Where?'

The man looked scared. 'Far end of the hall,' he said hastily.

Luke hurried the length of the building. At the end, a lecture theatre had been improvised, with a lectern, blackboard, and rows of chairs. Most of the audience had left, and attendants were already stacking the metal seats at the side of the room. But a small knot of eight or nine men remained in a corner, deep in discussion, surrounding a white-haired man who might have been the lecturer.

Luke's spirits fell. A few minutes ago, more than a

hundred scientists in his field had been here. Now there were just a handful, and it was quite possible that none of them knew him.

The white-haired man glanced up at him, then looked back at the others. It was impossible to know whether he had recognized Luke or not. He was speaking, and carried on without a pause. 'Nitromethane is almost impossible to handle. You can't ignore safety factors.'

'You can build safety into your procedures, if the fuel is good enough,' said a young man in a tweed suit.

The argument was a familiar one to Luke. A bewildering variety of rocket fuels had been tested, many of them more powerful than the standard combination of alcohol and liquid oxygen, but they all had drawbacks.

A man with a southern accent said: 'What about unsymmetrical dimethylhydrazine? I hear they're testing that at the Jet Propulsion Laboratory in Pasadena.'

Luke suddenly said: 'It works, but it's deadly poison.'

They all turned to him. The white-haired man frowned, looking slightly annoyed, resenting the interruption from a stranger.

Then the young man in the tweed suit looked shocked and said: 'My God, what are you doing in Washington, Luke?'

Luke felt so happy he could have wept.

PART 3

4.15 P.M.

A tape programmer in the tub varies the speed of rotation of the upper stages between 450 r.p.m. and 750 r.p.m., to avoid resonance vibrations that could cause the missile to break up in space.

Luke found he could not speak. The emotion of relief was so strong it seemed to constrict his throat. All day he had forced himself to be calm and rational, but now he was close to breaking down.

The other scientists resumed their conversation, oblivious to his distress, except for the young man in the tweed suit, who looked concerned and said: 'Hey, are you okay?'

Luke nodded. After a moment, he managed to say: 'Could we talk?'

'Sure, sure. There's a little office behind the Wright Brothers display. Professor Larkley used it earlier.' They headed for a door to one side. 'I organized this lecture, by the way.' He led Luke into a small, spartan room with a couple of chairs, a desk and a phone. They sat down. 'What's going on?' said the man.

'I've lost my memory.'

'My God!'

'Autobiographical amnesia. I still remember my science, that's how I found my way to you guys, but I don't know anything about myself.'

Looking shocked, the young man said: 'Do you know who I am?'

Luke shook his head. 'Heck, I'm not even sure of my own name.'

'Whew.' The man looked bewildered. 'I never came across anything like this in real life.'

'I need you to tell me what you know about me.'

'I guess you do. Uh . . . where shall I start?'

'You called me Luke.'

'Everyone calls you Luke. You're Dr Claude Lucas, but I guess you never liked "Claude". I'm Will McDermot.'

Luke closed his eyes, overwhelmed by relief and gratitude. He knew his name. 'Thank you, Will.'

'I don't know anything about your family. I've only met you a couple of times, at scientific conferences.'

'Do you know where I live?'

'Huntsville, Alabama, I guess. You work for the Army Ballistic Missile Agency. They're based at Redstone Arsenal in Huntsville. You're a civilian, though, not an army officer. Your boss is Wernher von Braun.'

'I can't tell you how good it is to know this stuff!'

'I was surprised to see you because your team is about to launch a rocket that will put an American satellite in space for the first time. They're all down in Cape Canaveral, and word is it could be tonight.'

'I read about it in the paper this morning – my God, did I work on that?'

'Yeah. The Explorer. It's the most important launch in the history of the American space programme – especially since the success of the Russian Sputnik and the failure of the Navy's Vanguard.'

Luke was exhilarated. Only hours ago he had imagined himself a drunken bum. Now it turned out he was a scientist at the peak of his career. 'But I ought to be there for the launch!'

'Exactly ... so do you have any idea why you're not?'

Luke shook his head. 'I woke up this morning in the men's room at Union Station. No idea how I got there.'

Will gave him a man-to-man grin. 'Sounds like you went to a great party last night!'

'Let me ask you seriously – is that the kind of thing I do? Get so drunk I pass out?'

'I don't know you well enough to answer that.' Will frowned. 'I'd be surprised, though. You know us scientists. Our idea of a party is to sit around drinking coffee and talking about our work.'

That sounded right to Luke. 'Getting drunk just doesn't seem interesting enough.' But he had no other explanation of how he had gotten into this scrape. Who was Pete? Why had people been following him? And who were the two men searching for him at Union Station?

He thought of talking to Will about all that, and

decided it sounded too strange. Will might begin to think he was nuts. Instead he said: 'I'm going to call Cape Canaveral.'

'Great idea.' Will picked up the phone on the desk and dialled zero. 'Will McDermot here. Can I make a long-distance call on this phone? Thank you.' He handed the phone to Luke.

Luke got the number from information and dialled.'This is Dr Lucas.' He felt inordinately pleased to be able to give his name: he would not have thought it could be so satisfying. 'I'd like to speak to someone on the Explorer launch team.'

'They're in hangars D and R,' said the male operator. 'Please hold the line.'

A moment later a voice said: 'Army security, Colonel Hide speaking.'

'This is Dr Lucas—'

'Luke! At last! Where the hell are you?'

'I'm in Washington.'

'Well, what the bejesus are you doing? We've been going crazy! We got Army Security looking for you, the FBI, even the CIA!'

That explained the two agents searching in Union Station, Luke thought. 'Listen, a strange thing has happened. I lost my memory. I've been wandering around town trying to figure out who I am. Finally I found some physicists who know me.'

'But that's extraordinary. How did it happen, for Christ's sake?'

'I was hoping you could tell me that, Colonel.'

'You always call me Bill.'

'Bill.'

'Okay, well, I'll tell you what I know. Monday morning you took off, saying you had to go to Washington. You flew from Patrick.'

'Patrick?'

'Patrick Air Force Base, near Cape Canaveral. Marigold made the reservations—'

'Who's Marigold?'

'Your secretary in Huntsville. She also booked your usual suite at the Carlton Hotel in Washington.'

There was a note of envy in the colonel's voice, and Luke wondered briefly about that 'usual suite', but he had more important questions. 'Did I tell anyone the purpose of the trip?'

'Marigold made an appointment for you to see General Sherwood at the Pentagon at ten a.m. yesterday – but you didn't keep the appointment.'

'Did I give a reason for wanting to see the general?'

'Apparently not.'

'What's his area of responsibility?'

'Army security – but he's also a friend of your family's, so the meeting could have been about anything.'

It must have been something highly important, Luke reflected, to take him away from Cape Canaveral just before his rocket was to take off. 'Is the launch going ahead tonight?'

'No, we've got weather problems. It's been postponed until tomorrow at ten-thirty p.m.'

Luke wondered what the hell he had been doing. 'Do I have friends here in Washington?'

'Sure. One of them's been calling me every hour. Bern Rothsten.' Hide read out a phone number.

Luke scribbled it on a scratchpad. 'I'll call him right away.'

'First you should talk to your wife.'

Luke froze. His breath was taken away. Wife, he thought. I have a wife. He wondered what she was like.

'You still there?' Hide said.

Luke started to breathe again. 'Uh, Bill . . .'

'Yes?'

'What's her name?'

'Elspeth,' he said. 'Your wife's name is Elspeth. I'll transfer you to her phone. Hold the line.'

Luke had a nervous sensation in his stomach. This was dumb, he thought. She was his wife.

'Elspeth speaking. Luke, is that you?'

She had a warm, low voice, with precise diction and no particular accent. He imagined a tall, confident woman. He said: 'Yes, this is Luke. I've lost my memory.'

'I've been so worried. Are you okay?'

He felt pathetically grateful for someone who cared how he was. 'I guess I am now,' he said.

'What on earth happened?'

'I really don't know. I woke up this morning in the men's room at Union Station, and I spent the day trying to find out who I am.'

'Everyone's been looking for you. Where are you now?'

'At the Smithsonian, in the Aircraft Building.'

'Is someone taking care of you?'

Luke smiled at Will McDermot. 'A fellow scientist has been helping me. And I have a number for Bern Rothsten. But I really don't need taking care of. I'm fine, I just lost my memory.'

Will McDermot stood up, looking embarrassed, and whispered: 'I'm going to give you some privacy. I'll wait outside.'

Luke nodded gratefully.

Elspeth was saying: 'So you don't remember why you took off for Washington in such a hurry.'

'No. Obviously I didn't tell you.'

'You said it was better for me not to know. But I was frantic. I called an old friend of ours in Washington, Anthony Carroll. He's in the CIA.'

'Did he do anything?'

'He called you at the Carlton on Monday night, and you arranged to meet him for breakfast early on Tuesday morning – but you didn't show up. He's been looking for you all day. I'm going to call him now and tell him everything's all right.'

'Obviously something happened to me between Monday evening and Tuesday morning.'

'You ought to see a doctor, get yourself checked out.'

'I feel fine. But there's a lot I want to know. Do we have children?'

'No.'

Luke felt a sadness that seemed familiar, like the dull ache of an old injury.

Elspeth went on: 'We've been trying for a baby ever since we got married, which was four years ago, but we haven't succeeded.'

'Are my parents alive?'

'Your Mom is. She lives in New York. Your Pa died five years ago.'

Luke felt a sudden wave of grief that seemed to come from nowhere. He had lost his memories of his father, and would never see him again. It seemed unbearably sad.

Elspeth went on: 'You have two brothers and a sister, all younger. Your baby sister Emily is your favourite, she's ten years younger than you, she lives in Baltimore.'

'Do you have phone numbers for them?'

'Of course. Hold on while I look them up.'

'I'd like to talk to them, I don't know why.' He heard a muffled sob at the other end of the line. 'Are you crying?'

Elspeth sniffed. 'I'm okay.' He imagined her taking a handkerchief out of her handbag. 'Suddenly I felt so sorry for you,' she said tearfully. 'It must have been awful.'

'There were some bad moments.'

'Let me give you those numbers.' She read them out.

'Are we rich?' he said when he had written down the phone numbers.

'Your father was a very successful banker. He left you a lot of money. Why?'

'Bill Hide told me I'm staying in my "usual suite" at the Carlton.'

'Before the war, your Pa was an adviser to the Roosevelt administration, and he liked to take his family with him when he went to Washington. You always had a corner suite at the Carlton. I guess you're keeping up the tradition.'

'So you and I don't live on what the army pays me.'

'No, though in Huntsville we try not to live very much better than your colleagues.'

'I could go on asking you questions all day. But what I really want is to find out how this happened to me. Would you fly up here tonight?'

There was a moment of silence. 'My God, why?'

'To figure out this mystery with me. I could use some help – and companionship.'

'You should forget about it and come down here.'

That was unthinkable. 'I can't forget about this. I have to know what it's all about. It's too strange to ignore.'

'Luke, I can't leave Cape Canaveral now. We're about to launch the first American satellite, for heaven's sake! I can't let the team down at a moment like this.'

'I guess not.' He understood, but all the same he was hurt by her refusal. 'Who's Bern Rothsten?'

'He was at Harvard with you and Anthony Carroll. He's a writer now.'

'Apparently he's been trying to reach me. Maybe he knows what this is all about.'

'Call me later, won't you? I'll be at the Starlite Motel tonight.'

'Okay.'

'Take care of yourself, Luke, please,' she said earnestly.

'I will, I promise.' He hung up.

He sat in silence for a moment. He felt emotionally drained. Part of him wanted to go to his hotel and lie down. But he was too curious. He picked up the phone again and called the number Bern Rothsten had left. 'This is Luke Lucas,' he said when the phone was answered.

Bern had a gravelly voice and the trace of a New York accent. 'Luke, thank God! What the hell happened to you?'

'Everybody says that. The answer is that I don't really know anything except that I've lost my memory.'

'You lost your memory?'

'Right.'

'Oh, shit. Do you know how this happened to you?'

'No. I was hoping you might have a clue.'

'I might.'

'Why have you been trying to reach me?'

'I was worried. You called me on Monday. You said you were on your way here, you wanted to see me, and you would call me from the Carlton. But you never did.'

'Something happened to me on Monday night.'

'Yeah. Listen, there's someone you have to call. Dr Billie Josephson is a world expert on memory.'

The name rang a bell. 'I think I came across her book in the library.'

'She's also my ex-wife, and an old friend of yours.'
Bern gave Luke the number.

'I'm going to call her right away. Bern . . .'

'Yeah.'

'I lose my memory, and it turns out that an old
friend of mine is a world expert on memory. Isn't that
a hell of a coincidence?'

'Ain't it just,' said Bern.

4.45 P.M.

The final stage, containing the satellite, is eighty inches long and only six inches across, and weighs just over thirty pounds. It is shaped like a stovepipe.

Billie had scheduled an hour-long interview with a patient, a football player who had been 'dinged' – concussed in a collision with an opponent. He was an interesting subject, because he could remember everything up to one hour before the game, and nothing after that until the moment when he found himself standing on the sideline with his back to the play, wondering how he got there.

She was distracted during the interview, thinking about the Sowerby Foundation and Anthony Carroll. By the time she got through with the football player and called Anthony, she was feeling frustrated and impatient. She was lucky, and reached him at his office on the first try. 'Anthony,' she said abruptly, 'what the hell is going on?'

'A lot,' he replied. 'Egypt and Syria have agreed to merge, skirts are getting shorter, and Roy Campanella broke his neck in a car wreck and may never catch for the Dodgers again.'

She controlled the impulse to yell at him. 'I was

passed over for the post of Director of Research here at the hospital,' she said with forced calm. 'Len Ross got the job. Did you know that?'

'Yeah, I guess I did.'

'I don't understand it. I thought I might lose to a highly qualified outsider – Sol Weinberg, from Princeton, or someone of that order. But everyone knows I'm better than Len.'

'Do they?'

'Anthony, come on! You know it yourself. Hell, you encouraged me in this line of research, years ago, at the end of the war, when we—'

'Okay, okay, I remember,' he interrupted. 'That stuff is still classified, you know.'

She did not believe that things they did in the war could still be important secrets. But it did not matter. 'So why didn't I get the job?'

'I'm supposed to know?'

This was humiliating, she felt, but her need to understand overrode her embarrassment. 'The Foundation is insisting on Len.'

'I guess they have the right.'

'Anthony, talk to me!'

'I'm talking.'

'You're part of the Foundation. It's very unusual for a trust to interfere in this kind of decision. They normally leave it to the experts. You must know why they took this exceptional step.'

'Well, I don't. And my guess is the step has not yet been taken. There certainly hasn't been a meeting about it – I'd know about that.'

'Charles was very definite.'

'I don't doubt it's true, unfortunately for you. But it's not the kind of thing that would be decided openly. More likely, the Director and one or two board members had a chat over a drink at the Cosmos Club. One of them has called Charles and given him the word. He can't afford to upset them, so he's gone along. That's how these things work. I'm just surprised Charles was so candid with you.'

'He was shocked, I think. He can't understand why they would do such a thing. I thought you might know.'

'It's probably something dumb. Is Ross a family man?'

'Married with four children.'

'The Director doesn't really approve of women earning high salaries when there are men trying to support a family.'

'For Christ's sake! I have a child and an elderly mother to take care of!'

'I didn't say it was logical. Listen, Billie, I have to go. I'm sorry. I'll call you later.'

'Okay,' she said.

When she had hung up, she stared at the phone, trying to sort out her feelings. The conversation rang false to her, and she asked herself why. It was perfectly plausible that Anthony might not know about machinations among the other board members of the Foundation. So why did she disbelieve him? Thinking back, she realized he had been evasive – which was not like him. In the end he had told her what little he knew, but reluctantly. It all added up to a very clear impression.

Anthony was lying.

5 P.M.

The fourth-stage rocket is made of lightweight titanium instead of stainless steel. The weight saving permits the missile to carry a crucial extra two pounds of scientific equipment.

When Anthony hung up the phone, it rang again immediately. He picked it up and heard Elspeth, sounding spooked. 'For God's sake, I've been on hold for a quarter of an hour!'

'I was talking to Billie, she—'

'Never mind. I just spoke with Luke.'

'Jesus, how come?'

'Shut up and listen! He was at the Smithsonian, in the Aircraft Building, with a bunch of physicists.'

'I'm on my way.' Anthony dropped the phone and ran out the door. Pete saw him and ran after him. They went down to the parking lot and jumped into Anthony's car.

The fact that Luke had spoken with Elspeth dismayed Anthony. It suggested that everything was coming unglued. But maybe if he got to Luke before anyone else, he could hold things together. It took them four minutes to drive to Independence Avenue and 10th Street. They left the car outside the back entrance to the museum and ran into the old hangar that was the Aircraft Building.

There was a payphone near the entrance, but no sign of Luke.

'Split up,' Anthony said. 'I'll go right, you go left.' He walked through the exhibits, scrutinizing the faces of the men as they gazed into the glass cases and stared up at the aircraft suspended from the ceiling. At the far end of the building he met up with Pete, who made an empty-hands gesture.

There were some restrooms and offices to one side. Pete checked the men's room and Anthony looked in the offices. Luke must have called from one of these phones, but he was not here now.

Pete came out of the men's room and said: 'Nothing.'

Anthony said: 'This is a catastrophe.'

Pete frowned. 'Is it?' he said. 'A catastrophe? Is this guy more important than you've told me?'

'Yes,' Anthony said. 'He could be the most dangerous man in America.'

'Christ.'

Against the end wall, Anthony saw stacked chairs and a movable lectern. A young man in a tweed suit was talking to two men in overalls. Anthony recalled that Elspeth had said Luke was with a bunch of physicists. Maybe he could still pick up the trail.

He approached the man in the tweed suit and said: 'Excuse me, was there a meeting of some kind here?'

'Sure, Professor Larkley gave a lecture on rocket

fuels,' the young man said. 'I'm Will McDermot, I organized it as part of International Geophysical Year.'

'Was Dr Claude Lucas here?'

'Yes. Are you a friend of his?'

'Yes.'

'Did you know he's lost his memory? He didn't even know his own name, until I told him.'

Anthony suppressed a curse. He had been afraid of this from the moment Elspeth had said she had spoken to Luke. He knew who he was.

'I need to locate Dr Lucas urgently,' Anthony said.

'What a shame, you just missed him.'

'Did he say where he was going?'

'No. I tried to encourage him to see a doctor, get himself checked out, but he said he was fine. I thought he seemed very shocked—'

'Yes, thank you, I appreciate your help.' Anthony turned and walked quickly away. He was furious.

Outside on Independence Avenue he saw a police cruiser. Two cops were checking out a car parked on the other side of the road. Anthony went closer and saw that the car was a blue-and-white Ford Fairlane. 'Look at that,' he said to Pete. He checked the licence plate. It was the car Nosy Rosy had seen from her Georgetown window.

He showed the patrolmen his CIA identification. 'Did you just spot this car illegally parked?' he said.

The older of the two men replied. 'No, we saw a man driving it on 9th Street,' he said. 'But he got away from us.'

'You let him escape?' Anthony said incredulously.

'He turned around and headed right into the traffic!' the younger cop said. 'Hell of a driver, whoever he is.'

'Few minutes later, we see the car parked here, but he's gone.'

Anthony wanted to knock their wooden heads together. Instead, he said: 'This fugitive may have stolen another car in this neighbourhood and made his getaway.' He took a business card out of his billfold. 'If you get a report of a car stolen nearby, would you please call me at this number?'

The older cop read the card and said: 'I'll make sure to do that, Mr Carroll.'

Anthony and Pete returned to the yellow Cadillac and drove away.

Pete said: 'What do you think he'll do now?'

'I don't know. He might go right to the airport and get a plane to Florida; he could go to the Pentagon; he may go to his hotel. Hell, he could take it into his head to go visit his mother in New York. We may have to spread ourselves kind of thin.' He was silent, thinking, while he parked and entered Q Building. Reaching his office, he said: 'I want two men at the airport, two at Union Station, two at the bus station. I want two men in the office calling all known members of Luke's family, friends and acquaintances, to ask if they're expecting to see him or if they've heard from him. I want you to go with two men to the Carlton Hotel. Take a room, then stake out the lobby. I'll join you there later.'

Pete went out and Anthony shut the door.

For the first time today, Anthony was scared. Now that Luke knew his own identity, there was no telling what else he might find out. This project should have been Anthony's greatest triumph, but it was turning into a foul-up that might end his career.

It might end his life.

If he could find Luke, he could still patch things up. But he would have to take drastic measures. It would no longer be enough simply to put Luke under surveillance. He had to solve the problem once and for all.

With a heavy heart, he went to the photograph of President Eisenhower that hung on the wall. He pulled on one side of the frame, and the picture swung out on hinges to reveal a safe. He dialled the combination, opened the door, and took out his gun.

It was a Walther P38 automatic. This was the handgun used by the German army in the Second World War. Anthony had been issued with it before he went to North Africa. He also had a silencer that had been specially designed by OSS to fit the gun.

The first time he had killed a man, it had been with this gun.

Albin Moulier was a traitor who had betrayed members of the French Resistance to the police. He deserved to die – the five men in the cell were agreed on that. They drew lots, standing in a derelict stable miles from anywhere, late at night, a single lamp throwing dancing shadows on the rough stone walls. Anthony might have been excused, as the only foreigner, but that way he would have lost respect, so he insisted on taking his chances with the rest. And he drew the short straw.

Albin was tied to the rusty wheel of a broken plough, not even blindfolded, listening to the discussion and watching the drawing of lots. He soiled himself when they pronounced the death sentence, and screamed when he saw Anthony take out the Walther. The screaming helped: it made Anthony want to kill him quickly, just to stop the noise. He shot Albin at close range, between the eyes, one bullet. Afterwards, the others told him he did it well, without hesitation or regrets, like a man.

Anthony still saw Albin in his dreams.

He took the silencer from the safe, fitted it over the barrel of the pistol, and screwed it tight. He put on his topcoat. It was a long camel-hair winter coat, single-breasted, with deep inside pockets. He placed the gun, butt down, in the right-hand pocket, with the silencer sticking up. Leaving the coat unbuttoned, he reached in with his left hand, pulled the gun out by the silencer, and transferred it to his right hand. Then he moved the thumb safety lever on the left of the slide up to the 'fire' position. The whole process took about a second. The silencer made the weapon cumbersome. It would be easier to carry the two parts separately. However, he might not have time to fit the silencer before shooting. This way was better.

He buttoned his coat and went out.

6 P.M.

The satellite is bullet-shaped, rather than spherical. In theory, a sphere should be more stable; but in practice, the satellite must have protruding antennae for radio communication, and the antennae spoil the round shape.

Luke took a taxicab to the Georgetown Mind Hospital and gave his name at the reception desk, saying he had an appointment with Dr Josephson.

She had been charming on the phone: concerned about him, pleased to hear his voice, intrigued to know that he had lost his memory, eager to see him as soon as she could. She spoke with a southern accent, and sounded as if laughter was forever bubbling up at the back of her throat.

Now she came running down the stairs, a short woman in a white lab coat, with big brown eyes and a flushed expression of excitement. Luke could not help smiling at the sight of her.

'It's so great to see you!' she said, and she threw her arms around him in a hug.

He felt an impulse to respond to her exuberance and squeeze her tightly. Afraid that he might do something to cause offence, he froze, his hands in the air like the victim of a hold-up.

She laughed at him. 'You don't remember what I'm like,' she said. 'Relax, I'm almost harmless.'

He let his arms fall around her shoulders. Her small body was soft and round under the lab coat.

'Come on, I'll show you my office.' She led him up the stairs.

As they crossed a broad corridor, a white-haired woman in a bathrobe said: 'Doctor! I like your boyfriend!'

Billie grinned and said: 'You can have him next, Marlene.'

Billie had a small room with a plain desk and a steel filing cabinet, but she had made it pretty with flowers and a splashy abstract painting in bright colours. She gave Luke coffee and opened a package of cookies, then asked him about his amnesia.

She made notes as he answered her questions. Luke had had no food for twelve hours, and he ate all the cookies. She smiled and said: 'Want some more? There's another pack.' He shook his head.

'Well, I have a pretty clear picture,' she said eventually. 'You have global amnesia, but otherwise you seem mentally healthy. I can't assess your physical state, because I'm not that kind of doctor, and it's my duty to advise you to have a physical as soon as you can.' She smiled. 'But you look all right, just shook up.'

'Is there a cure for this type of amnesia?'

'No, there's not. The process is generally irreversible.'

That was a blow. Luke had hoped everything might come back to him in a flash. 'Christ,' he muttered.

'Don't be downhearted,' Billie said kindly. 'Sufferers have all their faculties, and are able to relearn what has been forgotten; so they can usually pick up the threads of their lives and live normally. You're going to be fine.'

Even while he was hearing horrible news, he found himself watching her with fascination, concentrating his attention first on her eyes, which seemed to glow with sympathy, then her expressive mouth, then the way the light from the desk lamp fell on her dark curls. He wanted her to carry on talking for ever. He said: 'What might have caused the amnesia?'

'Brain damage is the first possibility to consider. However, there's no sign of injury, and you told me you don't have a headache.'

'That's right. So what else?'

'There are several alternatives,' she explained patiently. 'It can be brought on by prolonged stress, a sudden shock, or drugs. It's also a side effect of some treatments for schizophrenia involving a combination of electric shock and drugs.'

'Any way to tell which affected me?'

'Not conclusively. You had a hangover this morning, you said. If that wasn't booze, it might be the after-effects of a drug. But you're not going to get a final answer by talking to doctors. You need to find out what happened to you between Monday night and this morning.'

'Well, at least I know what I'm looking for,' he said. 'Shock, drugs or schizophrenia treatment.'

'You're not schizophrenic,' she said. 'You have a real good hold on reality. What's your next step?'

Luke stood up. He was reluctant to leave the company of this bewitching woman, but she had told him all she could. 'I'm going to see Bern Rothsten. I think he may have some ideas.'

'Got a car?'

'I asked the taxi to wait.'

'I'll see you out.'

As they walked down the stairs, Billie took his arm affectionately.

Luke said: 'How long have you been divorced from Bern?'

'Five years. Long enough to become friends again.'

'This is a strange question, but I have to ask it. Did you and I ever date?'

'Oh, boy,' said Billie. 'Did we ever.'

1943

On the day Italy surrendered, Billie bumped into Luke in the lobby of Q Building.

At first she did not know him. She saw a thin man of about thirty in a suit that was too big, and her eyes passed over him without recognition. Then he spoke. 'Billie? Don't you remember me?'

She knew the voice, of course, and it made her heart beat faster. But when she looked again at the emaciated man from whom the words issued, she gave a small scream of horror. His head looked like a skull. His once-glossy black hair was dull. His shirt collar was too large, and his jacket looked as if it were draped over a wire hanger. His eyes were the eyes of an old man. 'Luke!' she said. 'You look terrible!'

'Gee, thanks,' he said, with a tired smile.

'I'm sorry,' she said hastily.

'Don't worry. I've lost some weight, I know. There's not a lot of food where I've been.'

She wanted to hug him, but she held back, not sure he would like it.

He said: 'What are you doing here?'

She took a deep breath. 'A training course – maps, radio, firearms, unarmed combat.'

He grinned. 'You're not dressed for ju-jitsu.'

Billie still loved to dress stylishly, despite the war. Today she was wearing a pale yellow suit with a short bolero jacket and a daring knee-length skirt, and a big hat like an upside-down dinner plate. She could not afford to buy the latest fashions on her army wages, of course: she had made this outfit herself, using a borrowed sewing machine. Her father had taught all his children to sew. 'I'll take that as a compliment,' she said with a smile, beginning to get over her shock. 'Where have you been?'

'Do you have a minute to talk?'

'Of course.' She was supposed to be at a cryptography class, but to heck with that.

'Let's go outside.'

It was a warm September afternoon. Luke took off his suit coat and slung it over his shoulder as they walked alongside the Reflecting Pool. 'How come you're in OSS?'

'Anthony Carroll fixed it,' she said. The Office of Strategic Services was considered a glamorous assignment, and jobs here were much coveted. 'Anthony used family influence to get here. He's Bill Donovan's personal assistant now.' General 'Wild Bill' Donovan was head of OSS. 'I'd been driving a general around Washington for a year, so I was real pleased to get posted here. Anthony's used his position to bring in all his old friends from Harvard. Elspeth is in London, Peg is in Cairo, and I gather you and Bern have been behind enemy lines somewhere.'

'France,' Luke said.

'What was that like?'

He lit a cigarette. It was a new habit – he had not smoked at Harvard – but now he drew tobacco smoke into his lungs as if it were the breath of life. 'The first man I killed was a Frenchman,' he said abruptly.

It was painfully obvious that he needed to talk about it. 'Tell me what happened,' she said.

'He was a cop, a gendarme. Claude, same name as me. Not really a bad guy – anti-Semitic, but no more so than the average Frenchman, or a lot of Americans for that matter. He blundered into a farmhouse where my group was meeting. There was no doubt what we were doing – we had maps on the table and rifles stacked in the corner, and Bern was showing the Frenchies how to wire a time bomb.' Luke gave an odd kind of laugh, with no humour in it. 'Damn fool tried to arrest us all. Not that it made any difference. He had to be killed whatever he did.'

'What did you do?' Billie whispered.

'Took him outside and shot him in the back of the head.'

'Oh, my God.'

'He didn't die right away. It took about a minute.'

She took his hand and squeezed it. He held on, and they walked around the long, narrow pool hand in hand. He told her another story, about a woman Resistance fighter who had been captured and tortured, and Billie cried, tears streaming down her face in the September sunshine. The afternoon cooled, and still the grim details spilled out of him: cars blown up, German officers assassinated, Resistance comrades killed in shoot-outs, and Jewish families led away to unknown destinations, holding the hands of their trusting children.

They had been walking for two hours when he stumbled, and she caught him and prevented his falling. 'Jesus Christ, I'm so tired,' he said. 'I've been sleeping badly.'

She hailed a taxi and took him to his hotel.

Luke was staying at the Carlton. The army did not generally run to such luxury, but she recalled that his family was wealthy. He had a corner suite. There was a grand piano in the living room and – something she had never seen before – a telephone extension in the bathroom.

She called room service and ordered chicken soup and scrambled eggs, hot rolls and a pint of cold milk. He sat on the couch and began to tell another story, a funny one, about sabotaging a factory that made saucepans for the German army. 'I ran into this big metalworking shop, and there were about fifty enormous, muscle-bound women, stoking the furnace and hammering the moulds. I yelled: 'Clear the building! We're going to blow it up!' But the women laughed at me! They wouldn't leave, they all carried on working. They didn't believe me.' Before he could finish the story, the food came.

Billie signed the check, tipped the waiter, and put the plates on the dining table. When she turned around, Luke was asleep.

She woke him just long enough to get him into the

bedroom and onto the bed. 'Don't leave,' he mumbled, then his eyes closed again.

She took off his boots and gently loosened his tie. A mild breeze was blowing in through the open window: he did not need blankets.

She sat on the edge of the bed watching him for a while, remembering that long drive from Cambridge to Newport almost two years ago. She stroked his cheek with the outside edge of her little finger, the way she had that night. He did not stir.

She took off her hat and her shoes, thought for a moment, and slipped off her jacket and skirt. Then, in her underwear and stockings, she lay down on the bed. She got her arms around his bony shoulders, put his head on her bosom, and held him. 'Everything's all right, now,' she said. 'You just sleep as long as you want. When you wake up, I'll still be here.'

* * *

Night fell. The temperature dropped. She closed the window and pulled a sheet around them. Soon after midnight, with her arms wrapped around his warm body, she fell asleep.

At dawn, when he had been asleep for twelve hours, he got up suddenly and went to the bathroom. He returned a couple of minutes later and got back into bed. He had taken off his suit and shirt, and wore only his underwear. He put his arms around her and hugged her. 'Something I forgot to tell you, something very important,' he said.

'What?'

'In France, I thought about you all the time. Every day.'

'Did you?' she whispered. 'Did you really?'

He did not answer. He had gone back to sleep.

She lay in his embrace, thinking about him in France, risking his life and remembering her; and she was so happy she felt her heart would burst.

At eight o'clock in the morning, she went into the living room of the suite, phoned Q Building, and said she was sick. It was the first day she had taken off for illness in more than a year in the military. She had a bath and washed her hair, then got dressed. She ordered coffee and cornflakes from room service. The waiter called her Mrs Lucas. She was glad it was not a waitress, for a woman would have noticed that she wore no wedding ring.

She thought the smell of coffee might wake Luke, but it did not. She read the *Washington Post* from cover to cover, even the sports pages. She was writing a letter to her mother in Dallas, on hotel stationery, when he came stumbling out of the bedroom in his underwear, his dark hair mussed, his jaw blue with stubble. She smiled at him, happy that he was awake.

He looked confused. 'How long did I sleep?'

She checked her wristwatch. It was almost noon. 'About eighteen hours.' She could not tell what he was thinking. Was he pleased to see her? Embarrassed? Was he wishing she would go away?

'God,' he said. 'I haven't slept like that for a year.'

He rubbed his eyes. 'Have you been here all the time? You look as fresh as a daisy.'

'I took a little nap.'

'You stayed all night?'

'You asked me to.'

He frowned. 'I seem to remember . . .' He shook his head. 'Boy, I had some dreams.' He went to the phone. 'Room service? Let me have a T-bone steak, rare, with three eggs, sunnyside up. Plus orange juice, toast and coffee.'

Billie frowned. She had never spent the night with a man, so she did not know what to expect in the morning, but this disappointed her. It was so unromantic that she felt almost insulted. She was reminded of her brothers waking up – they, too, emerged from sleep stubbly, grouchy and ravenous. But, she recalled, they generally improved when they had eaten.

'Hold on,' he said into the phone. He looked at Billie. 'Would you like something?'

'Yeah, some iced tea.'

He repeated her order and hung up.

He sat beside her on the couch. 'I talked a lot yesterday.'

'That's the truth.'

'How long?'

'About five hours straight.'

'I'm sorry.'

'Don't be sorry. Whatever you do, please don't be sorry.' Tears came to her eyes. 'I'll never forget it as long as I live.'

He took her hands. 'I'm so glad we met again.'

Her heart jumped. 'Me, too.' This was more like what she had hoped for.

'I'd like to kiss you, but I've been in the same clothes for twenty-four hours.'

She felt a sudden sensation inside, like a spring breaking, and she was conscious of wetness. She was shocked at herself: it had never happened this fast before.

But she held back. She had not decided where she wanted this to go. She had had all night to make a decision, but she had not even thought about it. Now she was afraid that once she touched him she would lose control. And then what?

The war had brought about a new moral laxity in Washington, but she was not part of it. She clasped her hands in her lap and said: 'I sure don't aim to kiss you until you're dressed.'

He gave her a sceptical look. 'Are you afraid of compromising yourself?'

She winced at the irony in his voice. 'Just what does that mean?'

He shrugged. 'We spent the night together.'

She felt hurt and indignant. 'I stayed here because you begged me too!' she protested.

'All right, don't get mad.'

But her desire for him had turned, in a flash, to equally powerful anger. 'You were falling down with exhaustion, and I put you to bed,' she said wrathfully. 'Then you asked me not to leave you, so I stayed.'

'I appreciate it.'

'Then don't talk as if I've acted like a . . . whore!'

'That's not what I meant.'

'It sure is! You implied I've already compromised myself so much that anything else I might do makes no difference.'

He gave a big sigh. 'Well, I didn't intend to imply that. Jesus, you're making a hell of a fuss about a casual remark.'

'Too darn casual.' The trouble was, she *had* compromised herself.

There was a knock at the door.

They looked at one another. Luke said: 'Room service, I guess.'

She did not want a waiter to see her with an undressed man. 'Get in the bedroom.'

'Okay.'

'First, give me your ring.'

He looked at his left hand. He wore a gold signet ring on the little finger. 'Why?'

'So the waiter will think I'm married.'

'But I never take it off.'

That angered her even more. 'Get out of sight,' she hissed.

He went into the bedroom. Billie opened the suite door and a waitress brought in the room-service cart. 'There you go, Miss,' she said.

Billie flushed. There was an insult in that 'Miss'. She signed the check but did not tip. 'There you go,' she said, and turned her back.

The waitress left. Billie heard the shower running. She felt exhausted. She had spent hours in the grip of a profound romantic passion, then in a few minutes it had turned sour. Luke was normally so gracious, yet he had metamorphosed into a bear. How could such things happen?

Whatever the reason, he had made her feel cheap. In a minute or two, he would come out of the bathroom, ready to sit down and have breakfast with her as if they were a married couple. But they were not, and she was feeling more and more uncomfortable.

Well, she thought, if I don't like it, why am I still here? It was a good question.

She put on her hat. It was better to get out with what dignity she had left.

She thought about writing him a note. The sound of the shower stopped. He was about to reappear, smelling of soap, wearing a dressing gown, his hair wet and his feet bare, looking good enough to eat. There was no time for a note.

She left the suite, closing the door quietly behind her.

* * *

She saw him almost every day for the next four weeks.

At first he was in Q Building for daily debriefing sessions. He would seek her out at lunchtime, and they would eat together in the cafeteria or take sandwiches to the park. His manner reverted to his characteristic relaxed courtesy, making her feel respected and cared for. The sting of his behaviour in the Carlton eased. Maybe, she thought, he too had never spent the night with a lover; and, like her, he was not sure of the etiquette. He had treated her casually, as he might treat his sister – and perhaps his sister was the only girl who had ever seen him in his underwear.

At the end of the week he asked her for a date, and they saw the movie of *Jane Eyre* on Saturday night. On Sunday they went canoeing on the Potomac. There was a spirit of recklessness in the Washington air. The city was full of young men on their way to the front or back home on leave, men for whom violent death was an everyday event. They wanted to gamble, drink, dance, and make love because they might never have another chance. The bars were jammed, and a single girl never needed to spend an evening alone. The Allies were winning the war, but the bubble of exuberance was burst daily by news of relatives, neighbours, and college friends killed and wounded on the front line.

Luke put on a little weight and started to sleep better. The haunted look went from his eyes. He bought some clothes that fitted him, short-sleeved shirts and white pants and a navy flannel suit that he wore for their evening dates. A little of his boyishness came back.

They talked endlessly. She explained how the study of human psychology would eventually eliminate mental illness, and he told her how men could fly to the moon. They relived the fateful Harvard weekend that had changed their lives. They discussed the war, and when it might end: Billie thought the Germans could not last much longer, now that Italy had fallen, but Luke believed it would take years to clear the Japanese out of the Pacific. Sometimes they went out with Anthony and Bern, and argued politics in bars, just as they had when they were all at college together, in a different world. One weekend Luke flew to New York to see his family, and Billie missed him so badly she felt ill. She never tired of him, never came near to being bored. He was thoughtful and witty and smart.

They had a major fight about twice a week. Each followed the pattern of their first row, in his hotel suite. He would say something high-handed, or make a decision about their evening's plans without consulting her, or assume he knew better about some subject, radio or automobiles or tennis. She would protest hotly, and he would accuse her of overreacting. She would get more and more angry as she tried to make him understand what was wrong with his attitude, and he would start to feel like a hostile witness under cross-examination. In the heat of the argument, she would exaggerate, or make some wild assertion, or say something she knew to be false. Then he would accuse her of insincerity, and say there was no point in talking to her, because she was willing to say anything to win an argument. He would walk out, more convinced than ever that he was right. Within minutes, she would be distraught. She would seek him out and beg him to forget it and be friends. At first he would be stony-faced; then she would say something that made him laugh, and he would melt.

But in all that time she did not go to his hotel, and

when she kissed him it was a chaste brush of the lips, always in a public place. Even so, she felt the liquid sensation inside every time she touched him, and she knew she could go no farther without going the whole way.

The sunny September turned into a chilly October, and Luke was posted.

He got the news on a Friday afternoon. He was waiting for Billie in the lobby of Q Building when she left for the day. She could see by his face that something bad had happened. 'What's wrong?' she said immediately.

'I'm going back to France.'

She was dismayed. 'When?'

'I leave Washington early on Monday morning. Bern, too.'

'For God's sake, haven't you done your share?'

'I don't mind the danger,' he said. 'I just don't want to leave you.'

Tears came to her eyes. She swallowed hard. 'Two days.'

'I've got to pack.'

'I'll help you.'

They went to his hotel.

As soon as they were inside the door she grabbed him by his sweater, pulled him to her, and tilted her face to be kissed. This time there was nothing chaste about it. She ran the tip of her tongue along his lips, top and bottom, then opened her mouth to his tongue.

She slipped off her coat. She was wearing a dress with blue-and-white vertical stripes and a white collar. She said: 'Touch my breasts.'

He looked startled.

'Please,' she begged.

His hands closed over her small breasts. She shut her eyes and concentrated on the sensation.

They broke apart, and she stared at him hungrily, memorizing his face. She wanted never to forget the particular blue of his eyes, the lock of dark hair that fell over his forehead, the curve of his jaw, the soft cushion of his mouth. 'I want a photo of you,' she said. 'Do you have one?'

'I don't carry photographs of myself around,' he said with a grin. In a New York accent he added: 'What am I, Frank Sinatra?'

'You must have a picture of yourself somewhere.'

'I might have a family photo. Let me look.' He went into the bedroom.

She followed him.

His battered brown leather bag lay on a suitcase stand where, Billie guessed, it had been for four weeks. He took out a silver picture frame that opened up like a small book. Inside were two photographs, one on each side. He slipped a picture out and handed it to her.

It had been taken three or four years ago, and showed a younger, heavier Luke in a polo shirt. With him were an older couple, presumably his parents, plus twin boys of around fifteen, and a little girl. They were all dressed in beach clothes.

'I can't take this, it's your picture of your family,' she said, although she longed for it with all her heart.

'I want you to have it. That's me, I'm part of my family.'

That was what she loved about it. 'Did you take it to France with you?'

'Yes.'

It was so important to him, she could hardly bear to deprive him of it – yet that made it even more precious to her. 'Show me the other one,' she said.

'What?'

'There are two photos in that frame.'

He seemed reluctant, but opened it. The second picture had been cut out of the Radcliffe year book. It was a photo of Billie.

'You had that in France, too?' she said. She could not breathe properly, her throat felt constricted.

'Yes.'

She burst into tears. It was unbearable. He had cut her picture out of the year book and carried it, alongside the photo of his family, all that time his life was in such danger. She had had no idea that she meant so much to him.

'Why are you crying?' he said.

'Because you love me,' she replied.

'It's true,' he said. 'I was frightened to tell you. I've loved you ever since Pearl Harbor weekend.'

Her passion turned to rage. 'How can you say that, you bastard? You left me!'

'If you and I had become lovers then, it would have destroyed Anthony.'

'To hell with Anthony!' She hammered his chest with her fist, but he did not seem to feel it. 'How could you put Anthony's happiness before mine, you son of a bitch?'

'It would have been dishonourable.'

'But don't you see, we could have had each other for two years!' The tears streamed down her cheeks. 'Now we've only got two days – two lousy goddamn days!'

'Then stop crying and kiss me again,' he said.

She put her arms around his neck and pulled his head down. Her tears ran between their lips and into their mouths. He began to unfasten her dress. Impatient, she said: 'Please, just rip it.' He pulled hard, and the buttons flew off down to her waist. Another tug opened it completely. She slipped it back off her shoulders and stood in her slip and stockings.

He looked solemn. 'Are you sure you want to?'

She was afraid he would become paralysed by moral misgivings. 'I have to, I have to, please don't stop!' she cried.

He pushed her gently back to the bed. She lay on her back and he lay on top of her, resting his weight on his elbows. He looked into her eyes. 'I've never done this before.'

'That's all right,' she said. 'I haven't either.'

*   *   *

The first time was over quite quickly, but an hour later they wanted it again, and this time it took longer. She told him she wanted to do everything, give him every pleasure he had ever dreamed of, perform every possible act of sexual intimacy. They made love all weekend, frantic with desire and sorrow, knowing they might never meet again.

After Luke left on Monday morning, Billie cried for two days.

Eight weeks later she discovered she was pregnant.

6.30 P.M.

Scientists can only guess at the extremes of heat and cold the satellite will suffer in space as it moves from the deep darkness of the earth's shadow into the glare of naked sunlight. To mitigate the effects of this, the cylinder is partially coated with shiny aluminium oxide in stripes one-eighth of an inch wide, to reflect the sun's scorching rays, and insulated with glass fibre, to keep out the ultimate cold of space.

'Yes, we dated,' Billie said as they went down the stairs.

Luke's mouth was dry. He imagined holding her hand, looking at her face over a candlelit table, kissing her, watching her slip out of her clothes. He felt guilty, knowing he had a wife, but he could not remember his wife, and Billie was right here beside him, talking animatedly and smiling and smelling faintly of scented soap.

They came to the door of the building and stopped. 'Were we in love?' Luke asked. He looked hard at her, studying her expression. Until now, her face had been easy to read, but suddenly the book had been closed, and all he could see was a blank cover.

'Oh, sure,' she said, and although her tone was

light, there was a catch in her voice. 'I thought you were the only man in the world.'

How could he have let a woman like this slip away from him? It seemed a tragedy worse than losing all his memories. 'But you learned better.'

'I'm old enough now to know there's no Prince Charming, just a bunch of more or less flawed men. Sometimes they wear shining armour, but it's always rusty in spots.'

He wanted to know everything, every detail, but there were too many questions. 'So you married Bern.'

'Yes.'

'What's he like?'

'Clever. All my men have to be smart. Otherwise I get bored. Strong, too – strong enough to challenge me.' She smiled the smile of someone with a big heart.

He said: 'What went wrong?'

'Conflicting values. It sounds abstract, but Bern risked his life for the cause of freedom in two wars, the Spanish Civil War and then the Second World War – and for him, politics came above all else.'

There was one question Luke wanted to ask more than any. He could not think of a delicate, roundabout way of putting it, so he blurted it out. 'Do you have anyone now?'

'Sure. His name's Harold Brodsky.'

Luke felt foolish. Of course she had someone. She was a beautiful divorcée in her thirties, men would be queueing up to take her out. He smiled ruefully. 'Is he Prince Charming?'

'No, but he's smart, he makes me laugh, and he adores me.'

Envy stabbed Luke's heart. Lucky Harold, he thought. 'And I guess he shares your values.'

'Yes. The most important thing in his life is his child – he's a widower – and after that comes his academic work.'

'Which is?'

'Iodine chemistry. I feel the same about my work.' Billie smiled. 'I may not be starry-eyed about men, but I guess I'm still idealistic about unravelling the mysteries of the human mind.'

That brought Luke back to his immediate crisis. The reminder was like an unexpected blow, shocking and painful. 'I wish you could unravel the mystery of my mind.'

She frowned, and despite the weight of his problems he noticed how pretty she was when her nose wrinkled in puzzlement. 'It's strange,' she said. 'Maybe you suffered a cranial injury that left no visible trace, but in that case it's surprising you don't still have a headache.'

'Nope.'

'You're not an alcoholic or a drug addict, I can tell by looking at you. If you'd suffered some terrible shock, or been under prolonged stress, I probably would have heard about it, either from you or from our mutual friends.'

'Which leaves . . .?'

She shook her head. 'You certainly aren't schizophrenic, so there's no way you could have been given the combination drug-and-electrotherapy treatment that could have caused—'

She stopped suddenly, looking alluringly startled, mouth open, eyes wide.

'What?' Luke said.

'I just remembered Joe Blow.'

'Who's he?'

'Joseph Bellow. The name struck me because I thought it sounded made up.'

'And?'

'He was admitted late yesterday, after I'd gone home. Then he was discharged in the night – which was real strange.'

'What was wrong with him?'

'He was a schizophrenic.' She paled. 'Oh, shit.'

Luke began to see what she was thinking. 'So this patient . . .'

'Let's check his file.'

She turned and ran back up the stairs. They hurried along the corridor and entered a room marked Records Office. There was no one inside. Billie turned on the light.

She opened a drawer marked 'A—D', flipped through the file, and pulled out a folder. She read aloud: 'White male, six feet one inch tall, one hundred and eighty pounds, thirty-seven years old.'

Luke's guess was confirmed. 'You think it was me,' he said.

She nodded. 'The patient was given the treatment that causes global amnesia.'

'My God.' Luke was dismayed and intrigued at the

same time. If she was right, this had been done to him deliberately. That explained why he had been followed around – presumably by someone keen to make sure the treatment had worked. 'Who did this?'

'My colleague, Dr Leonard Ross, admitted the patient. Len's a psychiatrist. I'd like to know his rationale for authorizing the treatment. A patient should normally be kept under observation for some time, usually days, before any treatment is given. And I can't imagine the medical justification for discharging the patient immediately afterwards, even with the consent of relatives. This is very irregular.'

'Sounds like Ross is in trouble.'

Billie sighed. 'Probably not. If I complain, people will accuse me of sour grapes. They'll say I'm bitter because Len got the job I wanted, Director of Research here.'

'When did that happen?'

'Today.'

Luke was startled. 'Ross got promoted *today*?'

'Yes. I guess it's not a coincidence.'

'Hell, no! He was bribed. He was promised the promotion in return for doing this irregular treatment.'

'I can't believe it. Yes, I can. He's real weak.'

'But he's someone else's tool. A superior in the hospital hierarchy must have got him to do it.'

'No.' Billie shook her head. 'The trust that's funding the post, the Sowerby Foundation, insisted on Ross for the job. My boss told me. We couldn't figure out why. Now I know.'

'It all fits – but this is almost as baffling as before. Someone in the Foundation wanted me to lose my memory?'

'I can guess who,' Billie said. 'Anthony Carroll. He's on the board.'

The name rang a bell. Luke recalled that Anthony was the CIA man mentioned by Elspeth. 'That still leaves the question why.'

'But now we have someone to ask,' Billie said, and she picked up the phone.

While she dialled, Luke tried to organize his thoughts. The last hour had been a series of shocks. He had been told he was not going to get his memory back. He had learned that he had loved Billie and lost her, and he could not understand how he could have been such a fool. Now he had discovered that his amnesia had been deliberately inflicted on him and that someone in the CIA was responsible. Yet he still had no clue as to why this had been done.

'Let me speak to Anthony Carroll,' Billie said into the phone. 'This is Dr Josephson.' Her tone was peremptory. 'Okay, then tell him I need to speak to him urgently.' She looked at her watch. 'Have him call me at home in exactly one hour from now.' Her face suddenly darkened. 'Don't jerk me around, buster, I know you can get a message to him any time of the day or night, wherever he is.' She slammed the phone down.

She caught Luke's eye and looked abashed. 'Sorry,' she said. 'The guy said: "I'll see what I can do," like he was doing me a darn favour.'

Luke remembered Elspeth saying that Anthony Carroll was an old buddy who had been at Harvard with Luke and Bern. 'This Anthony,' he said. 'I thought he was a friend.'

'Yeah.' Billie nodded, a worried frown on her expressive face. 'So did I.'

7.30 P.M.

The temperature problem is a key obstacle to manned space flight. To gauge the efficacy of its insulation, the Explorer carries four thermometers: three in the outer shell, to measure skin temperature, and one inside the instrument compartment, to give the interior temperature. The aim is to keep the level between forty and seventy degrees Fahrenheit – a comfortable range for human survival.

Bern lived on Massachusetts Avenue, overlooking the picturesque gorge of Rock Creek, in a neighbourhood of large homes and foreign embassies. His apartment had an Iberian theme, with ornate Spanish colonial furniture, twisted shapes in dark wood. The stark white walls were hung with paintings of sun-baked landscapes. Luke recalled Billie saying that Bern had fought in the Spanish Civil War.

It was easy to imagine Bern as a fighter. His dark hair was receding now, and his waist hung over the belt of his slacks a little, but there was a hard set to his face and a bleak look in his grey eyes. Luke wondered if such a down-to-earth man would credit the strange story he had to tell.

Bern shook Luke's hand warmly and gave him

strong coffee in a small cup. On top of the console gramophone was a silver-framed photograph of a middle-aged man in a torn shirt holding a rifle. Luke picked it up. 'Largo Benito,' Bern explained. 'Greatest man I ever knew. I fought with him in Spain. My son is named Largo, but Billie calls him Larry.'

Bern probably looked back on the war in Spain as the best time of his life. Luke wondered enviously what had been the best time of his own life. 'I guess I must have had great memories of something,' he said despondently.

Bern gave him a sharp look. 'What the hell is going on, old buddy?'

Luke sat down and related what he and Billie had discovered at the hospital. Then he said: 'Here's what I think happened to me. I don't know if you're going to buy it, but I'll tell you anyway, because I'm really hoping you can shed some light on the mystery.'

'I'll do what I can.'

'I came to Washington on Monday, right before the launch of the rocket, to see an army general for some mysterious purpose that I wouldn't tell anyone about. My wife was worried about me and called Anthony, to ask him to keep an eye on me. Anthony made a breakfast date with me for Tuesday morning.'

'It makes sense. Anthony's your oldest friend. You were room-mates already when I met you.'

'The next bit is more speculative. I met Anthony for breakfast, before going to the Pentagon. He put something in my coffee to make me fall asleep, then got me into his car and drove me to Georgetown Mind

Hospital. He must have gotten Billie out of the way somehow, or maybe waited until she left for the day. Anyway, he made sure she didn't see me, and checked me in under a false name. Then he got hold of Dr Len Ross, whom he knew might be bribed. Using his position as a board member of the Sowerby Foundation, he persuaded Len to give me a treatment that would destroy my memory.'

Luke paused, waiting for Bern to say the whole thing was ludicrous, impossible, a figment of an overactive imagination. But he did not. To Luke's surprise, he simply said: 'But for God's sake, why?'

Luke began to feel better. If Bern believed him, he might help. He said: 'For the moment, let's concentrate on how, rather than why.'

'Okay.'

'To cover his tracks, he checked me out of the hospital, dressed me in rags – presumably while I was still unconscious from the treatment – and dumped me in Union Station, along with a sidekick whose job was to persuade me that I lived like that, and at the same time to keep an eye on me and make sure the amnesia treatment had worked.'

Now Bern did look sceptical. 'But he must have known you'd find out the truth sooner or later.'

'Not necessarily – not all of it, anyway. Sure, he had to calculate that after a few days or weeks I would figure out who I was. But he thought I'd still believe I had gone on a bender. People do lose their memories after drinking heavily, at least according to legend. If I did find it hard to believe, and asked a few questions, the trail would have gone cold. Billie probably would have forgotten about the mystery patient – and in case she remembered, Ross would have destroyed his records.'

Bern nodded thoughtfully. 'A risky plan, but one with a good chance of success. In clandestine work, that's generally the best you can hope for.'

'I'm surprised you're not more sceptical.'

Bern shrugged.

Luke pressed him. 'Do you have a reason for accepting the story so readily?'

'We've all been in secret work. These things happen.'

Luke felt sure Bern was keeping something back. There was nothing he could do but plead. 'Bern, if there's something else you know, for God's sake, tell me. I need all the help I can get.'

Bern looked anguished. 'There is something – but it's secret, and I don't want to get anyone into trouble.'

Luke's heart leaped in hope. 'Tell me, please. I'm desperate.'

Bern looked hard at him. 'I guess you are.' He took a deep breath. 'Okay, then, here goes. Toward the end of the war, Billie and Anthony worked on a special project for the OSS, the Truth Drug Committee. You and I didn't know about it at the time, but I found out later, when I was married to Billie. They were looking for drugs that would affect prisoners under interrogation. They tried mescaline, barbiturates, scopolamine, and cannabis. Their test subjects were soldiers suspected of communist sympathies. Billie and Anthony went to military camps in Atlanta, Memphis and New Orleans. They would win the confidence of the suspect soldier, give him a reefer, and see whether he betrayed secrets.'

Luke laughed. 'So a lot of grunts got a free high!'

Bern nodded. 'At that level, the whole thing was faintly comical. After the war, Billie went back to college and did her doctoral thesis on the effects of various legal drugs such as nicotine on people's mental states. When she finally became a professor, she continued to work on the same area, concentrating on how drugs and other factors affect memory.'

'But not for the CIA.'

'That's what I thought. But I was wrong.'

'Christ.'

'In 1950, when Roscoe Hillenkoetter was Director, the Agency started a project codenamed Bluebird, and Hillenkoetter authorized the use of unvouchered funds, so there was no paper trail. Bluebird was about mind control. They financed a whole series of legitimate research projects in universities, channelling the money through trusts to conceal their true source. And they financed Billie's work.'

'How did she feel about that?'

'We fought about it. I said it was wrong, the CIA was planning to brainwash people. She said that all scientific knowledge could be used for good or evil, she was doing invaluable research and she didn't care who paid the bill.'

'Is that why you divorced?'

'Sort of. I was writing a radio show called *Detective Story*, but I wanted to get into movies. In 1952 I wrote a screenplay about a secret government agency that brainwashed unsuspecting citizens. Jack Warner bought it. But I didn't tell Billie.'

'Why not?'

'I knew the CIA would get the film cancelled.'

'They can do that?'

'You bet your goddamn life.'

'So what happened?'

'The movie came out in 1953. Frank Sinatra played the nightclub singer who witnesses a political murder, then has his memory wiped by a secret process. Joan Crawford played his manager. It was a huge hit. My career was made – I was deluged with big-money offers from the studios.'

'And Billie?'

'I took her to the première.'

'I guess she was angry.'

He smiled ruefully. 'She went ape. She said I'd used confidential information that I got from her. She was sure the CIA would withdraw her funding, ruin her research. It was the end of our marriage.'

'That's what Billie meant when she said you had a conflict of values.'

'She's right. She should have married you – I never really understood why she didn't.'

Luke's heart missed a beat. He was curious to know why Bern had said that. But he postponed the question. 'Anyway, to return to 1953, I assume the CIA didn't cut off her funding.'

'No.' Bern looked bitterly angry. 'They destroyed my career instead.'

'How?'

'I was subjected to a loyalty investigation. Of course, I had been a communist, right up until the end of the war, so I made an easy target. I was blacklisted in Hollywood, and I couldn't even get back my old job in radio.'

'What was Anthony's role in that?'

'He did his best to protect me, Billie said, but he was overruled.' Bern frowned. 'After what you've just told me, I wonder if that was true.'

'What did you do?'

'I had a couple of bad years, then I thought of *The Terrible Twins*.'

Luke raised an eyebrow.

'It's a series of children's books.' He pointed to a bookcase. The bright jackets made a splash of colour. 'You've read them, as it happens – to your sister's kid.'

Luke was pleased he had a nephew or niece – or maybe several. He liked the idea of reading aloud to them.

There was so much he had to learn about himself.

He waved a hand at the expensive apartment. 'The books must be successful.'

Bern nodded. 'I wrote the first story under a pseudonym, and used an agent who was sympathetic to the victims of the McCarthy witch-hunt. The book was a big bestseller, and I've written two a year ever since.'

Luke got up and took a book from the shelf. He read:

*Which is stickier, honey or melted chocolate? The twins had
to know. That was why they did the experiment that made
Mom so mad.*

He smiled. He could imagine children loving this
stuff. Then he felt sad. 'Elspeth and I don't have any
kids.'

'I don't know why,' Bern said. 'You always wanted a
family so badly.'

'We tried, but it didn't happen.' Luke closed the
book. 'Am I happily married?'

Bern sighed. 'Since you ask, no.'

'Why?'

'Something was wrong, but you didn't know what.
You called me one time, to ask my advice, but I
couldn't help you.'

'A few minutes ago, you said Billie should have
married me.'

'You two used to be nuts about each other.'

'So what happened?'

'I don't really know. After the war, you had a big
quarrel. I'm not too sure what it was about.'

'I'll have to ask Billie.'

'I guess.'

Luke put the book back on the shelf. 'Anyway, now
I understand why you didn't react with total incredulity
to my story.'

'Yes,' Bern said. 'I believe Anthony did this.'

'But can you imagine why?'

'I don't have the slightest idea.'

8 P.M.

If temperature variations are higher than expected, it is possible that the germanium transistors will overheat, the mercury batteries will freeze, and the satellite will fail to transmit data back to Earth.

Billie sat at her dressing-table, freshening her make-up. She thought her eyes were her best feature, and she always did them carefully, with black eyeliner, grey eye shadow, and a little mascara. She left the bedroom door open, and she could hear television gunfire downstairs: Larry and Becky-Ma were watching *Wagon Train*.

She did not feel like a date tonight. The events of the day had stirred up strong passions. She was angry about not getting the job she wanted, bewildered by what Anthony had done, and confused and threatened to find that the old chemistry between herself and Luke was as powerful and dangerous as ever. She found herself reviewing her relationships with Anthony, Luke, Bern and Harold, wondering whether she had made the right decisions in life. After all that had happened, the prospect of spending the evening watching the Kraft Theater on TV with Harold seemed insipid, fond of him though she was.

The phone rang.

She jumped up from her stool and crossed the room to the extension by the bed, but Larry had already picked up in the hallway. She heard Anthony's voice say: 'This is the CIA. Washington is about to be invaded by an army of bouncing cabbages.'

Larry giggled. 'Uncle Anthony, it's you!'

'If you are approached by a cabbage do not, repeat, do not attempt to reason with it.'

'A cabbage can't talk!'

'The only way to deal with them is to beat them to death with sliced bread.'

'You're making this up!' Larry laughed.

Billie said: 'Anthony, I'm on the extension.'

Anthony said: 'Get your jammies on, Larry, okay?'

'Okay,' said Larry. He hung up.

Anthony's voice changed. 'Billie?'

'Here.'

'You wanted me to call – urgently. I gather you chewed out the duty officer.'

'Yeah. Anthony, what the hell are you up to?'

'You'll have to ask me a more specific question—'

'Don't screw around, for Christ's sake. I could tell you were lying last time we spoke, but I didn't know what the truth was then. Now I do. I know what you did to Luke at my hospital last night.'

There was a silence.

Billie said: 'I want an explanation.'

'I can't really talk about this on the phone. If we could meet some time in the next few days—'

'The hell with that.' She was not going to let him procrastinate. 'I want your story right now.'

'You know I can't—'

'You can do anything you damn well please, so don't pretend otherwise.'

Anthony protested: 'You ought to trust me. We've been friends for two decades.'

'Yeah, and you got me into trouble on our first date.'

There was a smile in Anthony's voice as he said: 'Are you still mad about that?'

Billie softened. 'Hell, no. I want to trust you. You're my son's godfather.'

'I'll explain everything if you'll meet me tomorrow.'

She almost agreed, then she remembered what he had done. 'You didn't trust me, last night, did you? You went behind my back, right in my own hospital.'

'I told you, I can explain—'

'You should have explained *before* you deceived me. Tell me the truth or I'll go to the FBI the minute I hang up. You choose.'

It was dangerous to threaten men – it often made them obstinate. But she knew how the CIA hated and feared interference from the FBI, especially when the Agency was working on the borderline of legality, which was most of the time. The Feds, who jealously guarded their exclusive right to hunt spies within the USA, would relish the chance to investigate illegitimate acts by the CIA on American soil. If whatever Anthony was doing was strictly on the up-and-up, then Billie's threat was empty. But if he were overstepping the limits of the law, he would be scared.

He sighed. 'Well, I'm on a pay phone, and I guess it's unlikely your line is tapped.' He paused. 'You may find this hard to believe.'

'Try me.'

'Well, here goes. Luke is a spy, Billie.'

For a moment she was dumbstruck; then she said: 'Don't be absurd.'

'He's a communist, an agent for Moscow.'

'For Christ's sake! If you think I'm going to fall for that—'

'I'm past caring whether you believe it or not.' Anthony's tone was suddenly harsh. 'He's been passing rocket secrets to the Soviets for years. How do you think they managed to put their Sputnik into orbit while our satellite was still on the laboratory bench? They're not ahead of us scientifically, for God's sake! They have the benefit of all our research as well as their own. And Luke is responsible.'

'Anthony, we've both known Luke for twenty goddamn years. He's never been interested in politics!'

'That's the best cover of all.'

Billie hesitated. Could it be true? No doubt a serious spy would pretend to have no interest in politics, or even to be a Republican. 'But Luke wouldn't betray his country.'

'People do. Remember, when he was with the French Resistance he was working with the com- munists. Of course, they were on our side then, but obviously he continued after the war. Personally, I think the reason he didn't marry you was that it would conflict with his work for the Reds.'

'He married Elspeth.'

'Yeah, but they never had children.'

Billie sat down on the stairs, feeling stunned. 'Do you have evidence?'

'I have *proof* – top-secret blueprints he gave to a known KGB officer.'

She was bewildered now, not knowing what to believe. 'But even if all this is true – why did you wipe out his memory?'

'To save his life.'

Now she was totally baffled. 'I don't understand.'

'Billie, we were going to kill him.'

'Who was going to kill him?'

'Us, the CIA. You know the army is about to launch our first satellite. If this rocket fails, the Russians will dominate outer space for the foreseeable future, the way the British dominated America for two hundred years. You have to understand that Luke was the worst threat to American power and prestige since the war. The decision to terminate him was made within an hour of our finding out about him.'

'Why not just put him on trial as a spy?'

'And have the whole world know that our security is so lousy the Soviets have been getting all our rocket secrets for years? Think what that would do to American influence – especially in all these underdeveloped countries that are flirting with Moscow. That option wasn't even tabled.'

'So what happened?'

'I persuaded them to try this. I went right to the top. Nobody knows what I'm doing, except the Director of the CIA and the President. And it would have worked, if Luke hadn't been such a resourceful fucking bastard. I could have saved Luke *and* kept the whole thing secret. If only he had believed that he lost his memory after a night of heavy drinking, and lived the life of a bum for a while, I could have kept the lid on. Even he would never have known what secrets he gave away.'

Billie had a selfish moment. 'You didn't hesitate to blight my career.'

'To save Luke's life? I didn't think you'd want me to hesitate.'

'Don't be so goddamn blasé, it always was your worst fault.'

'Anyway, Luke fouled up my plan – with your help. Is he with you now?'

'No.' Billie felt the hairs prickle on the back of her neck.

'I need to talk to him before he does himself any more damage. Where is he?'

Acting on instinct, Billie lied. 'I don't know.'

'You wouldn't hide anything from me, would you?'

'Sure I would. You've already said your organization wanted to kill Luke. It would be dumb of me to tell you where he is, if I knew. But I don't.'

'Billie, listen to me. I'm his only hope. Tell him to call me, if you want to save his life.'

'I'll think about it,' Billie said; but Anthony had already hung up.

8.30 P.M.

The instrument compartment has no doors or access hatches. To work on equipment inside, engineers at Cape Canaveral have to lift the entire cover. This is awkward but saves precious weight, a critical factor in the struggle to break free of Earth's gravity.

Luke put down the phone with a shaky hand.

Bern said: 'For Christ's sake, what did she say? You look like a ghost!'

'Anthony says I'm a Soviet agent,' Luke told him.

Bern narrowed his eyes. 'And . . .?'

'When the CIA found me out, they were going to kill me, but Anthony persuaded them that it would be just as effective to wipe my memory.'

'A vaguely plausible story,' Bern said coolly.

Luke was devastated. 'Jesus Christ, could it be true?'

'Hell, no.'

'You can't be sure of that.'

'Yes, I can.'

Luke hardly dared to hope. 'How?'

'Because I *was* a Soviet agent.'

Luke stared at him. What now? 'We could both have

been agents, without knowing about each other,' he said.

Bern shook his head. 'You ended my career.'

'How?'

'You want some more coffee?'

'No, thanks, it's making me dizzy.'

'You look like hell. When did you last eat?'

'Billie gave me some cookies. Forget food, will you? Tell me what you know.'

Bern stood up. 'I'm going to make you a sandwich, before you faint.'

Luke realized he was painfully hungry. 'That sounds great.'

They went into the kitchen. Bern opened the refrigerator and took out a loaf of rye bread, a stick of butter, some corned beef, and a bermuda onion. Luke's mouth began to water.

'It was in the war,' Bern said as he buttered four slices of bread. 'The French Resistance was divided into Gaullists and communists, and they were manoeu-vring for post-war position. Roosevelt and Churchill wanted to make sure the communists couldn't win an election. So the Gaullists were getting all the guns and ammunition.'

'How did I feel about that?'

Bern layered corned beef, mustard, and onion rings on the bread. 'You didn't have strong feelings about French politics, you just wanted to beat the Nazis and go home. But I had another agenda. I wanted to even things up.'

'How?'

'I tipped off the communists about a parachute drop we were expecting, so they could ambush us and steal our ordnance.' He shook his head ruefully. 'They screwed up royally. They were supposed to run into us on our way back to base, apparently by accident, and demand a friendly share-out. Instead, they attacked us at the drop point, as soon as the stuff hit the ground. So you knew we had been betrayed. And I was the obvious suspect.'

'What did I do?'

'You offered me a deal. I had to stop working for Moscow, right then, and you would keep quiet about what I had done, for ever.'

'And . . .?'

Bern shrugged. 'We both kept our promises. But I don't think you ever forgave me. Anyhow, our friendship was never the same afterwards.'

A grey Burmese cat appeared from nowhere and miaowed, and Bern tossed a sliver of meat to the floor. The cat ate it delicately and licked its paws.

Luke said: 'If I'd been a communist, I would have covered up for you.'

'Absolutely.'

Luke began to believe in his own innocence. 'But I might have become a communist after the war.'

'No way. It's something that happens to you when you're young, or not at all.'

That made sense. 'I might have spied for money, though.'

'You don't need money. Your family is wealthy.'

That was right. Elspeth had told him. 'So Anthony is mistaken.'

'Or lying.' Bern sliced the sandwiches and put them on two non-matching plates. 'Soda?'

'Sure.'

Bern took two bottles of Coke from the refrigerator and opened them. He handed Luke a plate and a bottle, picked up his own, and led the way back into the living room.

Luke felt like a starved wolf. He finished the sandwich in a few bites. Bern was watching with amusement. 'Here, have mine,' he said.

Luke shook his head. 'No, thanks.'

'Go ahead, take it. I ought to go on a diet anyway.'

Luke took Bern's sandwich and tore into it.

Bern said: 'If Anthony is lying, what was his *real* reason for making you lose your memory?'

Luke swallowed. 'It has to be connected with my sudden departure from Cape Canaveral on Monday.'

Bern nodded. 'Too much of a coincidence otherwise.'

'I must have learned something very important, so important that I had to rush to the Pentagon to talk to them about it.'

Bern frowned. 'Why didn't you tell the folks at Cape Canaveral what you had learned?'

Luke considered. 'It must be that I didn't trust anyone there.'

'Okay. Then, before you got to the Pentagon, Anthony intercepted you.'

'Right. And I guess I trusted him, and told him what I had found out.'

'And then?'

'He thought it was so important that he had to wipe my memory to make sure the secret never got out.'

'I wonder what the hell it was.'

'When I know that, I'll understand what happened to me.'

'Where will you start?'

'I guess my first step is to go to my hotel room and look through my stuff. Maybe I'll find a clue.'

'If Anthony wiped your memory, he must have gone through your possessions too.'

'He would have destroyed any obvious clues, but there may be something he didn't recognize as relevant. Anyway, I have to check.'

'And then?'

'The only other place to look would be Cape Canaveral. I'll fly back tonight...' He checked his watch. It was after nine o'clock. 'Or tomorrow morning.'

'Stay the night here,' Bern said.

'Why?'

'I don't know. I don't like the idea of you spending the night alone. Go to the Carlton, pick up your stuff, and come back here. I'll take you to the airport in the morning.'

Luke nodded. Feeling awkward, he said: 'You've been a heck of a good friend to me over this.'

Bern shrugged. 'We go back a long way.'

Luke was not satisfied with that. 'But you just told

me that after that incident in France, our friendship was never the same.'

'That's true.' Bern gave Luke a candid look. 'Your attitude was that a man who betrayed you once would betray you twice.'

'I can believe that,' Luke said thoughtfully. 'I was wrong, though, wasn't I?'

'Yes,' Bern said. 'You were.'

9.30 P.M.

The instrument compartment tends to overheat prior to take-off. The solution to this problem is typical of the crude but effective engineering of the rushed Explorer project. A container of dry ice is attached electromagnetically to the outside of the rocket. A thermostat switches on a fan whenever the compartment gets warm. Just before take-off, the magnet is disconnected and the cooling mechanism falls to the ground.

Anthony's yellow Cadillac Eldorado was parked on K Street between 15th and 16th, tucked in behind a line of taxis waiting to be summoned by the doorman of the Carlton Hotel. Sitting in the car, Anthony had a clear view of the hotel's curving driveway and brightly lit carriage porch. Pete was in the hotel, using the room he had rented, waiting for a phone call from one of the agents who were watching out for Luke all over town.

A part of Anthony hoped that none of them would call, that Luke would somehow make his escape. Then, at least, Anthony would be able to avoid making the most painful decision of his life. The other part of him was desperate to find out where Luke was and deal with him.

Luke was an old friend, a decent man, a loyal husband and a terrific scientist. It made no difference in the end. During the war, they had all killed good men who just happened to be on the wrong side. Luke was on the wrong side in the Cold War. It was knowing the guy that made it so hard.

Pete hurried out of the building. Anthony rolled down the window. Pete said: 'Ackie called in. Luke is at the apartment on Massachusetts Avenue, Bernard Rothsten's place.'

'At last,' Anthony said. He had posted agents outside Bern's building and Billie's house, anticipating that Luke might go to his old friends for help, and it gave him bleak satisfaction to have been right.

Pete added: 'When he leaves, Ackie will follow him on the motorcycle.'

'Good.'

'Do you think he'll come here?'

'He may. I'll wait.' There were two more agents in the hotel lobby who would alert Anthony if Luke should go in by another entrance. 'The other main possibility is the airport.'

'We have four men there.'

'Okay. I think we have all the exits covered.'

Pete nodded. 'I'll get back to the phone.'

Anthony brooded over the scene to come. Luke would be confused and uncertain, wary but keen to question Anthony. Anthony would try to get Luke alone somewhere. Once they were on their own, it would only be a few seconds before Anthony had the chance to draw the silenced gun from the inside pocket of his topcoat.

Luke would make a last-second bid for life. It was not his nature to accept defeat. He would jump at Anthony, or dive at the window, or run for the door. Anthony would be cool, he had killed before, he would keep his nerve. He would hold the gun steady and pull the trigger, aiming for Luke's chest, firing several times, confident of stopping Luke. Luke would fall. Anthony would move close to him, check his pulse, and if necessary administer the *coup de grâce*. And his oldest friend would be dead.

There would be no trouble about it. Anthony had the dramatic evidence of Luke's betrayal, the blueprints with Luke's handwriting on them. He could not actually prove that they had been taken from a Soviet agent, but his word was good enough for the CIA.

He would dump the body somewhere. It would be found, of course, and there would be an investigation. Sooner or later the police would discover that the CIA had been interested in the victim, and would start asking questions; but the Agency was experienced in fending off inquiries. The police would be told that the Agency's link with the victim was a matter of national security and therefore top secret, but had nothing to do with the murder.

Anyone who questioned that – cop, journalist, politician – would be subjected to a loyalty investigation. Friends, neighbours and relatives would be interviewed by agents who referred darkly to suspected communist affiliations. The investigation would never reach any conclusion, but all the same it would destroy the credibility of the subject.

A secret agency could do anything, he thought with grim confidence.

A taxicab pulled into the hotel's driveway, and Luke got out. He was wearing a navy topcoat and a grey hat that he must have bought or stolen sometime today. Across the street, Ackie Horwitz pulled up on his motorcycle. Anthony got out of his car and strolled toward the hotel entrance.

Luke looked strained, but wore an expression of grim determination. Paying the taxi driver, he glanced at Anthony but did not recognize him. He told the driver to keep the change, then walked into the hotel. Anthony followed.

They were the same age, thirty-seven. They had met at Harvard when they were eighteen, half a lifetime ago.

That it should come to this, Anthony thought bitterly. That it should come to this.

* * *

Luke knew he had been followed from Bern's apartment by a man on a motorcycle. Now he was strung taut, all his senses on alert.

The lobby of the Carlton looked like a grand drawing room, full of reproduction French furniture. Opposite the entrance, the reception desk and concierge's desk were set into alcoves so that they did not spoil the regular rectangle of the space. Two women in fur coats chatted with a group of men in tuxedos near the entrance to the bar. Bellhops in livery and desk staff in black tailcoats went about their business with quiet efficiency. It was a luxurious place, designed to soothe the nerves of jangled travellers. It did nothing for Luke.

Scanning the room, he quickly identified two men who had the air of agents. One sat on an elegant sofa reading a newspaper, the other stood near the elevator, smoking a cigarette. Neither looked as if he belonged here. They were dressed for work, in raincoats and business suits, and there was a daytime look to their shirts and ties. They definitely were not out for an evening in expensive restaurants and bars.

He thought of walking right out again – but where would that leave him? He approached the reception desk, gave his name, and asked for the key to his room. As he turned away, a stranger spoke to him. 'Hey, Luke!'

It was the man who had walked into the hotel behind him. He did not look like an agent, but Luke had vaguely noticed his appearance: he was tall, about Luke's height, and might have been distinguished, except that he was carelessly dressed. His expensive camel-hair topcoat was old and worn, his shoes looked as if they had never been shined, and he needed a haircut. However, he spoke with authority.

Luke said: 'I'm afraid I don't know who you are. I've lost my memory.'

'Anthony Carroll. I'm so glad I've caught up with you at last!' He held out his hand to shake.

Luke tensed. He still did not know whether Anthony was enemy or friend. He shook hands and said: 'I have a lot of questions to ask you.'

'And I'm ready to answer them.'

Luke paused, staring at him, wondering where to begin. Anthony did not look like the kind of man who would betray an old friend. He had an open, intelligent face, not handsome but appealing. In the end Luke said: 'How the hell could you do this to me?'

'I had to do it – for your own good. I was trying to save your life.'

'I'm not a spy.'

'It's not that simple.'

Luke studied Anthony, trying to guess what was in his mind. He could not decide whether he was telling the truth. Anthony looked earnest. There was no expression of slyness on his face. All the same, Luke felt sure he was holding something back. 'No one believes your story about my working for Moscow.'

'Who is no one?'

'Neither Bern nor Billie.'

'They don't know everything.'

'They know me.'

'So do I.'

'What do you know that they don't?'

'I'll tell you. But we can't talk here. What I have to say is classified. Shall we go to my office? It's five minutes away.'

Luke was not going to Anthony's office, not before

a whole lot of questions had been answered to his satisfaction. But he could see that the lobby was not a good place for a top-secret conversation. 'Let's go to my suite,' he said. That would get him away from the other agents, but leave him in control: Anthony on his own would not be able to overpower him.

Anthony hesitated, then seemed to make up his mind and said: 'Sure.'

They crossed the lobby and entered the elevator. Luke checked the number on his room key: 530. 'Fifth floor,' he said to the operator. The man closed the lift gate and threw the lever.

They did not speak as they went up. Luke looked at Anthony's clothes: the old coat, the rumpled suit, the nondescript tie. Surprisingly, Anthony managed to wear his untidy garments with something of a careless swagger.

Suddenly, Luke saw that the soft material of the coat sagged slightly on the right side. There was a heavy object in the pocket.

He felt cold with fear. He had made a bad mistake.

He had not thought that Anthony would have a gun.

Trying to keep his face expressionless, Luke thought furiously. Could Anthony shoot him right here in the hotel? If he waited until they were in the suite, no one would see. What about the noise? The gun might have a silencer.

As the elevator stopped at the fifth floor, Anthony unbuttoned his coat.

For a fast draw, Luke thought.

They stepped out. Luke did not know which way to go, but Anthony confidently turned right. He must have been to Luke's room already.

Luke was sweating under his topcoat. He felt as if this sort of thing had happened to him before, more than once, but a long time ago. He wished he had kept the gun of the cop whose finger he had broken. But he had had no idea, at nine o'clock this morning, what he was involved in – he had thought he had simply lost his memory.

He tried to make himself calm. It was still one man against another. Anthony had the gun, but Luke had guessed Anthony's intentions. It was about even.

Walking along the corridor, his heart racing, Luke looked for something to hit Anthony with: a heavy vase, a glass ashtray, a picture in a solid frame. There was nothing.

He had to do something before they entered the room.

Could he try to take the gun away from Anthony? He might succeed, but it was risky. The gun could easily go off in the struggle, and no telling which way it might be pointing at the crucial moment.

They reached the door and Luke took out his key. A bead of perspiration ran down his face. If he went inside, he was dead.

He unlocked the door and pushed it open.

'Come in,' he said. He stood aside to let his guest enter first.

Anthony hesitated, then walked past Luke and through the doorway.

Luke hooked his foot around Anthony's right ankle, put both hands flat on Anthony's shoulder blades, and pushed hard. Anthony went flying. He crashed into a small Regency table, knocking over a large vase of daffodils. In desperation he grabbed at a brass floor lamp with a pink silk shade, but the lamp fell with him.

Luke pulled the door shut and ran for his life. He hurtled along the corridor. The elevator had gone. He burst through the Fire Exit door on to the staircase and ran down. On the next floor, he crashed into a maid carrying a stack of towels. 'I'm sorry!' he called as the maid screamed and towels flew everywhere.

A few seconds later, he reached the foot of the staircase. He found himself in a narrow corridor. To one side, up a short flight of steps, through a small archway, he could see the lobby.

* * *

Anthony knew, before he did it, that it was a mistake to enter the room first; but Luke left him no choice. Fortunately he was not seriously hurt. After a stunned moment, he picked himself up. He turned, strode to the door, and opened it. Looking out, he saw Luke haring along the corridor. As he gave chase, Luke turned aside and disappeared, presumably into the stairwell.

Anthony followed, running as fast as he could, but he was afraid he might not be able to catch Luke, who was at least as fit as he. Would Curtis and Malone in the lobby have the sense to apprehend Luke?

On the next floor down, Anthony was momentarily delayed by a maid who was kneeling on the floor, picking up scattered towels. Anthony guessed Luke had crashed into her. He cursed, and slowed his pace to manoeuvre around her. As he did so, he heard the elevator arrive. His heart leaped: maybe he was in luck.

A dressed-up couple emerged, obviously tipsy from a celebration in the restaurant. Anthony barged past them into the elevator and said: 'Ground floor, and quick about it.'

The man slammed the doors and threw the lever. Anthony stared impotently at the descending floor numbers as they lit up in slow succession. The elevator reached the ground floor. The door slid aside and he stepped out.

* * *

Luke emerged into the lobby next to the elevator doors. His heart sank. The two agents he had spotted earlier were now standing in front of the main entrance, blocking his way out. A moment later, the elevator door opened beside him and Anthony stepped out.

He had to make a split-second decision: fight or flee.

He did not want to fight three men. They would almost certainly overpower him. Hotel security would join in. Anthony would show his CIA identification, and everyone would defer to him. Luke would end up in custody.

He turned and ran back along the corridor, into

the depths of the hotel. Behind him, he heard the pounding footsteps of Anthony giving chase. There had to be a back entrance – supplies could not possibly be delivered through the main lobby.

He pushed through a curtain and found himself in a little courtyard decorated like a Mediterranean outdoor café. A few couples were swaying on a small dance floor. Barging between the tables, he made it to an exit door. A narrow corridor stretched away to his left. He ran along it. He must be near the back of the hotel now, he figured, but he could see no way out.

He emerged into a kind of butler's pantry, where the finishing touches were applied to dishes cooked elsewhere. Half a dozen uniformed waiters were heating food in chafing dishes and arranging plates on trays. In the middle of the room was a staircase leading down. Luke pushed through the waiters and took the stairs, ignoring a voice that called: 'Excuse me, sir! You can't go down there!' As Anthony charged after him, the same voice said indignantly: 'What is this, Union Station?'

In the basement was the main kitchen, a sweaty purgatory where dozens of chefs cooked for hundreds of people. Gas jets flared, steam billowed, saucepans bubbled. Waiters shouted at cooks, and cooks shouted at kitchen hands. They were too busy to pay attention to Luke as he dodged between the refrigerators and the ranges, the plate stacks and the barrels of vegetables.

At the back of the kitchen, he found a staircase going up. He guessed it led to the delivery entrance. If not, he would be cornered. He took the chance and raced up the stairs. At the top, he burst through a pair of doors into the cold night air.

He was in a dark yard. A dim lamp over the door showed him giant garbage bins and stacked wooden pallets that looked as if they had contained fruit. Fifty yards away to his right was a high wire fence with a closed gate and, beyond that, a street which his sense of direction told him must be 15th.

He ran for the gate. He heard the door behind him bang open, and guessed that Anthony had come out. And they were alone.

He reached the gate. It was closed and secured with a big steel padlock. If only a pedestrian would come strolling by, Anthony would be afraid to shoot. But there was no one.

Heart pounding, Luke scrambled up the fence. As he reached the top, he heard the discreet cough of a silenced pistol. But he felt nothing. It was a hard shot, a moving target fifty yards away in the dark, but not impossible. He flung himself over the top. The pistol coughed again. He staggered and fell to the ground. He heard a third muffled shot. He sprang to his feet and ran, heading east. The gun did not speak again.

At the corner, he looked back. Anthony was nowhere in sight.

He had escaped.

*　*　*

Anthony's legs felt weak. He put a hand against the cold wall to steady himself. The yard smelled of rotting vegetables. He felt as if he were breathing corruption.

It had been the hardest thing he had ever done. By comparison, killing Albin Moulier had been easy. Pointing his gun at the figure of Luke scrambling over a wire fence, he had almost been unable to pull the trigger.

This was the worst possible outcome. Luke was still alive – and, having been shot at, he was on full alert, determined to learn the truth.

The kitchen door burst open, and Malone and Curtis appeared. Anthony discreetly slid the gun back into his inside pocket. Then, panting, he said: 'Over the fence – go after him.' He knew they would not catch Luke.

When they were out of sight, he started to look for the slugs.

10.30 P.M.

The design of the rocket is based on the V2 bomb used against London during the war. The engine even looks the same. The accelerometers, relays and gyros are all out of the V2. The pump for the propellants uses hydrogen peroxide passed over a cadmium catalyst, releasing energy that drives a turbine – and this, too, comes from the V2.

Harold Brodsky made a good dry martini, and Mrs Riley's tuna bake was as tasty as promised. For dessert, Harold served cherry pie and ice cream. Billie felt guilty. He was trying so hard to please her, but her mind was on Luke and Anthony, their shared past and their puzzling new entanglement.

While Harold made coffee, she called home and checked that all was well with Larry and Becky-Ma. Then Harold suggested they move to the living room and watch television. He produced a bottle of expensive French brandy and poured generous measures into two oversize snifters. Was he trying to stiffen his own courage, Billie wondered, or lower her resistance? She inhaled the vapours of the cognac but did not drink any.

Harold, too, was thoughtful. He was normally an

entertaining talker, witty and clever, and she generally laughed a lot when she was with him, but tonight he was preoccupied.

They saw a thriller called *Run, Joe, Run!* Jan Sterling played a waitress involved with ex-gangster Alex Nichol. Billie could not get interested in the imaginary dangers on the screen. Her mind drifted to the mystery of what Anthony had done to Luke. In OSS they had broken all kinds of laws, and Anthony was still in clandestine work, but all the same Billie was shocked that he had gone this far. Surely different rules applied in peacetime?

And what was his motive? Bern had called and told her of his confession to Luke, and that had confirmed what all her instincts told her, that Luke could not be a spy. But did Anthony believe it? If not, then what was the real reason for what he had done?

Harold turned off the TV and poured himself another brandy. 'I've been thinking about our future,' he said.

Billie's heart sank. He was going to propose. If he had done it yesterday, she would have accepted him. But today she could hardly think about it.

He took her hand. 'I love you,' he said. 'We get on well, we have the same interests, and we both have a child – but that's not why. I believe I'd want to marry you if you were a waitress who chewed gum and liked Elvis Presley.'

Billie laughed.

He went on: 'I just adore you, for no reason other than you're you. I know it's real, because it's happened to me before, just once, with Lesley. I loved her with all my heart, until she was taken away from me. So I'm not in any doubt. I love you, and I want us to be together for ever.' He looked at her, then said: 'How do you feel?'

She sighed. 'I'm fond of you. I'd like to go to bed with you, I think it would be great.' He raised his eyebrows at this, but did not interrupt. 'And I can't help thinking how much easier life would be if I had someone to share the burdens.'

'This is good.'

'Yesterday, it would have been enough. I would have said yes, I love you, let's get married. But today I met someone from my past, and I remembered what it was like to be in love at the age of twenty-one.' She gave him a candid look. 'I don't feel that way about you, Harold.'

He was not totally discouraged. 'Who does, at our age?'

'Maybe you're right.' She wished she could be crazy and wild again. But it was a foolish desire for a divorcée with a seven-year-old. To give herself time, she lifted the brandy goblet to her lips.

The doorbell rang.

Billie's heart leaped.

'Who the heck is that?' Harold said angrily. 'I hope Sidney Bowman doesn't want to borrow my car jack at this time of night.' He got up and went out to the hall.

Billie knew who it was. She put down her brandy untouched, and stood up.

She heard Luke's voice at the door. 'I need to talk to Billie.'

Billie wondered why she was so inordinately pleased.

Harold said: 'I'm not sure she wants to be disturbed right now.'

'It's important.'

'How did you know she was here?'

'Her mother told me. I'm sorry, Harold, I don't have time to dick around.' Billie heard a thump, followed by a cry of protest from Harold, and she guessed Luke had forced his way into the house. She went to the door and looked into the hallway. 'Just hold your horses, Luke,' she said. 'This is Harold's house.' Luke had ripped his coat and lost his hat, and he looked very shaken. 'What's happened now?' she said.

'Anthony shot at me.'

Billie was shocked. 'Anthony?' she said. 'My God, what got into him? He shot at *you*?'

Harold looked scared. 'What's this about a shooting?'

Luke ignored him. 'It's time to tell someone in authority about all this,' he said to Billie. 'I'm going to the Pentagon. But I'm worried I may not be believed. Will you come and back me up?'

'Sure,' she said. She took her coat off the hall stand.

Harold said: 'Billie! For God's sake – we were in the middle of a very important conversation.'

Luke said: 'I really need you.'

Billie hesitated. It was very hard on Harold. He had

obviously been planning this moment for some time. But Luke's life was in danger. 'I'm sorry,' she said to Harold. 'I have to go.' She lifted her face to be kissed, but he turned away.

'Don't be like that,' Billie said. 'I'll see you tomorrow.'

'Get out of my house, both of you,' Harold said furiously.

Billie walked out, with Luke behind her, and Harold slammed the door.

11 P.M.

The Jupiter programme cost 40 million dollars in 1956 and 140 million in 1957. In 1958 the figure is expected to be more than 300 million.

Anthony found some hotel stationery in the desk drawer of the room Pete had rented. He took out an envelope. From his pocket he took three distorted slugs and three cartridge cases, the rounds he had fired at Luke. He put them into the envelope and sealed it, then stuffed it into his pocket. He would dispose of it at the first opportunity.

He was doing damage control. He had very little time, but he had to be meticulous. He needed to wipe out all trace of this incident. The work helped to distract his mind from the self-loathing that tasted so bitter in his mouth.

The assistant manager on duty came into the room, looking wrathful. He was a small, neat man with a bald head. 'Sit down, please, Mr Suchard,' Anthony said. He showed the man his CIA identification.

'CIA!' Suchard said, and his indignation began to deflate.

Anthony took a business card from his billfold. 'The

card says State Department, but you can always reach me at that number if you need me.'

Suchard handled the card as if it might blow up. 'What can I do for you, Mr Carroll?' He had a slight accent which Anthony thought might be Swiss.

'First, I want to apologize for the little fracas we had earlier.'

Suchard nodded primly. He was not going to say it was okay. 'Fortunately, few guests noticed anything. Only the kitchen staff and a few waiters saw you chasing the gentleman.'

'I'm glad we didn't disrupt your fine hotel too much, even over a matter of national security.'

Suchard raised his eyebrows in surprise. 'National security?'

'Of course, I can't give you the details . . .'

'Of course.'

'But I hope I can rely on your discretion.'

Hotel professionals prided themselves on their discretion, and Suchard nodded vigorously. 'Indeed, you can.'

'It may not be necessary even to report the incident to your manager.'

'Possibly . . .'

Anthony took out a roll of bills. 'The State Department has a small fund for compensation in these instances.' He peeled off a twenty. Suchard accepted it. 'And if any staff members seem discontented, perhaps . . .' He slowly counted another four twenties and handed them over.

It was a huge bribe for an assistant manager. 'Thank

you, sir,' said Suchard. 'I'm sure we can meet your requirements.'

'If anyone should question you, it might be best to say you saw nothing.'

'Of course.' Suchard stood up. 'If there's anything else . . .'

'I'll be in touch.' Anthony nodded dismissively, and Suchard left.

Pete came in. 'The head of security for the army at Cape Canaveral is Colonel Bill Hide,' he said. 'He's staying at the Starlite Motel.' He handed Anthony a slip of paper with a phone number, and went out again.

Anthony dialled the number and got through to Hide's room. 'This is Anthony Carroll, CIA, Technical Services Division,' he said.

Hide spoke with a slow, unmilitary drawl, and sounded as if he might have had a couple of drinks. 'Well, what can I do for you, Mr Carroll?'

'I'm calling about Dr Lucas.'

'Oh, yes?'

He seemed faintly hostile, and Anthony decided to butter him up. 'I would appreciate your advice, if you could spare me a moment at this late hour, Colonel.'

Hide warmed up. 'Of course, anything I can do.'

That was better. 'I think you know that Dr Lucas has been behaving strangely, which is worrying in a scientist in possession of classified information.'

'It sure is.'

Anthony wanted Hide to feel in charge. 'What would you say is his mental state?'

'He seemed normal last time I saw him, but I talked to him a few hours ago and he told me he'd lost his memory.'

'There's more to it than that. He stole a car, broke into a house, got in a fight with a cop, stuff like that.'

'My God, he's in worse shape than I thought.'

Hide was buying the story, Anthony thought with relief. He pressed on. 'We think he's not rational, but you know him better than we do. What would you say is going on?' Anthony held his breath, hoping for the right answer.

'Hell, I think he's suffering some kind of breakdown.' This was exactly what Anthony wanted Hide to believe – but now Hide thought it was his own idea, and he proceeded to try to convince Anthony. 'Look, Mr Carroll, the army wouldn't employ a nutcase on a top secret project. Normally, Luke is as sane as you or me. Obviously something has destabilized him.'

'He seems to think there's some kind of conspiracy against him – but you're saying we shouldn't necessarily credit that.'

'Not for a minute.'

'So we should soft-pedal this stuff. I mean, we shouldn't alert the Pentagon.'

'God, no,' Hide said worriedly. 'In fact, I'd better call them and warn them that Luke seems to have lost his marbles.'

'As you wish.'

Pete came in and Anthony raised one finger for him to wait. He softened his voice and said into the phone: 'By happenstance, I'm an old friend of Dr and Mrs

Lucas. I'm going to try to persuade Luke to seek psychiatric help.'

'That sounds like a good idea.'

'Well, thank you, Colonel. You've set my mind at rest, and we will proceed along the lines you have suggested.'

'You're welcome. If there's anything you want to ask me or discuss with me, call me any time.'

'I sure will.' Anthony hung up.

Pete said: 'Psychiatric help?'

'That was just for his benefit.' Anthony reviewed the situation. There was no evidence here at the hotel. He had prejudiced the Pentagon against any report Luke might make. That just left Billie's hospital.

He stood up. 'I'll be back in an hour,' he said. 'I want you to stay here. But not in the lobby. Take Malone and Curtis and bribe a room-service waiter to let you into Luke's suite. I have a feeling he'll come back.'

'And if he does?'

'Don't let him get away again – no matter what.'

12 MIDNIGHT

The Jupiter C missile uses Hydyne, a secret, high-energy fuel that is 12 per cent more powerful than the alcohol propellant used in the standard Redstone missile. A toxic, corrosive substance, it is a blend of UDMH – unsymmetrical dimethyl hydrazine – and diethylene triamine.

Billie drove the red Thunderbird into the parking lot of the Georgetown Mind Hospital and killed the engine. Colonel Lopez from the Pentagon pulled alongside her in a Ford Fairlane painted olive drab.

'He doesn't believe a word I say,' Luke said angrily.

'You can't blame him,' Billie reasoned. 'The assistant manager of the Carlton says no one was chased through the kitchens, and there are no cartridge cases on the ground at the loading dock.'

'Anthony cleaned up the evidence.'

'I know that, but Colonel Lopez doesn't.'

'Thank God I've got you to back me up.'

They got out of the car and walked into the building with the colonel, a patient Hispanic man with an intelligent face. Billie nodded to the receptionist and led the two men up the stairs and along the corridor to the records office.

'I'm going to show you the file of a man named Joseph Bellow, whose physical characteristics match Luke's,' she explained.

The colonel nodded.

Billie went on: 'You'll see that he was admitted on Tuesday, treated, then discharged at 4 a.m. on Wednesday. You have to understand that it's very unusual for a schizophrenic patient to be given treatment without observation first. And I hardly need to tell you that it's unheard of for a patient to be released from a mental hospital at four o'clock in the morning.'

'I understand,' Lopez said non-committally.

Billie opened the drawer, pulled out the Bellow file, put it on the desk, and opened it.

It was empty.

'Oh, my God,' she said.

Luke stared at the cardboard folder in disbelief. 'I saw the papers myself less than six hours ago!'

Lopez stood up with a weary air. 'Well, I guess that's it.'

Luke had the nightmare feeling that he was living in a surreal world in which people could do what they liked to him, shoot at him and mess with his mind, and he could never prove it had happened. 'Maybe I am schizophrenic,' he said sombrely.

'Well, I'm not,' Billie said. 'And I saw that file too.'

'But it's not here now,' said Lopez.

'Wait,' Billie said. 'The daily register will show his admission. It's kept at the reception desk.' She slammed the file drawer shut.

They went down to the lobby. Billie spoke to the receptionist. 'Let me see the register, please, Charlie.'

'Right away, Dr Josephson.' The young black man behind the counter searched around for a moment. 'Dang, where did that thing go?' he said.

Luke muttered: 'Jesus Christ.'

The receptionist's face darkened with embarrassment. 'I know it was here a couple of hours ago.'

Billie's face was like thunder. 'Tell me something, Charlie. Has Dr Ross been here tonight?'

'Yes, mam. He left a few minutes ago.'

She nodded. 'Next time you see him, ask him where the register went. He knows.'

'I sure will.'

Billie turned away from the desk.

Luke said angrily: 'Let me ask you something, Colonel. Before we saw you tonight, had someone else talked to you about me?'

Lopez hesitated. 'Yes.'

'Who?'

Reluctantly, he said: 'I guess you're entitled to know. We got a call from a Colonel Hide down in Cape Canaveral. He said the CIA had been watching you and they reported that you were behaving irrationally.'

Luke nodded grimly. 'Anthony again.'

Billie said to Lopez: 'Hell, I can't think of anything else we can do to convince you. And I don't really blame you for not believing us, when we have no evidence.'

'I didn't say I don't believe you,' Lopez said.

Luke was startled, and looked at the colonel with new hope.

Lopez went on: 'I could believe you imagined that a CIA man chased you around the Carlton Hotel and shot at you in the alley. I might even accept that you and Dr Josephson conspired to pretend there used to be a file and it disappeared. But I don't believe that Charlie here is in on the conspiracy. There must be a daily register, and it's gone. I don't think you took it – why would you? But then who did? Someone has something to hide.'

'So you believe me?' Luke said.

'What's to believe? You don't know what this is all about. I don't know either. But something sure as hell is going on. And I believe it must have to do with that rocket we're about to launch.'

'What'll you do?'

'I'm going to order a full security alert at Cape Canaveral. I've been there, I know they're lax. Tomorrow morning they won't know what's hit them.'

'But what about Anthony?'

'I have a friend at the CIA. I'm going to tell him your story, and say I don't know whether it's true or not, but I'm concerned.'

'That's not going to get us far!' Luke protested. 'We need to know what's going on, why they wiped my memory!'

'I agree,' Lopez said. 'But I can't do any more. The rest is up to you.'

'Christ,' Luke said. 'So I'm on my own.'

'No, you're not,' said Billie. 'You're not on your own.'

PART 4

1 A.M.

The new fuel is based on a nerve gas and is very dangerous. It is delivered to Cape Canaveral on a special train equipped with nitrogen to blanket it if any escapes. A drop on the skin will be absorbed into the bloodstream instantly and will be fatal. The technicians say: 'If you smell fish, run like hell.'

Billie drove fast, handling the Thunderbird's three-speed manual gear change with confidence. Luke watched in admiration. They sped through the quiet streets of Georgetown, crossed the creek to downtown Washington, and headed for the Carlton.

Luke felt energized. He knew who his enemy was, he had a friend at his side, and he understood what he had to do. He was mystified by what had happened to him, but he was determined to unravel the mystery, and impatient to get on with it.

Billie parked around the corner from the entrance. 'I'll go first,' she said. 'If there's anyone suspicious in the lobby, I'll come right out again. When you see me take my coat off, you'll know it's all clear.'

Luke was not comfortable with this plan. 'What if Anthony's there?'

'He won't shoot me.' She got out of the car.

Luke contemplated arguing with her and decided against it. She was probably right. He presumed that Anthony had thoroughly searched his hotel room, and had destroyed anything he thought might be a clue to the secret he so badly wanted to keep. But Anthony also needed to maintain a semblance of normality, to support the fiction that Luke had lost his memory after a drinking bout. So Luke expected to find most of his own stuff. That would help him reorient himself. And there might be a clue that Anthony had overlooked.

They approached the hotel separately, Luke remaining on the opposite side of the street. He watched Billie go in, enjoying her jaunty walk and the swing of her coat. He could see through the glass doors into the lobby. A porter approached her immediately, suspicious of a glamorous woman arriving alone so late at night. He saw her speak, and guessed she was saying: 'I'm Mrs Lucas, my husband will be along in a moment.' Then she took off her coat.

Luke crossed the road and entered the hotel.

For the porter's benefit he said: 'I want to make a call before we go upstairs, honey.' There was an internal phone on the reception desk, but he did not want the porter to hear his conversation. Next to the reception desk was a little lobby that had a payphone in an enclosed booth with a seat. Luke went inside. Billie followed him and closed the door. They were very close together. He put a dime in the slot and called the hotel. He angled the handset so that Billie could hear. Tense though he was, he found it deliciously exciting to be so near to Billie.

'Sheraton-Carlton, good morning.'

It *was* morning, he realized – Thursday morning. He had been awake for twenty hours. But he did not feel sleepy. He was too tense. 'Room five-thirty, please.'

The operator hesitated. 'Sir, it's past one o'clock – is this an emergency?'

'Dr Lucas asked me to call no matter how late.'

'Very good.'

There was a pause, then a ringing tone. Luke felt very conscious of Billie's warm body in a purple silk dress. He had to resist the urge to put his arm around her small, neat shoulders and hug her to him.

After four rings, he was ready to believe that the room was empty – then the phone was picked up. So Anthony, or one of his men, was lying in wait. That was a nuisance; but Luke felt better knowing where the enemy was deployed.

A voice said: 'Hello?' The tone was uncertain. It was not Anthony, but it might have been Pete.

Luke put on a tipsy voice. 'Hey, Ronnie, this is Tim. We're all waitin' for ya!'

The man grunted with irritation. 'Drunk,' he muttered, as if speaking to someone else. 'You got the wrong room, buddy.'

'Oh, gee, I'm sorry, I hope I didn't wake—' Luke broke off as the phone was hung up.

'Someone there,' Billie said.

'Maybe more than one.'

'I know how to get them out.' She grinned. 'I did it in Lisbon, during the war. Come on.'

They left the phone booth. Luke noticed Billie discreetly pick up a book of matches from an ashtray by the elevator. The porter took them up to the fifth floor.

They found Room 530 and went quietly past it. Billie opened an unmarked door to reveal a linen closet. 'Perfect,' she said in a low voice. 'Is there a fire alarm nearby?'

Luke looked around and saw an alarm of the type that could be set off by breaking a pane of glass with the little hammer hanging next to it. 'Right there,' he said.

'Good.' In the closet, sheets and blankets stood in neat stacks on slatted wooden shelves. Billie unfolded a blanket and dropped it on the floor. She did the same with several more until she had a pile of loose fabric. Luke guessed what she was going to do, and his conjecture was confirmed when she took a breakfast order from a doorknob and lit it with a match. As it flared up, she put the flame to a pile of blankets.'This is why you should never smoke in bed,' she said.

As the flames blazed up, Billie piled on additional bedlinen. Her face was flushed with heat and excitement, and she looked more alluring than ever. Soon there was a roaring bonfire. Smoke poured out of the closet and began to fill the corridor.

'Time to sound the alarm,' she said. 'We don't want anyone to get hurt.'

'Right,' Luke said, and again the phrase came into

his mind: *They're not collaborators.* But now he understood it. In the Resistance, blowing up factories and warehouses, he must have worried constantly about innocent French people getting injured.

He grasped the little hammer that hung on a chain next to the fire alarm. He broke the glass with a light tap and pressed the large red button inside. A moment later, a loud ringing shattered the silence of the corridor.

Luke and Billie retreated along the corridor, moving away from the elevator, until they could only just see the door of Luke's suite through the smoke.

The door nearest them opened and a woman in a nightdress came out. She saw the smoke, screamed, and ran for the stairs. From another door, a man in shirtsleeves emerged with a pencil in his hand, obviously having been working late; then a young couple wrapped in sheets appeared, looking as if they had been interrupted making love; then a bleary-eyed man in rumpled pink pyjamas. A few moments later, the corridor was full of people coughing and fumbling through the smoke toward the stairwell.

The door to Room 530 opened slowly.

Luke saw a tall man step into the corridor. Peering through the murk, Luke thought he had a large wine-coloured birthmark on his cheek: Pete. He drew back to avoid being recognized. The figure hesitated, then seemed to make a decision and joined the rush for the stairs. Two more men came out and followed him.

'All clear,' Luke said.

Luke and Billie entered the suite, and Luke closed the door to keep the smoke out. He took off his coat.

'Oh, my God,' said Billie. 'It's the same room.'

* * *

She stared around, wide-eyed. 'I can't believe it,' she said. Her voice was hushed, and he could hardly hear her. 'This is the very suite.'

He stood still, watching. She was in the grip of a strong emotion. 'What happened here?' he asked her at last.

She shook her head wonderingly. 'It's hard to imagine that you don't remember.' She walked around. 'There was a grand piano in that corner,' she said. 'Imagine – a piano in a hotel room!' She looked into the bathroom. 'And a phone in here. I had never seen a phone in a bathroom.'

Luke waited. Her face showed sadness, and something else he could not quite make out. 'You stayed here in the war,' she said at last. Then, in a rush, she added: 'We made love here.'

He looked into the bedroom. 'On that bed, I guess.'

'Not just on the bed.' She giggled, then became solemn again. 'How young we were.'

The thought of making love to this enchanting woman was unbearably exciting. 'My God, I wish I could remember,' he said, and his voice sounded thick with desire.

To his surprise, she blushed.

He turned aside and picked up the phone. He dialled the operator. He wanted to make sure the fire did not have a chance to spread. After a long wait, the phone was answered. 'This is Mr Davies, I sounded the alarm,' Luke said rapidly. 'The fire is in a linen closet near room five-forty.' He hung up without waiting for a reply.

Billie was looking around, her emotional moment over. 'Your clothes are here,' she said.

He went into the bedroom. Lying on the bed were a pale grey tweed sport coat and a pair of charcoal flannel pants, looking as if they had come back from the dry cleaner. He guessed he had worn them on the plane and sent them for pressing. On the floor was a pair of dark tan wingtip shoes. A crocodile belt was neatly rolled up inside one of the shoes.

He opened the drawer of the bedside table and found a billfold, a cheque book and a fountain pen. More interesting was a slim appointments diary with a list of phone numbers in the back. He looked quickly through its pages and found the current week.

Sunday 26th
Call Alice (1928)

Monday 27th
Buy swim trunks
8.30 a.m. Apex mtg, Vanguard Mtl

Tuesday 28th
8 a.m. Bkfst w A.C., Hay Adams coffee shop

Billie stood beside him to see what he was reading. She put a hand on his shoulder. It was a casual gesture, but her touch gave him a thrill of pleasure. He said: 'Any idea who Alice might be?'

'Your kid sister.'

'How old?'

'Seven years younger than you, which makes her thirty.'

'So she was born in 1928. I guess I talked to her on her birthday. I could call her now, ask her if I said anything unusual.'

'Good idea.'

Luke felt good. He was reconstructing his life. 'I must have gone to Florida without my swimsuit.'

'Who thinks of swimming in January?'

'So I made a note to buy one on Monday. That morning I went to the Vanguard Motel at eight-thirty.'

'What's an Apex meeting?'

'I think it must have to do with the curve followed by the missile in flight. I don't remember working on it, of course, but I know there's an important and tricky calculation that has to be made. The second stage has to be fired precisely at the apex, in order to put the satellite into a permanent orbit.'

'You could find out who else was at the meeting and talk to them.'

'I will.'

'Then, on Tuesday, you had breakfast with Anthony in the coffee shop of the Hay Adams hotel.'

'After that, there are no appointments in the book.'

He turned to the back of the diary. There were phone numbers for Anthony, Billie and Bern, for

Mother and Alice, and twenty or thirty others that meant nothing to him. 'Anything strike you?' he said to Billie. She shook her head.

There were some leads worth following up, but no obvious clues. It was what he had expected, but all the same he felt deflated. He pocketed the diary and looked around the room. A well-worn black leather suitcase rested open on a stand. He rummaged through it, finding clean shirts and underwear, a notebook half full of mathematical calculations, and a paperback book called *The Old Man and the Sea* with a corner turned down at page 143.

Billie looked into the bathroom. Shaving gear, toiletry bag, toothbrush.

Luke opened all the cupboards and drawers in the bedroom, and Billie did the same in the living room. Luke found a black wool topcoat and a black Homburg hat in a closet, but nothing else. 'Zilch,' he called out. 'You?'

'Your phone messages are here on the desk. From Bern, from a Colonel Hide, and from someone called Marigold.'

Luke figured that Anthony had read the messages, judged them harmless, and decided there was no point in creating suspicion by destroying them.

Billie said: 'Who's Marigold, do you know?'

Luke thought for a moment. He had heard the name at some point during the day. It came back to him. 'She's my secretary in Huntsville,' he said. 'Colonel Hide said she had made my flight reservations.'

'I wonder if you told her the purpose of the trip.'

'I doubt it. I didn't tell anyone at Cape Canaveral.'

'She's not at Cape Canaveral. And you might trust your own secretary more than anyone else.'

Luke nodded. 'Anything's possible. I'll check. It's the most promising lead so far.' He took out the diary and looked again at the phone numbers in the back. 'Bingo,' he said. 'Marigold – home.' He sat at the desk and dialled the number. He wondered how much longer he had before Pete and the other agents came back.

Billie seemed to read his mind, and started packing his stuff into the black leather bag.

The phone was answered by a sleepy woman with a slow Alabama accent. Luke guessed from her voice that she was black. He said: 'I'm sorry to call so late. Is this Marigold?'

'Dr Lucas! Thank God you've called. How are you?'

'I'm fine, I think, thank you.'

'Well, what in heaven happened to you? No one knew where you were at – and now I hear tell you lost your memory. Is that so?'

'Yes.'

'Well, now, how did that come to pass?'

'I don't know, but I'm hoping you might help me figure it out.'

'If I can . . .'

'I'd like to know why I suddenly decided to go to Washington on Monday. Did I tell you?'

'You sure didn't, and I was curious.'

It was the answer Luke expected, but still he felt disappointed. 'Did I say anything that gave you a hint?'

'No.'

'What *did* I say?'

'You said you needed to fly to Washington via Huntsville, and you asked me to make reservations on MATS flights.'

MATS was the military airline, and Luke guessed he was entitled to use it when on army business. But there was something he did not understand. 'I flew via Huntsville?' No one else had mentioned that.

'You said you wanted to stop over here for a couple of hours.'

'I wonder why.'

'Then you said something kind of strange. You asked me not to tell anyone that you were coming to Huntsville.'

'Ah.' Luke felt sure this was an important clue. 'So it was a secret visit?'

'Yes. And I've kept it secret. I've been questioned by army security and the FBI, and I didn't tell either one of them, because you said not to. I didn't know if I was doing right or not, when they said you had disappeared, but I figured I better stick with what you told me. Did I do right?'

'Gosh, Marigold, I don't know. But I appreciate your loyalty.' The fire alarm stopped ringing. Luke realized he had run out of time. 'I have to go now,' he told Marigold. 'Thanks for your help.'

'Well, you bet. Now you just take care, hear?' She hung up.

'I've packed your stuff,' Billie said.

'Thanks,' he said. He took his own black coat and

hat from the closet and put them on. 'Now let's get out of here before the spooks come back.'

* * *

They drove to an all-night diner near the FBI building, around the corner from Chinatown, and ordered coffee. 'I wonder when the first flight to Huntsville leaves in the morning,' Luke said.

'We need the Official Airline Guide,' Billie said.

Luke looked around the diner. He saw a pair of cops eating doughnuts, four drunk students ordering hamburgers, and two underdressed women who might have been prostitutes. 'I don't think they'll keep it behind the counter here,' he said.

'I bet Bern has one. It's the kind of thing writers like. They're always looking stuff up.'

'He's probably asleep.'

Billie stood up. 'Then I'll wake him. Got a dime?'

'Sure.' Luke still had a pocket full of the change he had stolen yesterday.

Billie went to the payphone beside the restrooms. Luke sipped his coffee, watching her. As she talked into the phone she smiled and tilted her head, being charming to someone she had woken up. She looked bewitching, and he ached with desire for her.

She returned to the table and said: 'He's going to join us and bring the book.'

Luke checked his watch. It was two a.m. 'I'll probably go straight to the airport from here. I hope there's an early flight.'

Billie frowned. 'Is there a deadline?'

'There might be. I keep asking myself: What could have made me drop everything and rush to Washington? It has to be something to do with the rocket. And what could that be if not a threat to the launch?'

'Sabotage?'

'Yes. And if I'm right, I have to prove it before ten-thirty tonight.'

'Do you want me to fly to Huntsville with you?'

'You have to take care of Larry.'

'I can leave him with Bern.'

Luke shook his head. 'I don't think so . . . thanks.'

'You always were an independent son of a gun.'

'It's not that,' he said. He wanted her to understand. 'I'd love you to come with me. That's the trouble – I'd like it too much.'

She reached across the plastic tabletop and took his hand. 'It's okay,' she said.

'This is confusing, you know? I'm married to someone else, but I don't know how I feel about her. What's she like?'

Billie shook her head. 'I can't talk to you about Elspeth. You have to rediscover her yourself.'

'I guess so.'

Billie brought his hand to her lips and kissed it softly.

Luke swallowed. 'Did I always like you so much, or is this new?'

'This is not new.'

'It seems we get on really well.'

'No. We fight like hell. But we adore one another.'

'You said we were lovers, once – in that hotel suite.'

'Stop it.'

'Was it good?'

She looked at him with tears in her eyes. 'The best.'

'Then how come I'm not married to you?'

She began to cry, soft sobs that shook her small frame. 'Because . . .' She wiped her face and took a deep breath, then started crying again. At last she blurted out: 'You got so mad at me, you didn't speak to me for five years.'

1945

Anthony's parents had a horse farm near Charlottesville, Virginia, a couple of hours from Washington. It was a big white timber-framed house with rambling wings that contained a dozen bedrooms. There were stables and tennis courts, a lake and a stream, paddocks and woodland. Anthony's mother had inherited it from her father, along with five million dollars.

Luke arrived there on the Friday after Japan surrendered. Mrs Carroll welcomed him at the door. She was a nervous blonde woman who looked as if she had once been very beautiful. She showed him to a small, spotlessly clean bedroom with a polished board floor and a high old-fashioned bed.

He changed out of his uniform – he now held the rank of major – and put on a black cashmere sport coat and grey flannel pants. As he was tying his tie, Anthony looked in. 'Cocktails in the drawing room whenever you're ready,' he said.

'I'll be right there,' Luke said. 'Which room is Billie's?'

A worried frown flickered across Anthony's face. 'The girls are in the other wing, I'm afraid,' he said.

'The Admiral is old-fashioned about that sort of thing.' His father had spent his life in the navy.

'No problem,' Luke said with a shrug. He had spent the last three years moving around occupied Europe at night: he would be able to find his lover's bedroom in the dark.

When he went downstairs at six o'clock he found all his old friends waiting. As well as Anthony and Billie, there were Elspeth, Bern, and Bern's girlfriend Peg. Luke had spent much of the war with Bern and Anthony, and every leave with Billie, but he had not seen Elspeth or Peg since 1941.

The Admiral handed him a martini and he took a satisfying gulp. This was a time to celebrate if ever there was one. The conversation was noisy and high-spirited. Anthony's mother looked on with a vaguely pleased expression, and his father drank cocktails faster than anyone else.

Luke studied them all over dinner, comparing them with the golden youths who had been so worried, four years ago, about being expelled from Harvard. Elspeth was painfully thin after three years on iron rations in wartime London: even her magnificent breasts seemed smaller. Peg, who had been a dowdy girl with a big heart, was now smartly dressed, but her skilfully made-up face looked hardened and cynical. Bern at twenty-seven looked ten years older. This had been his second war. He had been wounded three times, and he had the gaunt face of a man who has known too much suffering, his own and other people's.

Anthony had come through best. He had seen some

action, but had spent most of the war in Washington. His confidence, his optimism and his offbeat humour had survived intact.

Billie, too, seemed little changed. She had known hardship and bereavement in childhood, and perhaps that was why the war had not bruised her. She had spent two years undercover in Lisbon, and Luke knew – though the others did not – that she had killed a man there, cutting his throat with silent efficiency in the yard behind the café where he had been about to sell secrets to the enemy. But she was still a small bundle of radiant energy, gay at one moment and fierce at the next, her constantly changing face a study that Luke never tired of.

It was remarkably lucky that they were all still alive. Most such groups would have lost at least one friend. 'We should drink a toast,' he said, lifting his wine glass. 'To those who survived – and those who did not.'

They all drank, then Bern said: 'I have another. To the men who broke the back of the Nazi war machine – the Red Army.'

They all drank again, but the Admiral looked displeased and said: 'I think that's enough toasts.'

Bern's communism was still strong, but Luke felt sure he was no longer working for Moscow. They had made a deal, and Luke believed Bern had kept the bargain. Nevertheless, their relationship had never returned to its old warmth. Trusting someone was like holding a little water in your cupped hands – it was so easy to spill the water, and you could never get it back. Luke was sad every time he recalled the comradeship he and Bern had shared, but he felt helpless to regain it.

Coffee was served in the drawing room. Luke handed the cups around. As he offered cream and sugar to Billie, she said in a low voice: 'East wing, second floor, last door on the left.'

'Cream?'

She raised an eyebrow.

He smothered a laugh and passed on.

At ten-thirty the Admiral insisted the men move to the billiard room. Hard liquor and Cuban cigars were laid out on a sideboard. Luke refused more booze: he was looking forward to sliding between the sheets next to Billie's warm, eager body, and the last thing he wanted to do then was fall asleep.

The Admiral poured himself a big tumbler of bourbon and took Luke to the far end of the room to show him his guns, standing in a locked display rack on the wall. Luke's family were not hunters, and guns to him were for killing people, not animals, so he took no pleasure in them. He also felt strongly that guns and liquor made a bad combination. However, he feigned interest in order to be polite.

'I know and respect your family, Luke,' the Admiral said as they examined an Enfield rifle. 'Your father is a very great man.'

'Thank you,' Luke said. This sounded like the preamble to a rehearsed speech. His father had spent the war helping to run the Office of Price Administration, but the Admiral probably still thought of him as a banker.

'You'll have to think of your family when you choose a wife, my boy,' the Admiral went on.

'Yes, sir, I will.' Luke wondered what was on the old man's mind.

'Whoever becomes Mrs Lucas will have a place waiting for her in the upper reaches of American society. You must pick a girl who can carry that off.'

Luke began to see where this was going. Annoyed, he abruptly put the rifle back in the rack. 'I'll bear that in mind, Admiral,' he said, and he turned away.

The Admiral put a hand on his arm, stopping him. 'Whatever you do, don't throw yourself away.'

Luke glared at him. He was determined not to ask the Admiral what he was getting at. He thought he knew the answer, and it would be better if it were not said.

But the Admiral was determined. 'Don't get stuck with that little Jewess – she's not worthy of you.'

Luke gritted his teeth. 'If you'll excuse me, this is something I'd rather discuss with my own father.'

'But your father doesn't know about her, does he?'

Luke flushed. The Admiral had scored a point. Luke and Billie had not met one another's parents.

There had hardly been time. Their love affair had been conducted in snatched moments during a war. But that was not the only reason. Deep in Luke's heart a small, mean-spirited voice told him that a girl from a dirt-poor Jewish family was not his parents' idea of the right wife for their son. They would accept her, he felt sure – indeed, they would come to love her, for all the reasons he loved her. But at first they might be a little disappointed. Consequently, he was eager to introduce her to them in the right circumstances, on a relaxed occasion when they would have time to get to know her.

The fact that there was a grain of truth in the Admiral's insinuation made Luke even angrier. With barely controlled aggression, he said: 'Forgive me if I *warn* you that these remarks are personally offensive to me.'

The room went quiet, but Luke's veiled threat passed right over the head of the drunk Admiral. 'I understand that, son, but I've lived longer than you, and I know what I'm talking about.'

'Pardon me, you don't know the people involved.'

'Oh, but I think I may know more about the lady in question than you do.'

Something in the Admiral's tone sounded a warning, but Luke was angry enough to ignore it. 'The hell you do,' he said with deliberate rudeness.

Bern tried to intervene. 'Hey, guys, lighten up, will you? Let's shoot some pool.'

But nothing could stop the Admiral now. He put his arm around Luke's shoulders. 'Look, son, I'm a man, I understand,' he said with an assumption of intimacy that Luke resented. 'So long as you don't take matters too seriously, there's no harm in pronging a little tart, we've all—'

He never finished the sentence. Luke turned towards him, put both hands on his chest, and shoved him away. The Admiral staggered back, arms flailing, and his glass of bourbon went flying through the air.

He tried to regain his balance, failed, and sat down hard on the rug. Luke shouted at him: 'Now knock it off before I close your filthy mouth with my fist!'

Anthony, white-faced, grabbed Luke's arm, saying: 'Luke, for Christ's sake, what do you think you're doing?'

Bern stepped between them and the fallen Admiral. 'Calm down, both of you,' he said.

'The hell with *calm*,' Luke said. 'What kind of man invites you to his house then insults your girlfriend? It's about time someone taught the old fool a lesson in manners!'

'She is a tart,' the Admiral said from his sitting position. 'I should know, goddam it.' His voice rose to a roar. 'I paid for her abortion!'

Luke was stunned. 'Abortion?'

'Hell, yes.' He struggled to his feet. 'Anthony got her pregnant, and I paid a thousand dollars for her to get rid of the little bastard.' His mouth twisted in a spiteful grin of triumph. 'Now tell me I don't know what I'm talking about.'

'You're lying.'

'Ask Anthony.'

Luke looked at Anthony.

Anthony shook his head. 'It wasn't my baby. I told my father it was, so that he'd give me the thousand dollars. But it was your baby, Luke.'

Luke blushed to the roots of his hair. The drunk old Admiral had made a complete fool of him. He was the ignorant one. He thought he knew Billie, yet she had kept something as big as this a secret from him.

He had fathered a child, and his girlfriend had had an abortion, and they knew about it but he did not. He was utterly humiliated.

He stormed out of the room. He crossed the hall and burst into the drawing room. Only Anthony's mother was there: the girls must have gone to bed. Mrs Carroll saw his face and said: 'Luke, my dear, is something wrong?' He ignored her and went out, slamming the door.

He ran up the stairs and along the east wing. He found Billie's room and went in without knocking.

She was lying naked on the bed, reading, her head resting on her hand, her curly dark hair falling forward like a breaking wave. For a moment, the sight of her took his breath away. Light from a bedside lamp painted a line of gold at the edge of her body, from her neat small shoulder, along her hip, and down one slender leg to her red toenail. But her beauty only made him angrier.

She looked up at him with a happy smile, then her face darkened when she saw his expression.

He yelled: 'Have you ever deceived me?'

She sat upright, scared. 'No, never!'

'That fucking admiral says he paid for you to have an abortion.'

Her face paled. 'Oh, no,' she said.

'Is it true?' Luke shouted. 'Answer me!'

She nodded, began to cry, and buried her face in her hands.

'So you did deceive me.'

'I'm sorry,' she sobbed. 'I wanted to have your baby

– wanted it with all my heart. But I couldn't talk to you. You were in France, and I didn't know if you were ever coming back. I had to decide all on my own.' She raised her voice. 'It was the worst time of my life!'

Luke was dazed. 'I fathered a child,' he said.

Her mood changed in a flash. 'Don't get maudlin,' she said scornfully. 'You weren't sentimental about your sperm when you fucked me, so don't start now – it's too damn late.'

That stung him. 'You should have told me. Even if you couldn't reach me at the time, you should have told me at the first opportunity, the next time I came home on leave.'

She sighed. 'Yes, I know. But Anthony thought I shouldn't tell anyone, and it's not difficult to persuade a girl to keep something like that a secret. No one need ever have known, if not for Admiral goddamn Carroll.'

Luke was maddened by the calm way she talked about her treachery, as if the only thing she had done wrong was to get caught. 'I can't live with this,' he said.

Her voice went quiet. 'What do you mean?'

'After you've deceived me – and over something so important – how can I ever trust you again?'

She looked anguished. 'You're going to tell me it's over.' He said nothing. She went on: 'I can tell, I know you too well. I'm right, aren't I?'

'Yes.'

She began to cry afresh. 'You idiot!' she said through the tears. 'You don't know anything, do you, despite the war.'

'The war taught me that nothing counts as much as loyalty.'

'Bullshit. You still haven't learned that when humans are under pressure, we're all willing to lie.'

'Even to people we love?'

'We lie *more* to our loved ones, because we care about them so damn much. Why do you think we tell the truth to priests and shrinks and total strangers we meet on trains? It's because we don't love them, so we don't care what they think.'

She was infuriatingly plausible. But he despised such easy excuses. 'That's not my philosophy of life.'

'Lucky you,' she said bitterly. 'You come from a happy home, you've never known bereavement or rejection, you have troops of friends. You had a hard war, but you weren't crippled or tortured, and you don't have enough imagination to be a coward. Nothing bad has ever happened to you. Sure, you don't tell lies – for the same reason Mrs Carroll doesn't steal cans of soup.'

She was incredible – she had convinced herself that he was in the wrong! It was impossible to talk to someone who could fool herself so thoroughly. Disgusted, he turned to leave. 'If that's how you think of me, you must be glad our relationship is over.'

'No, I'm not glad.' Tears ran down her face. 'I love you, I've never loved another guy. I'm sorry I deceived you, but I'm not going to prostrate myself with guilt because I did a bad thing in a moment of crisis.'

He did not want her to prostrate herself with guilt. He did not want her to do anything at all. He just wanted to get away from her and their friends and Admiral Carroll and this hateful house.

Somewhere in the back of his mind, a small voice told him he was throwing away the most precious thing he had ever had, and warned that this conversation would cause him a regret so bitter that it would burn in his soul for years. But he was too angry, too humiliated, and too painfully wounded to listen.

He went to the door.

'Don't leave,' she pleaded.

'Go to hell,' he said, and he went out.

2.30 A.M.

The new fuel and a larger fuel tank have boosted the Jupiter's thrust to a force of 83,000 pounds, and extended the burning time from 121 seconds to 155 seconds.

'Anthony was a true friend to me then,' Billie said. 'I was desperate. A thousand dollars! There was nowhere I could find that kind of money. He got it from his father, and he took the blame. He was a mensch. That's why it's so hard to understand what he's doing now.'

'I can't believe I gave you up,' Luke said. 'Didn't I understand what you'd been through?'

'It wasn't all your fault,' Billie said wearily. 'I thought it was, at the time, but now I can see my own role in the whole mess.' She looked as if the telling of the story had exhausted her.

They sat in silence for a while, hushed by regret. Luke wondered how long it would take Bern to drive here from Georgetown; then his thoughts reverted to the story Billie had told. 'I don't much like what I'm learning about myself,' he said after a while. 'Did I really lose my two best friends, you and Bern, just by being unforgiving and pig-headed?'

Billie hesitated, then she laughed. 'Why mince words? Yes, that's exactly what you did.'

'And so you married Bern.'

She laughed again. 'You can be so egocentric!' she said amiably. 'I didn't marry Bern because you left me. I married him because he's one of the best men in the world. He's smart, he's kind, and he's good in bed. It took me years to get over you, but when I did, I fell in love with Bern.'

'And you and I became friends again?'

'Slowly. We always loved you, all of us, even if you could be a stiff-necked son of a gun. I wrote to you when Larry was born, and you came to see me. Then, the following year, Anthony had a huge party on his thirtieth birthday and you showed up. You were back at Harvard, getting your doctorate, and the rest of us were in Washington – Anthony and Elspeth and Peg working for the CIA, me doing research at George Washington University, and Bern writing scripts for radio – but you came to town a couple of times a year, and we would get together.'

'When did I marry Elspeth?'

'Nineteen fifty-four – the year I divorced Bern.'

'Do you know why I married her?'

She hesitated. The answer should have been easy, Luke thought. She should have said: 'Because you loved her – of course!' But she did not. 'I'm the wrong person to answer that question,' she said at last.

'I'll ask Elspeth.'

'I wish you would.'

He looked at her. There was an edge to that last

remark. Luke was figuring out how to tease out her meaning when a white Lincoln Continental pulled up outside, and Bern jumped out and came into the diner. Luke said: 'I'm sorry we woke you.'

'Forget it,' Bern said. 'Billie does not subscribe to the belief that when a man is asleep you should leave him be. If she's awake, everyone should be awake. You'd know that, if you hadn't lost your memory. Here.' He tossed a thick booklet on to the table. The cover said: OFFICIAL AIRLINE GUIDE – PUBLISHED MONTHLY. Luke picked it up.

Billie said: 'Look for Capital Airlines – they fly to the south.'

Luke found the right pages. 'There's a plane that leaves at six fifty-five – that's only four hours from now.' He looked more closely. 'But, shit, it stops at every small town in Dixie, and gets to Huntsville at two twenty-three this afternoon, local time.'

Bern put on a pair of spectacles and read over his shoulder. 'The next plane doesn't leave until nine o'clock, but it has fewer stops, and it's a Viscount, so it gets you to Huntsville earlier, a few minutes before noon.'

'I'd get the later plane, but I don't relish hanging around Washington any longer than I have to,' Luke said.

Bern said: 'You have two more problems. Number one, I think Anthony will have men at the airport.'

Luke frowned. 'Maybe I could leave here by car, and pick up a plane somewhere down the line.' He looked at the timetable. 'The early flight's first stop is a place called Newport News. Where the hell is that?'

'Near Norfolk, Virginia,' Billie said.

'It lands there at two minutes past eight. Can I get there in time?'

'It's two hundred miles,' Billie said. 'Say four hours. You can make it with an hour to spare.'

Bern said: 'More, if you take my car. It has a top speed of a hundred and fifteen.'

'You'd lend me your car?'

Bern smiled. 'We've both saved each other's lives. A car is nothing.'

Luke nodded. 'Thanks.'

'But you have a second problem,' Bern said.

'What's that?'

'I was followed here.'

3 A.M.

The fuel tanks contain baffles to prevent sloshing. Without the baffles, the movement of the liquid is so violent that it caused a test missile, Jupiter 1B, to disintegrate after 93 seconds of flight.

Anthony sat at the wheel of his yellow Cadillac a block from the diner. He had parked tight up against the rear of a truck, so that his distinctive automobile was mostly shielded from view, but he could clearly see the diner and the stretch of sidewalk brightened by the light spilling from its windows. It appeared to be a cop hang-out: there were two patrol cars parked outside, along with Billie's red Thunderbird and Bern's white Continental.

Ackie Horwitz had been stationed outside Bern Rothsten's apartment, with instructions to stay there unless Luke showed up; but, when Bern left in the middle of the night, Ackie had had the good sense to disobey orders and follow on his motorcycle. As soon as Bern arrived at the diner, Ackie had called Q Building and alerted Anthony.

Now Ackie came out of the diner in his motorcycle leathers, carrying a container of coffee in one hand

and a candy bar in the other. He came to Anthony's
window. 'Lucas is in there,' he said.

'I knew it,' Anthony said with malevolent
satisfaction.

'But he's changed his clothes. He has a black coat
and a black hat now.'

'He lost his other hat at the Carlton.'

'Rothsten is with him, and the girl.'

'Who else is in there?'

'Four cops telling dirty jokes, an insomniac reading
the early edition of tomorrow's *Washington Post*, and
the cook.'

Anthony nodded. He could not do anything to Luke
with the cops present. 'We wait here until Luke comes
out, then we both follow him. This time, we're not
going to lose him.'

'Gotcha.' Ackie went to his motorcycle, behind
Anthony's car, and sat in the saddle to drink his coffee.

Anthony planned ahead. They would catch up with
Luke in a quiet street, overpower him, and take him to
a CIA safe house in Chinatown. At that point Anthony
would get rid of Ackie. Then he would kill Luke.

He felt coldly determined. He had suffered a
moment of emotional weakness at the Carlton earlier,
but afterwards he had hardened his heart, resolving
not to think about friendship and betrayal until this
was all over. He knew he was doing the right thing. He
would deal with regrets after he had done his duty.

The door of the diner opened.

Billie came out first. The bright lights were behind
her, so Anthony could not see her face, but he

recognized her small figure and the characteristic sway of her walk. Next came a man in a black coat and black hat: Luke. They went to the red Thunderbird. The figure in the trench coat bringing up the rear got into the white Lincoln.

Anthony started his engine.

The T-bird moved away, followed by the Lincoln. Anthony waited a few seconds, then pulled out. Ackie tucked in behind on his motorcycle.

Billie headed west, and the little convoy followed. Anthony stayed a block and a half behind, but the streets were deserted, so they were sure to notice they were being tailed. Anthony felt fatalistic about it. There was no further point in deception: this was the showdown.

They came to 14th Street and stopped for a red light, and Anthony came up behind Bern's Lincoln. When the light turned green, Billie's Thunderbird suddenly shot forward, while the Lincoln remained stationary.

Cursing, Anthony reversed a few yards, then threw the shift into drive and stamped on the gas pedal. The big car shot forward. He swung around the standing Lincoln and raced after the others.

Billie zigzagged through the neighbourhood at the back of the White House, shooting red lights, defying No Turn signs, and driving the wrong way on one-way streets. Anthony did the same, desperately trying to stay on her tail, but the Cadillac could not match the T-bird for manoeuvrability, and she drew away.

Ackie passed Anthony and stayed right on Billie's

tail. However, as she increased her lead over Anthony, he guessed that her game plan was first to shake the Cadillac by twisting and turning, then get on to a freeway and outrun the motorcycle, which could not match the T-bird's top speed of 125. 'Hell,' he said.

Then luck intervened. Screeching around a corner, Billie ran into a flood. Water was gushing out of a drain at the kerbside, and the entire width of the road was two or three inches under. She lost control of her car. The tail of the Thunderbird swung around in a wide arc, and the vehicle spun through a half-circle. Ackie veered around her, his bike slipped from under him, and he fell off and rolled in the water, but got up immediately. Anthony jammed on the brakes of the Cadillac and skidded to a halt at the intersection. The Thunderbird came to a halt slewed across the street, with its trunk an inch from a parked car. Anthony pulled across its front, blocking it in. Billie could not get away.

Ackie was already at the driver's door of the Thunderbird. Anthony ran to the passenger side. 'Get out of the car!' he yelled. He drew the gun from his inside pocket.

The door opened, and the figure in the black coat and hat got out.

Anthony saw immediately that it was not Luke, but Bern.

He turned and looked back the way they had come. There was no sign of the white Lincoln.

Rage boiled up inside him. They had switched coats, and Luke had escaped in Bern's car. 'You fucking idiot!' he screamed at Bern. He felt like shooting him on the spot. 'You don't know what you've done!'

Bern was infuriatingly calm. 'Then tell me, Anthony,' he said. 'What have I done?'

Anthony turned away and stuffed the gun back into his coat.

'Wait a minute,' Bern said. 'You've got some explaining to do. What you did to Luke is illegal.'

'I don't have to explain one goddamn thing to you,' Anthony spat.

'Luke's not a spy.'

'How would you know a thing like that?'

'I know.'

'I don't believe you.'

Bern gave him a hard look. 'Sure you do,' he said. 'You know perfectly well that Luke is not a Soviet agent. So why the hell are you pretending otherwise?'

'Go to hell,' Anthony said, and he walked away.

* * *

Billie lived in Arlington, a leafy suburb on the Virginia side of the Potomac river. Anthony drove along her street. As he passed her house, he saw on the other side of the road a dark-coloured Chevrolet sedan belonging to the CIA. He turned a corner and parked.

Billie would come home in the next couple of hours. She knew where Luke had gone. But she would not tell Anthony. He had lost her trust. She would stay loyal to Luke now – unless Anthony put her under extraordinary pressure.

So that was what he would do.

Was he crazy? A small voice in his head kept asking if the race was worth the prize. Was there any justification for what he was about to do? He pushed his doubts aside. He had chosen his destiny long ago, and he was not to be deflected from it, not even by Luke.

He opened the trunk of his car and took out a black leather case, the size of a hardcover book, and a pencil flashlight. Then he walked back to the Chevy. He slid into the passenger seat beside Pete and sat looking at the dark windows of Billie's little house. He thought: This will be the worst thing I have ever done.

He looked at Pete. 'Do you trust me?' he said.

Pete's disfigured face twisted in an embarrassed grin. 'What kind of question is that? Yes, I trust you.'

Most of the young agents hero-worshipped Anthony, but Pete had an extra reason for being loyal to him. Anthony had discovered something about Pete that could get him fired – the fact that he had once been arrested for soliciting a prostitute – but he had kept it secret. Now, to remind Pete of that, he said: 'If I did something that seemed wrong to you, would you still back me up?'

Pete hesitated, and when he spoke his voice was choked with emotion. 'Let me tell you something.' He looked ahead, through the windscreen, at the lamplit street. 'You've been like a father to me, that's all.'

'I'm going to do something you won't like. I need you to trust me that it's the right thing to do.'

'I'm telling you – you got it.'

'I'm going in,' Anthony said. 'Honk if anyone arrives.'

He walked softly up the driveway, circled around the garage and went to the back door. He shone his flashlight through the kitchen window. The familiar table and chairs stood in darkness.

He had lived a life of deception and betrayal, but this, he thought with a surge of self-loathing, was the lowest he had ever sunk.

The kitchen door had an old-fashioned two-way lock with a key on the inside. Anthony could have opened it with a pencil. He put the flask in his mouth, then unzipped the leather case and took out an instrument like a dental probe. He slid it into the keyhole, pushing the key out on the far side. It fell on to the mat with no sound. He twisted the probe and unlocked the door.

Silently, he stepped into the darkened house. He knew his way around. He checked the living room first, then Billie's bedroom. Both were empty. Next he looked in on Becky-Ma. She was fast asleep, her hearing aid on the bedside table. Last he went into Larry's room.

He shone his flash on the sleeping child, feeling sick with guilt. He sat on the edge of the bed and switched on the light. 'Hey, Larry, wake up,' he said. 'Come on.'

The boy's eyes opened. After a disoriented moment, he grinned. 'Uncle Anthony!' he said, and he smiled.

'Time to get up,' Anthony said.

'What time is it?'

'It's early.'

'What are we going to do?'

'It's a surprise,' Anthony said.

4.30 A.M.

Fuel shoots into the combustion chamber of the rocket engine at a speed of about 100 feet per second. Burning begins the instant the fluids meet. The heat of the flame soon evaporates the liquids. Pressure rises to several hundred pounds per square inch, and the temperature soars to 5,000 degrees Fahrenheit.

Bern said to Billie: 'You're in love with Luke, aren't you.'

They were sitting in her car outside his building. She did not want to go in: she was impatient to get home to Larry and Becky-Ma.

'In love?' she said evasively. 'Am I?' She was not sure how much she wanted to share with her ex-husband. They were friends, but not intimate.

'It's okay,' he said. 'I realized long ago that you should have married Luke. I don't think you ever stopped loving him. You loved me, too, but in a different way.'

That was true. Her love for Bern was a gentle, calm feeling. With him she had never felt the hurricane of passion that engulfed her when she was with Luke. And when she asked herself what she felt for Harold –

the easy affection or the whirlwind of excitement – the answer was depressingly obvious. Thinking about Harold gave her a pleasant but mild sense of pleasure. She had little experience of men – the only ones she had slept with were Luke and Bern – but instinct told her that with Harold she would never have the feeling Luke gave her of a sexual craving that left her weak and helpless with desire.

'Luke's married,' she said. 'To a beautiful woman.' She thought for a moment. 'Is Elspeth sexy?'

Bern frowned. 'Hard to say. She could be, with the right guy. To me she seemed cold, but she never had eyes for anyone but Luke.'

'Not that it matters. Luke is the faithful type. He'd stay with her if she was an iceberg, just out of a sense of duty.' She paused. 'There's something I have to say to you.'

'Okay.'

'Thank you. For not saying "I told you so." I sure appreciate your restraint.'

Bern laughed. 'You're thinking about our great quarrel.'

She nodded. 'You said my work would be used to brainwash people. Now your prediction has come true.'

'All the same, I was wrong. Your work had to be done. We need to understand the human brain. People may use knowledge to do evil, but we can't hold up scientific progress. But, listen, do you have a theory about what Anthony is up to?'

'Best I could come up with: I imagine Luke

discovered a spy down there at Cape Canaveral, and came to Washington to tell the Pentagon about it. But the spy is really a double agent, working for us, so Anthony is desperate to protect the guy.'

Bern shook his head. 'Not good enough. Anthony could have dealt with that simply by telling Luke that the spy was a double. He didn't have to wipe his memory.'

'I guess you're right. And Anthony *shot* at Luke a few hours ago. I know this secret agent work tends to go to men's heads, but I can't believe the CIA would actually kill an American citizen to protect a double agent.'

'Sure they would,' Bern said. 'But it wouldn't have been necessary. Anthony could just have trusted Luke.'

'Do you have a better theory?'

'No.'

Billie shrugged. 'I'm not sure it matters any more. Anthony has deceived and betrayed his friends – who cares why? Whatever strange purpose has driven him to this, we've lost him. And he was a good friend.'

'Life sucks,' Bern said. He kissed her cheek and got out of the car. 'If you hear from Luke tomorrow, call me.'

'Okay.'

Bern walked into the building, and Billie drove off.

She crossed the Memorial Bridge, skirted the National Cemetery, and zigzagged through the suburban streets to her home. She reversed into the driveway, a habit she had developed because she was usually in a hurry when leaving. She entered the house, hung her coat on the hall stand, and went straight upstairs, unbuttoning her dress and pulling it off over her head as she did so. She threw it over a chair, kicked off her shoes, and went to check on Larry.

When she saw the empty bed, she screamed.

She looked into the bathroom, then Becky-Ma's room. 'Larry!' she yelled at the top of her voice. 'Where are you?' She ran downstairs and went into every room. Still in her underwear, she left the house and looked in the garage and the yard. Going back inside, she went into every room again, opening closets and checking under beds, looking into every space large enough to hold a seven-year-old.

He had gone.

Becky-Ma came out of her bedroom, fear written on her lined face. 'What's happening?' she said shakily.

'Where's Larry?' Billie shouted.

'In his bed, I thought,' she said, her voice becoming a moan of misery as she realized what had happened.

Billie stood still for a moment, breathing hard, fighting down panic. Then she went into Larry's bedroom and studied it.

The room was tidy, with no signs of struggle. Checking his closet, she saw the blue teddy-bear pyjamas he had worn last night neatly folded on a shelf. The clothes she had set out for school today had gone. Whatever had happened, he had got dressed before leaving. It looked as if he had gone with someone he trusted.

Anthony.

At first she felt relief. Anthony would not harm

Larry. But then she thought again. Wouldn't he? She would have said Anthony would not harm Luke, but he had shot at him. There was no telling any more what Anthony would do. At the very least, Larry must have been frightened, to be woken up so early and made to get dressed and leave the house without seeing his mother.

She had to get him back fast.

She ran downstairs to call Anthony. Before she got to the phone, it rang. She snatched it up. 'Yes?'

'This is Anthony.'

'How could you do it?' she screamed. 'How could you be so cruel?'

'I have to know where Luke is,' he said coolly. 'It's unimaginably important.'

'He's gone—' She stopped herself. If she gave him the information, she would have no weapons left.

'Gone where?'

She took a breath. 'Where's Larry?'

'He's with me. He's fine, don't worry.'

That enraged her. 'How could I not worry, you dumb prick!'

'Just tell me what I need to know, and everything will be all right.'

She wanted to believe him, to blurt out the answer and trust him to bring Larry home, but she resisted the temptation fiercely. 'Listen to me. When I see my son, I'll tell you where Luke is.'

'Don't you trust me?'

'Is that a joke?'

He sighed. 'Okay. Meet me at the Jefferson Memorial.'

She felt a small surge of triumph. 'When?'

'Seven o'clock.'

She checked her watch. It was after six. 'I'll be there.'

'Billie . . .'

'What?'

'Be alone.'

'Yeah.' She hung up.

Becky-Ma was standing by her side, looking frail and old. 'What is it?' she said. 'What's going on?'

Billie tried to give an impression of calm. 'Larry's with Anthony. He must have come in and got him while you were asleep. I'm going to pick him up now. We can stop worrying.'

She went upstairs and threw on some clothes. Then she picked up the dressing-table chair and placed it in front of the wardrobe. Standing on the chair, she took a small suitcase from on top of the wardrobe. She placed the case on the bed and opened it.

She unwrapped a cloth to reveal a .45 Colt Automatic.

They had all been issued with Colts in the war. She had kept hers as a souvenir, but some instinct made her clean and oil it regularly. Once you had been shot at, you were never comfortable unless you had a firearm someplace, she guessed.

She pressed the thumb release on the left side of the grip, behind the trigger, and drew the magazine out of the grip. There was a box of bullets in the case. She loaded seven into the magazine, pushing them in one by one against the spring, then slid the magazine back into the butt until she felt it lock. She worked the slide to chamber a round.

She turned around to see Becky-Ma standing in the doorway, staring at the gun.

She looked back at her mother in silence for a moment.

Then she ran out of the house and jumped into her car.

6.30 A.M.

The first stage contains approximately 25,000 kilograms of fuel. This will be used up in two minutes and thirty-five seconds.

Bern's Lincoln Continental was a joy to drive, a sleek, long-legged car that cruised at a hundred, effortlessly flying over the deserted roads of sleeping Virginia. In getting out of Washington, Luke felt he was leaving the nightmare behind, and his early-hours journey had the exhilarating air of an escape.

It was still dark when he arrived at Newport News and pulled into the small parking lot next to the closed airport building. No lights showed except the solitary bulb of a phone booth next to the entrance. He turned off his engine and listened to the silence. The night was clear, and the airfield was starlit. The parked planes seemed peculiarly still, like horses asleep on their feet.

He had been up more than twenty-four hours, and he felt desperately weary, but his mind was racing. He was in love with Billie. Now that he was two hundred miles away from her, he could admit that to himself. But what did it mean? Had he always loved her? Or was it a one-day infatuation, a repeat of the crush he had developed so quickly back in 1941? And what about Elspeth? Why had he married her? He had asked Billie that, and she had refused to answer. 'I'll ask Elspeth,' he had said.

He checked his watch. He had more than an hour until take-off. There was plenty of time. He got out of the car and went to the phone booth.

She picked up fast, as if she was already awake. The hotel operator advised her that the phone charge would be added to her bill, and she said: 'Sure, sure, put him on.'

Suddenly he felt awkward. 'Uh, good morning, Elspeth.'

'I'm so glad you called!' she said. 'I've been out of my mind with worry – what's happening?'

'I don't know where to begin.'

'Are you okay?'

'Yes, I'm fine, now. Basically, Anthony caused me to lose my memory, by giving me a combination of electric shock and drugs.'

'Good God. Why would he do a thing like that?'

'He says I'm a Soviet spy.'

'That's absurd.'

'It's what he told Billie.'

'So you've been with Billie?'

Luke heard the note of hostility in Elspeth's voice. 'She's been kind,' he said defensively. He recalled that he had asked Elspeth to come to Washington and help him, but she had refused.

Elspeth changed the subject. 'Where are you calling from?'

He hesitated. His enemies might easily have tapped Elspeth's phone. 'I don't really want to say, in case someone is listening.'

'All right, I understand. What are you going to do next?'

'I need to find out what it was that Anthony wanted me to forget.'

'How will you do that?'

'I'd rather not say over the phone.'

Her voice betrayed exasperation. 'Well, I'm sorry you can't tell me anything.'

'Matter of fact, I called to ask you some things.'

'Okay, fire away.'

'Why can't we have children?'

'We don't know. Last year, you went to a fertility specialist, but he couldn't find anything wrong. A few weeks ago, I saw a woman doctor in Atlanta. She ran some tests. We're waiting for the results.'

'Would you tell me how we came to get married?'

'I seduced you.'

'How?'

'I pretended to have soap in my eye, in order to make you kiss me. It's the oldest trick in the book, and I'm embarrassed that you fell for it.'

He could not tell whether she was being amusing, or cynical, or both. 'Tell me what the circumstances were, how I proposed.'

'Well, I didn't see you for years, then we met again

in 1954, in Washington,' she began. 'I was still with the CIA. You were working at the Jet Propulsion Laboratory in Pasadena, but you flew in for Peg's wedding. We were seated together at the breakfast.' She paused, remembering, and he waited patiently. When she resumed, her voice had softened. 'We talked and talked – it was as if thirteen years had never happened, and we were still a couple of college kids with all of life ahead of us. I had to leave early – I was conductor of the 16th Street Youth Orchestra, and we had a rehearsal. You came with me . . .'

1954

The children in the orchestra were all poor, and most of them were black. The rehearsal took place at a church hall in a slum neighbourhood. The instruments were begged, borrowed, and bought from pawnshops. They were rehearsing the overture from a Mozart opera, *The Marriage of Figaro*. Against the odds, they played well.

Elspeth was the reason. She was an exacting teacher, noticing every false note and rhythmic misstep, but she corrected her pupils with infinite patience. A tall figure in a yellow dress, she conducted the orchestra with enormous verve, her red hair flying, her long, elegant hands drawing the music from them with passionate gestures.

The rehearsal lasted two hours and Luke sat through the whole thing, mesmerized. He could see that all the boys were in love with Elspeth and all the girls wanted to be like her.

'These children have as much music in them as any rich kid with a Steinway in the drawing room,' she said in the car afterwards. 'But I get into lots of trouble.'

'Why, for God's sake?'

'I'm called a nigger-lover,' she said. 'And it's pretty much ended my career at the CIA.'

'I don't understand.'

'Anyone who treats Negroes like human beings is suspected of being a communist. So I'll never be more than a secretary. Not that it's a great loss. Women never get higher than case officer anyway.'

She took him to her place, a small, uncluttered apartment with a few pieces of angular modern furniture. Luke made martinis and Elspeth started to cook spaghetti in the tiny kitchen. Luke told her about his job.

'I'm so happy for you,' she said with generous enthusiasm. 'You always wanted to explore outer space. Even back at Harvard, when we were dating, you used to talk about it.'

He smiled. 'And in those days, most people thought it was a foolish dream of science-fiction writers.'

'I guess we still can't be sure it will happen.'

'I think we can,' he said seriously. 'The big problems were all solved by German scientists in the war. The Germans built rockets that could be fired in Holland and land on London.'

'I was there, I remember – we called them buzz-bombs.' She shuddered briefly. 'One nearly killed me. I was walking to my office in the middle of an air raid, because I had to brief an agent who was to be dropped into Belgium a few hours later. I heard a bomb go off behind me. It makes a horrible noise like *crump*, then there's the sound of breaking glass and masonry collapsing, and a kind of wind full of dust and little bits of stone. I knew that if I turned around to look, I'd panic and throw myself to the ground, and just curl up in a ball with my eyes shut. So I looked straight ahead and kept walking.'

Luke was moved by the picture of the young Elspeth walking through the dark streets as the bombs fell around her, and he felt grateful that she had survived. 'Brave woman,' he murmured.

She shrugged. 'I didn't feel brave, just scared.'

'What did you think about?'

'Can't you guess?'

He recalled that whenever she was idle she thought about math. 'Prime numbers?' he hazarded.

She laughed. 'Fibonacci's numbers.'

Luke nodded. The mathematician Fibonacci had imagined a pair of rabbits that produced two offspring every month, offspring that began to breed at the same rate one month after birth, and asked how many pairs of rabbits there would be after a year. The answer was 144, but the number of pairs of rabbits each month was the most famous sequence of numbers in mathematics: 1, 1, 2, 3, 5, 8, 13, 21, 34, 55, 89, 144 ... You could always work out the next number by adding up the previous two.

Elspeth said: 'By the time I got to my office, I had worked out the fortieth Fibonacci number.'

'Do you remember what it is?'

'Of course: one hundred and two million, three hundred and thirty-four thousand, one hundred and five. So, our missiles are based on the German buzz-bombs?'

'More on their V2 rocket, to be exact.' Luke was not supposed to talk about his work, but this was Elspeth, and anyway she probably had a higher security rating than he did. 'We're building a rocket that can take off in Arizona and explode in Moscow. And, if we can do that, we can fly to the moon.'

'So it's just the same thing on a larger scale?'

She showed more interest in rocketry than any other girl he had ever met. 'Yes. We need larger engines, more efficient fuel, better guidance systems, that kind of thing. None of these problems are insurmountable. Plus, those German scientists are working for us now.'

'I think I heard that.' She changed the subject. 'And what about life in general? Are you dating someone?'

'Not right now.' He had dated several girls since his break-up with Billie nine years ago, and had slept with some of them, but the truth – which he did not want to tell Elspeth – was that none had meant much.

There had been one woman he might have loved, a tall girl with brown eyes and wild hair. She had the kind of energy and *joie de vivre* that he loved about Billie. He had met her at Harvard while he was doing his doctorate. Late one evening, as they strolled together through Harvard Yard, she had taken his hands and said: 'I have a husband.' Then she had kissed him and walked away. That was the nearest he had come to giving his heart.

'How about you?' he asked Elspeth. 'Peg's married, Billie's already getting divorced – you've got some catching-up to do.'

'Oh, you know about us government girls.' The

phrase was a newspaper cliché. So many young women worked for the government in Washington that they outnumbered single men by five to one. Consequently they were stereotyped as sexually frustrated and desperate for dates. Luke did not believe Elspeth was like that, but if she wanted to evade his question, she was entitled.

She asked him to watch the stove while she freshened up. There was a big pan of spaghetti and a smaller one of bubbling tomato sauce. He took off his jacket and tie, then stirred the sauce with a wooden spoon. The martini had made him mellow, the food smelled good, and he was with a woman he really liked. He felt happy.

He heard Elspeth call out, with an uncharacteristic note of helplessness: 'Luke – could you come here?'

He stepped into the bathroom. Elspeth's dress hung on the back of the door, and she stood in a strapless peach-coloured brassiere and matching half-slip, stockings and shoes. Although she was wearing more clothes than if she had been on the beach, Luke found it unbearably sexy to see her in her underwear. Her hand was to her face. 'I got soap in my eye, damn it,' she said. 'Would you try to wash it out?'

Luke ran cold water into the washbasin. 'Bend down, get your face close to the bowl,' he said, encouraging her with his left hand between her shoulder blades. The pale skin of her back was soft and warm to his touch. He cupped water in his right hand and raised it to her eye.

'That helps,' she said.

He rinsed her eye again and again until she said the stinging had stopped. Then he stood her upright and patted her face dry with a clean towel. 'Your eye is a little bloodshot, but I guess it's okay,' he said.

'I must look a mess.'

'No.' He looked hard at her. Her eye was red and her hair on that side was wet in patches, but nevertheless she was as stunning as she had been on the day he first set eyes on her, more than a decade ago. 'You're absolutely beautiful.'

Her head was still tilted up, though he had stopped drying her face. Her lips were parted in a smile. It was the easiest thing in the world to kiss her. She kissed him back, hesitantly at first, then she put her hands behind his neck and pulled his face to hers and kissed him hard.

Her bra pressed against his chest. It should have been sexy, but the wiring was so stiff that it scratched his chest through the fine cotton of his shirt. After a moment he pulled away, feeling foolish. 'What?' she said.

He lightly touched the brassiere and said with a grin: 'It hurts.'

'You poor thing,' she said with mock pity.

She reached behind her back and unfastened the bra with a swift movement. It fell to the floor.

He had touched her breasts a few times, all those years ago, but he had never seen them. They were white and round, and the pale nipples were puckered with excitement. She put her arms around his neck and pressed her body to his. Her breasts were soft and warm. 'There,' she said. 'That's how it should feel.'

After a while he picked her up, stepped into the bedroom, and laid her on the bed. She kicked off her shoes. He touched the waistband of her half-slip and said: 'May I?'

She giggled. 'Oh, Luke, you're so polite!'

He grinned. It was kind of silly, but he did not know how else to be. She lifted her hips and he pulled off the slip. Her pink panties matched the rest of her underwear.

'Don't ask,' she said. 'Just take them off.'

When they made love it was slow and intense. She kept pulling his head to hers and kissing his face while he moved in and out of her. 'I've wanted this for so long,' she whispered into his ear; and then she cried out with pleasure, several times, and lay back, exhausted.

Soon Elspeth fell into a deep sleep, but Luke lay awake, thinking about his life.

He had always wanted a family. For him, happiness was a big, noisy house full of children and friends and pets. Yet here he was, thirty-three and single, and the years seemed to go by faster and faster. Since the war, his career had been his priority, he told himself. He had gone back to college, making up for the lost years. But that was not the real reason he was unmarried. The truth was that only two women had ever touched his heart – Billie and Elspeth. Billie had deceived him, but Elspeth was here beside him. He looked at her voluptuous body in the faint glow of the lights of Dupont Circle outside. Could there be anything better than spending every night like this, with a girl who was smart, brave as a lion, wonderful with children, and – on top of all that – stunningly beautiful?

At daybreak he got up and made coffee. He brought it into the bedroom on a tray, and found Elspeth sitting up in bed, looking sleepily delectable. She smiled happily at him.

'I have something to ask you,' he said. He sat on the edge of the bed and took her hand. 'Will you marry me?'

Her smile disappeared and she looked troubled. 'Oh, my God,' she said. 'Can I think about it?'

7 A.M.

The exhaust gases pass through the nozzle of the rocket like a cup of hot coffee being poured down the throat of a snowman.

Anthony drove up to the Jefferson Memorial with Larry sitting in the front seat between him and Pete. It was still dark, and the area was deserted. He turned the car around and parked so that its headlights would shine at any other car that came along.

The monument was a double circle of pillars with a domed roof. It stood on a high platform approached by steps at the rear. 'The statue is nineteen feet high and weighs ten thousand pounds,' he told Larry. 'It's made of bronze.'

'Where is it?'

'You can't see it from here, but it's inside those pillars.'

'We should have come in the daytime,' Larry whined.

Anthony had taken Larry out before. They had gone to the White House and the zoo and the Smithsonian. They would get hot dogs for lunch and eat ice cream in the afternoon, and Anthony would buy Larry a toy before taking him home again. They always had a good time. Anthony was fond of his godson. But today Larry knew something was wrong. It was too early and he wanted his mother and he probably sensed the tension in the car.

Anthony opened the door. 'Stay here a second, Larry, while I talk to Pete,' he said. The two men got out. Their breath misted in the cold air.

Anthony said to Pete: 'I'll wait here. You take the kid and show him the monument. Stay this side, so that she'll see him when she arrives.'

'Right.' Pete's voice was cold and abrupt.

'I hate this,' Anthony said. In truth, he was past caring. Larry was unhappy, and Billie was frantic with fear, but they would get over it, and he was not going to allow sentiment to get in his way. 'We're not going to harm the kid, or his mother,' he said, trying to reassure Pete. 'But she'll tell us where Luke has gone.'

'Then we give back the kid.'

'No.'

'We don't?' Pete's expression was concealed by the darkness, but his voice betrayed dismay. 'Why not?'

'In case we need more information from her later.'

Pete was troubled, but he would acquiesce, at least for now, Anthony thought. He opened the car door. 'Come on, Larry. Uncle Pete's going to show you the statue.'

Larry got out. With careful politeness he said: 'After we've seen it, I think I'd like to go home.'

Anthony's breath caught in his throat. Larry's bravery was almost too much. After a moment,

Anthony replied in a calm voice: 'We'll check with Mommy. Now go ahead.'

The child took Pete's hand and they walked around the monument toward the steps at the back. A minute later they appeared in front of the pillars, lit by the car's headlights.

Anthony checked his watch. Sixteen hours from now, the rocket would have taken off, and it would all be over, one way or another. Sixteen hours was a lot, plenty of time for Luke to do unlimited damage. Anthony had to catch him, fast.

Billie should be here by now. He suffered a pang of doubt. Surely she would come? She was too frightened and panicky to call the cops, or pull any kind of stunt, he felt certain.

He was right. A few moments later, another car arrived. Anthony could not see the colour, but it was a Ford Thunderbird. It parked twenty yards from Anthony's Cadillac and a small, slight figure jumped out, leaving the engine running.

'Hello, Billie,' said Anthony.

She looked from him to the monument and saw Pete and Larry up on the raised platform, looking into the circle. She stood frozen, staring.

Anthony walked toward her. 'Don't try anything dramatic – it would upset Larry.'

'Don't talk to me about upsetting him, you son of a bitch.' Her voice cracked with strain. She was near to tears.

'I had to do this.'

'Nobody *has* to do something like this.'

Her hostility was hardly surprising, but all the same her contempt stung him. He said: 'Do you know the quote from Thomas Jefferson that appears inside this monument, in letters two feet high? It says: "I have sworn upon the altar of God eternal hostility against every form of tyranny over the mind of man." That's why I'm doing it.'

'The hell with your motives. You've lost sight of whatever ideals you once had. Nothing good can survive this kind of treachery.'

It was a waste of time arguing with her. 'Where's Luke?' he said abruptly.

There was a long pause. At last she said: 'Luke caught a plane to Huntsville.'

Anthony breathed a deep sigh of satisfaction. He had what he needed.

He was also surprised at the answer. 'Why Huntsville?'

'It's where the army designs the rockets.'

'I know that. But why would he go there today? Florida is where it's all happening.'

'I don't know why.'

Anthony tried to read her face, but it was too dark. 'I think you're holding something back.'

'I don't care what you think. I'm going to take my son and leave.'

'No, you're not,' Anthony said. 'We're keeping him for a while.'

Billie's voice was a cry of anguish. 'Why? I've told you where Luke went!'

'There may be other ways you can help us.'

'It's not fair!'

'You'll live.' He turned away.

That was his mistake.

* * *

Billie had been half-expecting this.

As Anthony stepped towards his car, she rushed him. With her right shoulder, she hit him in the small of the back. She weighed only 120 pounds, and he had to be fifty pounds heavier, but she had surprise and rage on her side. He stumbled and fell forward, coming down on his hands and knees. He grunted with surprise and pain.

Billie took the Colt from her coat pocket.

As Anthony tried to get up, she charged him again, this time from the side. He crashed to the ground, rolling. As he came face up, she dropped to one knee beside his head and shoved the barrel of the gun forcefully into his mouth. She felt a tooth break.

He froze.

Deliberately, she moved the safety catch up to the firing position. She looked into his eyes and saw fear. He had not expected the gun. A trickle of blood appeared on his chin.

Billie looked up. Larry and the man with him were still gazing at the monument, unaware of the fracas. She returned her attention to Anthony. 'I'm going to take the gun out of your mouth,' she said, panting. 'If you move, I'll kill you. If you're still alive, you're going to call to your colleague and tell him what I say.' She took the gun out of Anthony's mouth and pointed it at his left eye. 'Now,' she said. 'Call him.'

Anthony hesitated.

She touched the barrel of the pistol to his eyelid.

'Pete!' he shouted.

Pete looked around. There was a pause. Pete said in a puzzled tone: 'Where are you?' Anthony and Billie were outside the range of the headlights.

Billie said: 'Tell him to stay where he is.'

Anthony said nothing. Billie pressed the gun into his eye. Anthony shouted: 'Stay where you are!'

Pete put his hand to his forehead, peering into the dark, looking for the source of the voice. 'What's happening?' he called. 'I can't see you.'

Billie shouted: 'Larry, this is Mom. Get in the T-bird!'

Pete grabbed Larry's arm.

'The man won't let me!' Larry screamed.

'Stay calm!' Billie yelled. 'Uncle Anthony's going to tell the man to let you go.' She pressed the gun barrel harder into Anthony's eye.

'All right!' Anthony cried. She eased the pressure. He shouted: 'Let the kid go!'

Pete said: 'Are you sure?'

'Do what I say, for Christ's sake – she's got a gun on me!'

'Okay!' Pete released Larry's arm.

Larry headed toward the back of the monument then reappeared, seconds later, at ground level. He ran towards Billie. 'Not this way,' she said, struggling to keep her voice calm. 'Get in the car, quickly.'

Larry ran to the Thunderbird and jumped in, slamming the door.

With a quick lashing movement, Billie hit Anthony on both sides of his face with the gun, as hard as she could. He cried out in pain, but before he could move she pushed the gun into his mouth again. He lay still, groaning. She said: 'Remember that if you're ever tempted to kidnap a child again.'

She stood up, withdrawing the gun from his mouth. 'Stay still,' she commanded. She backed towards her car, keeping the gun on him. She glanced up at the monument. Pete had not moved.

She got into her car.

Larry said: 'Have you got a gun?'

She stuffed the Colt inside her jacket. 'Are you okay?' she asked him.

He started to cry.

She shoved the gearshift into first and tore away.

8 A.M.

The smaller rockets that power the second, third and last stages use a solid fuel known as T17-E2, a polysulphide with ammonium perchlorate as oxidizer. Each rocket generates about 1,600 pounds of thrust in space.

Bern poured warm milk over Larry's cornflakes while Billie beat up an egg for french toast. They were giving their child comfort food, but Billie felt the adults needed comfort too. Larry was eating heartily and listening to the radio at the same time.

'I'm going to kill that son of a bitch Anthony,' Bern muttered, speaking quietly so that Larry would not hear. 'I swear to God, I'll fucking kill him.'

Billie's rage had evaporated. Pistol-whipping Anthony had gotten rid of it all. Now she was worried and frightened – partly for Larry, who had had a nasty fright, and partly for Luke. 'I'm afraid Anthony may try to kill Luke,' she said.

Bern dropped a knob of butter into a hot frying pan, then dipped a slice of white bread into the egg mixture Billie had made. 'Luke won't kill easy.'

'But he thinks he's escaped – he doesn't know I've told Anthony where he is.' While Bern fried the egg-soaked bread, Billie walked up and down the kitchen, biting her lip. 'Anthony is probably on his way to Huntsville now. Luke's on a slow plane. Anthony could get a MATS flight and be there first. I have to find a way to warn Luke.'

'Leave a message at the airport?'

'It's not reliable enough. I think I have to go there myself. There was a Viscount that left at nine, wasn't there? Where's that airline guide?'

'Right on the table.'

Billie picked it up. Flight 271 left Washington at exactly nine. Unlike Luke's flight, this one stopped only twice, landing at Huntsville four minutes before noon. Luke's flight did not land until two twenty-three. She could be waiting for him at the airport. 'I can do it,' she said.

'Then you should.'

Billie hesitated, looking at Larry, torn by conflicting urges.

Bern read her mind. 'He'll be okay.'

'I know, but I don't want to leave him, today of all days.'

'I'll take care of him.'

'Would you keep him out of school?'

'Yes, I think that'd be a good idea, at least for today.'

Larry said: 'I've finished my cornflakes.'

Bern said: 'Then you must be just about ready for some french toast.' He slid a slice on to a plate. 'Want some maple syrup with that?'

'Yeah.'

'Yes, what?'

'Yes, please.'

Bern poured syrup from a bottle.

Billie sat opposite her son and said: 'I want you to skip school today.'

'But I'll miss swimming!' he protested.

'Maybe Daddy will take you swimming.'

'But I'm not sick!'

'I know, honey, but you had kind of a tiring morning, and you need to rest.' Larry's protests reassured Billie. He seemed to be recovering fast. All the same, she would not be comfortable letting him go to school, not until this whole business was over.

But she could leave him with his father. Bern was a trained agent and could protect his kid from just about anything. She made a decision. She would go to Huntsville. 'Have a fun day with Daddy and maybe you'll go to school tomorrow, okay?'

'Okay.'

'Mommie has to go now.' She did not want to make a drama of saying goodbye, for that would only scare the child. 'I'll see you later,' she said casually.

As she went out, she heard Bern say: 'I bet you couldn't eat another slice of that french toast.'

'I could too!' Larry replied.

Billie closed the door.

PART 5

10.45 A.M.

The missile will take off vertically, then be tilted into a trajectory inclined forty degrees to the horizon. The first stage is guided, during powered flight, by aerodynamic tail surfaces and by movable carbon vanes in the engine exhaust jet.

Luke fell asleep as soon as he had fastened his seat belt, and he was unaware of the take-off from Newport News. He slept heavily while the plane was in the air, but woke up every time it bumped down at yet another airstrip on its stop-go flight west across Virginia and North Carolina. Each time his eyes opened he felt a rush of anxiety, and checked his watch to see how many hours and minutes were left until the launch. He would fidget in his seat while the little aircraft taxied across the apron. A few people would leave, one or two more would get on, and the plane would take off again. It was like riding the bus.

The plane refuelled at Winston-Salem, and the passengers got off for a few minutes. Luke called Redstone Arsenal from the terminal and got his secretary, Marigold Clark, on the phone.

'Dr Lucas!' she said. 'Are you okay?'

'I'm fine, but I only have a minute or two. Is the launch still scheduled for tonight?'

'Yes, ten-thirty.'

'I'm on my way to Huntsville – my plane lands at two twenty-three. I'm trying to figure out why I went there on Monday.'

'You still don't have your memory back?'

'No. Now, you don't know why I made that trip.'

'Like I said, you didn't tell me.'

'What did I do there?'

'Well, now, let me see. I met you at the airport in an army car and brought you here to the base. You went into the Computation Lab, then drove yourself down to the south end.'

'What's there, at the south end?'

'The static test pads. I imagine you went into the Engineering Building – you sometimes work there – but I don't know for sure, because I wasn't with you.'

'And then?'

'You asked me to drive you to your home.' Luke heard a prim note enter her voice. 'I waited in the car while you stepped inside for a minute or two. Then I took you to the airport.'

'That's it?'

'That's all I know.'

Luke grunted with frustration. He had felt sure Marigold would come up with some clue.

Desperately, he cast about for another line of questioning. 'How did I look?'

'Okay, but your mind was someplace else. Preoccupied, that's the word I'm searching for. I figured you were worried about something. Happens all the time with you scientists. I don't let it trouble me.'

'Wearing my usual clothes?'

'One of them nice tweed jackets.'

'Carrying anything?'

'Just your little suitcase. Oh, and a file.'

Luke stopped breathing for a moment. 'A file?' he said. He swallowed.

A stewardess interrupted him. 'Time to board the aircraft, please, Dr Lucas.'

He covered the mouthpiece with his hand and said: 'Just one minute.' Then he said to Marigold: 'Was it any special kind of file?'

'A standard army file folder, thin cardboard, buff-coloured, large enough to hold business letters.'

'Any idea what was in it?'

'Just papers, it looked like.'

Luke tried to breathe normally. 'How many sheets of paper? One, ten, a hundred?'

'Maybe fifteen or twenty, I guess.'

'Did you happen to see what was on the sheets?'

'No, sir, you didn't take them out.'

'And did I still have this file when you took me to the airport?'

There was a silence at the other end.

The stewardess returned. 'Dr Lucas, if you won't board the plane, we'll have to go without you.'

'I'm coming, I'm coming.' He began to repeat his question to Marigold. 'Did I still have the file—'

'I heard you,' she interrupted. 'I'm trying to remember.'

He bit his lip. 'Take your time.'

'Whether you had it at the house, I can't tell.'

'But at the airport?'

'You know, I don't believe you had it then. I'm picturing you walking away from me into the terminal, and I see you have your bag in one hand, and in the other . . . nothing.'

'Are you sure?'

'Yes, now I am. You must have left that file here somewhere, either at the base or at home.'

Luke's mind was racing. The file was the reason for his trip to Huntsville, he felt sure. It contained the secret he had found out, the one that Anthony was so desperate for him to forget. Maybe it was a Xerox copy of the original, and he had stashed it somewhere for safe keeping. That was why he had asked Marigold not to tell anyone of his visit. It seemed ultra-cautious, but not doubt he had learned such habits in the war.

Now, if he could find the file, he could discover the secret.

The stewardess had abandoned him, and he saw her running across the tarmac. The plane's propellers were already turning.

'I think that file could be very important,' he told Marigold. 'Could you look around and see if it's there?'

'My lord, Dr Lucas, this is the army! Don't you know there must be a million of them buff-coloured file folders here? How would I know which is the one you were carrying?'

'Just check around, see if there's one someplace

where it shouldn't be. As soon as I land at Huntsville, I'll go to the house and search there. Then, if I don't find it, I'll come to the base.' Luke hung up and ran for the plane.

11 A.M.

The flight plan is programmed in advance. During flight, signals telemetered to the computer activate the guidance system to keep it on course.

The MATS flight to Huntsville was full of generals. Redstone Arsenal did more than design space rockets. It was the headquarters of the Army Ordnance Missile Command. Anthony, who kept track of this kind of thing, knew that a whole range of weapons were being developed and tested at the base – from the baseball-bat-sized Redeye, for ground troops to use against enemy aircraft, up to the huge surface-to-surface Honest John. The base undoubtedly saw a lot of brass.

Anthony wore sunglasses to conceal the two black eyes Billie had given him. His lip had stopped bleeding, and the broken tooth showed only when he talked. Despite his injuries, he felt energized: Luke was within his grasp.

Should he simply take the first opportunity to kill him? It was temptingly simple. But he worried that he did not know exactly what Luke was up to. He had to make a decision. However, by the time he boarded the plane he had been awake for forty-eight hours straight, and he fell asleep. He dreamed he was twenty-one again, and there were new leaves on the tall trees in Harvard Yard, and a life full of glorious possibilities stretched before him like an open road. Next thing he knew, Pete was shaking him as a corporal opened the aircraft door, and he woke up inhaling a warm Alabama breeze.

Huntsville had a civilian airport, but this was not it. MATS flights came down on the airstrip within Redstone Arsenal. The terminal building was a small wooden hut, the tower an open steel gantry with a one-room flight-control post on top.

Anthony shook his head to clear it as he walked across the parched grass. He was carrying the small bag that held his gun, a false passport, and five thousand dollars in cash, the emergency kit without which he never caught a plane.

Adrenalin enlivened him. In the next few hours he would kill a man, for the first time since the war. His stomach tensed as he thought of it. Where would he do it? One option was to wait for Luke at Huntsville Airport, follow him as he left, and gun him down on the road somewhere. But that was high-risk. Luke might well spot the tail and escape. He would never be an easy target. He could yet slip away, if Anthony were not extremely careful.

It might be best to find out where Luke was planning to go, then get there ahead and ambush him. 'I'm going to make some inquiries at the base,' he said to Pete. 'I want you to go to the airport and keep watch. If Luke arrives, or anything else happens, try to reach me here.'

At the edge of the airstrip, a young man in the uniform of a lieutenant waited with a card that read: 'Mr Carroll, State Department.' Anthony shook his hand. 'Colonel Hickam's compliments, sir,' the lieutenant said formally. 'As requested by the State Department, we have provided you with a car.' He pointed to an olive-drab Ford.

'That'll be fine,' Anthony said. He had called the base before catching his plane, brazenly pretending he was under orders from CIA Director Alan Dulles, and demanded army cooperation for a vital mission the details of which were classified. It had worked: this lieutenant seemed eager to please.

'Colonel Hickam would be glad if you would drop by headquarters at your convenience.' The lieutenant handed Anthony a map. The base was enormous, Anthony realized. It stretched several miles south, all the way to the Tennessee River. 'The headquarters building is marked on the map,' the soldier went on. 'And we have a message, asking you to call Mr Carl Hobart in Washington.'

'Thank you, Lieutenant. Where's Dr Claude Lucas's office?'

'That'll be the Computation Laboratory.' He took out a pencil and made a mark on the map. 'But all those guys are down to Cape Canaveral this week.'

'Does Dr Lucas have a secretary?'

'Yes – Mrs Marigold Clark.'

She might know Luke's movements. 'Good.

Lieutenant, this is my colleague Pete Maxell. He needs to get to the civilian airport to meet a flight.'

'I'd be glad to drive him there, sir.'

'I appreciate that. If he needs to reach me here at the base, what's the best way?'

The lieutenant looked at Pete. 'Sir, you could always leave a message at Colonel Hickam's office, and I would try to get it to Mr Carroll.'

'Good enough,' Anthony said decisively. 'Let's get going.'

He got into the Ford, checked the map, and started out. It was a typical army base. Arrow-straight roads ran through rough woodland broken by neat rectangles of lawn close-cropped like a conscript's haircut. The buildings were all flat-roofed structures of tan brick. It was well signposted, and he easily found the Computation Lab, a T-shaped building two storeys high. Anthony wondered why they needed so much space to make calculations, then realized they must have a powerful computer in there.

He parked outside and thought for a few moments. He had a simple question to ask: where in Huntsville did Luke plan to go? Marigold probably knew, but she would be defensive of Luke and wary of a stranger, especially one with two black eyes. However, she had been left behind here when most of the people she worked with had gone to Cape Canaveral for the big event, so she was probably also feeling lonely and bored.

He went into the building. In an outer office were three small desks, each with a typewriter. Two were vacant. The third was occupied by a Negro woman of about fifty wearing spectacles with diamanté rims, and a flowered cotton dress printed with daisies. 'Good afternoon,' he said.

She looked up. He took off his sunglasses. Her eyes widened in surprise at his appearance. 'Hello! How can I help you?'

With mock sincerity, he said: 'Ma'am, I'm looking for a wife who won't beat me up.'

Marigold burst out laughing.

Anthony pulled up a chair and sat to one side of her desk. 'I'm from Colonel Hickam's office,' he said. 'I'm looking for Marigold Clark. Where is she?'

'That's me.'

'Oh, no. The Miz Clark I'm looking for is a grown woman. You're just a young girl.'

'Now, you stop your jive,' she said, but she smiled broadly.

'Dr Lucas is on his way here – I guess you knew that.'

'He called me this morning.'

'What time do you expect him?'

'His plane lands at two twenty-three.'

That was useful. 'So he'll be here around three.'

'Not necessarily.'

Ah. 'Why not?'

She gave him what he wanted. 'Dr Lucas said he's going home first, then he'll stop by here.'

That was perfect. Anthony could hardly believe his luck. Luke was going from the airport straight to his house. Anthony could go there and wait, then shoot Luke as soon as he walked in the door. There would be no witnesses. If he used the silencer, no one would even hear a shot. Anthony would leave the body where it fell and drive away. With Elspeth in Florida, the corpse might not be found for days.

'Thank you,' he said to Marigold. He stood up. 'It was a pleasure to meet you.' He left the room before she could ask his name.

He returned to the car and drove to the headquarters building, a long three-storey monolith that looked like a prison. He found Colonel Hickam's office. The colonel was out, but a sergeant showed him to an empty room with a phone.

He called Q Building, but did not speak to his boss, Carl Hobart. Instead he asked for Carl's superior, George Cooperman. 'What's up, George?' he said.

'Did you shoot at someone last night?' said Cooperman, his smoker's voice sounding even more gravelly than usual.

With an effort, Anthony put on the swashbuckling persona that appealed to Cooperman. 'Aw, hell, who told you that?'

'Some colonel from the Pentagon called Tom Ealy in the Director's office, and Ealy told Carl Hobart, who had an orgasm.'

'There's no proof. I picked up all the slugs.'

'This colonel found a hole in the fucking wall about nine millimetres wide and he guessed what caused it. Did you hit anybody?'

'Unfortunately not.'

'You're in Huntsville now, right?'

'Yeah.'

'You're supposed to come back immediately.'

'Then it's a good thing I didn't talk to you.'

'Listen, Anthony, I always cut you as much slack as I can, because you get results. But I can't do any more for you on this one. You're on your own from here, buddy.'

'That's how I like it.'

'Good luck.'

Anthony hung up and sat staring at the phone. He did not have much more time. His Billy the Kid act was wearing thin. He could disobey orders for only so long. He needed to wrap this up fast.

He called Cape Canaveral and got Elspeth on the phone. 'Have you talked to Luke?' he asked her.

'He called me at six-thirty this morning.' She sounded shaky.

'Where from?'

'He wouldn't say where he was, where he was going, or what he intended to do, because he was afraid my phone might be tapped. But he told me you were responsible for his amnesia.'

'He's on his way to Huntsville. I'm at Redstone Arsenal now. I'm going to your house to wait for him there. Will I be able to get in?'

She answered with another question. 'Are you still trying to protect him?'

'Of course.'

'Will he be okay?'

'All I can do is my best.'

There was a moment's pause, then she said: 'There's a key under the bougainvillea pot in the back yard.'

'Thanks.'

'Take care of Luke, won't you?'

'I said I would do my best!'

'Don't snap at me,' she said with some of her more usual spirit.

'I'll take care of him.' He hung up.

He stood up to go, and the phone rang.

He wondered whether to answer. It might be Hobart. But Hobart did not know he was in Colonel Hickam's office. Only Pete knew that . . . he thought.

He picked up.

It was Pete. 'Dr Josephson's here!' he said.

'Shit.' Anthony had felt sure she was out of the picture. 'She just got off a plane?'

'Yeah, it must have been a faster flight than the one Lucas is on. She's sitting in the terminal building, like she's waiting.'

'For him,' Anthony said decisively. 'Damn her. She's come to warn him that we're here. You have to get her out of there.'

'How?'

'I don't care – just get rid of her!'

12 NOON

The Explorer's orbit will be at thirty-four degrees to the equator.
Relative to the Earth's surface, it will head south-east across
the Atlantic Ocean to the southern tip of Africa, then north-
east across the Indian Ocean and Indonesia to the Pacific.

Huntsville Airport was small but busy. The single
terminal building had a Hertz desk, some vending
machines and a row of phone booths. As soon as she
arrived, Billie checked on Luke's flight and learned it
was running almost an hour late, and would land in
Huntsville at three fifteen. She had three hours to
kill.

She got a candy bar and a Dr Pepper from a
machine. She put down the attaché case that contained
her Colt and stood leaning against a wall, thinking.
How was she going to handle this? As soon as she saw
Luke, she would warn him that Anthony was here.
Luke would be on his guard, and could take
precautions – but he could not go into hiding. He had
to find out what he had done here on Monday, and
for that he would need to move around. He had to
take risks. Could she do anything to help protect him?

As she was racking her brains, a girl in Capital

Airlines uniform approached her. 'Are you Dr Josephson?'

'Yes.'

'I have a phone message for you.' She handed over an envelope.

Billie frowned. Who knew she was here? 'Thanks,' she muttered, tearing it open.

'You're very welcome. Please let us know if there's any way we can be of further service.'

Billie looked up and smiled. She had forgotten how polite people were in the South. 'I sure will,' she said. 'I appreciate that.'

The girl walked away, and Billie read her message: 'Please call Dr Lucas on Huntsville JE 6–4231.'

She was bewildered. Could Luke be here already? And how had he known she would be here?

There was only one way to find out. She dropped her pop bottle in a trash can and found a payphone.

The number she dialled answered immediately, and a man's voice said: 'Components test lab.'

It sounded as if Luke was already at Redstone Arsenal. How had he done that trick? She said: 'Dr Claude Lucas, please.'

'Just one moment.' After a pause the man came back. 'Dr Lucas stepped out for a minute. Who is this, please?'

'Dr Bilhah Josephson, I have a message to call him on this number.'

The man's tone changed immediately. 'Oh, Dr Josephson, I'm so glad we found you! Dr Lucas is very concerned to contact you.'

'What's he doing here? I thought he was still in the air.'

'Army security pulled him off the plane at Norfolk, Virginia, and laid on a special flight. He's been here more than an hour.'

She felt relieved he was safe, but at the same time she was puzzled. 'What's he doing there?'

'I think you know.'

'Okay, I guess I do. How is it going?'

'Fine – but I can't give you details, especially over the phone. Can you get yourself down to us?'

'Where are you?'

'The lab is about an hour out of town on the Chattanooga road. I could send an army driver to pick you up, but it would be quicker for you to get a cab, or rent a car.'

Billie took a notebook out of her bag. 'Give me directions.' Then, remembering her Southern manners, she added: 'If you would, please.'

1 P.M.

*The first-stage engine must be switched off sharply, and
separated immediately, otherwise gradual thrust decay could
cause the first stage to catch up with the second and misalign
it. As soon as pressure drops in the fuel lines, the valves are
closed, and the first stage is separated five seconds later by
detonation of spring-loaded explosive bolts. The springs
increase the speed of the second stage by 2.6 feet per second,
ensuring that it separates cleanly.*

Anthony knew the way to Luke's house. He had spent
a weekend there, a couple of years back, soon after
Luke and Elspeth had moved from Pasadena. He
reached the place in fifteen minutes. It was on Echols
Hill, a street of large older homes a couple of blocks
from downtown. Anthony parked around the corner,
so that Luke would not be forewarned that he had a
visitor.

He walked back to the house. He should have felt
quietly confident. He held all the cards: surprise, time,
and a gun. But instead he was nauseated with
apprehension. Twice already he had felt he had Luke
in his hands, and Luke had eluded him.

He still did not know why Luke had chosen to fly

to Huntsville rather than Cape Canaveral. This inexplicable decision suggested there was something Anthony did not know about, an unpleasant surprise that might leap out at him at any moment.

The house was a white turn-of-the-century Colonial with a pillared verandah. It was too grand for an army boffin, but Luke had never pretended to live on what he made as a scientist. Anthony opened a gate in a low wall and entered the yard. The place would have been easy to break into, but that would not be necessary. He circled around to the back. By the kitchen door was a terracotta planter with bougainvillea spilling out of it, and under the pot was a big iron key.

Anthony let himself in.

The outside was pleasantly old-fashioned, but the interior was right up to the minute. Elspeth had every kind of gadget in the kitchen. There was a big hall decorated in bright pastel colours, a living room with a console TV and a record player, and a dining room with modern splayed-leg chairs and sideboards. Anthony preferred traditional furniture, but he had to admit this was stylish.

As he stood in the living room, staring at a curved couch upholstered in pink vinyl, he recalled vividly the weekend he had spent here. He had known within an hour that the marriage was in trouble. Elspeth had been flirtatious, always a sign of tension with her, and Luke had adopted a forced air of cheery hospitality that was quite uncharacteristic.

They had given a cocktail party on the Saturday night and invited the young crowd from Redstone

Arsenal. This room had been full of badly dressed scientists talking about rockets, junior officers discussing their prospects for promotion, and pretty women gossiping about the intrigues of life on a military base. The gramophone had been stacked with long-playing jazz records, but that night the music had sounded plaintive, not joyous. Luke and Elspeth had got drunk – a rare thing for both of them – and Elspeth had grown more flirty while Luke became quieter and quieter. Anthony had found it painful to see two people he liked and admired so unhappy, and the whole weekend had depressed him.

And now the long drama of their interwoven lives was playing out its inevitable conclusion.

Anthony decided to search the house. He did not know what he was looking for. But he might turn up something that would give him a clue to why Luke was coming here, and warn him of unforeseen danger. He put on a pair of rubber gloves that he found in the kitchen. There would be a murder investigation eventually, and he did not want to leave fingerprints.

He started in the study, a small room lined with shelves full of scientific books. He sat at Luke's desk, which looked out on to the back yard, and opened the drawers.

Over the next two hours, he searched the house from top to bottom. He found nothing.

He looked in every pocket of every suit in Luke's well-filled closet. He opened every book in the study to check for papers concealed between the pages. He took the lids off every piece of Tupperware in the enormous double-door refrigerator. He went into the garage and searched the handsome black Chrysler 300C – the fastest stock sedan in the world, according to the newspapers – from its streamlined headlamps to its rocket-ship tail fins.

He learned a few intimate secrets along the way. Elspeth coloured her hair, used sleeping pills that were prescribed by a doctor, and suffered from constipation. Luke used a dandruff shampoo and subscribed to *Playboy* magazine.

There was a small pile of mail on a table in the hall – put there by the maid, presumably. Anthony shuffled the letters, but there was nothing of interest: a flyer from a supermarket, *Newsweek*, a postcard from Ron and Monica in Hawaii, envelopes with the cellophane address window that indicated a business letter.

The search had been fruitless. He still did not know what Luke might have up his sleeve.

He went into the living room. He chose a position from which he could see through the venetian blinds to the front yard, and also through the open door into the hallway. He sat down on the pink vinyl couch.

He took out his gun, checked that it was fully loaded, and fitted the silencer.

He tried to reassure himself by imagining the scene ahead. He would see Luke arrive, probably in a taxicab from the airport. He would watch him walk into the front yard, take out his key, and open his own front door. Luke would step into the hall, close the door, then head for the kitchen. As he passed the living room, he would glance through the open doorway and see Anthony on the couch. He would stop, raise his eyebrows in surprise, and open his mouth to speak. In his mind would be some phrase such as: 'Anthony? What the hell—?' But he would never say the words. His eyes would drop to the gun held perfectly level in Anthony's lap, and he would know his fate a split second before it happened.

Then Anthony would shoot him dead.

3 P.M.

A system of compressed-air nozzles, mounted in the tail of the instrument compartment, will control the tilt of the nose section when in space.

Billie was lost.

She had known it for half an hour. Leaving the airport in a rented Ford a few minutes before one o'clock, she had driven into the centre of Huntsville, then taken Highway 59 toward Chattanooga. She had wondered why the components testing laboratory should be an hour away from the base, and imagined it might be for safety reasons: perhaps there was a danger that components would explode under testing. But she had not thought very hard about it.

Her directions were to take a country road to the right exactly thirty-five miles from Huntsville. She had zeroed her trip meter on Main Street, but when the revolving figures reached 35 she could not see a right turn. Feeling only mildly anxious, she went on and took the next road on the right, a couple of miles farther.

The directions, which had seemed so precise as she wrote them down, never quite corresponded with the roads on which she found herself, and her anxiety grew, but she carried on, making the likeliest interpretation. Obviously, she thought, the man she had spoken to had not been as reliable as he had sounded. She wished she had been able to speak to Luke personally.

The landscape gradually became wilder, the farmhouses ramshackle, the roads potholed and the fences broken-down. The disparity between what she expected and the landmarks she saw around her grew until she threw up her hands in despair and admitted to herself that she could be anywhere. She was furious with herself and with the fool who had given her directions.

She turned around and tried to find her way back, but soon she was on unfamiliar roads again. She began to wonder if she were going around in a huge circle. She stopped beside a field where a Negro in dungarees and a straw hat was turning the hard earth with a walking plough. She stopped her car and spoke to him. 'I'm looking for the components testing lab of Redstone Arsenal,' she said.

He looked surprised. 'The army base? That's all the way back to Huntsville and across to the other side of town.'

'But they have some kind of facility out this way.'

'Not that I ever see.'

This was hopeless. She would have to call the lab and ask for fresh directions. 'Can I use your phone?'

'Ain't got no phone.'

She was about to ask him where the nearest pay

phone was when she saw a look of fear in his eyes. She realized that she was putting him in a situation that made him anxious: alone in a field with a white woman who was not making sense. She quickly thanked him and drove away.

After a couple of miles, she came upon a dilapidated feed store with a payphone outside. She pulled over. She still had Luke's message with the phone number. She put a dime in the slot and dialled.

The phone was answered immediately. A young man's voice said: 'Hello?'

'May I speak to Dr Claude Lucas?' she said.

'You got the wrong number, honey.'

Can't I do anything right? she thought desperately. 'Isn't this Huntsville JE 6–4231?'

There was a pause. 'Yep, that's what it says on the dial.'

She double-checked the number on the message. She had not made a mistake. 'I was trying to call the components testing lab.'

'Well, you reached a payphone in Huntsville airport.'

'A *pay*phone?'

'Yes, mam.'

Billie began to realize she had been hoodwinked.

The voice at the other end of the line went on: 'I'm about to call my Mom and tell her to come get me, and when I pick up the phone I hear you asking for some guy named Claude.'

'Shit!' Billie said. She slammed the phone down, furious with herself for being so gullible.

Luke had not been taken off his plane in Norfolk and put on an army flight, she realized, and he was not at the components testing lab, wherever that was. That whole story was a lie designed to get her out of the way – and it had succeeded. She looked at her watch. Luke must have landed by now. Anthony had been waiting for him – and she might as well have been in Washington, for all the use she had been.

With despair in her heart, she wondered if Luke were still alive.

If he was, maybe she could still warn him. It was too late to leave a message at the airport, but there must be someone she could call. She racked her brains. Luke had a secretary at the base, she remembered; a name like a flower . . .

Marigold.

She called Redstone Arsenal and asked to speak to Dr Lucas's secretary. A woman with a slow Alabama voice came on the line. 'Computation Laboratory, how may I help you?'

'Is that Marigold?'

'Yes.'

'I'm Dr Josephson, a friend of Dr Lucas.'

'Yes.' She sounded suspicious.

Billie wanted this woman to trust her. 'We've spoken before, I think. My first name is Billie.'

'Oh, sure, I remember. How are you?'

'Worried. I need to get a message to Luke urgently. Is he with you?'

'No, mam. He went to his house.'

'What's he doing there?'

'Looking for a file folder.'

'A file?' Billie saw the significance of that immediately. 'A file he left here on Monday, maybe?'

'I don't know nothing about that,' said Marigold.

Of course, Luke had told Marigold to keep his Monday visit secret. But none of that was important now. 'If you see Luke, or if he calls you, would you please give him a message from me?'

'Of course.'

'Tell him Anthony is in town.'

'That's all?'

'He'll understand. Marigold . . . I hesitate to say this, in case you think I'm some kind of nut, but I guess I should. I believe Luke is in danger.'

'From this Anthony?'

'Yes. Do you believe me?'

'Stranger things have happened. Is this all tied up with him losing his memory?'

'Yes. If you get that message to him, it could save his life. I mean it.'

'I'll do what I can, Doctor.'

'Thank you.' Billie hung up.

Was there anyone else Luke might talk to? She thought of Elspeth.

She called the operator and asked for Cape Canaveral.

3.45 P.M.

After discarding the burnt-out first stage, the missile will coast through a vacuum trajectory while the spatial-attitude-control system aligns it so that it is exactly horizontal with respect to the Earth's surface.

Everyone was bad-tempered at Cape Canaveral. The Pentagon had ordered a security alert. Arriving this morning, eager to get to work on the final checks for the all-important rocket launch, staff had been made to wait in line at the gate. Some had been there for three hours in the Florida sun. Gas tanks had run dry, radiators had boiled over, air-conditioners had failed, and engines had stalled, then refused to restart. Every car had been searched – hoods lifted, golf bags taken out of trunks, spare wheels removed from covers. Tempers frayed as all briefcases were opened, each lunch pail unpacked, and every woman's purse dumped out on to a trestle table so that Colonel Hide's military police could paw through her lipsticks, love letters, tampons and Rolaids.

But that was not the end of it. When workers reached their laboratories and offices and engineering shops, they were disrupted all over again by teams of men who went through their drawers and filing cabinets, looked inside their oscillators and vacuum cabinets, and took the inspection plates off their machine tools. 'We're trying to launch a goddamn rocket here,' people said again and again, but the security men just gritted their teeth and carried on. Despite the disruption, the launch was still scheduled for 10.30 p.m.

Elspeth was glad of the upset. It meant nobody noticed she was too distraught to do her job. She made mistakes in her timetable and produced her updates late, but Willy Fredrickson was too distracted to reprimand her. She did not know where Luke was and she no longer felt sure she could trust Anthony.

When the phone at her desk rang a few minutes before four o'clock, her heart seemed to stop.

She snatched up the handset. 'Yes?'

'This is Billie.'

'*Billie?*' Elspeth was taken by surprise. 'Where are you?'

'I'm in Huntsville, trying to contact Luke.'

'What's he doing there?'

'Looking for a file he left here on Monday.'

Elspeth's jaw dropped. 'He went to Huntsville on Monday? I didn't know that.'

'Nobody knew, except Marigold. Elspeth, do you understand what's going on?'

She laughed humourlessly. 'I thought I did . . . but not any more.'

'I believe Luke's life is in danger.'

'What makes you say so?'

'Anthony shot at him in Washington last night.'

Elspeth went cold. 'Oh, my God.'

'It's too complicated to explain right now. If Luke calls you, will you tell him that Anthony is in Huntsville?'

Elspeth was trying to recover from the shock. 'Uh . . . sure, of course I will.'

'It could save his life.'

'I understand. Billie . . . one more thing.'

'Yeah.'

'Look after Luke, won't you?'

There was a pause. 'What do you mean?' Billie asked. 'You sound like you're going to die.'

Elspeth did not answer. After a moment, she broke the connection.

A sob came to her throat. She fought fiercely to control herself. Tears would not help anyone, she told herself severely. She made herself calm.

Then she dialled her home in Huntsville.

4 P.M.

Explorer's elliptical orbit will take it as far as 1,800 miles into space and swing it back within 187 miles of the Earth's surface. Orbiting speed of the satellite is 18,000 miles per hour.

Anthony heard a car. He looked out of the front window of Luke's house and saw a Huntsville taxicab pull up at the curb. He thumbed the safety catch on his gun. His mouth went dry.

The phone rang.

It was on one of the triangular side tables at the ends of the curved couch. Anthony stared at it in horror. It rang a second time. He was paralysed by indecision. He looked out of the window and saw Luke getting out of the cab. The call could be trivial, nothing, a wrong number. Or it could be vital information.

Terror bubbled up inside him. He could not answer the phone and shoot someone at the same time.

The phone rang a third time. Panicking, he snatched it up. 'Yes?'

'This is Elspeth.'

'What? What?'

Her voice was low and strained. 'He's looking for a file he stashed in Huntsville on Monday.'

Anthony understood in a flash. Luke had made not one but two copies of the blueprints he had found on Sunday. One set he had brought to Washington, intending to take them to the Pentagon – but Anthony had intercepted him, and Anthony now had those copies. Unfortunately, he had not imagined there might be a second set, hidden somewhere as a precaution. He had forgotten that Luke was a Resistance veteran, security-conscious to the point of paranoia. 'Who else knows about this?'

'His secretary, Marigold. And Billie Josephson – she told me. There may be others.'

Luke was paying the driver. Anthony was running out of time. 'I have to have that file,' he said to Elspeth.

'That's what I thought.'

'It's not here – I just searched the house from top to bottom.'

'Then it must be at the base.'

'I'll have to follow him while he looks for it.'

Luke was approaching the front door.

'I'm out of time,' Anthony said, and he slammed down the phone.

He heard Luke's key scrape in the lock as he ran through the hall and into the kitchen. He went out the back door and closed it softly. The key was still in the outside of the lock. He turned it silently, bent down, and slipped it under the flowerpot.

He dropped to the ground and crawled along the verandah, keeping close to the house and below window level. In that position he turned the corner and reached the front of the house. From here to the street there was no cover. He just had to take a chance.

It seemed best to make a break for it while Luke was putting down his bag and hanging up his coat. He was less likely to look out of the window now.

Gritting his teeth, Anthony stepped forward.

He walked quickly to the gate, resisting the temptation to look behind him, expecting at every second to hear Luke shout: 'Hey! Stop! Stop, or I shoot!'

Nothing happened.

He reached the street and walked away.

4.30 P.M.

The satellite contains two tiny radio transmitters powered by mercury batteries no bigger than flashlight batteries. Each transmitter carries four simultaneous channels of telemetry.

On top of the console TV in the living room, next to a bamboo lamp, was a matching bamboo picture frame containing a colour photograph. It showed a strikingly beautiful redhead in an ivory silk wedding dress. Beside her, wearing a grey cutaway and a yellow vest, was Luke.

He studied Elspeth in the picture. She could have been a movie star. She was tall and elegant, with a voluptuous figure. Lucky man, he thought, to be marrying her.

He did not like the house so much. When he had first seen the outside, and the wisteria climbing the pillars of the shady verandah, it had gladdened his heart. But the inside was all hard edges and shiny surfaces and bright paint. Everything was too neat. He knew, suddenly, that he liked to live in a house where the books spilled off the shelves, and the dog was asleep right across the hallway, and there were coffee rings on the piano, and a tricycle stood upside down in the driveway and had to be moved before you could put your car in the garage.

No kids lived in this house. There were no pets, either. Nothing ever got messed up. It was like an advertisement in a women's magazine, or the set of a television comedy. It made him feel that the people who appeared in these rooms were actors.

He began to search. A buff-coloured army file folder should be easy enough to find – unless he had removed the contents and thrown away the folder. He sat at the desk in the study – *his* study – and looked through the drawers. He found nothing of significance.

He went upstairs.

He spent a few seconds looking at the big double bed with the yellow-and-blue covers. It was hard to believe that he shared that bed every night with the ravishing creature in the wedding photo.

He opened the closet and saw, with a shock of pleasure, the rack of navy blue and grey suits and tweed sport coats, the shirts in bengal stripes and tattersall checks, the stacked sweaters and the polished shoes on their rack. He had been wearing this stolen suit for more than twenty-four hours, and he was tempted to take five minutes to shower and change into some of his own clothes. But he resisted. There was no time to spare.

He searched the house thoroughly. Everywhere he looked, he learned something about himself and his wife. They liked Glen Miller and Frank Sinatra, they read Hemingway and Scott Fitzgerald, they drank

Dewar's scotch and ate All-Bran and brushed their teeth with Colgate. Elspeth spent a lot on expensive underwear, he discovered as he went through her closet. Luke himself must be fond of ice cream, because the freezer was full of it, and Elspeth's waist was so small she could not possibly eat much of anything at all.

At last he gave up.

In a kitchen drawer he found keys to the Chrysler in the garage. He would drive to the base and search there.

Before leaving, he picked up the mail in the hall and shuffled the envelopes. It all looked straight-forwardly official, bills and suchlike. Desperate for a clue, he ripped open the envelopes and glanced at each letter.

One was from a doctor in Atlanta.

It began:

Dear Mrs Lucas,
Following your routine check-up, the results of your
blood tests have come back from the lab, and everything is
normal.
However . . .

Luke stopped reading. Something told him it was not his habit to read other people's mail. On the other hand, this was his wife, and that word 'However' was ominous. Perhaps there was a medical problem he should know about right away.

He read the next paragraph.

However, you are underweight, you suffer insomnia,
and when I saw you, you had obviously been crying,
although you said nothing was wrong. These are
symptoms of depression.

Luke frowned. This was troubling. Why was she
depressed? What kind of husband must he be?

Depression may be caused by changes in body
chemistry, by unresolved mental problems such as marital
difficulties, or by childhood trauma such as the early
death of a parent. Treatment may include antidepressant
medication and/or psychiatric therapy.

This was getting worse. Was Elspeth mentally ill?

In your case, I have no doubt that the condition is
related to the tubal ligation you underwent in 1954.

What was a tubal ligation? Luke stepped into his
study, turned on the desk lamp, took from the
bookshelf the *Family Health Encyclopedia*, and looked it
up. The answer stunned him. It was the commonest
method of sterilization for women who did not want to
have children.

He sat down heavily and put the encyclopedia on
the desk. Reading the details of the operation, he
realized that this was what women meant when they
spoke of having their tubes tied.

He recalled his conversation with Elspeth this

morning. He had asked her why they could not have children. She had said: 'We don't know. Last year, you went to a fertility specialist, but he couldn't find anything wrong. A few weeks ago, I saw a woman doctor in Atlanta. She ran some tests. We're waiting for the results.'

That was all lies. She knew perfectly well why they could not have children – she had been sterilized.

She *had* gone to a doctor in Atlanta, but not for fertility testing – she had simply had a routine check-up.

Luke was sick at heart. It was a terrible deception. Why had she lied? He looked at the next paragraph.

This procedure may cause depression at any age, but in your case, having it six weeks before your wedding—

Luke's mouth fell open. There was something terribly wrong here. Elspeth's deception had begun shortly before they got married.

How had she managed it? He could not remember, of course. But he could guess. She could have told him she was having a minor operation. She might even have said vaguely that it was a 'feminine thing'.

He read the whole paragraph.

This procedure may cause depression at any age, but in your case, having it six weeks before your wedding, it was almost inevitable, and you should have returned to your doctor for regular consultations.

Luke's anger subsided as he realized how Elspeth had suffered. He reread the line: 'You are underweight, you suffer insomnia, and when I saw you, you had obviously been crying, although you said nothing was wrong.' She had put herself through some kind of personal hell.

But although he pitied her, the fact remained that their marriage had been a lie. Thinking about the house he had just searched, he realized that it did not feel much like a home to him. He was comfortable here in the little study, and he had felt a start of recognition on opening his closet, but the rest of the place presented a picture of married life that was alien to him. He did not care for kitchen appliances and smart modern furniture. He would rather have old rugs and family heirlooms. Most of all, he wanted children – yet children were the very thing she had deliberately denied him. And she had lied about it for four years.

The shock paralysed him. He sat at his desk, staring through the window, while evening fell over the hickory trees in the back yard. How had he let his life go so wrong? He considered what he had learned about himself in the last thirty-six hours, from Elspeth, Billie, Anthony and Bern. Had he lost his way slowly and gradually, like a child wandering farther and farther from home? Or was there a turning point, a moment when he had made a bad decision, taken the wrong fork in the road? Was he a weak man, who had drifted into misfortune for lack of a purpose in life? Or did he have some crucial flaw in his character?

He must be a poor judge of people, he thought. He had remained close to Anthony, who had tried to kill him, yet had broken with Bern, who had been a faithful friend. He had quarrelled with Billie and married Elspeth, yet Billie had dropped everything to help him and Elspeth had deceived him.

A large moth bumped into the closed window, and the noise startled Luke out of his reverie. He looked at his watch and was shocked to see that it was past seven.

If he hoped to unravel the mystery of his life, he needed to start with the elusive file. It was not here, so it had to be at Redstone Arsenal. He would turn out the lights and lock up the house, then he would get the black car out of the garage and drive to the base.

Time was pressing. The launch of the rocket was scheduled for ten-thirty. He had only three hours to find out whether there was a plot to sabotage it. Nevertheless, he remained sitting at his desk, staring through the window into the darkened garden, seeing nothing.

7.30 P.M.

One radio transmitter is powerful but short-lived – it will be dead in two weeks. The weaker signal from the second will last two months.

There were no lights on in Luke's house when Billie drove by. But what did that mean? There were three possibilities. One: the house was empty. Two: Anthony was sitting in the dark, waiting to shoot Luke. Three: Luke was lying in a pool of blood, dead. The uncertainty made her crazy with fear.

She had screwed up royally, maybe fatally. A few hours ago, she had been well placed to warn Luke and save him – then she had allowed herself to be diverted by a simple ruse. It had taken her hours to get back to Huntsville and find Luke's house. She had no idea whether either of her warning messages had reached him. She was furious with herself for being so incompetent, and terrified that Luke might have died because of her failure.

She turned the next corner and pulled up. She breathed deeply and made herself think calmly. She had to find out who was in the house. But what if Anthony were there? She contemplated sneaking up, hoping to surprise him; but that was too dangerous. It was never a good idea to startle a man with a gun in his hand. She could go right up to the front door and ring the bell. Would he shoot her down in cold blood, just for being there? He might. And she did not have the right to risk her life carelessly – she had a child who needed her.

On the passenger seat beside her was her attaché case. She opened it and took out the Colt. She disliked the heavy touch of the dark steel on the palm of her hand. The men she had worked with, in the war, had enjoyed handling guns. It gave a man sensual pleasure to close his fist around a pistol grip, spin the cylinder of a revolver, or fit the stock of a rifle into the hollow of his shoulder. She felt none of that. To her, guns were brutal and cruel, made to tear and crush the flesh and bones of living, breathing people. They made her skin crawl.

With the pistol in her lap, she turned the car around and returned to Luke's house.

She screeched to a halt outside, threw the car door open, grabbed her gun and leaped out. Before anyone inside might have time to react, she jumped the low wall and ran across the lawn to the side of the house.

She heard no sound from within.

She ran around to the back, ducked past the door, and looked in at a window. The dim light of a distant street lamp enabled her to see that it was a simple casement with a single latch. The room seemed empty. She reversed her grip on the gun and smashed the glass, all the time waiting for the gunshot that would end her life. Nothing happened. She reached through the broken pane, undid the latch, and pulled open the window. She climbed in, holding the gun in her right hand, and flattened herself against a wall. She could make out vague shapes of furniture, a desk and some bookshelves. This was a little study. Her instinct told her she was alone. But she was terrified of stumbling over Luke's body in the dark.

Moving slowly, she crossed the room and located the doorway. Her dark-accustomed eyes saw an empty hall. She stepped cautiously out, gun at the ready. She moved through the house in the gloom, dreading at every step that she would see Luke on the floor. All the rooms were empty.

At the end of her search she stood in the largest bedroom, staring at the double bed where Luke slept with Elspeth, wondering what to do next. She felt tearfully grateful that Luke was not lying here dead. But where was he? Had he changed his plans, and decided not to come here? Or had the body been spirited away? Had Anthony somehow failed to kill him? Or had one of her warnings got through?

One person who might have some answers was Marigold.

Billie returned to Luke's study and turned on the light. A medical encyclopedia lay on the desk, open at the page about female sterilization. Billie frowned in puzzlement, then put aside her questions. She called information and asked for a number for Marigold Clark. After a moment the voice on the line gave her a Huntsville number.

A man answered. 'She gone to singing practice,' he said. Billie guessed he was Marigold's husband. 'Miz Lucas is down to Florida, so Marigold conducting the choir till she come back.'

Billie recalled that Elspeth had been conductor of the Radcliffe Choral Society, and later of an orchestra for black kids in Washington. It seemed she was doing something of that sort here in Huntsville, and Marigold was her deputy. 'I need to talk to Marigold real bad,' Billie said. 'Do you think it would be all right if I interrupted the choir for a minute?'

'Guess so. They're at the Calvary Gospel Church on Mill Street.'

'Thank you, I sure appreciate it.'

Billie went out to her car. She found Mill Street on the Hertz map and drove there. The church was a fine brick building in a poor neighbourhood. She heard the choir as soon as she opened the car door. When she stepped inside the church, the music washed over her like a tidal wave. The singers stood at the far end. There were only about thirty men and women, but they sounded like a hundred. The hymn went: 'Everybody's gonna have a wonderful time up there – oh! Glory, hallelujah!' They clapped and swayed as they sang. A pianist played a rhythmic barrelhouse accompaniment, and a large woman with her back to Billie conducted vigorously.

The pews were neat rows of wooden folding seats. She sat in the rear, conscious that hers was the only white face in the place. Despite her anxiety, the music tugged at her heartstrings. She had been born in Texas and, to her, these thrilling harmonies represented the soul of the South.

She was impatient to question Marigold, but she felt sure she would get a better response by showing respect and waiting for the end of the song.

They finished on a high chord, and the conductor immediately looked around. 'I wondered what happened to disturb your concentration,' she said to the choir. 'Take a short break.'

Billie walked up the aisle. 'I'm sorry to interrupt,' she said. 'Are you Marigold Clark?'

'Yes,' she said warily. She was a woman of about fifty, wearing fancy spectacles. 'But I don't know you.'

'We spoke on the phone earlier, I'm Billie Josephson.'

'Oh, hi, Dr Josephson.'

They walked a few steps away from the others. Billie said: 'Have you heard from Luke?'

'Not since this morning. I expected him to show up at the base this afternoon, but he didn't. Do you think he's all right?'

'I don't know. I went to his house, but there was no one there. I'm afraid he might have been killed.'

Marigold shook her head in bewilderment. 'I've worked for the army twenty years and I never heard of anything like this.'

'If he is alive, he's in great danger,' Billie said. She looked Marigold in the eye. 'Do you believe me?'

Marigold hesitated for a long moment. 'Yes, ma'am, I do,' she said at last.

'Then you have to help me,' Billie told her.

9.30 P.M.

The radio signal from the more powerful transmitter may be picked up by radio hams all over the world. The weaker signal from the second can be picked up only by specially equipped stations.

Anthony was at Redstone Arsenal, sitting in his army Ford, peering through the darkness, anxiously watching the door of the Computation Laboratory. He was in the parking lot in front of the headquarters building, a couple of hundred yards away.

Luke was in the lab, searching for his file folder. Anthony knew he would not find it there, just as he had known Luke would not find it at his home – because he had already searched there. But Anthony was no longer able to anticipate Luke's movements. He could only wait until Luke decided where to go next, then try to follow him.

However, time was on his side. Every minute that passed made Luke less dangerous. The rocket would be launched in one hour. Could Luke ruin everything in an hour? Anthony knew only that over the last two days his old friend had proved again and again that he should not be underestimated.

As he was thinking this, the door to the lab opened, spilling yellow light into the night, and a figure emerged and approached the black Chrysler parked at the curb. As Anthony had expected, Luke was empty-handed. He got in and drove off.

Anthony's heartbeat quickened. He started his engine, switched on his headlights, and followed.

The road went south in a dead-straight line. After about a mile, Luke slowed in front of a long one-storey building and pulled into its parking lot. Anthony drove past, accelerating into the night. A quarter of a mile down the road, out of sight of Luke, he turned around. When he came back, Luke's car was still there, but Luke had gone.

Anthony pulled into the parking lot and killed his engine.

* * *

Luke had felt sure he would find the folder in the Computation Lab, where his office was. That was why he had spent so long there. He had looked at every file in his own room, then in the main office where the secretaries sat. And he had found nothing.

But there was one more possibility. Marigold had said that he also went to the Engineering Building on Monday. There must have been a reason for that. Anyway, it was his last hope. If the file were not here, he did not know where else to look. And anyway, he would by then have run out of time. In a few minutes, the rocket would either be launched – or be sabotaged.

Engineering had an atmosphere quite different

from that of the Computation Lab. Computation was spotlessly clean, as it had to be for the sake of the massive computers that calculated thrust and speed and trajectories. Engineering was scruffy by comparison, smelling of oil and rubber.

He hurried along a corridor. The walls were painted dark green below waist level and light green above. Most of the doors had nameplates beginning 'Dr', so he presumed they were the offices of scientists but, to his frustration, none said 'Dr Claude Lucas'. Most likely he did not have a second office, but maybe he had a desk here.

At the end of the corridor he came upon a large open room with half a dozen steel tables. On the far side, an open door led into a laboratory with granite bench tops above green metal drawers and, beyond the benches, a big double door that looked as if it led to a loading bay outside.

Along the wall to Luke's immediate left was a row of lockers, each with a name plate. One was his. Maybe he had stashed the file here.

He took out his key ring and found a likely key. It worked, and he opened the door. Inside he saw a hard hat on a high shelf. Below that, hanging from a hook, was a set of blue overalls. On the floor stood a pair of black rubber boots that looked like his size.

There, beside the boots, was a buff-coloured army file folder. This had to be what he was looking for.

The folder contained some papers. When he took them out, he could see immediately that they were blueprints for parts of a rocket.

His heart hammering in his chest, Luke moved quickly to one of the steel tables and spread the papers out under a lamp. After a few moments' rapid study, he knew without doubt that the drawings showed the Jupiter C rocket's self-destruct mechanism.

He was horrified.

Every rocket had a self-destruct mechanism so that, if it should veer off course and threaten human life, it could be blown up in mid-air. In the main stage of the Jupiter rocket, a Primacord igniter rope ran the length of the missile. A firing cap was attached to its top end, and two wires stuck out of the cap. If a voltage was applied across the wires, Luke could see from the drawings, the cap would ignite the Primacord, which would rip the tank, causing the fuel to burn and be dispersed, and destroying the rocket.

The explosion was triggered by a coded radio signal. The blueprints showed twin plugs, one for the transmitter on the ground and the other for the receiver in the satellite. One turned the radio signal into a complex code; the other received the signal and, if the code was correct, applied the voltage across the twin wires. A separate diagram, not a blueprint but a hastily drawn sketch, showed exactly how the plugs were wired, so that anyone having the diagram could duplicate the signal.

It was brilliant, Luke realized. The saboteurs had no need of explosives or timing devices – they could use what was already built in. They did not need access to the rocket. Once they had the code, they did not even have to get inside Cape Canaveral. The radio signal could be broadcast from a transmitter miles away.

The last sheet was a photocopy of an envelope addressed to Theo Packman at the Vanguard Motel. Had Luke prevented the original being mailed? He could not be sure. Standard counter intelligence procedure was to leave a spy network in place and use it for disinformation. But if Luke had confiscated the original, the sender would have mailed another set of blueprints. Either way, Theo Packman was now somewhere in Cocoa Beach with a radio transmitter, ready to blow up the rocket seconds after it took off.

But now Luke could prevent that. He glanced at the electric clock on the wall. It was ten-fifteen. He had time to call Cape Canaveral and have the launch postponed. He snatched up the phone on the desk.

A voice said: 'Put it down, Luke.'

Luke turned slowly, phone in hand. Anthony stood in the doorway in his camel-hair coat, with two black eyes and a swollen lip, holding a gun with a silencer, pointing it at Luke.

Slowly and reluctantly, Luke cradled the phone. 'You were in the car behind me,' he said.

'I figured you were in too much of a rush to check.'

Luke stared at the man whom he had so misjudged. Was there some sign he should have noticed, some feature that should have warned him he was dealing with a traitor? Anthony had a pleasantly ugly face that suggested considerable force of character, but not duplicity. 'How long have you been working for Moscow?' Luke asked him. 'Since the war?'

'Longer. Since Harvard.'

'Why?'

Anthony's lips twisted into a strange smile. 'For a better world.'

Once upon a time, Luke knew, a lot of sensible people had believed in the Soviet system. But he also knew their faith had been undermined by the realities of life under Stalin. 'You still believe that?' he said incredulously.

'Sort of. It's still the best hope, despite all that has happened.'

Maybe it was. Luke had no way of judging. But that was not the real issue. For him, it was Anthony's personal betrayal that was so hard to understand. 'We've been friends for two decades,' he said. 'But you *shot* at me last night.'

'Yes.'

'Would you kill your oldest friend? For this cause that you only half believe in?'

'Yes, and so would you. In the war, we both put lives at risk, our own and other people's, because it was right.'

'I don't think we lied to one another, let alone shot at one another.'

'We would have, if necessary.'

'I don't think so.'

'Listen. If I don't kill you now, you'll try to stop me escaping – won't you?'

Luke was scared, but he angrily told the truth. 'Hell, yes.'

'Even though you know that if I'm caught, I'll finish up in the electric chair.'

'I guess so . . . yes.'

'So you're willing to kill your friend, too.'

Luke was taken aback. Surely he could not be classified with Anthony? 'I might bring you to justice. That's not murder.'

'I'd be just as dead, though.'

Luke nodded slowly. 'I guess you would.'

Anthony raised the gun with a steady hand, aiming at Luke's heart.

Luke dropped behind the steel table.

The silenced gun coughed, and there was a metallic clang as the bullet hit the top of the table. It was cheap furniture, and the steel of which it was made was thin, but it had been enough to deflect the shot.

Luke rolled under the table. He guessed Anthony was now running across the room, trying to get another shot at him. He raised himself so that his back was against the underside of the table. Grabbing the two legs at one end of the table he heaved, standing upright at the same time. The table came up off the floor and teetered forward. As it toppled, Luke blindly ran with it, hoping to collide with Anthony. The table crashed to the floor.

But Anthony was not beneath it.

Luke tripped and tumbled onto the inverted table. He fell on his hands and knees, and banged his head on a steel leg. He rolled sideways and came up into a sitting position, hurt and dazed. He looked up to see

Anthony facing him, framed by the doorway that led into the lab, braced with his feet apart, aiming his gun two-handed. He had dodged Luke's clumsy charge and got behind him. Luke was now, literally, a sitting target, and the end of his life was a second away.

Then a voice rang out: 'Anthony! Stop!'

It was Billie.

Anthony froze, gun pointed at Luke. Luke slowly turned his head and looked behind him. Billie stood by the door, her sweater a flash of red against the army-green wall. Her red lips were set in a determined line. She held an automatic pistol in a steady hand, levelled at Anthony. Behind her was a middle-aged Negro woman, looking shocked and scared.

'Drop the gun!' Billie yelled.

Luke half expected Anthony to shoot him anyway. If he was a truly dedicated communist, he might be willing to sacrifice his life. But that would achieve nothing, for Billie would still have the blueprints, and they told the whole story.

Slowly, Anthony lowered his arms, but he did not drop the gun.

'Drop it, or I'll shoot!'

Anthony gave his twisted smile again. 'No, you won't,' he said. 'Not in cold blood.' Still pointing the gun at the floor, he began to walk backwards, making for the open door that led into the laboratory. Luke remembered noticing a door there that looked as if it led to the outside.

'Stop!' Billie cried.

'You don't believe that a rocket is worth more than

a human life, even if it's a traitor's life,' Anthony said, continuing to walk backward. He was now two steps from the door.

'Don't test me!' she cried.

Luke stared at her, not knowing whether she would shoot or not.

Anthony turned and darted through the doorway.

Billie did not shoot.

Anthony leaped over a lab bench, then threw himself at a double door. It burst open, and he disappeared into the night.

Luke leaped to his feet. Billie came towards him with her arms wide. He looked at the clock on the wall. It said ten twenty-nine. He had a minute left to warn Cape Canaveral.

He turned away from Billie and picked up the phone.

10.29 P.M.

The scientific instruments on board the satellite have been designed to withstand take-off pressure of more than 100 gravities.

When the phone was picked up in the blockhouse, Luke said: 'This is Luke, give me the launch conductor.'

'Right now he's—'

'I know what he's doing! Put him on, quick!'

There was a pause. In the background, Luke could hear the countdown: 'Twenty, nineteen, eighteen—'

A new voice came on the line, tense and impatient. 'This is Willy – what the hell is it?'

'Someone has the self-destruct code.'

'Shit! Who?'

'I'm pretty sure it's a spy. They're going to blow up the rocket. You have to abort the launch.'

The background voice said: 'Eleven, ten—'

'How do you know?' Willy asked.

'I've found diagrams of the wiring of the coded plugs, and an envelope addressed to someone called Theo Packman.'

'That's not proof. I can't cancel the launch on such a flimsy basis.'

Luke sighed, suddenly feeling fatalistic. 'Oh, Christ, what can I say? I've told you what I know. The decision is yours.'

'Five, four—'

'Hell!' Willy raised his voice. 'Stop the countdown!'

Luke slumped in his chair. He had done it. He glanced up at the anxious faces of Billie and Marigold. 'They've aborted the launch,' he said.

Billie lifted the hem of her sweater and stuffed the pistol into the waistband of her ski pants.

'Well,' said Marigold, somewhat lost for words. 'Well, I declare.'

Over the phone, Luke heard a buzz of angry questions in the blockhouse. A new voice came on the line. 'Luke? This is Colonel Hide. What the hell is going on?'

'I've discovered what made me take off for Washington in such a hurry on Monday. Do you know who Theo Packman is?'

'Uh, yeah, I think he's a freelance journalist on the missile beat, writes for a couple of European newspapers.'

'I found an envelope addressed to him containing blueprints of the Explorer's self-destruct system, including a sketch of the wiring of the coded plugs.'

'Jesus! Anyone who had that information could blow up the rocket in mid-air!'

'That's why I persuaded Willy to abort the launch.'

'Thank God you did.'

'Listen, you have to find this Packman character right now. The envelope was addressed to the Vanguard Motel, you may find him there.'

'Got it.'

'Packman was working with someone in the CIA, a double agent called Anthony Carroll. He's the one who intercepted me in Washington before I could get to the Pentagon with the information.'

'I talked to him!' Hide sounded incredulous.

'I'm sure of it.'

'I'll call the CIA and tell them.'

'Good.' Luke hung up. He had done all he could.

Billie said: 'What next?'

'I guess I'll go to Cape Canaveral. The launch will be rescheduled for the same time tomorrow. I'd like to be there.'

'Me, too.'

Luke smiled. 'You deserve it. You saved the rocket.' He stood up and embraced her.

'Your life, you goop. To heck with the rocket, I saved your life.' She kissed him.

Marigold coughed. 'You've missed the last plane from Huntsville airport,' she said in a businesslike tone.

Luke and Billie separated reluctantly.

'Next one is a MATS flight that leaves from the base at 5.30 a.m.,' Marigold went on. 'Or there's a train on the Southern Railway System you could catch. It runs from Cincinnati to Jacksonville and stops in Chattanooga around one a.m. You could get to Chattanooga in a couple of hours in that nice new car of yours.'

Billie said: 'I like the train idea.'

Luke nodded. 'Okay.' He looked at the upturned

table. 'Someone's going to have to talk to army security about these bullet holes.'

Marigold said: 'I'll do it in the morning. You don't want to be waiting around here answering questions.'

They went outside. Luke's car and Billie's rental were in the parking lot. Anthony's car had gone.

Billie embraced Marigold. 'Thank you,' she said. 'You were wonderful.'

Marigold was embarrassed, and turned practical again. 'You want me to return your rental to Hertz?'

'Thank you.'

'Off you go, leave everything to me.'

Billie and Luke got into his Chrysler and drove away.

When they were on the highway, Billie said: 'There's a question we haven't talked about.'

'I know,' Luke said. 'Who sent the blueprints to Theo Packman?'

'It must be someone inside Cape Canaveral, someone on the scientific team.'

'Exactly.'

'Do you have any idea who?'

Luke winced. 'Yes.'

'Why didn't you tell Hide?'

'Because I don't have any evidence, or even much of a reason, for my suspicions. It's just instinct. But, all the same, I'm sure.'

'Who?'

With a heart full of grief, Luke said: 'I think it's Elspeth.'

11 P.M.

The telemetry encoder uses hysteresis loop core materials to establish a series of input parameters from satellite instruments.

Elspeth could not believe it. Just a few seconds before ignition, the launch had been postponed. She had been so close to success. The triumph of her life had been within her grasp – and had slipped through her fingers.

She was not in the blockhouse – that was restricted to key personnel – but on the flat roof of an administration building, with a small crowd of secretaries and clerks, watching the floodlit launch pad through binoculars. The Florida night was warm, the sea-air moist. Their fears had grown as the minutes ticked by and the rocket remained on the ground; and now a collective groan went up as technicians in overalls swarmed out of their bunkers and began the complex procedure of standing down all systems. Final confirmation came when the mobile service tower slowly moved forward on its railway tracks to take the white rocket back into its steel arms.

Elspeth was in an agony of frustration. What the hell had gone wrong?

She left the others without a word and walked back to Hangar R, her long legs covering the ground with purposeful strides. When she reached her office, the phone was ringing. She snatched it up. 'Yes?'

'What's happening?' The voice was Anthony's.

'They've aborted the launch. I don't know why – do you?'

'Luke found the papers. He must have called.'

'Couldn't you stop him?'

'I had him in my sights – literally – but Billie walked in, armed.'

Elspeth had a sick feeling in the pit of her stomach at the thought of Anthony pointing a gun at Luke. It only made things worse that it was Billie who had intervened. 'Is Luke all right?'

'Yes – and so am I. But Theo's name is on those papers, remember?'

'Oh, hell.'

'They'll be on their way to arrest him already. You have to find him first.'

'Let me think . . . he's on the beach . . . I can be there in ten minutes . . . I know his car, it's a Hudson Hornet . . .'

'Then get going!'

'Yep.' She slammed down the phone and rushed out of the building.

She ran across the parking lot and jumped into her car. Her white Bel Air was a convertible, but she kept the top up and the windows tightly shut because of the mosquitoes that plagued the Cape. She drove fast to the gate and was waved through:

security was heavy coming in, but not going out. She headed south.

There was no regular road to the beach. From the highway several narrow, unpaved tracks led between the dunes to the shore. She planned to take the first, then continue south on the beach. That way she could not miss Theo's car. She peered at the rough brush alongside the road, trying to pick out the track in the light of her headlamps. She had to go slowly, even though she was in such a hurry, for fear of missing the turn-off. Then she saw a car emerging.

It was followed by another, and another. Elspeth flashed her left-turn indicator and slowed down. A constant stream of cars was coming from the beach. The spectators had figured out that the launch was cancelled – no doubt they, too, had seen, through their binoculars, the service gantry returning to position – and they were all going home.

She waited to turn left. Infuriatingly, the track was too narrow for two-way traffic. A car behind her honked impatiently. She grunted with exasperation as she saw she was not going to be able to get to the beach this way. She flicked off the indicator and floored the gas pedal.

She soon came to another turn-off, but the picture was the same: an unbroken line of cars emerging from a track too narrow to allow two cars to pass. 'Hell!' she said aloud. She was sweating now, despite the air-conditioning in her car. There was no way for her to get to the beach. She would have to think of something else. Could she wait on the highway in the hope of spotting his car? It was too chancy. What would Theo do after he left the beach? Her best option was to go to his motel and wait there.

She sped on, driving fast through the night. She wondered if Colonel Hide and army security were already at the Vanguard Motel. They might first have called the police or the FBI. They needed a warrant to arrest Theo, she knew – although law enforcement people generally had ways around such inconveniences. Whatever happened, it would take them a few minutes to get themselves together. She had a chance of beating them if she hurried.

The Vanguard was in a short business strip alongside the highway, between a gas station and a bait-and-tackle store. It had a large parking lot out front. There was no sign of police or army security: she was in time. But Theo's car was not there. She parked near the motel office, where she was sure to see anyone going in or out, and switched off her engine.

She did not have to wait long. The yellow-and-brown Hudson Hornet pulled in a couple of minutes later. Theo eased into a slot at the far end of the lot, near the road, and got out, a small man with thinning hair, dressed in chinos and a beach shirt.

Elspeth got out of her own car.

She opened her mouth to call to Theo across the lot. At that moment, two police cruisers arrived.

Elspeth froze.

They were Cocoa County Sheriff's vehicles. They came in fast, but without flashing lights or sirens. Behind them followed two unmarked cars. They parked across the entry, making it impossible for cars to leave.

At first Theo did not see them. He headed across the lot, toward Elspeth and the motel office.

She knew in a flash what she had to do – but it would take a steady nerve. Stay cool, she told herself. She took a deep breath, then started walking towards him.

As he came close he recognized her and said loudly: 'What the hell happened? Did they abort the launch?'

Elspeth said in a low voice: 'Give me your car keys.' She held out her hand.

'What for?'

'Look behind you.'

He glanced over his shoulder and saw the police cars. 'Fuck, what do they want?' he said shakily.

'You. Stay calm. Give me the keys.'

He dropped them into her open hand.

'Keep walking,' she said. 'The trunk of my car is not locked. Get inside.'

'Into the trunk?'

'*Yes!*' Elspeth went on past him.

She recognized Colonel Hide and another vaguely familiar face from Cape Canaveral. With them were four local cops and two tall, well-dressed young men who might have been FBI agents. None of them was looking her way. They gathered around Hide. Distantly, Elspeth heard him say: 'We need two men to check the licence plates of the cars here in the lot while the rest come inside.'

She reached Theo's car and opened the trunk. Inside was the leather suitcase containing the radio transmitter – powerful, and heavy. She was not sure she could carry it. She pulled it to the lip of the trunk and dragged it over the edge. It hit the ground with a thud. She closed the trunk lid quickly.

She looked around. Hide was still giving orders to his men. At the other end of the lot, she saw the trunk lid of her own car slowly closing, as if of its own volition. Theo was inside. That was half the problem solved.

Gritting her teeth, she grasped the handle of the suitcase and lifted it. It felt like a box of lead. She walked a few yards, holding it as long as she could. When her fingers became numb with strain, she dropped the case. Then she picked it up with her left hand. She managed another ten yards before the pain overcame her will and she dropped the case again.

Behind her, Colonel Hide and his men were crossing the lot towards the motel office. She prayed Hide would not look at her face. The darkness made it less likely he would recognize her. Of course, she could make up some story to explain her presence here, but what if he asked to look in the case?

Once more she changed sides and grasped the handle with her right hand. She could not lift the transmitter this time. Giving up, she began to drag it across the concrete, hoping the noise would not attract the attention of the cops.

At last she reached her car. As she opened the trunk, one of the uniformed police approached her with a cheerful smile. 'Help you with that, ma'am?' he said politely.

Theo's face stared at her from inside the trunk, white and scared.

'I got it,' she said to the cop out of the corner of her mouth. With both hands, she heaved up the suitcase and slid it in. There was a quiet grunt of pain from Theo as a corner dug into him. With a quick movement, Elspeth slammed the trunk lid and leaned on it. Her arms felt as if they would fall off.

She looked at the cop. Had he spotted Theo? He gave a puzzled grin. Elspeth said: 'My daddy taught me never to pack a bag I couldn't lift.'

'Strong girl,' the cop said in a mildly resentful tone.

'Thanks, anyway.'

The other men went past, heading purposefully towards the motel office. Elspeth was careful not to catch Hide's eye. The cop lingered a moment. 'Checking out?' he said.

'Yeah.'

'All alone?'

'That's right.'

He bent to the window and looked into the car, front and back seats, then straightened up again. 'Drive safely.' He walked on.

Elspeth got into her car and started the engine.

Two more uniformed cops had stayed behind and were checking licence plates. She pulled up next to one of them. 'Are you going to let me out, or do I have to stay here all night?' she said. She tried a friendly smile.

He checked her licence plate. 'Are you alone?'

'Yes.'

He looked through the window into the back seat. She held her breath. 'Okay,' he said at last. 'You can go.'

He sat in one of the cruisers and moved it out of the way.

She drove through the gap and pulled onto the highway, then floored the gas pedal.

Suddenly she felt limp with relief. Her arms trembled, and she had to slow the car. 'God almighty,' she breathed. 'That was too damn close.'

12 MIDNIGHT

Four whip antennae, protruding from the satellite cylinder, broadcast radio signals to receiving stations around the globe. Explorer will broadcast on a frequency of 108 MHz.

Anthony had to get out of Alabama. The action was in Florida now. Everything he had worked towards for twenty years would be decided at Cape Canaveral in the next twenty-four hours, and he had to be there.

Huntsville Airport was still open, lights blazing on the runway. That meant there was at least one more plane in or out tonight. He parked his army Ford at the roadside in front of the terminal building, behind a limousine and a couple of taxicabs. The place seemed deserted. He did not trouble to lock the car but hurried inside.

The place was quiet but not empty. One girl sat behind an airline counter writing in a book, and two black women in overalls were mopping the floor. Three men stood around waiting, one in chauffeur uniform and the others in the creased clothes and peaked caps of cab drivers. Pete was sitting on a bench.

Anthony had to get rid of Pete, for the man's own sake. The scene in the Engineering Building at

Redstone Arsenal had been witnessed by Billie and Marigold, and one of them would soon report it. The army would complain to the CIA. George Cooperman had already said he could not shield Anthony any longer. Anthony had to give up the pretence that he was on a legitimate CIA mission. The game was up, and Pete had better go home before he got hurt.

Pete might have been bored after twelve hours waiting at the airport, but instead he seemed excited and tense as he jumped to his feet. 'At last!' he said.

'What's flying out of here tonight?' Anthony said abruptly.

'Nothing. One more flight is due in, from Washington, but nothing is leaving before seven a.m.'

'Damn. I have to get to Florida.'

'There's a MATS flight from Redstone at five-thirty going to Patrick Air Force Base, near Cape Canaveral.'

'That'll have to do.'

Pete looked embarrassed. Seeming to force the words out, he said: 'You can't go to Florida.'

So that was why he was so tense. Anthony said coolly: 'How so?'

'I talked to Washington. Carl Hobart spoke to me himself. We have to go back – and no argument, to quote him.'

Anthony felt wild with rage, but he pretended to be merely frustrated. 'Those assholes,' Anthony said. 'You can't run a field operation from headquarters!'

Pete was not buying this. 'Mr Hobart says we have to accept there is no operation now. The army is handling this from here on.'

'We can't let them. Army security is totally incompetent.'

'I know, but I don't think we have a choice, sir.'

Anthony made an effort to breathe calmly. This had to happen sooner or later. The CIA did not yet believe he was a double agent, but they knew he had gone rogue, and they wanted to put him out of action as quietly as possible.

However, Anthony had carefully cultivated the loyalty of his men over the years, and he should still have some credit left. 'Here's what we'll do,' he said to Pete. 'You go back to Washington. Tell them I refused to obey orders. You're out of it – this is my responsibility now.' He half turned away, as if taking Pete's consent for granted.

'Okay,' Pete said. 'I guessed you would say that. And they can't expect me to kidnap you.'

'That's right,' Anthony said casually, concealing his relief that Pete was not going to argue.

'But there's something else,' Pete said.

Anthony rounded on him, letting his irritation show. 'What now?'

Pete blushed, and the birthmark on his face turned purple. 'They told me to take your gun.'

Anthony began to fear he might not be able to get out of this situation easily. There was no way he was giving up his weapon. He forced a smile and said: 'So you'll tell them I refused.'

'I'm sorry, sir, I can't tell you how sorry I am. But Mr Hobart was very specific. If you won't hand it over, I have to call the local police.'

Anthony realized then that he had to kill Pete.

For a moment he was swamped by grief. What depths of treachery he had been led into. It hardly seemed possible that this was the logical conclusion of his commitment, made two decades ago, to dedicate his life to a noble cause. Then a deadly calm descended on him. He had learned about hard choices in the war. This was a different war, but the imperatives were the same. Once you were in, you had to win, whatever it took. 'In that case, I guess it's all over,' he said with a sigh that was genuine. 'I think it's a dumb decision, but I believe I've done all I can.'

Pete made no attempt to conceal his relief. 'Thank you,' he said. 'I'm so glad you're taking it this way.'

'Don't you worry. I won't hold this against you. I know you have to follow a direct order from Hobart.'

Pete's face took on a determined expression. 'So, do you want to give me the firearm now?'

'Sure.' The gun was in Anthony's coat pocket, but he said: 'It's in my trunk.' He wanted Pete to go with him to the car, but he pretended the opposite. 'Wait here, I'll get it.'

As he had expected, Pete feared he was trying to escape. 'I'll come with you,' Pete said hastily.

Anthony pretended to hesitate and then give in. 'Whatever.' He walked through the door, with Pete following. The car was parked at the kerb, thirty yards from the airport entrance. There was no one in sight.

Anthony thumbed the trunk lid and threw it open. 'There you go,' he said.

Pete bent over to look in the trunk.

Anthony drew the gun, silencer attached, from inside his coat. For a moment, he was tempted by a mad impulse to put the barrel in his own mouth and pull the trigger, bringing the nightmare to an end.

That moment of delay was a crucial mistake.

Pete said: 'I don't see any gun,' and he turned around.

He reacted fast. Before Anthony could level his gun with its cumbersome silencer, Pete stepped sideways, away from the muzzle, and swung a fist. He caught Anthony with a bone-jarring blow to the side of the head. Anthony staggered. Pete hit him with the other fist, connecting with his jaw, and Anthony stumbled backwards and fell; but as he hit the ground he brought the gun up. Pete saw what was going to happen. His face twisted in fear and he lifted his hands, as if they could protect him from a bullet; then Anthony pulled the trigger three times in rapid succession.

All three bullets found their target on Pete's chest, and blood spurted from three holes in his grey mohair suit. He fell to the road with a thud.

Anthony scrambled to his feet and pocketed the gun. He looked up and down. No one was arriving at the airport, and no one had come out of the building. He bent over Pete's body.

Pete looked at him. He was not dead.

Fighting down nausea, Anthony picked up the bleeding body and tumbled it into the open trunk of the car. Then he drew his gun again. Pete lay in the trunk, twisted in pain, staring at him with terrified eyes. Chest wounds were not always fatal: Pete could live if he were treated in hospital soon. Anthony pointed the gun at Pete's head. Pete tried to speak, and blood came out of his mouth. Anthony pulled the trigger.

Pete slumped, and his eyes closed.

Anthony slammed the trunk lid and collapsed onto it. He had been hit seriously hard for the second time in a day, and his head was swimming; but worse than the physical damage was the knowledge of what he had done.

A voice said: 'Are you okay, buddy?'

Anthony came upright, stuffing the gun inside his coat, and turned around. A taxi had pulled up behind and the driver walked up, looking concerned. He was a black man with greying hair.

How much had the man seen? Anthony did not know if he had the heart to kill him, too.

The cabbie said: 'Whatever you were loading into your trunk, looks like it was heavy.'

'A rug,' Anthony said, breathing hard.

The man looked at him with the candid curiosity of small-town people. 'Someone give you a black eye? Or two?'

'A little accident.'

'Come inside, get a cup of coffee or something.'

'No, thanks. I'm okay.'

'Please yourself.' The driver ambled slowly into the terminal.

Anthony got into his car and drove away.

1.30 A.M.

The first task of the radio transmitters is to provide signals enabling the satellite to be followed by tracking stations on Earth – to prove that it is in orbit.

The train pulled slowly out of Chattanooga. In the cramped roomette, Luke took off his jacket and hung it up, then perched on the edge of the lower bunk and unlaced his shoes. Billie sat cross-legged on the bunk, watching him. The lights of the station flickered then faded as the locomotive gathered speed, heading into the Southern night, bound for Jacksonville, Florida.

Luke undid his tie. Billie said: 'If this is a striptease, it doesn't have much oomph.'

Luke grinned ruefully. He was going slowly because he was undecided. They had been forced to share the roomette: only one was available. He was longing to take Billie in his arms. Everything he had learned about himself and his life told him that Billie was the woman he should be with. Yet, all the same, he hesitated.

'What?' she said. 'What are you thinking?'

'That this is too quick.'

'Seventeen years is nothing?'

'To me it's been a couple of days, that's all I can remember.'

'It feels like forever.'

'I'm still married to Elspeth.'

Billie nodded solemnly. 'But she's been lying to you for years.'

'So I should jump out of her bed into yours?'

She looked offended. 'You should do what you want.'

He tried to explain. 'I don't like the feeling that I'm seizing an excuse.' She said nothing in reply, so he added: 'You don't agree, do you?'

'Hell, no,' she said. 'I want to make love to you tonight. I remember what it was like, and I want it again, right now.' She glanced out of the window as the train flew through a small town: ten seconds of streaking lights and they were in darkness again. 'But I know you,' she went on. 'You've never been one to live for the moment, even when we were kids. You need time to think things through and convince yourself that you're doing the right thing.'

'Is that so bad?'

She smiled. 'No. I'm glad you're like that. It makes you rock-solid reliable. If you weren't this way, I guess I wouldn't have . . .' Her voice tailed off.

'What were you going to say?'

She looked him in the eye. 'I wouldn't have loved you this much, this long.' She was embarrassed, and covered up by saying something flip. 'Anyway, you need a shower.'

It was true. He had been wearing the same clothes since he had stolen them thirty-six hours ago. 'Every time I thought about changing, there was something more urgent to do,' he said. 'I have fresh clothes in my bag.'

'No matter. Why don't you climb up on top, and give me room to take off my shoes.'

Obediently, he climbed the little ladder and lay down on the top bunk. He turned on his side, elbow on the pillow, head resting on his hand. 'Losing your memory is like a new start in life,' he said. 'Like being born again. Every decision you ever made can be revisited.'

She kicked off her shoes and stood up. 'I'd hate that,' she said. With a swift movement, she slipped off her black ski pants and stood there in her sweater and brief white panties. Catching his eye, she grinned and said: 'It's okay, you can watch.' She reached under her sweater at the back and unfastened her brassiere. Then she drew her left arm out of her sleeve, reached inside with her right hand to pull the strap off her shoulder, thrust her left arm back into the sleeve, and drew her bra out of her right sleeve with a conjurer's flourish.

'Bravo,' he said.

She gave him a thoughtful look. 'So, we're going to sleep now?'

'I guess.'

'Okay.' She stood on the edge of the lower bunk and raised herself to his level, tilting her face to be kissed. He leaned forward and touched her lips with his own. She closed her eyes. He felt the tip of her tongue flick over his lips, then she pulled away and her face disappeared.

He lay on his back, thinking about her lying a few

inches below, with her round breasts inside the soft angora sweater, her neat bare legs. In a few moments he was asleep.

He had an intensely erotic dream. He was Bottom in *A Midsummer Night's Dream*, with donkey's ears, and he was being kissed all over his hairy face by Titania's fairies, who were naked girls with slim legs and round breasts. Titania herself, the queen of the fairies, was unbuttoning his pants, while the wheels of the train drummed an insistent beat . . .

He woke up slowly, reluctant to leave fairyland and return to the world of railroads and rockets. His shirt was open and his pants were undone. Billie lay beside him, kissing him. 'Are you awake?' she murmured in his ear – a normal ear, not a donkey's. She giggled. 'I don't want to waste this on a guy who's asleep.'

He touched her, running his hand along her side. She still had on the sweater, but her panties had gone. 'I'm awake,' he said thickly.

She lifted herself on hands and knees so that she was over him, poised in the narrow space below the ceiling of the roomette. Looking into his eyes, she lowered her body onto his. He sighed with intense pleasure as he slid inside her. The train rocked from side to side, and the tracks sang to an erotic rhythm.

He reached inside her sweater to touch her breasts. Her skin was soft and warm. She whispered in his ear: 'They missed you.'

He felt as if he were still half in the dream, as the train rocked and Billie kissed his face and America flew by the window, mile after mile. He wound his arms around her back and held her tightly, to convince himself that she was made of flesh and blood, not fairy gossamer. Just as he was thinking that he wanted this to go on forever, his body took control, and he clung to her as waves of pleasure broke over him.

As soon as it was over she said: 'Keep still. Hold me tight.' He did not move. She buried her face in his neck, her breath hot on his skin. As he lay prone, still inside her, she seemed to twitch with an internal spasm, time and time again, until at last she sighed deeply and relaxed.

They lay still a few minutes longer, but Luke was not sleepy. Billie evidently felt the same, for she said: 'I have an idea. Let's wash.'

He laughed. 'Well, I sure need it.'

She rolled off him and climbed down, and he followed. In the corner of the roomette was a tiny washbasin with a cupboard over it. Billie found a hand towel and a little cake of soap in the cupboard. She filled the basin with hot water. 'I'll wash you, then you can wash me,' she said. She soaked the towel, rubbed soap on it, and began.

It was delightfully intimate and sexy. He closed his eyes. She soaped his belly, then kneeled to wash his legs. 'You missed a bit,' he said.

'Don't worry, I'm leaving the best part till last.'

When she had finished, he did the same for her, which was even more arousing. Then they lay down again, this time on the lower bunk.

'Now,' she said, 'do you remember oral sex?'

'No,' he said. 'But I think I can figure it out.'

PART 6

8.30 A.M.

To help track the satellite accurately, the Jet Propulsion Laboratory has developed a new radio technique called Microlock. The Microlock stations use a phased-lock loop tracking system which is able to lock on to a signal of only one-thousandth of a watt from as far as 20,000 miles away.

Anthony flew to Florida in a small plane that bumped and bucked with every gust of wind all the way across Alabama and Georgia. He was accompanied by a general and two colonels who would have shot him on sight if they had known the purpose of his trip.

He landed at Patrick Air Force Base, a few miles south of Cape Canaveral. The air terminal consisted of a few small rooms at the rear of an aircraft hangar. In his imagination he saw a detachment of FBI agents, with their neat suits and shiny shoes, waiting to arrest him; but there was only Elspeth.

She looked drained. For the first time, he saw signs of approaching middle age in her. The pale skin of her face showed the beginnings of wrinkles, and the posture of her long body was a little stooped. She led him outside to where her white Corvette was parked in the hot sun.

As soon as they were inside the car, he said: 'How's Theo?'

'Pretty shook, but he'll be okay.'

'Do the local police have his description?'

'Yes – Colonel Hide gave it out.'

'Where's he hiding?'

'In my motel room. He'll stay there until dark.' She drove out of the base onto the highway and turned north. 'What about you? Will the CIA give out your description to the police?'

'I don't think so.'

'So you can move around fairly freely. That's good, because you'll need to buy a car.'

'The Agency likes to solve its own problems. Right now, they think I've gone rogue, and their only concern is to take me out of circulation before I embarrass them. Once they start listening to Luke, they'll realize they've been harbouring a double agent for years – but that may make them even more concerned to hush up the whole thing. I can't be sure, but my guess is there will be no high-profile search for me.'

'And no shadow of suspicion has fallen on me. So all three of us are still in play. That gives us a good chance. We can still pull this thing off.'

'Luke doesn't suspect you?'

'He has no reason to.'

'Where is he now?'

'On a train, according to Marigold.' A note of bitterness entered her voice. 'With Billie.'

'When will he get here?'

'I'm not sure. The overnight train takes him to Jacksonville, but from there he has to get a slow train down the coast. Some time this afternoon, I guess.'

They drove in silence for a while. Anthony tried to make himself calm. In twenty-four hours, it would be all over. They would have struck a historic blow for the cause to which they had devoted their lives, and they would go down in history – or they would have failed, and the space race would once again be a two-horse contest.

Elspeth glanced across at him. 'What will you do after tonight?'

'Leave the country.' He tapped the small case in his lap. 'I have everything I need – passports, cash, a few simple items of disguise.'

'And then?'

'Moscow.' He had spent much of the flight thinking about this. 'The Washington desk at the KGB, I imagine.' Anthony was a major in the KGB. Elspeth had been an agent longer – had, in fact, recruited Anthony, back at Harvard – and she was a colonel. 'They'll give me some kind of senior advisory-consultative role,' he went on. 'After all, I'll know more about the CIA than anyone else in the Soviet bloc.'

'How will you like life in the USSR?'

'In the workers' paradise, you mean?' He gave her a wry grin. 'You've read George Orwell. Some animals are more equal than others. I guess a lot will depend on what happens tonight. If we pull this off, we'll be heroes. And if not . . .'

'You're not nervous?'

'Sure I am. I'll be lonely at first – no friends, no family, and I don't speak Russian. But maybe I'll get married and raise a brood of little comrades.' His flip answers disguised the depth of his anxiety. 'I decided, a long time ago, to sacrifice my personal life to something more important.'

'I made the same decision, but I'd still be frightened by the thought of moving to Moscow.'

'It's not going to happen to you.'

'No. They want me to stay in place, at all costs.'

She had obviously talked to her controller, whoever that was. Anthony was not surprised by the decision to leave Elspeth in place. For the last four years, Russian scientists had known everything about the US space programme. They saw every important report, all the test results, each blueprint produced by the Army Ballistic Missile Agency – thanks to Elspeth. It was as good as having the Redstone team working for the Soviet programme. Elspeth was the reason the Soviets had beaten the Americans into space. She was easily the most important spy of the Cold War.

Her work had been done at enormous personal sacrifice, Anthony knew. She had married Luke in order to spy on the space programme. But her love for him was genuine, and it had broken her heart to betray him. However, her triumph was the Soviet victory in the space race, which would be sealed tonight. That would make everything worthwhile.

Anthony's own triumphs were second only to Elspeth's. A Soviet agent, he had penetrated to the highest levels of the CIA. The tunnel he had been responsible for in Berlin, which had tapped into Soviet communications, had in fact been a channel for disinformation. The KGB had used it to mislead the CIA into wasting millions shadowing men who were not spies, penetrating organizations that were never communist fronts, and discrediting Third World politicians who were in fact pro-American. If he was lonely in his Moscow flat, he would think of what he had achieved, and it would warm his heart.

Among the palm trees on the roadside ahead, he saw a huge model of a space rocket above a sign that read 'Starlite Motel'. Elspeth slowed the car and pulled in. The office was in a low building with angular buttresses that gave it a futuristic look. Elspeth parked as far as possible from the road. The rooms were in a two-storey building around a large pool where a few early birds were already sunbathing. Beyond the pool, Anthony could see the beach.

Despite the assurances he had given Elspeth, he wanted to be seen by as few people as possible, so he pulled his hat low and walked quickly as they went from the car to her upstairs room.

The motel was making the most of the space-programme connection. The lamps were shaped like rockets, and there were pictures of stylized planets and stars on the walls. Theo was standing at the window, looking out over the ocean. Elspeth introduced the two men and ordered coffee and doughnuts from room service. Theo said to Anthony: 'How did Luke find me out – did he explain that to you?'

Anthony nodded. 'He was using the Xerox machine in Hangar R. There's a security log book beside the machine. You have to note the date and time and the number of copies you made, and sign the log. Luke noticed that twelve copies had been signed for by "WvB", meaning Wernher von Braun.'

Elspeth said: 'I always used von Braun's name, because no one would dare to question the boss about the Xerox copies he needed.'

Anthony went on: 'But Luke knew something you and everyone else didn't know – that von Braun was in Washington that day. Luke's instinct rang an alarm bell. He went to the mail room and found the copies in an envelope addressed to you. But he had no clue as to who had sent the package. He decided he couldn't trust anyone down here, so he flew to Washington. Fortunately, Elspeth called me and I was able to intercept Luke before he could tell anyone.'

Elspeth said: 'But now we're right back where we were on Monday. Luke has rediscovered what we made him forget.'

Anthony asked her: 'What do you think the army will do now?'

'They could launch the rocket with the self-destruct mechanism disabled. But if it got out that they had done so, there would be hell to pay, and the fuss might spoil the triumph. So my guess is they'll change the code, so that a different signal is required to trigger the explosion.'

'How would they do that?'

'I don't know.'

There was a knock at the door. Anthony tensed, but Elspeth said: 'I ordered coffee.' Theo went into the bathroom. Anthony turned his back to the door. To look natural, he opened the closet and pretended to study the clothes inside. There was a suit of Luke's hanging there, a light grey herringbone, and a stack of blue shirts. Instead of letting the waiter in, Elspeth stood in the doorway to sign the bill, tipped the man, then took the tray from him and closed the door.

Theo came out of the bathroom and Anthony sat down again.

Anthony said: 'What can we do? If they change the code we can't make the rocket self-destruct.'

Elspeth put down the coffee tray. 'I have to find out what their plan is, and figure out a way around it.' She picked up her handbag and slung her jacket over her shoulders. 'Buy a car. Drive to the beach as soon as it's dark. Park as near as you can to the Cape Canaveral fence. I'll meet you there. Enjoy your coffee.' She went out.

After a moment, Theo said: 'You have to give her credit, she's got a cool nerve.'

Anthony nodded. 'It's what she needs.'

4 P.M.

A string of tracking stations stretches from north to south roughly along the line of longitude 65 degrees west of the Greenwich meridian. The network will receive signals from the satellite every time it passes overhead.

The countdown stood at X minus 390 minutes.

Countdown time was moving in step with real time, so far, but Elspeth knew that might not last. If something unexpected happened, causing a delay, the countdown would stop. After the problem had been solved, the countdown would resume where it had left off, even though ten or fifteen minutes had passed. As the moment of ignition approached, the gap often broadened, and countdown time fell farther behind real time.

Today the countdown had started half an hour before noon, at X minus 660 minutes. Elspeth had moved about the base restlessly, updating her timetable, alert for any change in procedure. So far she had gained no clue as to how the scientists planned to guard against sabotage – and she was beginning to feel desperate.

Everyone knew Theo Packman was a spy. The desk

clerk at the Vanguard had told people that Colonel Hide had raided the motel with four cops and two FBI men, and asked at the desk for Theo's room number. The space community quickly linked the news with the last-second cancellation of the launch. The explanation given, that a late weather report had indicated a worsening of the jet stream, was not believed by anyone inside Cape Canaveral's perimeter fence. By this morning everyone had been talking about sabotage. But no one seemed to know what was being done about it; or, if they did, they were not spreading the news. As midday cooled into afternoon, Elspeth's tension mounted. So far she had not asked direct questions, for fear of arousing suspicion, but before too long she would have to abandon caution. If she did not learn the plan soon, it would be too late for her to act to counter it.

Luke had not shown up yet. She was longing to see him, and dreading it at the same time. She missed him when he was not beside her at night. But when he was there, she thought all the time about how she was working to destroy his dream. Her deceit had poisoned their marriage, she knew. All the same, she yearned to see his face, to hear his grave, courteous voice, to touch his hand and make him smile.

The scientists in the blockhouse were taking a break, eating sandwiches and drinking coffee where they sat at their panels. There was normally some joshing when an attractive woman entered the room, but today the atmosphere was quiet and tense. They were waiting for something to go wrong: a warning light, an overload, a broken part or a malfunctioning system. As soon as a glitch appeared, the mood would change: they would all become more cheerful as they got immersed in the problem, trying out explanations, brainstorming solutions, jury-rigging a repair. They were the kind of men who were happiest fixing something.

She sat next to Willy Fredrickson, her boss, who had his headphones around his neck while he ate a grilled-cheese sandwich. 'I guess you know everyone's talking about an attempt to sabotage the rocket,' she said conversationally.

Willy looked disapproving, which she took as a sign that he knew exactly what she was talking about. Before he could reply, a technician at the back of the room said: 'Willy,' and touched his own headphones.

Willy put down his sandwich and replaced his headset, then said: 'Fredrickson here.' He listened for a minute. 'Okay,' he said into his mouthpiece. 'Quick as you can.' Then he looked up and said: 'Stop the countdown.'

Elspeth tensed. Was this the clue she was waiting for? She lifted her notebook and pencil expectantly.

Willy took off his headphones. 'There'll be a ten-minute delay,' he said. His tone of voice betrayed only the normal irritation with any glitch. He took another bite of his sandwich.

Fishing for more information, Elspeth said: 'Shall I say why?'

'We have to replace a feed-through capacitor that seems to be chattering.'

It was possible, Elspeth thought. Capacitors were essential to the tracking system, and 'chattering' – random small electrical discharges – could be a sign that the device was going to fail. But she was not convinced. She made up her mind to check it out, if she could.

She scribbled a note, then got up and left with a cheery wave. Outside the blockhouse, the afternoon shadows were lengthening. The white shaft of the rocket stood like a signpost to the heavens. She imagined it taking off, lifting with agonizing slowness from the launch pad on its tail flame and rising into the night. Then she saw a flash of light brighter than the sun as the rocket exploded, fragments of metal scattering like shards of glass, a ball of red-and-black flame in the night sky, and a roaring sound like the triumphant shout of all the earth's poor and wretched.

She walked briskly across the sandy lawn to the concrete launch pad, circled around the gantry to the back and entered the steel cabin in its base that housed the offices and machinery. The gantry supervisor, Harry Lane, was speaking into a phone, making notes with a thick pencil. When he hung up, she said: 'Ten minutes' delay?'

'Could be more.' He did not look at her, but that did not mean much: he was always rude, not liking to see women on the launch pad.

Writing in her notebook, she said: 'Reason?'

'Replacing a malfunctioning component,' he said.

'Would you care to tell me *which* component?'

'No.'

It was maddening. She still could not tell whether he was covering up for security reasons or being just plain awkward. She turned away. Just then, a technician in oily overalls walked in. 'Here's the old one, Harry,' he said.

In his dirty hand he held a plug.

Elspeth knew exactly what it was: the receiver for the coded self-destruct signal. The pins that stuck out from it were cross-wired in a complex manner, so that only the correct radio signal would cause it to ignite the firing cap.

She walked quickly out the door before Harry could see the triumphant expression on her face. Heart thumping with excitement, she hurried back to her jeep.

She sat in the driving seat, working it out. To prevent sabotage they were replacing the plug. The new one would be wired differently, to work on a different code. A matching broadcast plug must have been fitted to the transmitter. The new plugs had probably been flown here from Huntsville earlier in the day.

It made sense, she thought with satisfaction. At last she knew what the army was doing. But how could she outmanoeuvre them?

The plugs were always made in sets of four, the duplicate pair being a spare in case of malfunction. It was the duplicate pair that Elspeth had examined, last Sunday, when she had sketched the wiring so that Theo could mimic the radio code and trigger the explosion. Now, she thought worriedly, she had to do the same all over again: find the duplicate set, dismantle the transmitter plug, and sketch its wiring.

She started the jeep and drove fast back to the hangars. Instead of going into Hangar R, where her desk was, she entered Hangar D and went to the telemetry room. This was where she had found the duplicate plugs the last time.

Hank Mueller was leaning on a bench with two other scientists, looking solemnly at a complex electrical device. When he saw her he brightened and said: 'Eight thousand.'

His colleagues groaned in mock despair and moved away.

Elspeth suppressed her impatience. She would have to play the numbers game with him before anything else. 'It's the cube of twenty,' she said.

'Not good enough.'

She thought for a moment. 'Okay, it's the sum of four consecutive cubes: $11^3+12^3+13^3+14^3$ equals 8,000.'

'Very good.' He gave her a dime and looked expectant.

She racked her brains for a curious number, then said: 'The cube of 16,830.'

He frowned, and looked affronted. 'I can't work that out, I need a computer!' he said indignantly.

'You haven't heard of it? It's the sum of all the consecutive cubes from 1,134 to 2,133.'

'I didn't know that!'

'When I was in high school, the number of my parents' house was 16,830, that's how I know.'

'This is the first time you've ever kept my dime.' He looked comically despondent.

She could not search the lab: she had to ask him. Fortunately, the other men were out of earshot, just. She blurted out: 'Do you have the duplicate set of new plugs from Huntsville?'

'No,' he replied, looking even more despondent. 'They say security is not good enough here. They put the plugs in a safe.'

She was relieved that he did not question her need to know. 'What safe?'

'They didn't tell me.'

'Never mind.' She pretended to make a note in her book, and went out.

She hurried to Hangar R, running across the sandy earth in her high-heeled shoes. She felt optimistic. But she still had a lot to do. It was getting dark already, she noticed.

There was only one safe that she knew of, in Colonel Hide's office.

Back at her desk, she rolled an army envelope into her typewriter and marked it: 'Dr W. Fredrickson – Eyes Only.' Then she folded two blank sheets of paper, slid them into the envelope, and sealed it.

She went to Hide's office, tapped at the door, and walked in. He was alone, sitting behind his desk, smoking a pipe. He looked up and smiled: like most of the men, he was generally pleased to see a pretty face. 'Elspeth,' he said in his slow drawl. 'What can I do for you?'

'Would you keep this in the safe for Willy?' She handed him the envelope.

'Sure,' he said. 'What is it?'

'He didn't tell me.'

'Naturally.' He spun around in his chair and opened a cupboard behind him. Looking over his shoulder, Elspeth saw a steel door with a dial. She moved closer. The dial was graduated from 0 to 99, but only multiples of 10 were marked with a figure, the other numbers being indicated by a notch. She peered at the dial. She had sharp eyesight, but still it was difficult to see exactly where Hide stopped the dial. She strained forward, leaning over the desk to get closer.

The first number was easy: 10. Then he dialled a number just below 30, either 29 or 28. Finally he moved the dial to between 10 and 15. The combination was something like 10–29–13. It must be his birthday, either the 28th or 29th of October, in 1911, 1912, 1913 or 1914. That gave a total of eight possibilities. If she could get in here alone, she could try them all in a few minutes.

Hide opened the door. Inside were two plugs. 'Eureka,' Elspeth whispered.

'What was that?' Hide said.

'Nothing.'

He grunted, tossed the envelope into the safe, closed the door and spun the dial.

Elspeth was already on her way out. 'Thank you, Colonel.'

'Any time.'

Now she had to wait for him to leave his office. She could not quite see his door from her desk. However, he was farther down the corridor, so he had to pass her office to get out. She propped her door open.

Her phone rang. It was Anthony. 'We're leaving here in a few minutes,' he said. 'Do you have what we need?'

'Not yet, but I will.' She wished she felt as sure as she sounded. 'What kind of car did you buy?'

'A light green Mercury Monterey, fifty-four model, the old-fashioned style, no tail fins.'

'I'll recognize it. How's Theo?'

'Asking me what he should do after tonight.'

'I assumed he'd fly to Europe and continue to work for *Le Monde*.'

'He's afraid they may track him down there.'

'I guess they might. Then he should go with you.'

'He doesn't want to.'

'Promise him anything,' she said impatiently. 'Just make sure he's ready for tonight.'

'Okay.'

Colonel Hide passed her door. 'I gotta go,' she said, and hung up.

She went out, but Hide had not disappeared. He stood in the next doorway, talking to the girls in the typing pool. He was still in sight of his door: Elspeth could not go in. She loitered for a minute, wishing he would move on. But, when he did, he returned to his office.

He stayed there for two hours.

Elspeth almost went crazy. She had the combination, she only needed to get in there and open the safe, and he would not go away. He sent his secretary to get coffee from the mobile refreshment stall they called the Roach Coach. He did not even go to the bathroom. Elspeth began to dream up ways of putting him out of action. She had been taught, in OSS, how to strangle someone with a nylon stocking, but she had never tried it. Anyway, Hide was a big man, he would put up a hell of a struggle.

She did not leave her office. Her timetable was forgotten. Willy Fredrickson would be furious, but what did that matter?

She looked at her wristwatch every few minutes. At eight twenty-five Hide at last walked past. She sprang up and went to her door. She saw him heading down the stairs. Launch was now only a couple of hours away: he was probably heading for the blockhouse.

Another man was walking along the corridor towards her. He said: 'Elspeth?' in an uncertain voice that she recognized. Her heart stopped, and she met his eye.

It was Luke.

8.30 P.M.

Information from the satellite's recording instruments is transmitted via radio by a musical tone. The different instruments use tones of different frequencies, so that the 'voices' can be separated, electronically, when they are received.

Luke had been dreading this moment.

He had dropped Billie off at the Starlite. She planned to check in and freshen up, then get a cab to the base in time to see the launch. Luke had gone straight to the blockhouse and learned that take-off was now scheduled for 10.45 p.m. Willy Fredrickson had explained the precautions the team had taken to prevent the sabotage of the rocket. Luke was not completely reassured. He wished Theo Packman had been arrested, and he would have liked to know where Anthony was. However, neither of them could do anything with the wrong code. And the new plugs were locked in a safe, Willy told him.

He would feel less worried when he had seen Elspeth. He had not told anyone about his suspicions of her – partly because he could not bear to accuse her, partly because he had no evidence. But when he looked into her eyes and asked her to tell him the truth, he would know.

He came up the stairs in Hangar R with a heavy heart. He had to talk to Elspeth about her betrayal, and he had to confess that he had been unfaithful to her. He did not know which was worse.

As he reached the top of the stairs he passed a man in colonel's uniform who spoke without stopping. 'Hey, Luke, good to have you back, see you in the blockhouse.' Then he saw a tall redhead emerge from an office along the corridor, looking anxious. There was a poised tension to her slender body as she stood in the doorway, looking past Luke at the colonel going down the stairs. She was more beautiful than her wedding photograph. Her pale face had a faint glow, like the surface of a lake at dawn. He felt a jolt of emotion like a shot in the arm, a strong feeling of tenderness for her.

He spoke to her, and then she noticed him. 'Luke!' She came quickly towards him. Her smile of welcome showed genuine pleasure, but he saw fear in her eyes. She threw her arms around him and kissed his lips. He realized he should not have been surprised – she was his wife, and he had been away all week. A hug was the most natural thing in the world. She had no idea that he suspected her, so she was continuing to act like a normal wife.

He cut short the kiss and detached himself from her embrace. She frowned and looked hard at him, trying to read his expression. 'What is it?' she said. Then she sniffed, and sudden anger suffused her face.

'You son of a bitch, you smell of sex.' She pushed him away. 'You fucked Billie Josephson, you bastard!' A passing scientist looked startled to hear such language, but she took no notice. 'You fucked her on the goddamn train.'

He did not know what to say. Her betrayal was worse than his, but all the same he was ashamed of what he had done. Anything he said was going to sound like an excuse, and he hated excuses, they made a man pathetic. So he said nothing.

Her mood switched again, just as quickly. 'I don't have time for this,' she said. She looked up and down the corridor, seeming impatient and distracted.

Luke was suspicious. 'What do you have to do that is more important than this conversation?'

'My job!'

'Don't worry about that.'

'What the hell are you talking about? I have to go. We'll talk later.'

'I don't think so,' he said firmly.

She reacted to his tone. 'What do you mean, you don't think so?'

'When I was at the house I opened a letter addressed to you.' He took it out of his jacket pocket and gave it to her. 'It's from a doctor in Atlanta.'

The blood drained from her face. She pulled the letter out of the envelope and began to read it. 'Oh, my God,' she whispered.

'You had your tubes tied six weeks before our wedding,' he said. Even now he could hardly believe it.

Tears came to her eyes. 'I didn't want to do it,' she said. 'I had to.'

He recalled what the doctor had said about Elspeth's state – insomnia, loss of weight, sudden crying, depression – and he felt a surge of compassion. His voice fell to a whisper. 'I'm so sorry you've been unhappy,' he said.

'Don't be nice to me, I couldn't stand it.'

'Let's go into your office.' He took her arm and led her into the room, closing the door. She went automatically to her desk and sat down, fumbling in her purse for a handkerchief. He got the big chair from behind the boss's desk and pulled it over so that he could sit close to her.

She blew her nose. 'I almost didn't have the operation,' she said. 'It broke my heart.'

He looked carefully at her, trying to be cool and detached. 'I guess they forced you to,' he said. He paused. Her eyes widened. 'The KGB,' he went on, and she stared at him. 'They ordered you to marry me so that you could spy on the space programme, and they made you get sterilized so that you would not have children to divide your loyalties.' He saw a terrible grief in her eyes, and he knew he was right. 'Don't lie,' he said quickly. 'I won't believe you.'

'All right,' she said.

She had admitted it. He sat back. It was all over. He felt breathless and bruised, as if he had fallen out of a tree.

'I kept changing my mind,' she said, and tears rolled down her face as she spoke. 'In the morning I'd be determined to do it. Then at lunch time I'd call you on the phone, and you'd say something about a house with a big yard for children to run around in, and I'd make up my mind to defy them. Then, alone in bed at night, I'd think how badly they needed the information I could get if I was married to you, and I'd resolve all over again to do what they wanted.'

'You couldn't do both?'

She shook her head. 'As it was I could hardly stand it, loving you and spying on you at the same time. If we'd had children I never could have done it.'

'What made you decide, in the end?'

She sniffed and wiped her face. 'You're not going to believe me. It was Guatemala.' She gave a queer little laugh. 'Those wretched people only wanted schools for their children and a trade union to protect them and the chance to earn a living. But it would have put a few cents on the price of bananas, and United Fruit didn't want that, so what did the US do? We overthrew their government and put in a fascist puppet. I was working for the CIA at the time, so I knew the truth. It made me so angry – that those greedy men in Washington could screw a poor country, and get away with it, and tell lies about it, and have the press tell Americans that it was a revolt by local anti-communists. You'll say it's a strange thing to get emotional about, but I can't tell you how mad I was.'

'Mad enough to do damage to your body.'

'And betray you, and ruin my marriage.' She lifted her head, and a proud look came over her face. 'But what hope is there for the world, if a nation of penniless peasants can't try to climb up out of the mud without being crushed under the jackboot of Uncle Sam? The only thing I regret is denying you children. That was wicked. The rest, I'm proud of.'

He nodded. 'I guess I understand.'

'That's something.' She sighed. 'What are you going to do? Call the FBI?'

'Should I?'

'If you do, I'll end up in the electric chair, like the Rosenbergs.'

He winced as if someone had stabbed him. 'Christ.'

'There's an alternative.'

'What?'

'Let me go. I'll catch the first plane out. I'll go to Paris, Frankfurt, Madrid, anywhere in Europe. From there I can get a flight to Moscow.'

'Is that what you want to do? Live out your days there?'

'Yes.' She gave a wry grin. 'I'm a KGB colonel, you know. I'd never be a colonel in the US.'

'You'd have to go now, immediately,' he said.

'Okay.'

'I'll escort you to the gate, and you'll have to give me your pass so you can't get back in.'

'Okay.'

He looked at her, trying to imprint her face on his memory. 'I guess this is goodbye.'

She picked up her purse. 'Can I go to the ladies' room first?'

'Of course,' he said.

9.30 P.M.

The main scientific purpose of the satellite is to measure cosmic rays, in an experiment designed by Dr James Van Allen of the State University of Iowa. The most important instrument inside it is a Geiger counter.

Elspeth walked out of her office, turned left, passed the door of the ladies' room, and entered Colonel Hide's office.

It was empty.

She closed the door behind her and stood leaning against it, trembling with relief. The office swam in her sight as her eyes filled with tears. The triumph of her life was within her grasp, but she had just ended her marriage to the best man she had ever known; and she was committed to leave the country of her birth and spend the rest of her days in a land she had never seen.

She closed her eyes and made herself breathe slowly and deeply: one, out, two, out, three, out. After a moment she felt better.

She turned the key in the office door. Then she went to the cupboard behind Hide's desk and kneeled in front of the safe. Her hands were shaking. With an effort of will, she made them steady. For some reason she recalled her Latin lessons at school and the proverb *Festina lente* – hurry slowly.

She repeated the actions Hide had performed when she watched him opening the safe. First she spun the dial four times anticlockwise, stopping at ten. Next she turned it three times in the other direction, stopping at 29. Then she turned it twice anticlockwise, stopping at 14. She tried to turn the handle. It would not move.

She heard footsteps outside, and a woman's voice. The sounds from the corridor seemed unnaturally loud, like noises in a nightmare. But the footsteps receded and the voice faded.

She knew the first number was 10. She dialled it again. The second number could have been 29 or 28. She dialled 28 this time, then 14 again.

The handle still would not turn.

She had tried only two possibilities out of the eight. Her fingers were slippery with sweat, and she wiped them on the hem of her dress. Next she tried 10, 29, 13, then 10, 28, 13.

She was half way through the list.

She heard a distant hooter give a warning blast – two shorts and a long, sounded three times in succession. This meant that all personnel should clear the launch-pad area. The launch was an hour away. She glanced involuntarily at the door, then returned her attention to the dial.

The combination 10, 29, 12 did not work.

But 10, 28, 12 did.

Jubilant, she turned the handle and pulled open the heavy door.

The two plugs were still there. She allowed herself a smile of triumph.

There was no time now to dismantle them and sketch the wiring. She would have to take them to the beach. Theo could either copy the wiring or use the actual plug in his own transmitter.

A danger occurred to her. Was it possible someone might notice the absence of the duplicate plugs during the next hour? Colonel Hide had gone to the blockhouse and was unlikely to return before blast-off. She had to take the risk.

There were footsteps outside the office again, and this time someone tried the door.

Elspeth stopped breathing.

A man's voice called: 'Hey, Bill, you in there?' It sounded like Harry Lane. What the hell did he want? The doorknob rattled. Elspeth kept still and silent. Harry said: 'Bill doesn't normally keep his door locked, does he?'

Another voice replied: 'I don't know, I guess the head of security is entitled to lock his door if he wants to.'

She heard departing footsteps, then the waning voice of Harry, saying: 'Security, hell, he doesn't want anyone stealing his Scotch.'

She grabbed the plugs from the safe and stuffed them into her purse. Then she closed the safe, spun the dial, and shut the cupboard.

She went to the office door, turned the key, and opened it.

Harry Lane was standing outside.

'Oh!' she said in shock.

He frowned accusingly. 'What were you doing in there?'

'Oh, nothing,' she said feebly, and tried to walk around him.

He grabbed her arm in a firm grasp. 'If it was nothing, why did you lock the door?' He squeezed her until it hurt.

That made her mad, and she stopped acting guilty. 'Let go of my arm, you big brainless bear, or I'll scratch your damn eyes out.'

Startled, he let go and stepped back; but he said: 'I still want to know what you were up to in there.'

She was struck by inspiration. 'I had to adjust my garter belt, and the ladies' room was full, so I used Bill's office in his absence. I'm sure he wouldn't mind.'

'Oh.' Harry looked foolish. 'No, I guess he wouldn't.'

Elspeth softened her tone. 'I know we have to be security-conscious, but there was no need to bruise my arm.'

'Yeah, sorry.'

She walked past him, breathing hard.

She re-entered her office. Luke was sitting where she had left him, looking grim. 'I'm ready,' she said.

He stood up. 'After you leave here, you'll go straight to the motel,' he said.

447

He was sounding brisk and practical, but she could see by his face that he was suppressing powerful emotions. She just said: 'Yes.'

'In the morning, you'll drive to Miami and get on a plane out of the United States.'

'Yes.'

He nodded, satisfied. Together they went down the steps and out into the warm night. Luke walked her to her car. As she opened the door, he said: 'I'll take your security pass now.'

She opened her purse and suffered a moment of sheer panic. The plugs were right there, on top of a yellow silk make-up bag, glaringly visible. But Luke did not see them. He was looking away, too polite to peek into a lady's purse. She took out her Cape Canaveral security pass and gave it to him, then closed her purse with a snap.

He pocketed the pass and said: 'I'll follow you to the gate in the jeep.'

She realized this was goodbye. She found herself unable to speak. She got into her car and slammed the door.

She swallowed her tears and drove off. The lights of Luke's jeep came on and followed her. Passing the launch pad, she saw the gantry inching back on its railroad tracks, ready for take-off. It left the huge white rocket standing alone in the floodlights, looking precarious, as if a careless nudge from a passer-by might topple it. She checked her watch. It was a minute before ten. She had forty-six minutes left.

She drove out of the base without stopping. The

headlights of Luke's jeep diminished in her rear-view mirror and finally disappeared as she rounded a bend. 'Goodbye, my love,' she said aloud, and she began to cry.

This time she could not control herself. As she drove down the coast road, she cried unrestrainedly, tears pouring down her face, her chest heaving with anguished sobs. The lights of other cars swept by in blurred streaks. She almost overshot the beach road. When she saw it, she jammed on her brakes and slewed across the highway in the path of the oncoming traffic. A taxicab braked hard and swerved, honking and skidding, and narrowly missed the tail of her Bel Air. She bumped onto the uneven sand of the beach track and slowed to a halt, heart pounding. She had almost ruined everything.

She wiped her face on her sleeve and drove on, more slowly, to the beach.

* * *

After Elspeth left, Luke stayed at the gate in his jeep, waiting for Billie to arrive. He felt breathless and stunned, as if he had run full-tilt into a wall, and was now lying on the ground trying to recover his senses. Elspeth had admitted everything. He had been sure, for the last twenty-four hours, that she was working for the Soviets, but nonetheless it was shocking to have his beliefs confirmed. Of course there were spies, everyone knew that, and Ethel and Julius Rosenberg had both died in the electric chair for espionage; but reading about such things in the newspapers was nothing. He had been married to a spy for four years. He could hardly take it in.

Billie arrived at ten-fifteen in a taxicab. Luke signed her in with security, then they got in the jeep and headed for the blockhouse. 'Elspeth has gone,' Luke said.

'I think I saw her,' Billie replied. 'Is she in a white Bel Air?'

'Yes, that's her.'

'My cab nearly hit her car. She pulled across the road right in front of us. I saw her face in the headlights. We missed her by about an inch.'

Luke frowned. 'Why did she pull in front of you?'

'She was turning off the road.'

'She told me she'd go straight back to the Starlite.'

Billie shook her head. 'No, she was heading for the beach.'

'The beach?'

'She went down one of those little tracks between the dunes.'

'Shit,' said Luke, and he turned the jeep around.

* * *

Elspeth drove slowly along the beach, staring at the groups of people who had gathered for the launch. Wherever she saw children or women, her eye moved on quickly. But there were many all-male groups of rocket buffs, standing around their cars in shirtsleeves with binoculars and cameras, smoking cigarettes and drinking coffee or beer. She stared hard at their vehicles, looking for a four-year-old Mercury Monterey.

Anthony had told her it was green, but there was not enough light to see colours.

She started at the crowded end of the beach, nearest to the base, but Anthony and Theo were not there, and she guessed they had chosen a more isolated spot. Terrified of missing them, she worked her way gradually south.

At last she saw a tall man in old-fashioned braces leaning against a light-coloured car and looking through binoculars towards the glow of the Cape Canaveral lights. She stopped the car and jumped out. 'Anthony!' she said.

He lowered the binoculars and she saw that it was not him. 'I'm sorry,' she said. She drove on.

She checked her watch. It was ten-thirty. She was almost out of time. She had the plugs, everything was ready: she just had to find two men on a beach.

The cars thinned out until they were a hundred yards or so apart. Elspeth picked up speed. She drove close to a car that looked right, but it seemed to be empty. She accelerated again – then the car honked.

She slowed down and looked back. A man had got out of the car and was waving at her. It was Anthony. 'Thank God!' she said. She reversed back to him and leaped out of the car. 'I've got the duplicate plugs,' she said.

Theo got out of the other car and opened its trunk. 'Give them to me,' he said. 'Quickly, for God's sake.'

10.48 P.M.

The countdown reaches zero.

In the blockhouse, the launch conductor says: 'Firing command!' A crewman pulls a metal ring and twists it. This is the action that fires the rocket.

Prevalves open to let the fuel start flowing. The liquid oxygen vent is closed, and the halo of white smoke around the missile suddenly vanishes.

The launch conductor says: 'Fuel tanks pressurized.'

For the next eleven seconds, nothing happens.

The jeep tore along the beach at top speed, dodging in and out of family groups. Luke scanned the cars, ignoring the cries of protest as his tyres showered people with sand. Billie was standing up beside him, holding the top of the windshield. He shouted over the wind noise: 'See a white Bel Air?'

She shook her head. 'It should be easy to spot!'

'Yeah,' Luke said. 'So where the hell are they?'

* * *

The last connection hose drops away from the missile. A second later, the priming fuel ignites, and the first-stage engine thunders into life. A huge orange firelick bursts from the base of the rocket as thrust builds.

* * *

Anthony said: 'For Christ's sake, Theo, hurry!'

'Shut up,' Elspeth told him.

They were bent over the open trunk of the Mercury, watching Theo fiddle with his radio transmitter. He was attaching wires to the pins of one of the plugs Elspeth had given him.

There was a roaring sound like distant thunder, and they all looked up.

* * *

With painful slowness, Explorer I lifts off the launch pad.

In the blockhouse, someone yells: 'Go, baby!'

* * *

Billie saw a white Bel Air parked next to a darker sedan. 'There!' she screamed.

'I see them,' Luke shouted back.

At the rear of the sedan, three people were clustered around the open trunk. Billie recognized Elspeth and Anthony. The other man was presumably Theo Packman. But they were not looking into the trunk. Their heads were raised and they were staring across the sand dunes towards Cape Canaveral.

Billie read the situation instantly. The transmitter was in the trunk. They were in the process of setting it to broadcast the detonation signal. But why were they looking up? She turned towards Cape Canaveral.

There was nothing to see, but she heard a deep, rumbling roar like the sound of a blast furnace in a steel mill.

The rocket was taking off.

'We're out of time!' she yelled.

'Hold tight!' Luke said.

She gripped the windshield as he swung the jeep around in a wide arc.

* * *

The rocket picks up speed suddenly. At one instant it seems to be hovering hesitantly over the launch pad. At the next it moves like a bullet out of a gun, shooting into the night sky on a tail of fire.

* * *

Over the roar of the rocket, Elspeth heard another sound, the scream of a car engine being raced. A second later, the beam of headlights fell on the group around the trunk of the Mercury. She looked up and saw a jeep heading for them at top speed. She realized it was going to ram them. 'Hurry!' she screamed.

Theo connected the last wire.

On his transmitter were two switches, one marked 'Arm' and the other 'Destroy'.

The jeep was on them.

Theo threw the 'Arm' switch.

* * *

On the beach, a thousand faces tip backwards, watching the rocket rise straight and true, and a huge cheer goes up.

* * *

Luke drove straight for the back of the Mercury.

The jeep had slowed as he turned, but he was still travelling at about twenty miles per hour. Billie jumped out, hit the ground running, then fell and rolled.

At the last second Elspeth threw herself out of the way. Then there was a deafening bang and the crash of breaking glass.

The Mercury's rear end crumpled, it jumped forward a yard, and its trunk lid came down with a bang. Luke thought either Theo or Anthony had been crushed between the cars, but he could not be sure. He was thrown forward violently. The bottom of the steering wheel caught his lower chest, and he felt the sharp pain of cracked ribs. A moment later, his forehead hit the top edge of the wheel, and he sensed hot blood flowing down his face.

Luke pulled himself upright and looked at Billie. She seemed to have fared better than he. She was sitting on the ground rubbing her forearms, but she did not appear to be bleeding.

He looked across the hood of the jeep. Theo lay on the ground in a spread-eagle position, not moving. Anthony was on his hands and knees, looking shaken but unhurt. Elspeth had escaped injury and was scrambling to her feet. She dashed to the Mercury and tried to open the trunk.

Luke leaped out of the jeep and ran at her. As the trunk lid lifted, he shoved her aside. She fell to the sand.

Anthony yelled: 'Hold it!'

Luke looked at him. He was standing over Billie with a pistol held to the back of her head.

Luke looked up. The red firetail of the missile was a bright shooting star in the night sky. As long as that was visible, Explorer could still be destroyed. The first stage would burn out when it was sixty miles high. At that point, the rocket would become invisible – for the lesser fire of the second stage would not be bright enough to be seen from the Earth – and this would be the sign that the self-destruct system would no longer work. The first stage, which contained the explosive detonator, would separate and fall away, eventually to splash down in the Atlantic Ocean. After separation, it could no longer damage the satellite.

And separation would take place two minutes and twenty-five seconds after ignition. Luke figured the rocket had been ignited roughly two minutes ago. There had to be about twenty-five seconds left.

It was plenty of time to throw a switch.

Elspeth got to her feet again.

Luke looked at Billie. She was on one knee, like a sprinter at the starting line, frozen in position with the long silencer of Anthony's gun pressing into her curly black hair. Anthony's hand was rock-steady.

Luke asked himself if he was ready to sacrifice Billie's life for the rocket.

The answer was No.

But what would happen, he thought, if he moved? Would Anthony shoot Billie? He might.

Elspeth again bent over the trunk of the car.

Then Billie moved.

She jerked her head to one side, then threw herself backwards, hitting Anthony's legs with her shoulders.

Luke lunged at Elspeth and pushed her away from the car.

The silenced gun coughed as Anthony and Billie fell in a heap.

Luke stared in dread. Anthony had fired, but had he hit Billie? She rolled away from him, apparently unhurt, and Luke breathed again. Then Anthony lifted his gun arm, aiming at Luke.

Luke looked death in the face, and a peculiar calm possessed him. He had done all he could.

There was a long moment of hesitation. Then Anthony coughed, and blood came out of his mouth. Pulling the trigger as he fell, he had shot himself, Luke realized. Now his limp hand dropped the gun and he slumped back on the sand, his eyes staring up at the sky but seeing nothing.

Elspeth sprang to her feet and bent over the transmitter a third time.

Luke looked up. The firetail was a glow-worm in space. As he watched, it winked out.

Elspeth threw the switch and looked up into the sky, but she was too late. The first stage had burned out and separated. The Primacord had probably detonated, but there was no fuel left to burn, and anyway the satellite was no longer connected to the first stage.

Luke sighed. It was all over. He had saved the rocket.

Billie put her hand on Anthony's chest, then checked his pulse. 'Nothing,' she said. 'He's dead.'

At the same moment, Luke and Billie looked at Elspeth. 'You lied again,' Luke said to her.

Elspeth stared at him with a hysterical light in her eyes. 'We weren't wrong!' she yelled. 'We were not wrong!'

Behind her, families of spectators and tourists were beginning to pack their belongings. No one had been close enough to notice the fighting: all eyes had been turned to the sky.

Elspeth looked at Luke and Billie as if she had more to say; but after a long moment she turned away. She got into her car, slamming the door, and started the engine.

Instead of turning towards the road, she headed for the ocean. Luke and Billie watched in horror as she drove straight into the water.

The Bel Air stopped, waves lapping at its fenders, and Elspeth got out. In the car's headlights, Luke and Billie saw her begin to swim out to sea.

Luke moved to go after her, but Billie grabbed his arm and held him back.

'She'll kill herself!' he said in agony.

'You can't catch her now,' Billie said. 'You'll kill yourself!'

Luke still wanted to try. But then Elspeth passed beyond the headlights' beam, swimming strongly, and he realized he would never find her in the dark. He bowed his head in defeat.

Billie put her arms around him. After a moment, he hugged her back.

Suddenly the strain of the last three days fell on him like a tree. He staggered, about to fall, and Billie held him upright.

After a moment he felt better. Standing on the beach, with their arms around one another, they both looked up.

The sky was full of stars.

EPILOGUE

1969

Explorer 1's Geiger counter recorded cosmic radiation a thousand times higher than expected. This information enabled scientists to map the radiation belts above the Earth that became known as the Van Allen belts, named after the State University of Iowa scientist who designed the experiment.

The micrometeorite experiment determined that about two thousand tons of cosmic dust rain down on the Earth annually.

The shape of the Earth turned out to be about one per cent flatter than previously thought.

Most important of all, for the pioneers of space travel, the temperature data from the Explorer showed that it was possible to control the heat inside a missile sufficiently for human beings to survive in space.

Luke was on the NASA team that put Apollo 11 on the moon.

By then he was living in a big, comfortable old house in Houston with Billie, who was Head of Cognitive Psychology at Baylor. They had three children: Catherine, Louis, and Jane. (Luke's stepson, Larry, also lived with them, but that July he was visiting his father, Bern.)

Luke happened to be off duty on the evening of 20 July. Consequently, at a few minutes before nine o'clock, Central time, he was watching TV with his family, as was half the world. He sat on the big couch with Billie beside him and Jane, the youngest, on his lap. The other kids were on the carpet with the dog, a yellow Labrador called Sidney.

When Neil Armstrong stepped on the moon, a tear rolled down Luke's cheek.

Billie took his hand and squeezed it.

Catherine, the nine-year-old, who had Billie's colouring, looked at him with solemn brown eyes. Then she whispered to Billie: 'Mommy, why is Daddy crying?'

'It's a long story, honey,' Billie said. 'I'll tell it to you, one day.'

* * *

Explorer 1 was expected to remain in space for two to three years. In fact, it orbited the Earth for twelve years. On 31 March 1970 it finally re-entered the atmosphere over the Pacific Ocean near Easter Island, and burned up at 5.47 a.m., having circled the Earth 58,376 times and travelled a total of 1.66 billion miles.

THE END.

ACKNOWLEDGEMENTS

Many people generously gave time and effort to help me get the background details right for this story. Most of them were found for me by Dan Starer, of Research for Writers in New York City, who has worked with me on every book since *The Man from St Petersburg* back in 1981. Special thanks to the following:

In Cambridge, Massachusetts: Ruth Helman, Isabelle Yardley, Fran Mesher, Peg Dyer, Sharon Holt and the students of Pforzheimer House, and Kay Stratton.

At the St Regis hotel, formerly the Carlton, in Washington DC: concierge Louis Alexander, bellhop José Muzo, general manager Peter Walterspiel and Mr Walterspiel's assistant, Pat Gibson.

At Georgetown University: archivist Jon Reynolds, retired physics professor Edward J. Finn, and Val Klump of the Astronomy Club.

In Florida: Henry Magill, Ray Clark, Henry Paul, and Ike Rigell, all of whom worked on the early space programme; and Henri Landwirth, the former manager of the Starlite Motel.

In Huntsville, Alabama: Tom Carney, Cathey Carney, and Jackie Gray, of *Old Huntsville* magazine;

Roger Schwerman of Redstone Arsenal; Michael Baker, Command Historian of the US Army Aviation & Missile Command; David Albert, Curator of the US Space & Rocket Center; Dr Ernst Stuhlinger.

Several family members read drafts and offered criticism, including my wife Barbara Follett, my stepdaughters Jann Turner and Kim Turner, and my cousin John Evans. I'm much indebted to editors Phyllis Grann, Neil Nyren, and Suzanne Baboneau; and to agents Amy Berkower, Simon Lipskar and, most of all, Al Zuckerman.